ALL
THE
WORDS
UNSPOKEN

T0159849

ALL
THE
WORDS
UNSPOKEN

SERENA KAUR

Red Door

Published by RedDoor
www.reddoorpress.co.uk

© 2020 Serena Kaur

The right of Serena Kaur to be identified as author of this Work has been
asserted by her in accordance with sections 77 and 78 of the Copyright,
Designs and Patents Act 1988

ISBN 978-1-913062-12-5

All rights reserved. No part of this publication may be reproduced, stored in a
retrieval system, copied in any form or by any means, electronic, mechanical,
photocopying, recording or otherwise transmitted without written permission
from the author

This is a work of fiction. Names, characters, businesses, places, events and
incidents are either the products of the author's imagination or used in a
fictitious manner. Any resemblance to actual persons, living or dead, or actual
events is purely coincidental.

A CIP catalogue record for this book is available from the British Library

Cover design: Emily Courdelle

Typesetting: Fuzzy Flamingo

Printed and bound in Denmark by Nørhaven

For my husband, Hinesh
Thank you for believing in me
when I couldn't believe in myself

CHAPTER 1

Maybe she should've told him what she was doing. Some part of her knew he deserved to be told. But telling him would invite discussion and what good would talking about it do? Like Newton's cradle, they'd go backwards and forwards, stuck in an endless sway as they explored the outcomes, each swoop from left to right making the problem harder to ignore and, one day, forget. To speak of it would give it the chance to grow roots and fixtures – to take residence in reality. No, she was right. She shouldn't have told him.

As she stared at the pill in front of her, her fears rose like dust in the air and clawed the back of her throat. What if she regretted her decision? What if she couldn't purge herself later for committing the act? She feared the onset of too much guilt, but equally feared a dearth of it – the palpable absence of it, confirming a fear too great to handle. The fear that she, Maansi Cavale, was a terrible person. She dug her fingertips into her knees and squeezed. How did she get herself into this mess?

'Miss Cavale?' came a woman's silvery voice.

Maansi snapped back to the cool, colourless office of the clinic. The smell of disinfectant roamed the room and stung her eyes, encouraging them to water. The formal quiet bothered her. She could feel it, as it settled over her head like an airtight, plastic bag. She didn't want to speak to the woman any more, or look upon the information laid out in glossy leaflets before her. She cast her eyes towards the sink at the rear of the room, seeking a moment's distraction. A bulb of water gathered at the tap's nozzle and trembled, resisting the fall and final splash against stainless steel.

'It's not too late to change your mind,' the nurse said, trying for her attention once more. Maansi met her face. Her cerulean eyes were empty of the warmth required from them. Her lily-white skin told her she'd never understand. People like her could go one way or the other, without concern or consequence. Maansi winced. No, that wasn't fair. It'd be a hard decision for anyone to make.

'I'm not going to change my mind.'

She tried to remember where she was when the absence of her monthly bleed began niggling at her mind. What had she been doing, when she allowed herself, just for a moment, to imagine that the worst thing had happened? When she let herself think that she, of all people, had somehow... The idea was laughable, at the time. She was convinced stress had interfered. Then, as the days leapt ahead and her uterus continued to resist release, she held the common cold accountable. Whatever it was, it wasn't that. Her bodily systems had just been thrown out of balance. There was nothing to worry about. She waited for the initial stirrings of a menstrual cramp. She checked her underwear for the first, reassuring drop of pomegranate-pink. Nothing came, except waves of nausea and two distinct bands on a stick. She checked the Clearblue packet. Over ninety-nine per cent accurate.

She pushed her weight into the hard-backed chair. The violent impulse to run out and chase after the safety of last month gripped her. She was a student. She should've been worrying about making morning lectures on time, or making them at all. Any distress she felt should've been because of trivial things, like microwaves ruining the integrity of leftover pizza. She thought back to the appetite-sating pleasures beneath the sheets, her body wrapped up with Lewis's. For a touch of time, she must have been sloppy and careless, not just surrendering her body, but the last hunks of a working mind. Had they gone too fast? Had the protective barrier torn? Where the hell did it all go wrong?

'Would you like me to go over anything again?' the nurse continued. 'If you have any questions for me, now would be the time to ask.'

'No. No more questions.'

They'd already been over the details three times.

Her stomach spasmed as she remembered what her mother had told her some years ago. They'd just finished watching Aamir Khan's TV show: *Satyamev Jayate*. The famed actor had brought guests on to discuss India's problem with female foeticide. Maansi's mother, with ears pricked, readied her own lecture regarding the action of *garbhpat*.

'Everyone goes through the cycle of birth, death and rebirth until they can meet with God again. If you terminate, you ruin a soul's progress towards God,' her mum had said, issuing the loaded statement while sifting through dried lentils, hunting for those hidden, molar-breaking stones that sometimes slipped through and spoiled a good daal. 'For women that do it, there are consequences, Maansi. Severe spiritual consequences.'

Sweat wriggled like larvae down Maansi's spine. Because of her careless mistake, she must interfere with a soul's cycle. If she didn't, she'd be cast out – sullied and depraved like a criminal. She could already feel them – the 'sanctified' members of the community – clawing at her like starved beasts, attempting to snatch what was hers. She'd have to surrender what she held before she could even understand her feelings towards it, or else risk their hell-powered judgements. All because she was unmarried.

She picked up the pill. It layered the tips of her fingers with a fine, white powder. A trace of the substance slid off

3

and jammed itself beneath her nail, masquerading as flaking skin. She'd dig it out later. Obvious or not, she'd remove any evidence that clung to her.

'So, if there are any problems, or if I have questions…'

'You can ring the twenty-four-hour number. They'll be able to advise you or address any concerns you might have.'

She held her breath. Now or never, she told herself. In one swift motion, she popped the pill into her mouth, brought the paper cup to her lips and swallowed the lukewarm water. She pictured the pill journeying down her throat and into her belly, where it would dissolve like sugar and begin the process of erasure.

She told herself it'd be all right. Of course it would. God wouldn't hate her. She was a good person and she was sorry. That would be enough. And anyway, maybe there weren't any Gods or souls. Maybe Hinduism was wrong and all she did was delete a lifeless collection of cells from her body. Maybe each action didn't have a karmic value. She sighed. Somehow, telling herself the world was void of souls and meaning wasn't making her feel better.

Maansi leaned back in her chair, ignoring the nurse's questions about how she felt and whether she needed a moment. She focused on keeping her tears at bay. It seemed wrong to her that a thing so important and weighted could be resolved in such a way. It was too simple; like knocking back paracetamol to quell a mild headache.

'I'm all right,' Maansi croaked. 'Thank you. I'd like to go.'

'Of course. Remember, you'll need to take your second pill in twenty-four hours. If you have any questions, please don't hesitate to call.'

She'd forgotten about the second pill. How was she going to find the strength to do it again? She stood to leave, surprised her trembling legs could hold her and carry her out.

Outside the clinic, she brushed herself down, smeared lip balm over her cracked lips and began her journey back to campus, her senses sedated. She was deaf to the passing of cars along the main road. She couldn't hear the primary school children skipping ahead of her, hand-in-hand with red bookbags precariously swinging at their sides. The sounds around her were muffled and fading, as if she were trapped beneath the surface of water, dropping lower and lower until she was several feet beneath its sun-dappled ceiling.

She found Lewis waiting for her outside her room, one hand fidgeting with his university-branded clothing, and the other winding the strands of his chestnut hair into tight loops. He'd gone home for reading week and wasn't due to return until the following day. She hadn't expected to see him immediately after what she'd done. Her feet slowed their pace as she reworked her face into a blank, expressionless mask. She could already feel the bile rising in her throat. Did he know? Is that why he was there? No, there was no way he knew. She hadn't told a soul.

'Lewis,' she began, fixing a smile on to her face. She forced herself to hug him. Her arms were limp and boneless around his shoulders. Her head reeled as the smell of Lynx body spray flooded her nostrils.

'Maansi, listen,' he said, without looking at her. 'We need to talk.'

The hairs on her neck rose like mummies from their tombs. No, he didn't know. She was sure of that. But that line – 'We need to talk' – signposted an upcoming break-up in every TV programme she'd ever watched. Her legs weakened and her arms grew more leaden. She should've known it was coming. Over the holidays, he stopped messaging her and became too busy to call. His attention wandered. They barely spoke.

As she let him into her room, she fought back her tears. If she were in a different headspace, she'd stop him. She'd do everything in her power to prevent him from throwing their relationship down the drain like old, contaminated soup. For her, Lewis was it. He was the one. They met at the first freshers' meet and greet. While the other males staggered about drunk, unable to string two words together, he drew her into voluble conversation. He was witty, charming and full of charisma. The eyes of other girls sought him among the crowds, but his eyes were on her. There was an instant and easy connection between them. Like her, he listened to old records, was concerned with the greater meaning of life and had a fondness for fruity bubble teas. Who could argue with physical appeal and sparkling conversation? It wasn't long before they got together. But now…

'Are you OK?' he asked, pulling at the hem of his T-shirt, failing to project the same confidence and self-assurance he had had when she met him. 'You seem a bit… peaky.'

She wiped the moisture from her forehead. 'I'm fine. Time of the month. What is it, then? What did you need to tell me?'

'Maybe you should sit down.'

She remained standing by the door, her hand pressed against her desk for balance. She'd endure whatever he needed to say as she was. She could take it. And if she couldn't, it was easier to storm out of the room from a standing position.

'All right. I'm just going to come out and say it.' He took a deep breath, his eyes crinkling shut before reopening again. 'You know I like you. I think you're amazing. But lately, I don't know. I've been thinking we may not be right for each other.'

'Really?' she asked, faking indifference. 'And why is that?'

'You know why.'

She snorted. No, she didn't. What he was saying made no sense to her. She thought of their dates, regularly filled with gusts of laughter and excitable hands, hovering towards each other, unable to resist the fierce magnetic pull. She thought of their late-night talks of their future journeys across Europe, spoken in sighs and whispers beneath the burnt orange lights of university accommodation. He told her he loved her. He made her feel secure. What was he talking about?

'Is there someone else?' she asked. She wouldn't pretend she hadn't seen the images online of him and some golden-haired girl from his home city. It had to be another girl. Or was it something else? As far as she knew, she'd done nothing wrong. Or had she? Of course, she could be a handful at times. She needed extra support and could lose herself to fits of tears, or could be ensnared by long, interminable silences; but he understood all of that. He wouldn't leave her because of that.

'There's no one else. It's just, you're difficult for me to handle sometimes. And with me studying medicine...'

She froze. Oh God, she thought. It was that.

'I don't understand. You never said there was a problem before. And this year has been good. I've got better control of my mental health now.'

'No, you haven't.' He sighed. 'Lately, you've been even more withdrawn and emotional. It's become too much.'

'No, no. Look, I know I've come across worse but it's for a different reason. I swear. The depression is totally under control.' A part of her begged her to tell him, but she bit her tongue and reminded herself the truth couldn't surface. Besides, she'd dealt with it. There was nothing to tell. The problem had gone.

'Maansi...'

'I've just had a rough few weeks.'

He shook his head in disbelief. How many times had she said that before? There was no way he'd believe her.

'So, you want to be that guy, do you? You want to leave a girl because of her depression? Fine. Be that guy.' The words exploded out of her, unplanned and unwanted. She had to say something to change his mind and make him see the error of his thinking. Anything.

'Maansi, don't. There are other reasons!'

'Like what?'

'Like, I don't know. We're different.'

'Different? What does that even mean?'

'I don't know. We're from different cultures, for one.'

Her eyes widened. It took her a second to process his words and absorb them into her body. Then, she heard nothing and did nothing but steep in heated rage. Of course, he would pull that card. That card had always been there, snug in his front pocket, its back emblazoned with a golden 'A'. He was taking the easy way out.

'Wow. Get the hell out.'

'Maansi, I don't mean it like—'

'Didn't you hear me? I said get out!'

'No, look. You're taking it the wrong way. If you just—'

Before she could stop herself, she grabbed a hardcover from the pile of books on her desk and hurled one with as much force as she could gather. She hit the wall and left it marked with a diffident grey. Only a few weeks ago, her greatest worry was losing her deposit. In that moment, she no longer cared. She wanted to embroil her surroundings into the moment and erupt with intensely matte paints of crimsons and blacks. She wanted to capture the chaos breeding in her body.

'You have no idea! No idea what I've just been through. Now you're going to pull that shit?'

Her tears fell freely, streaking her cheeks as they slipped down, one hot drop after the other.

'Maansi. Please.' He squirmed, uncomfortable with the way she allowed herself to break down like a goaded animal.

'Different cultures? I'm from Leicester, not Jaipur!'

He blinked repeatedly, as he did when confronted with an overzealous salesman or a homeless person asking for change – in other words, whenever he felt awkward and desperate to abandon a situation. 'I'm sorry, Maansi. It's all too much. I'm in my final year of medicine. I need to focus.'

How long had he been feeling that way? Had he been hiding his true feelings? As much as she wanted to scream about it, she couldn't permit herself to get angry over concealed truths. She was anything but a hypocrite.

'Just go,' she said.

After a stretched pause, he nodded and slipped out of her room, closing the door gently behind him.

She wiped away her tears. Maybe this was the punishment God was dishing out, knowing it would rip her own soul apart, as if it were constructed from nothing but frail tissue paper.

'Fine!' she said to the ceiling above her. She'd bear it.

She lay in bed and breathed. If Lewis couldn't handle her before, she knew he couldn't handle what was to come. Her depression had been birthed out of nothing. Its shadowy figure leaned over her for years, trying to dictate each turn and step without cause or reason. Normally, she could manage it and leave it flailing in the background. But now, she gave it a reason for being. If man could find himself renewed when met with purpose, she wondered how her depression would transform. She pictured the removal of pure light from her body and watched as the depression planted itself in the evacuated space, ready to grow.

She closed her eyes. She could hear Lewis pacing outside.

He was probably trying to come up with something more to tell her. A better explanation? Words of comfort? She didn't care. Maybe the death of their relationship was for the best.

Maansi clutched her lower abdomen. She could never tell him what she'd done.

CHAPTER 2

Maansi stepped through each day dissociated from the world, feeling less like a human being and more like an apparition. She couldn't recall the details of the days, nor find any emotion attached to them. The passing moments stowed themselves away in her once technicoloured mind as flat, paper-thin memories. She struggled with the vivacity of the world around her, with the glow of life bounding from the faces of others. Everything was too much. Too amplified. She wished someone would turn down the volume.

It became a habit to stay in her room as her flatmates gathered to watch the *X Factor* in the kitchen. She'd hear them through the walls, erupting into high-pitched squeals and low warbles of laughter. She hated hearing them. It seemed unnatural for them to respond to the world with anything other than neutrality. Still, she had to give them credit. Even though she'd chosen to hide away, they afforded her the same kindness and the same smiles, as if nothing had changed.

Then the porridge incident happened.

'Maansi, can you please clean up after yourself? You've left porridge there for three days now. Seriously. It's not OK,' one of the female flatmates said, her arms folded. 'It's growing mould.'

She lived in a large flat with five others. Three of them were present in the kitchen, nodding along and expressing their horror at the hardened clumpy mess cleaving to the Wilko's Functional bowl. They waited for her to respond. They waited for her to apologise and begin tackling the cemented mess, so they could all move on and continue in harmony. Out of all the things to be bothered about in the world, she couldn't give a damn about some porridge.

'You know what?' she began, collecting fire in her throat. 'Fuck the porridge!'

Without seeing their reactions, she stormed into her bedroom and slammed the door shut. The pile of books on her desk collapsed as the violent sound reverberated through her room. Forget them. They were just people she lived with. She still had her course friends. Although, she hadn't been paying much attention to them either. She'd sit in her lectures and seminars, gawping at her tutor – an incomplete portrait of a corpse, missing the spinning halo of flies above her head and a clot of spittle stuck to the corner of her mouth. Information would enter one ear and leave the other. The nudges from her friends and the questions darted at her from her tutor did nothing to revive her.

The minute a seminar or lecture ended, she'd shuffle home. She'd slip into bed, haul the duvet over her and try to quiet the guilt as it tapped away in her head, producing a hard patter, like rain hitting tin roofs or fingers tapdancing on frame drums – constant and merciless.

The days limped on. The forward, plodding movement of life made her want to scream. Some days, she'd hold a piece of ice in her hand, allowing the cold to penetrate the centre of her palm. The feeling of nothingness remained.

Soon enough, she found herself in the exam hall and the tapping song in her head met with the ticking of the clock. The sound of time passing, once a gentle reminder, merged with the frame drum and took her attention. She read the question before her more than once, struggling to understand what it wanted from her, though the words were written in simple, unpretentious English. She scribbled along the margins with pencil. The exams would determine her future and all she could hear was *tic-toc tic-toc tic-toc*, the fingers tapping and rain pattering, reminding her there would be no arrival of a gentler pitter-patter, and it was all her fault.

She pressed her head to the desk, pleading for silence.

In the end, she didn't meet her predicted grades. But she passed. She guessed that was enough. The chapter was over. She could move on. She left for her graduation ceremony, a cut of ice melting in her hand.

When Maansi returned home, she got the full weekend to herself, before her parents started probing her for information about her relationship status. All she could say was it ended because he didn't want to commit. Of course, they had a field day.

'We told you, didn't we? These *goray*, they don't want to marry,' her mum said, tittering as she pottered around the kitchen in her over-worn joggers. Even with the pressure cooker going, her mother yammered on, her orotund voice effortlessly scything through the sharp shrieks. 'English people are not goal-orientated like us. They go out with somebody for years, live with them for another ten years, and then decide they don't want to marry. We think about marriage from the start.'

'Mum, seriously, don't.'

'Why live and sleep together, but not get married? It's shameful. Our people have values. None of this boyfriend-girlfriend rubbish or hanky-panky before marriage.'

Maansi shook her head. She was fattened with these kinds

13

of lectures daily. Maansi's mother and father wore an air of superiority when discussing white people and what they did. Nevertheless, their showy thrones would shrink the minute a fairer face entered their home. They would fester in shame while trying to disguise the smell of Indian cooking. They would change the channel from Star Plus to BBC One. They would, rather ruefully, nudge statues of Gods to less conspicuous positions on the mantelpiece, too desperate to curtail the offensiveness of their culture. A culture hemmed with scarlets and golds. A culture too boisterous, too flavoursome – too different. Even though her generation were beginning to embrace their cultures, her parents hoped to squeeze into the picture of polished people in the country, sipping Yorkshire brew from dainty teacups, their fingertips resting on tablecloths of Victorian lace as they spouted words like 'wonderful' and 'quite' between tiny, civilised sips. They could be 'quintessentially' English, they convinced themselves. Although, from the gruffness of his voice and his professed inability to sit still, Mark the plumber – the last Englishman to visit – would surely loathe the unreality they invented for him. Her parents wished they could name the song he whistled while he worked. Their guess was Robbie Williams.

Since Maansi was a child, she'd been keenly aware of the shame that lurked around the edges, blunting the corners of an otherwise strong pride in their culture. Maansi's parents clung on to Indian values and traditions, as a man dangling off a precipice would cling on to the rocky edge. Their views on marriage were fixed and immutable. The topic encouraged her parents to burst forth from their shells like voracious tigers.

'They are always getting divorced! Indian people never get divorced,' her mother tossed out another false statement as she tackled a slab of dough with her rolling pin. Even when faced with conflicting evidence, these statements were treated as complete and utter truth.

Maansi sighed at the kitchen table. She looked longingly at her ring-finger, marking its nakedness. She remembered when Lewis had suggested they move to London after graduating.

'I'll start practising as a junior doctor, and you'll find work you want to do. London's full of opportunity,' he told her as he walked her to her seminar.

'My parents would never allow that unless we were engaged,' she replied. 'I'm getting by with them now by saying you have every intention of marrying me one day.' He looked terrified. She laughed at his reaction and said she'd think of something. In the end, she couldn't conjure up an argument her parents would accept for moving in with a boy, so her search history suffered an incursion of links to engagement rings. She lost herself in the lappets of the idea, the romance of it. She sent him an image of a princess-cut and told him it was for future reference. She'd been a fool. Maybe that was what he meant by 'different cultures'. She'd been raised on different ideas.

There was a knock at the front door, snatching Maansi away from her thoughts. She groaned as her mother bumbled out of the kitchen to answer it. Company was forever coming in and out of the house. Her mother had a habit of inviting her friends over every few days. They would twitter and gossip over cups of tea and chocolate digestives before launching into discussions about their favourite books. In their last session, they sparked a painful debate over the ethics behind Will's decision in Jojo Moyes's *Me Before You*.

Whenever Maansi's father returned home from his accounting job, she'd talk his ear off about all the things she'd discovered about so-and-so's husband or daughter, never sparing a single, thirst-quenching detail, before throwing a book at him and telling him if he'd just read they'd have more to talk about. Then, he'd feel guilty for not taking an interest and would make a firm decision to open a book, all to set off a sparkle in her eyes. Without fail, he'd fall asleep after the first couple of chapters and, after waking, would beg Maansi to print off a detailed synopsis.

This time, it wasn't one of her mother's friends at the door. A young woman entered the kitchen. She had a tall, angular body and straight hair stretching towards the small of her back. She wore a plain but fitted T-shirt, black jeans and a pair of Mary Janes. Rakhee was the last person Maansi expected to see.

'Hello Maansi,' she spoke in that soft, fragile voice of hers.

'Hey, Rakhs. What are you doing here?'

'I was on my way to the shops. I thought I'd stop by. See how you are.'

It was nice of Rakhee to think of Maansi. They weren't exactly friends. At least, not close friends. Their fathers were close, so they found themselves stuck with each other. Rakhee was all right. But she wasn't the kind of person you could confide in. Nor was she the kind of person you could have a terribly interesting conversation with.

Maansi endured Rakhee's eyes as they moved up and down her body like a lift, taking in her ragged appearance. Her hair was tied into a scruffy bun and she was sporting mismatching pyjamas, patterned with a cluster of mysterious stains (one she knew to be three-day-old barbecue sauce). Her mother, who hadn't noticed before, expressed her embarrassment.

'Maansi, why haven't you got ready? It's already noon. Do you want your friends to see you like this? Every day, you wake up late, you do nothing all day, except eat. All the time, bloody eating. Are you planning on hibernating this winter?'

'Mum, please stop.'

'I'll stop when you stop. Look at Rakhee, so pretty and presentable. Oh, and when are you going to start applying for jobs? You can't sit here like a queen. This isn't a hotel.'

Maansi rose and gestured for Rakhee to follow her upstairs, before her mother launched into one of her full-blown lectures. As they reached the landing, they could still hear her as she switched between loud protests and inaudible grumbles.

'When's the last time you opened your curtains?' Rakhee said, as she entered Maansi's bedroom. Her eyes sank into her skull as she surveyed the room. Maansi's wardrobe was empty, its contents in several piles and lumps across the floor. The room smelt of stale perfume and was covered with thick gobbets of dust.

'Oh, leave the curtains. The light will just make the mess in here look worse.'

Rakhee shuddered. 'So, are you coming to Nanika's reception tonight?' she asked, perching on the edge of Maansi's bed, taking care to avoid the pair of knickers hanging on the bedstead. She folded her hands in her lap, as was her habit. Maansi found this contained and elegant way of sitting disingenuous. Too controlled. She considered Rakhee's question for a moment.

'No.'

'Why not? It'll be fun.'

'Your idea of fun is sitting quietly at a table, folding napkins and nibbling at finger foods.'

Rakhee stuck up her nose. 'Well, Sejal will be there. You two can drink and dance until you fall down and embarrass yourselves.' She must've meant for a light-hearted delivery, but her tone was peppery. She quickly changed the subject before Maansi could respond. 'Anyway, how is the job hunt going?'

'Don't ask.' Maansi dropped on to her bed. She couldn't face the subject. For her sanity, that door had to remain closed. Its handle alone was hot enough to scald. 'Let's just say nothing is going on in my life right now.'

'Well, I have some news. If you're interested.' Rakhee looked down at her slender hands. They were slicked with blush polish and filed to the exact same length and shape. Rakhee Joshi led her life with a clinical perfection. She was the girl at school that colour coordinated and underlined her titles with care and precision. She went slowly, with one eye closed and the tip of her tongue sticking out, as if threading a needle through the fog of myopia.

'What news?'

'Someone told my dad they are interested in me for their son. They saw my biodata and now I have a suitor.'

'Oh God. Not this arranged marriage bullshit again,' Maansi moaned. Rakhee reddened at her easy use of coarse language. 'You're really going to let your dad decide who you marry?'

'I'll obviously get a say.'

'Yes, but you only go on what? Four dates before you decide?'

'I trust my parents. They'll know who to choose.'

'Your parents aren't going to have to sleep with him!' As Maansi spoke these words, she realised she couldn't quite frame a picture of Rakhee getting physical with anyone. She imagined her laying on her back, straight as a rod and eyes vacant. Rakhee grew even more florid, but her body remained as contained and unmovable as steel. 'Don't you want to choose someone for yourself? Fall in love?'

Rakhee looked at Maansi and regurgitated the timeworn response advocates of arranged marriages waved like banners: 'Love will grow.'

Maansi snorted. She hated that antiquated mode of thinking. She knew some of her anger came from knowing her own biodata wouldn't impress. She had dark skin, despite repeated abuse of skin-lightening creams. Though she'd finally come to love her deep, earthy tones, others chose to devalue her for them. She had a degree below an upper second-class honours and she couldn't cook or speak a single Indian language. Rakhee, on the other hand, had skin as pale and radiant as Kareena Kapoor's. She was devoted to Hinduism. She was domesticated and sensible. She was what a lot of people wanted in a daughter-in-law.

'Come to the reception, OK? If you want, I can show you the guy.'

'He'll be there?' Her curiosity ignited. Her mind worked to conjure up the image of the kind of man that'd agree to an arranged marriage. Staid, boring and shy? She pictured both him and Rakhee, soundlessly sitting with their hands folded on their laps, picking at spring rolls and avoiding the small but soul-bearing intimacy of eye contact. Rakhee's cheeks would brew as crimson as the wedding dress she'd soon be dressed in. Maansi felt the urge to poke at the situation with Sejal – someone who'd understand the ridiculousness of it all. Maybe she'd go after all. She needed to at least try to remove herself from the quicksand that neither swallowed her nor ceded its hold. She stood, a rush of fatigue threatening to push her back down.

She opened her wardrobe to locate her favourite magenta and silver-hued lehenga. She worried it would no longer fit and felt a deep, interminable contempt for her body. She was no longer a slim size eight but an assertive size twelve with (what she deemed) 'unloving love-handles' that protruded through the most forgiving of fabrics. She sighed. What was she thinking? Her body could not, even with her best efforts, squeeze into her favourite dress, so she hung up her lehenga with a sigh and fished out an ochre Punjabi suit.

'So, is this boy part of your caste?'

'Of course. My dad won't let me marry someone that isn't Brahmin.' Brahmin: the caste of priests. Brahmin foreheads were anointed with the mark of God, however indiscernible the mark may be.

'Of course.' She was glad her parents gave her the freedom to choose. It was the twenty-first century after all. Inter-caste marriages weren't thought of as senseless occurrences any more, and many committed to those they loved.

As she readied herself for the reception, Maansi thought about the vast ocean and how some could cast their nets far across it, while others sat with a mere mugful of it, dunking their fingers in and awaiting the feel of a wriggly tailfin. Even then, they may only catch a trout, leaving them pining after the Moorish idols and regal tangs, swimming freely beyond the constraints of caste.

CHAPTER 3

The hall seethed with heat stemming from the fulsome and gregarious crowds. The bride and groom had invited every friend, relative and acquaintance to boast a wedding fit for royalty. Men wore black suits and faded into the shadows of women in luminous, colour-splashed saris. The frequented wedding soundtrack of *Dilwale Dulhania Le Jayenge* ricocheted off the walls and fell on the lips of those caught in nostalgia, pining after a less 'untoward' era of Bollywood. Tables were decorated with ostentatious centrepieces and platefuls of samosas, bhajias and chilli paneer, pulling in an onslaught of gluttonous children, ready to pile their plates high with their favourite fried snacks. The bride sat at the top of the hall with her husband and wore a gilded gown and such heavy jewellery Maansi wondered if she could move. She could never remember where Nanika was positioned on her multibranched family tree. After all, her family considered the extended families of the extended family their family too. They joined together like a set of magician's linking rings.

Rakhee and Maansi stood by the entrance, reluctant to enter. Rakhee, even with her near-perfections, struggled in social situations and was used to playing the wallflower. She inched behind Maansi, her shoulders high, while Maansi scoured the hall for Sejal. In a matter of moments, she found her, running towards her with the energy of a Duracell bunny. She threw herself at Maansi.

'Maaaaaansi! I am so happy you're here. Oh my God!'

Sejal's sprightly character spoke through the streaks of electric blue coursing through her hair. She wore a lightly embroidered chiffon dress, fusing English and Indian tastes in a bold turquoise. Maansi loved Sejal for her reluctance, or even inability, to conform. She felt lighter around her, as though she had removed duck cloth from her body and slipped into organza.

'Where have you been, woman? I haven't heard from you in a while.'

'Oh. I've just been busy,' Maansi replied, drawing her eyes downwards. Busy staying in bed and doing nothing, she meant, while feeling as if she were doing everything. Getting up to shower and brushing her teeth had become taxing activities; every motion and activity was pilfered from her and wore her down. It was difficult to keep in touch with friends when her mind was focused on performing the basics. For Sejal's sake, she'd try to be the same old Maansi Cavale. She owed her that much.

Sejal noticed Rakhee and gave her a brief nod. 'Is she going to stay with us?' she whispered to Maansi.

She peered back at Rakhee and sighed. 'Sejal, I can't ditch her. She's still my mate. She's got a man here, though, so maybe she'll spend some time with him.'

'What? Really? I thought she was allergic to men.'

'This is different. She has a suitor.'

'Whoa. Really? See, that makes more sense. Do we even call them suitors?'

Sejal and Maansi walked to the bar, with Rakhee trailing behind them, her arms folded and her eyes scanning the room for aunties gossiping about her and her twittering, vodka-worshipping friends.

'Let's get smashed. I'm so done with receptions,' Sejal said. Rakhee fidgeted, keeping her distance from them by a few feet as they ordered their drinks. She didn't approve of drinking. Thinking about it, Maansi realised there was always something Rakhee was uncomfortable with. On her list, below alcohol, were halter-neck dresses, Coca-Cola and public displays of affection.

'Oh look! My mum's calling me,' she piped up, her voice packed with relief. 'I'll see you in a moment...'

Maansi and Sejal watched her mince towards her mother, who stood across the room, repressing a tendril of hair behind her ear as she shook hands with a towering man and his significantly smaller wife. Maansi zoned in on the pair. This couple was the second focal point after the bride and groom. They stood still and confident, like the sun, while others orbited around them, enlivened by their presence. It was easy to tell from a mile off. These were distinguished people.

As Rakhee's mother introduced her daughter, the couple nodded and a young man, perhaps in his early twenties, emerged between them. Rakhee gave a coy smile as he shook her hand. After a few exchanges and inflated grins and beams from both sides, the young man led her away to an empty table.

'Is that him?' Sejal asked. Maansi noticed their mouths were wide open.

'He doesn't look like an ugly, old man.'

'Yeesh, Maansi. Men who opt for arranged marriages aren't all bad looking and old. Bet he's a freshie though! Let's go have a look.'

They positioned themselves at a nearby table to get a closer look. They discerned a fair-skinned male with pleasing facial features and an athletic build. As he spoke, their ears detected the nuances of a British accent.

'He looks ethnically ambiguous, like he could be Mexican or Iranian or something,' Sejal sighed. 'Bet that works in his favour.'

23

'Yeah. Like the sort they cast on Indian television.' It was an unspoken requirement for a heroine to be fair, but more often than not, the hero of the series would have the same moonlit skin. Whiteness was synonymous with beauty. Maansi couldn't count how many times relatives had commented on her dark complexion, lamenting that she hadn't taken after her mother, telling her how much 'luckier' in love she'd be if she had. She'd call out 'bullshit' and the topic would shift from her skin to her dirty mouth.

'Maansi. He's actually... fit,' Sejal said, chewing on her fingernails. 'He looks a little like Avan Jogia!'

'He does. Why would he agree to an arranged marriage?'

They didn't need to brainstorm possible reasons. They conjectured it was parental pressure.

Instead of digging into the platefuls of spice-laden food in front of them, Maansi and Sejal kept their eyes fixed on the pair. The mystery man did the most amount of talking. Rakhee, as statuesque as ever, nodded and offered him meagre, one-word answers, her eyes planted on the offence of his alcoholic drink. He took long swigs of the golden elixir for every ounce of silence she gave him. They watched as he became cognisant of the food laid before him by waiters in bowties and glittering vests. He leaned forward and said something to Rakhee, making her eyes swell like balloons. She delivered a seemingly curt response and he sighed, reaching for his liquid saviour again.

'Doesn't look like it's going well, does it?' Maansi spoke, feeling sorry for Rakhee at that moment. She was bound to be rejected. Nonetheless, there was a sweet, sadist's pleasure roiling in her at the thought, making her question what kind of friend she was being. Hadn't she once cared? She guzzled her own drink, wondering how she'd let herself become so numb.

'He's going to the bar. Want to ask Rakhee his name?' Sejal

waved her phone at her and winked. Of course, with a name, they could begin a session of strategic stalking; a complete ransacking of his social media profiles to get the information they craved. They'd been to so many receptions, they were beginning to lose their minds. They had to find some way to regale themselves...

'You know what. I'm going to get another drink.'

'To get a closer look I bet!' Sejal teased. 'Isn't he beautiful? I'll see if Rakhee's all right. She looks miserable.'

Maansi stood next to the nameless suitor at the bar. She observed him from her peripheral vision as he tapped his fingers against the curved counter, craning his neck to find the barman who was busy filling orders on the other side. She caught the faint notes of Giorgio Armani's *Acqua Di Gio Pour Homme* as it melded with the scent of dark rum. The ocean-fresh and husky meeting in an unsettling but seductive scent that snaked its hot body around him.

'Bride or groom?' Maansi dared herself to ask.

'Groom,' he answered, without glancing in her direction. She was hit with a pang of irritation. She tried again.

'So, I saw you talking to Rakhee. How do you know her?'

He faced her then, eyebrows raised. 'I just met her today. She your friend?'

'Sort of. My dad knows her dad. Family friends,' she said. 'So, what do you think of her then?'

He hesitated. 'She's... fine.' Of course, he wasn't going to tell her the truth. He didn't know her. But from reading his body language earlier, she didn't believe his assessment of Rakhee was a positive one.

'Well, if you want to impress her, I wouldn't buy another drink.'

His fingers ended their impatient tapping and his eyes narrowed. 'I suppose you know why we're speaking.'

'I might. Here's some free advice. She thinks poorly of those who drink, eat meat and smoke. Basically, anyone who isn't a monk.'

'I figured. She freaked when I said they should've offered some non-veg options too,' he said, again facing away from her as he spoke. Maansi wondered why Rakhee's parents were interested in this man at all. Sure, he was a looker, but where were his manners? She always imagined they had a full and detailed criterion to match men against, working with the refined skill of espionage agents during the screening process. Why would her strict, religious parents filter this renegade through? It crossed her mind: financial security or status. Those were big players in the marriage game. She caught the gleam of the Rolex wound around his wrist.

'Well, thanks for the advice,' he said, though he proved not to care for it. The barman came around and he ordered a pint of San Miguel.

Maansi's phone rang from her sequinned clutch bag. It was Sejal. She turned to see her mouthing something and gesticulating towards the man beside her, her arms flapping like a distressed bird's wings.

'What was that?' he sniggered beside her.

'Sorry?'

'Your ringtone. One Direction?'

Before he could align a series of corrosive remarks about her favourite band, she jumped in. 'Yes. One Direction. I love them. It breaks me every day that they split up.'

He shook his head and released a small, breathy laugh. 'What are you? Twelve? Let me guess. Harry Styles is your favourite and you sleep with his cardboard cut-out in your pre-teen, One Direction-themed room,' he theorised, wearing a platina of self-importance she couldn't quite stomach.

'No,' she scowled. 'I'm more a Liam Payne kind of girl, actually. And hey, Rakhee's a fan too. So, if you both click, I'm sure there'll be a few songs playing at your reception!'

He didn't laugh or crack a smile at her remark. Had she overstepped a line? She twirled a loose strand of hair around her finger, unsure of how to save the conversation. His eyes clouded over and the air between them settled as a thick, palpable mass.

'Are you OK?' she asked, after a handful of silences. He seemed to be meditating over something, wearing the expression of a poet beset with nihilism. He shook off whatever roved about his mind and offered her a placating smile. He told her he had to get back to Rakhee.

'OK, it was nice meeting you,' Maansi called after him as he strode away. He didn't turn to respond. 'Rude,' she muttered to herself. Then again, maybe he hadn't heard her over the recycled Bollywood tracks. She retreated to her table where an animated Sejal waited for her.

'When are they going to put on bhangra?' Maansi whinged, plonking herself down on the chair. She didn't care much for dancing and thought again of her bed and the safe comfort of it, but the old Maansi loved bhangra and never napped. Sejal gripped her arm.

'Forget that! What did he say?' she said, bouncing like a rubber ball.

'Not much. Small talk. What did Rakhee say?'

'His name. It's Aryan Alekar.' She passed her phone to Maansi. His Facebook page occupied the entire screen, yet all that was visible was a picture of him, dapper in a navy suit and teal tie. A corporate man, she presumed. His personal life, his interests, his friends were all shrouded behind an unyielding privacy setting. 'Add him as a friend.'

'What? No.'

'How else will we get access to his profile? Come on, you just spoke to him. It won't be weird. Aren't you curious? It's your duty as Rakhee's friend to vet him.'

Sejal pleaded with Maansi until the groom's brother called for silence. The string of never-ending speeches began and they tried to endure them as best they could. During the best man's speech, where embarrassing moments were plucked from the groom's history and laid out to behold like underwear on a washing line, Sejal stole Maansi's phone from her bag.

'Added,' Sejal said, smirking as she pushed Maansi's phone into her hand.

'What the f–'

'OK, ladies and gentlemen. It's time for the first dance,' the best man announced.

Maansi tried to calm down. She hovered over the 'cancel friend request' option. Would Facebook inform him that she'd made a request and then cancelled? Or would he never know a request was made? She wanted to tear her hair out. He'd think she was snooping. No, she didn't care, she told herself. Why the hell should she care? She hid her phone away and let the oncoming dance distract her. Nanika's husband led his new, shiny wife to the dancefloor. They airily swayed like willow-tree leaves to the soft, romance-soused song: *Tum Hi Ho*. Her husband couldn't centre his gaze and let his eyes shift from side to side like panicked prey, too embarrassed to lock his eyes with hers. After all, love and affection had to be muted beneath the prodding eyes of the elders. Though many, like Maansi, were still hoping someone would slash the polyethylene barrier and 'kiss the bride' – without thought, as others did around the world. She remembered her cousins kissing their partners on the cheek, or omitting the kiss for a hug at their respective registries, too afraid of offending someone. Meanwhile, Bollywood actors and actresses were brushing their lips against each other's necks beneath the rise and fall of sheer dupattas, the women's stomachs often bare; their movements a slow dance. These sensual scenes, more wholesome than a single, fleeting kiss upon the lips.

As the song came to a finish, Maansi caught a glimpse of the man she now knew as Aryan Alekar on the other side of the hall. His eyebrows knitted together as he fingered his phone. She gulped. His face shot up and he found her within a matter of seconds. She turned away, her skin burning beneath the searing heat of his gaze. He must have seen the request. She rose, telling Sejal she'd be back in a moment.

She travelled to the back of the hall where the music was less likely to activate a form of tinnitus. A group of chatty, middle-aged women whipped their heads around as they saw her approach, like voracious crows towards a field mouse.

'Maansi. Come say hello,' said one of the aunties – Priya Soni, her mother's friend from work. She was introduced as Roshni's daughter, which made the other women 'ooh' and 'aah' as they skimmed her like a book. They fussed around her, trading their analyses of her as they took her in, acting as if she wasn't present among them.

'She has grown so much, *heina*?'

'Yes, she graduated only a while ago.'

'Any job yet?'

'She'll be getting married and having children before we know it.'

One of the ladies asked Maansi whether she achieved a first-class honours, like her own daughter, and another planted and grew the image of her marrying and having children, as if this 'sure' eventuality was the sole reason for her existence. Their talk skewered her, dragging forward the ache of undead memories. The pills, the clinic, the blood and passing of large clots. The image of the baby she'd accidentally drawn awakened in her mind and opened its tired eyes. She knew her face would soon be strewn with tears if she didn't desert the women around her. She apologised and burst through the exit doors, leaving them with something else to read into and talk about. Her rudeness, her emotional instability… whatever they could dig up.

Finally, out of the unventilated hall, she inhaled the cold air, but her body wasn't accepting it. Her chest tightened as if she had overstretched an elastic band to manage just one final loop over her rib cage, and now it was seconds away from either snapping her or itself, in two.

Her breathing was shallow. Fast. She brought her hands towards her head as it lightened. She didn't understand why this was happening again. She thought for sure she'd got a handle on her emotions.

'You again?'

She turned. Aryan was behind her, lighting the cigarette nestled between his front teeth. She didn't answer. She couldn't. She lowered herself on to a step and tried to capture the whispers of wind passing her lips. She was going to die. She was sure of it. She wanted to ask for help but words wouldn't come out. Stubbing out his cigarette, Aryan settled beside her. She wished he'd go away. She didn't need anyone to witness her in that state. She continued gasping for air.

'Breathe with me,' he spoke with purpose.

He counted in their inhalations and exhalations. Her chest

would loosen, but she'd relapse and grab his arm while the stricture replaced itself, squeezing her like a piece of soft-fleshed fruit. They kept focusing on her breathing, until she was calm enough and her body loose enough to feel the bite of the cold. Her moist hand was still wrapped around his forearm. It took her a moment too many to realise and remove it.

'Are you all right?' he asked her. 'Do you need me to get someone?'

'N-no. I'm fine. Thank you,' she managed to say through chattering teeth. 'How did you know, just now, what to do?' She couldn't work out why he was so calm. He must've thought she was an escapee from a psychiatric ward.

'I just know,' he said. 'What happened?'

She shook her head and let her face sink into her knees. She was too embarrassed and ashamed to lift her face, which continued to dampen with careless tears. She couldn't explain herself to a stranger.

'Go back in. Get a drink. You'll feel better.' He rose, rolling his shoulders to work out the cracks.

'You're going to just leave me here?'

'You're all right, aren't you?'

'Well, I...' She gave a perfunctory nod, wiping away a few stray tears. He lingered for a second or two, his eyes scoring through her, before heading back into the hall.

She kicked a stone beneath her feet and grumbled. Maybe he'd be good for Rakhee. He seemed phlegmatic enough. What kind of man was he anyway? The kind of person that'd save a drowned kitten, yet leave it in a shivering lump on the pavement?

After a few more deep breathing exercises, she gathered enough mettle to re-enter the hall. She scanned the hall for Sejal and found her at the bar, tossing her head back in raucous laughter, her hand on Aryan's shoulder. She should have known Sejal would make her way to him. Maansi considered what they might be discussing. What was so funny that Sejal had to roar with laughter like that? Rakhee was seated at her table watching them too, reproaching them with dagger-flinging glares, her mother shaking her head at the spectacle.

'Maansi, there you are,' Sejal said as Maansi approached. 'Drink with us.'

The barman neatly lined up shots of Jager Bombs in front of them. 'Here. Feel better,' Aryan winked, handing her a shot glass. She flushed, refusing to take it.

'Aryan said you weren't feeling well,' Sejal said. 'You were gone so long. I came and asked if he'd seen you. What happened?'

'Nothing,' she replied, hoping he hadn't divulged any details. Sejal didn't know about any of it. The unpredictable and ruthless panic attacks, the daily switches between feeling wholly separate from the world, then feeling it burrow into your belly, squeezing into a space too small to accommodate it. 'Should you really be drinking this much in front of the aunties and uncles? And shouldn't you be getting back to Rakhee?'

'No one will notice. Everyone's focused on the bride and groom. Come on, Maansi. Live a little.' She tantalised her, swilling the liquorice-scented liquid inches from her face. Maansi was about to decline but the vision of Aryan's pompous grin made her grab the glass and down the contents. She slammed the glass down on to the counter, wiping the edge of her mouth with her hand. 'That's my girl!' Sejal celebrated. They each swept through a fair few, laughing and talking about nothing of worth: the people around them, the reactions of aunties noticing them and the wacky dance moves of uncles. Sejal drank the most and soon gave way to a drunken sway. She wobbled towards Aryan, dipping dangerously close to his chest and slurring her apologies through pouting lips. Her flirtations had never been subtle.

'So, Aryan, if you had to. Like say you *had to*, choose between me and Rakhee. Who would you choose?' Sejal asked, shaping her hand into a gun and aiming it at his head. Maansi tried to peel her off him.

'Sejal, you're embarrassing yourself,' she whispered. Sejal shook her off and told her to stop being silly. However, she soon ceased her pursuit and dawdled off to the bathroom with a full bladder, leaving Maansi alone with him. She left it to him to start the conversation, but he was captivated by something on his phone. Only moments ago, she'd been vulnerable in front of him. In front of a stranger. How was she to start? She considered asking him a question about himself. What did he do? How old was he? But her thoughts were interrupted by the intent stare of a woman. The one half of the power couple she saw earlier sitting at a nearby table, watching her.

'Is that your mum?' Maansi asked. 'She keeps staring.'

'Ignore her. She's upset I'm not continuing my conversation with Rakhee,' Aryan replied. 'Want another drink?'

Aryan's mother released the same condemnatory energy as Rakhee did. It annoyed her, the way some still formed a negative opinion of you for just drinking and talking to a member of the opposite sex. The woman's stare burned through Maansi's inhibitions and the conversation starters she searched for poured from her mouth.

'So how are you related to the groom?' she asked Aryan.

'He's my second cousin. I think.'

'I think Nanika's my second cousin, once removed. That's just a guess though. Can never be sure.'

As they spoke about the reception, she let herself become more liberal with him, talking louder and even patting his arm, giving his mother something to feed off. Honey Singh surged through the speakers as she knocked back another drink. It was one of her favourite songs.

'Do you want to dance?' she asked.

'I'm not much of a dancer.'

'Oh, come on! It'll be fun.'

She would not be judged for failing to be demure and quiet. As she reached the floor, leading Aryan with her clinging hand, she realised she was drunker than she'd thought. She began to move, getting into the rhythm of the music, her hips rocking side to side, until she lost her balance and almost toppled over. Aryan caught her and straightened her up. His hands were strong and his eyes were penetrating beneath the flitting party lights. She weakened, her head replete with powdery balls of fuzz.

'Are you OK? Maybe you should go and sit down,' he suggested. 'You clearly can't handle your drink.'

'I'm fine,' she replied with umbrage. 'Just the shoes.'

She kicked off her stilettos and continued dancing, but when she almost fell again he led her to a table and fetched her a glass of water. She brought it to her lips and spilt the water down her front.

'You're a mess,' Aryan said coolly, offering her a serviette. She seized it and started dabbing at her chest, her hands working with the speed of an accomplished typist.

'Yes, thank you for that,' she said, masking her embarrassment through gritted teeth and the best scathing tone she could produce. He only laughed.

'Aryan!' a man called from a group comprised of three others. They gestured for him to join them.

'I better go. See you around,' he said, leaving her soaked – the drowned kitten after all. He departed the moment Sejal returned. She slouched in the chair next to Maansi and started picking at the decorative hearts scattered along the table, disappointment clear in her face.

'Shame he's gone. He's cute, don't you think? Lucky Rakhee. What did you guys talk about?' she asked Maansi.

'Nothing really.' She disapproved of Sejal's dreamy eyes. She wasn't one to fall so easily. 'Last one to the dancefloor buys the next round!'

They didn't need a man around to have fun. She hit the dancefloor with her friend, determined to dance until her feet hurt and drink until she could no longer feel the pain. They even dragged Rakhee on at one point, who chastised them for 'borrowing' Aryan, then complained about his flaws in the gaps between songs. 'I would never marry him. No matter what he looks like. We're just too different.'

As the evening approached its end and their faces were hot with pleasure from dancing without care, Maansi and Sejal took a breather at the back of the hall. It was here they saw Aryan and his mother talking. His mother looked as if she was imploring him, her hands pressed together and her doe-eyes wide and wobbling. Aryan shook his head and dismissed her with a sharp flip of a hand. She crossed her arms, her gentle features hardening. He bowed his head in apology before he marched off.

'Do you think it's about Rakhee? We shouldn't have borrowed him,' Sejal said. 'Not our fault though, right? It wasn't going well. She needed saving!'

Aryan's mother looked at Maansi. Really looked at her. Maansi quickly pretended to be engrossed in something else. Once she judged it safe to look over again, she noticed the mother was making an enquiry of the lady next to her. The guest then pointed towards another woman at the front of the hall. Maansi's forehead wrinkled as Aryan's mother strutted towards her own mother.

'Is she going to talk to my mum?' Maansi said to Sejal. 'Why is she doing that?'

Sejal shrugged, kneading her feet beneath the table. 'Maybe to complain about what a naughty girl you are. "*Behenji*, your daughter brushed arms with my son! I beg you whip her into shape with your best *chappal*."'

Maansi laughed. She wasn't concerned. She surveyed the dancefloor from a safe distance. Though the majority couldn't dance, everyone on the floor enjoyed themselves. At that moment, she couldn't understand why it mattered whether you were fair, or dark, or from a low caste or high caste, a doctor or a cashier at Asda. Everybody looked as foolish as each other, with their buoyant hearts and their inner-children visible and unguarded beneath the flare of disco lights.

CHAPTER 4

Maansi typed 'graduate' in the search box of another online job board. She didn't specify a location this time. Beggars couldn't be choosers, she told herself. Especially with her mediocre achievement. She imagined having to move to the back of beyond and shuddered. Although she was indifferent to Leicester at the best of times, she couldn't imagine being anywhere else. Leicester was diverse and cultured. Leicester was big without being overwhelming. Life burned at the centre of her city. She'd never been anywhere else. Even the university she attended resided in the same county.

A number of 'highly competitive' and 'intensive' graduate schemes popped up, each unequivocally demanding at least an upper second-class degree. Some companies stated they'd consider someone that didn't meet the grade requirements, if they proved to be the right candidate. She wondered if she was made of the 'right' stuff. She supposed not. She wasn't convinced she could offer anything of much worth to these corporate companies with their cohorts of debonair graduates, dressed in sleek blazers and winning smiles. She cringed at the thought of sitting in front of an interviewer, trying to sell herself through a set of grinning teeth and the façade of a bubbly, confident personality. 'I have exceptional communication skills, I am positive, confident...' She wasn't sure she could fake it. They'd stamp her application with the word FRAUD, in fat red letters.

She read more about each scheme she came across. Her

palms began to moisten. The intensive nature of these schemes was clear and left her fraught with anxiety. 'This fourteen-month, intensive, employer-led programme...' 'This intensive tailor-made programme will mould graduates...' 'Our graduate scheme is an intensive two-year programme designed to fast-track graduates...'

She was tired. She lacked motivation and felt like an insatiable leech had settled into her body to feed off every morsel of energy she produced. Her whole body had become slow and heavy, moving as if it were wading through water. It was in a long state of protest and she let it beat on.

She viciously clicked out of the job sites. What was the point, anyway?

She signed into Facebook. It was the worst thing to do when she felt low, but she couldn't help it. Her body compelled her to log on, though she knew the last thing she needed was to look upon the lives of others. She'd stew in jealousy, looking upon photos of people doing remarkable things as part of their remarkable lives. Facebook didn't show the menial and mundane moments. She wouldn't see that they too consumed too many shows on Netflix and lounged around in their onesies for hours a day, stuffing their faces with guilt-inducing snacks and scrolling through their news feeds, wondering why others had it so good. Their holidays, their parties, their friends – their snapshots of moments that seemed to be lit beneath the glow of candles – pinioned her to the bed and made her loath to leave it.

As if she were a masochist pleading for pain, she visited Lewis's profile. She had unfriended him, leaving most of his content locked away from her prying eyes. But right there, visible for the world to see, were his holiday pictures with a golden-haired girl, tagged as Katie McHugh. The caption to accompany the slew of oncoming pictures read: 'having fun in

Majorca with this one'. The girl stood there in her coral bikini and honey-hued skin, with Lewis's arm securely fastened around her waist. They flashed their whiter-than-milk teeth at the camera. They fit together, like the right pair of jigsaw pieces, finally found among the pile of thousands.

Maansi flicked through the album. Other photos showed them standing on a balcony together, peering at saffron skies. She imagined the uncaptured bed, standing only a few steps away. She pictured their bodies intertwining in the Mediterranean heat and felt overcome with nausea. More images surfaced, of him kissing her on the cheek, of them drinking with a group of other happy couples. They were quite the pair. Everyone thought so. 'You look so cute together', 'adorable couple', 'nice one mate' the comments read. And they all pasted in little hearts to reaffirm how much they meant what they said. Katie and Lewis, how bloody perfect.

She hated herself for looking at his profile, but she was curious. Like a child told not to touch a hot plate, she had to do it. She had to know what she didn't know, even at the risk of burning skin.

'Maansi!' her mother shouted from downstairs. 'Maansi come down, this moment!'

Maansi rolled her eyes. She was probably about to be served another one of her mother's infamous lectures about unwashed dishes. Her parents always made a big deal out of everything.

'This is a big deal,' her father began as she entered the living room. He leaned forward in his favourite armchair, the meaty pads of his fingertips pressed together. Maansi immediately distrusted the twinkle in his eye. 'Somebody has taken an interest in you.' At last, the day had arrived.

'Oh for fuck's–'

'Maansi!' her mother warned her, her eyes popping out of her skull like bloated globes.

'Please, don't do this to me. You said I could marry whomever I want,' she moaned.

'And you still can,' her father said, his chocolate-button eyes seeking to appease her. He held up his hands. 'We are not forcing you, but maybe consider this person.'

'You know I won't.' She was twenty-three and fresh out of university. It wasn't the right time to think about marriage. 'I don't want to marry some sad loser that needs his mummy and daddy to find him a girl because he hasn't got the balls, sorry, I mean guts to find one himself. What's wrong with him then?'

'Nothing, Maansi,' her father said. He spoke in flute-like tones, as he often did when trying to calm her down. She saw his cheeks spasm. He was trying to suppress a smile that longed to spread across his chubby face. 'The boy's family are very wealthy. Millionaires. They are Brahmin and Hindu-Punjabi, like us. And he is good-looking.'

She was stunned into silence. What did he mean? Millionaires? Interested in her? They were clearly mistaken. Who would be interested in her? Besides, she had never expressed a desire to marry to her parents. She was too young. But hearing the word millionaire roused something in her. It was natural to be curious. 'I don't understand. Why me? Not that I care, because I don't. But, well, I'm not a Rakhee.'

How did these people come to find her? She sincerely hoped her mother hadn't created a profile for her on shaadi.com. She imagined the sort of profile her mother would produce. Up popped an 'about me' description riddled with exaggerations, accompanied with pictures taken beneath sheaths of too-white light to mask the colour of her skin – her rich, clay-pot skin.

'They don't want a girl like Rakhee. They said they want a lively girl. Somebody their son will enjoy the company of,' her dad continued.

'Oh, really? And how do they know what I'm like?'

'The parents saw you at the reception. They think you might form a connection with him and want to see,' her dad continued. 'They said he looked like he enjoyed himself with you.'

'I'm sorry, whose parents?'

'The parents of Aryan Alekar. Very handsome boy. Very well-to-do.'

Maansi's mouth dropped a little. She vaguely recalled Aryan's mother speaking to hers. What was she asking? Did her mother talk her up too much? Her stomach lurched as she remembered dancing with him. She recalled how his hands held her up. The alcohol made her forget how risky such contact was with her mother around. Did Aryan ask his parents to get in touch with hers? Was *he* the one interested? Or was she another selection made by his mum? She wondered what Rakhee would do if she knew.

'Think about it. You two can speak and if you think you might like each other, we'll have a formal meeting with his parents and see if we are happy.' Her father smiled encouragingly at her. 'You'd have a good lifestyle. Imagine *beti*. You wouldn't even have to work.'

'No. No way. I told you arranged marriages are a stupid idea. It's completely backwards. You can't decide who you want to marry just like that. It takes years!'

She retreated into her bedroom, having given her final word. Her parents had clearly forgotten her stance on arranged marriages. Deciding to make a life partner of someone after a few meetings? You might as well flip a coin. And for parents to

41

have any say in marriage made no sense to Maansi. The whole thing spelt madness.

She thought she shut the door hard and fast on the idea. However, a few days passed by and Maansi realised she couldn't quite forget what her dad said about not having to work. Her inability to find a job was making her feel worse. Even if she could find one, she pictured sitting at an office with the same black cloud hovering over her head, opening to unleash rain on her until her fingers trembled with the chill. She could foresee herself locked in a bathroom cubicle, begging for time to make haste.

Then, another image spawned in her mind, sparkling and revolving upon a turntable like a brand-new car. She imagined waking up with money and an attractive man. An attractive, rich husband, living in London – a different world, away from her darker world. She knew it was wrong to be shallow, but when she considered her belief in marrying for love, she only saw the torn slivers of her broken heart, pinned against her banner that screamed 'love does not grow!' Love had snapped and stunted her. Maybe, just maybe, there were advantages to arranged marriages she was blind to. She'd be foolish to deny the possibility.

When her parents brought the subject up again, she fought the impulse to answer them with rolling eyes and stomping feet. She didn't passionately denounce arranged marriage and strut away, too dignified to have the conversation. She said, in a feeble voice: 'I'll think about it.' They celebrated, and she knew they expected her to agree to a meeting. They told her they'd tell his parents she'd consider it. Feeling out of her depth, she called Sejal and asked her what she thought. She spoke to her friend of a handsome, wealthy man of her age, never disclosing his name.

'I don't know, Maansi. I've always thought you should see

42

someone as long as humanly possible before marrying them. But, I mean, we all want rich, good-looking men. What if he's really nice too? Maybe just see him. It could be destiny.' Sejal's words and her parents' eagerness meddled with her mind.

Maansi settled in her room one night and switched on the laptop. The worries about her future made her brain twinge with the vigour of a stitch. She feared she'd be stuck doing nothing for ever.

An email arrived from one of the graduate schemes she applied to. It began 'Thank you for your recent application. We are sorry to inform you...' She closed the email and felt tears gently simmer around her eyes. It happened again. She'd been rejected so many times, she was sure she'd become immune to the sting, yet her heart shrivelled up like a raisin once more. But this time, she was saved from her fall into self-pity with a bell-toned ping. A notification arrived from Facebook: Aryan Alekar had accepted her friend request.

She felt her heart bouncing erratically, suddenly a sugar-flushed child on a pogo stick. She navigated to his profile and the pictures and information that were under lock and key spilt across her screen. The unveiling of Aryan Alekar's life began.

She was disheartened to find that he was only a sporadic user of Facebook. Pictures and statuses were posted months apart and revealed little about him. A reserved picture here and there, of him with a couple of friends in unmentioned locations. Nothing to indicate hobbies, likes or passions. It was all neutral. She dipped further into his past. He used to frequent social media a long time ago. At the age of seventeen, his profile was rife with photos, videos and posts. He was a lot younger then, but still attractive. She could imagine having admired him as a teenager. From the sheer number of likes and comments he received, she could see he was popular. Most of his pictures belonged to an album titled 'Boarding School' – a testament to his family's wealth. She wanted to know more.

As if the universe were responding to her unspoken wish, a chat box opened, delivering a message from him to her. It said: 'Hey. My parents think we'd make a good match and, apparently, so do yours. Do you want to speak?'

She was surprised by the inclusion of punctuation and complete words in a simple Facebook message. She supposed something like this, if to be discussed at all, was to be discussed properly. Maansi's fingers twitched as she tried to figure out what to say. A 'good match' meant a good pair for marriage. They were talking about marriage! It rattled her. She still wondered why she was agreeing to marriage so soon. Was she insane for considering it?

'Maybe we could meet at a café and speak there?' she typed back.

'I live in London. We'd have to speak on the phone or Skype,' came the reply.

'To make this kind of decision?'

'Sorry. Best I can do.'

He couldn't have sounded more uninterested.

CHAPTER 5

He called every Friday evening to talk to her. He was unnervingly quiet to begin with. Finding the weavings of vacant silences unbearable, she tried to steer him into a conversation about her obsession with boybands. She hoped for playful derision or a train of sarcastic remarks on his part but got nothing. Instead, she suffered small talk, and she soon believed she was going to be another Rakhee: discarded like a plastic doll that once promised hours of fun as it shone in the shop window, but in truth inspired nothing.

Every time Maansi thought about telling her parents it was a no-go, she'd fill with an anxiety that'd build to a harsh crescendo, remembering she would have to find a job, deal with Lewis and Katie as a couple, cope with what she'd done and how she let it affect her grades. Worst of all, she'd have to tackle her depression in a home where depression was an unrecognisable entity.

'People don't have depression in India,' she had heard before. According to her mother, people in the UK are too absorbed in themselves. 'In India, it's about the community. There is none of this individualism, so how can anybody sulk around and get "depressed"?' she would say. Maansi hated the implication. She did not lure her depression in through being an egocentric individual. Rather, it snatched her and absorbed her into its black, tarry belly. Thankfully, her father was a little better. He'd approached her one day, sitting at the foot of her bed while she buried herself under her unicorn-themed duvet, mugs and used plates.

'Don't listen to your mother. Do you want me to pay for you to see someone?' he asked her. 'I watched Deepika Padukone talk about depression. It sounds difficult. I don't know how to help, so you tell me.'

In the end, she told him private counselling would cost too much, so she'd have it for free, knowing her position on the waiting list meant waiting for a long amount of time. She wondered if leading a new lavish lifestyle with a new man, in a new place, would force the depression to dissipate into nothing.

Knowing what was at stake, she tried harder to engage Aryan's interest. She constantly asked him about his life. What was he doing? What shows did he like? He was difficult to pry open, like a window sealed shut by the iced tongue of winter. Even on Skype, he didn't care to occupy the centre of his webcam's focus. He was ungraspable.

Saturday at Bru café, she told him. It was difficult, but she convinced him to travel to Leicester to see her. It was the only way she could get him to focus on her.

'What should I wear?' she asked Sejal, who sat cross-legged on the bed, watching Maansi fling clothes about the room.

'I don't know,' she answered. Maansi stopped. Sejal loved picking out outfits for her. It was her greatest pleasure in life to conduct people on how to be aesthetically appealing. She was prone to getting herself into trouble because of it, blurting out comments such as, 'Well, that colour drains you out and makes you look old, Mum.'

'What's wrong? Have you got the hump?'

'It just seems weird,' she said. 'You agreeing to an arranged marriage.'

'I haven't agreed yet. I don't even know if he will.'

Maansi pulled out a dark-blue skater dress with daisies climbing the front of the fabric. She held it in front of her, examining it for lint or faded patches. Would it even fit? She took a handful of the extra fat wheeling around her body, wishing it'd stretch further and break off like dough.

'But he rejected your friend. Ain't her dad mates with yours?'

Maansi did wonder how her family's relationship with Rakhee's family would be affected. She tried broaching the subject with her parents. It seemed they'd found justification through the Alekar wealth and status.

'Rakhee's dad will understand,' her dad had told her. 'I just want what is best for our daughter.'

Why couldn't Sejal understand that this really could be the best thing for her? She couldn't comprehend why her so-called friend was being so negative. She never once cared for Rakhee and treated her like an insect to be shaken off.

'Since when were you so bothered about Rakhee anyway? Trust me, he isn't her type. I'm doing her a favour.' She flinched, finding the sudden depth of her voice, the strength and unerring quality of it, grating and wrong.

Sejal rolled her eyes and began picking at the fraying fibres of her burgundy jumper.

'I know what this is,' Maansi began. She twisted her body from the mirror to face Sejal. 'You're jealous.'

'Excuse me?'

'Don't pretend you weren't ogling at him at Nanika's reception. You're jealous because he picked me.' Had those words really erupted from her mouth?

'His mum picked you, you delusional cow,' Sejal said. 'And anyway, I just heard some very interesting rumours about him. His cousin is mates with my sister and–'

'Oh please, can you ever stop gossiping? Seriously,' she spumed, surprised by her fiery reaction but unable to douse it.

'What is wrong with you? You're acting so weird. And if

47

you want to treat your friends like shit, then fine. I don't have to take this.' Sejal sprung off the bed and made for the door.

'Good. Go!'

Before she shut the door behind her, she spoke with a snake-like hiss sailing beneath her words: 'You know, maybe this mean streak of yours is why Lewis left you.' The following slam of the door was a sharp slap to the face. Maansi frothed with fury. She was sick of the past affecting her. She could feel it. The air was concentrated with it and stuck with her like a sceptre. Sejal was supposed to help her unpick this situation, to help her study it from every angle. She was supposed to help her in making one of the biggest decisions of her life.

She put on the blue, floral dress and produced various vials and pots of designer cosmetics from her drawers. She lined her eyes with kohl and painted her lips a sweet-tempered red. She sprayed her body with an aquatic scent – *Fijian Water Lotus* – remembering how he had given off the scent of an ocean breeze. She straightened her stubborn curls, until her hair fell just below her ribcage, and planted her feet in a pair of kitten heels. Finally, she tugged at her dress, exposing just the right amount of cleavage. She left the house.

She entered Bru café, feverish with anxiety. Her eyes scrutinised the place but she found no Aryan Alekar. She exhaled, glad she had arrived first and could comfortably order without his eyes upon her. She forwent her usual mocha, afraid the caffeine would only make her more tremulous. Her voice erupted in a rippling lilt as she ordered her hot chocolate. Her palms were clammy and she was beginning to question her deodorant's protective abilities. She sat down in a quiet corner of the café and took out her phone. It was a safety crutch for her. She needn't look up and meet his eyes as he walked in.

Half an hour passed and the remainder of her hot chocolate coagulated at the bottom of her mug. She was beginning to believe she'd been stood up. As she reached for her bag, she heard a voice.

'I'm sorry I'm late.'

Her eyes flickered upwards. He stood before her, more handsome than she remembered and proffering her a full-bosomed rose. Its lips were puckered, proposing a conciliatory kiss. She took it and her disappointment dissolved.

'I thought you weren't coming,' she said.

'I'm sorry. Really. Can I get you a cake or something, to make it up to you?'

She nodded cheekily and he soon returned with a chocolate cake for her and a hot drink for himself. She rubbed her hands together. This was her first date with an actual suitor.

'They are good at that don't you think?' she said, indicating the leaf-pattern settled on the milky froth of his cappuccino. He nodded and looked at it in a strange wistful manner, as if there was more of the leaf in his cup than just the rough, cocoa-powdered outline. Silence ensued. How were these things supposed to go?

'So, this is a bit awkward, right?' Maansi said, immediately hating herself for it.

He offered a mild-mannered smile. 'Sorry. I guess I haven't been giving you much attention recently. How is your job hunt going? I hear you want to work for the United Nations one day?'

Her cheeks flushed as he said this. Had her mum said that? She'd been avoiding speaking about careers and her future ambitions with him, veering him towards trivial matters such as his favourite TV shows, food and what football team he supported. Thinking about it, she realised they had mostly spoken about him and his interests. Perhaps it was better that way. What was she supposed to say? 'Hey there, I'm a jobless depressed loser that binge-eats in the dark because I'm too sad to open my bedroom curtains?' He'd run a mile.

'Yes, I'm still looking for jobs. I'm not so sure about the United Nations thing. I'm keeping my options open,' she said. He nodded, his eyes void of expression. 'Anyway, what about you? You work for your dad's company?'

'Yeah. He runs a property development company. He wants me to eventually take over as CEO.'

'That's amazing,' Maansi replied in a plasticised voice. She was having a difficult time being herself in front of him. He had an aura that left her disorientated and dizzied. She pulled at the hem of her dress. It was failing to imbue her with the kind of confidence she expected from it. He noticed her fidgeting.

'You look nice.'

'Not really,' she said.

'Oh God, you're not one of those girls, are you?' He leaned back in his chair and shook his head.

'Pardon? One of what girls?'

'A girl that cannot take a compliment. Riddled with insecurities. Takes every opportunity to put herself down...' He rolled his eyes and she immediately felt reactive. This was definitely the guy she met at the reception.

'No! I'm very comfortable in my skin, thank you very much!' She hoped he couldn't tell she was lying. 'I'm not one of those girls.'

'OK. So, what kind of girl are you?'

'How am I supposed to answer that?'

'Come on. We kind of need to fast-track here. Get to know each other quickly,' he said. 'Here. Tell me, the worst thing that's ever happened to you, followed by the best and the craziest.'

Maansi was a little bit taken aback by his directness, but acquiesced. The grains of sand were gathering in the lower bulb of their hourglass, slipping through the gap without vacillation. She could be marrying this man. Could she tell him the truth about her? She didn't want to let truth's full, alarming face bloom in her answers. She'd give him just enough.

'The worst thing that happened to me was learning my boyfriend was unfaithful.' That wasn't true. She didn't believe he started seeing that Katie girl while seeing her. It was just something she'd been telling herself to make herself feel better. And even then, Lewis leaving her wasn't the worst thing that ever happened.

He raised his eyebrows. 'So, this means you're a bad judge of character?'

'What? No.'

He took another sip of his cappuccino. 'OK. Continue.'

'Craziest moment…' She began to think and then threw her face in her hands as she remembered. 'Oh, I can't tell you that.'

'You've got to. That's the deal.'

'OK, but this is just to prove I am comfortable in my own skin,' she began. 'I ran the naked quarter mile.'

'The what?'

'In my first year of living in halls, if you were brave enough, you ran the quarter mile track naked.'

'And you did that?'

'Yes. Well, sort of. I wore my underwear.'

'That doesn't count.'

'Yes it does! Running in a bra and knickers is still pretty gutsy. This was in the middle of December at midnight. You have to give that to me.' As she defended herself with force, people put down their cups to stare. She shielded her face and refocused her attention on her chocolate cake.

He quietly laughed. 'OK, fine. Best thing?'

Maansi frowned. 'I don't know. I guess, the best thing was what the worst thing came out of.' Before it all went downhill, her days with Lewis had been joyful, pleasant, edged with an astral glow. 'I'm waiting for the best thing.'

He nodded, as if he understood what she was talking about. His eyes traced the little leaf in his cup again.

'OK. Your turn then.'

He blinked. It seemed he forgot he was up for interrogation too. 'No, you can't use my questions. Ask me something else.'

'What? No way.'

'I don't make the rules.'

'Uhr, yes you do.' She expelled a laugh. He had some nerve. 'OK. If you insist. Why are you agreeing to an arranged marriage? I mean, you're only twenty-three. You still have time, right?'

'It's hard to find girls ready to commit,' he began. He seemed to be selecting his words with care, like a junior copywriter at an advertising firm, using all their mental energy to prove their worth. 'They play games, so finding one by myself wasn't an easy task. My parents also want someone from the same caste, so even more difficult to find a girl like that. And with only being twenty-three, well, I have my life sorted. I have a high salary, my own place, why wait?'

The word 'commit' rang like a gentle-toned bell in her ear. She welcomed it. 'So, what was wrong with Rakhee?'

'Not my type. Filled my parents' brief but not mine.'

'And what is it you want?' she asked.

'A free thinker. Someone with a bit of passion. Someone a little bit wild. Maybe someone willing to run the naked quarter mile?' he grinned. Maansi grimaced, the temperature in her cheeks rising again.

'I get it, with Rakhee,' she said, picking at her cake. The chocolate ganache oozed down the sides and spread across the plate. 'She's a sweet girl. Sometimes a bit judgemental. She feeds into the whole "what will people say" mentality. Who cares?'

'I hate that. What will the community think? All the time.'

'*Log Kya Kahenge?*'

'You know Hindi?'

She bit her tongue. 'Not even a little bit. Although, I love the odd Shah Rukh Khan movie. Thank God for subtitles!'

She felt herself finally scramble through the debris and arrive within her body. They were engaging. They were laughing. He leaned in to talk to her now, and she dared to meet his eyes. She could see translucent, amber specks afloat on two golden-brown pools.

'So, I might have cyber-stalked you a little. Only because of the whole possibly getting married thing,' she said, delicately spooning chocolate cake into her mouth. The last thing she wanted was chocolate smeared across her face. 'You went to a boarding school?'

'Yes. Brookside School in East Anglia. I was there from year seven to thirteen,' he said in a matter-of-fact way.

'Oh wow. So, you were away from home at a young age. Was it difficult? Being away?'

'It was difficult returning home, actually. I'd been away for so long. My parents wanted me to live at home while I went to university to make up for lost time. It was a nightmare,' he swallowed the bitter memory. 'But I have my own place now. So, if we decided... well, you wouldn't have to live with my parents.'

She peered bashfully at her hands. They were still moist

and tormented by persistent but weak tremors. 'Should we talk about that? You know, directly?' She was sure he was peering down too.

'I'm under pressure to make a decision. You seem like a nice girl. I'm fine with taking this further. But if you want to talk more or meet up again, we can do that.'

The word 'commit' popped into her mind once more and she heard the same direct tone again in his voice. He was different. He wasn't like Lewis. Straight to the point – a little sarcastic, sure – but he didn't beat around the bush. She couldn't imagine him force-feeding her sticky sweet talks like a daily vitamin. And she had a great time. If she didn't move forward with him, she worried she'd be stuck, forever wallowing in the pit of the past in her parents' home, unable to get a job. Unable to move. That terrified her. How could she not take this chance?

'I'm happy to move along,' she said. As soon as she said it, she bit her tongue. She was being beyond impulsive. They'd spoken for a while over the phone, yes, but this was only their first date. She was supposed to return home, demand more dates and consider the prospect in great detail.

'OK. I'll let my parents know and, I guess, they'll be in touch.' His face altered as he remembered something. 'Oh, I was meaning to ask you. The little breakdown at the reception…'

'Oh, that was a one off,' she spoke hastily. Relief flashed like a sprig of lightning across his features.

'OK. Just need to know these things. Your mum said you're in perfect health. You are, right? Mentally and physically?'

She gave a slight nod – nothing too pronounced to engender suspicion. She didn't want to lie to him. Besides, she bet she could remove the issue before anything progressed between them.

'Cool. I am too.'

They both sat up and smiled at each other. Maansi held back and cautiously selected her next movement and word. It was an intense game, but one she played well. She wondered if the other was a proficient player.

CHAPTER 6

Things escalated faster than she expected, almost knocking her off her feet. Only a couple of weeks following their first date, the Alekar and Cavale families resolved to meet. Maansi and her two parents sat on one of their ragged, leather sofas and the Alekars on the opposite one, a coffee table filled with sweetmeats and fancy china cups acting as a wall between them. The house was impeccably clean. In all the years she and her family had lived there, Maansi had never seen it so tidy.

'These are big people. What are they going to think of our small house?' her mother fretted, as she swept, washed and polished each and every surface, her teeth gritted. Four hours later, she still wasn't satisfied but surrendered, unable to argue with the piercing pain in her back. Before the Alekars arrived, she encased the living room with the saccharine scent of cherry blossoms by jamming an Air Wick plug in into the wall. The Alekars were used to the better things in life – the finer details. They couldn't match but they'd have to try, she told Maansi.

'You have a lovely home,' spoke Damini Alekar, Aryan's petite mother.

'Oh no, this is nothing,' Maansi's mother laughed, trying to conceal her embarrassment towards her shoebox home. She patted her wiry hair and smoothed down her best but tired Punjabi suit, all the while gawping at Damini Alekar's emerald wrap dress and her elegantly coiffed hair.

'So Maansi, what are you looking to do now that you have graduated?' Damini asked.

Before Maansi could open her mouth, her mother leapt in.

'Oh, she has only just begun applying for jobs. We are confident she will get something good.'

'What grade did you get?'

'She got a high second-class honours. Isn't it, Maansi?' her mother raised her eyebrows at Maansi, encouraging her to comply.

'Oh. Um. Y-yeah. I did.' She felt uncomfortable lying. Technically, she did achieve a second-class honours degree, though not of the upper division. She knew her mum would ignore her when she later complained about lying. She'd claim it was partly true and they were just embellishing, stretching the truth a little, to make her appear desirable. Everybody did it.

'Good' spoke Aryan's father. Dhruv Alekar had an engulfing presence, like an assertive flag on top of a tower, informing every one of its presence and significance. Maansi was sure everybody felt it. Although polite, he came across as a sober, calculating man. He wasn't tucking into the sweetmeats, nor was he sipping tea. His eyes were a deep tone of sterling grey. The kind of expressionless eyes that bore into you and stripped you down to your most quivering vulnerabilities.

Maansi's and Aryan's mothers did most of the talking. Churning out line after line about them, as if they weren't in the room.

'Yes, Aryan is very business-minded. He is going to take over from my husband one day.'

'Oh, how lovely. Maansi is very clever too. You know at university she ran a charity event. She has good values. She always goes to *mandir* with us.'

During the meeting, Aryan's and Maansi's eyes met. Her initial instinct was to tear away, but his eyes held hers there, locking them to his. She wondered what he was trying to say.

Was he finding this process as insufferable as she was? She felt frozen beneath a probing spotlight. Her mother would nudge her every twenty minutes, urging her to offer the Alekars something.

'More tea, auntie? Uncle?' She was too afraid to ask him: her potential husband. She was sure he detected her hesitancy and was amused by it.

'Anyway, we are happy for Aryan and Maansi to get married,' Damini said. Maansi's parents couldn't subdue the smiles and let them grow the full width of their faces. They firmly agreed to the match. Maansi's stomach stirred. It was happening. The parents told her and Aryan to go and spend some time in the next room together. They were happy to talk among themselves for ten minutes and discuss wedding plans.

Maansi led Aryan into the spare room downstairs, which had nothing but a single sofa and old television in it. She was alone with him, away from the intrusive eyes of others. She wasn't sure she could handle it. This man was going to be her husband. Her actual swear-to-God husband!

'Well, I guess this is happening then,' she said.

'I guess it is,' he said, his voice flat. Why was it flat? She worried he had suddenly become disenchanted with her. Did her family put him off? She knew her parents could be a bit embarrassing and weren't the wealthiest, but they weren't that bad. In all honesty, she loved her parents. If he didn't like them… 'This whole process is exhausting,' he continued.

'Oh, right. Yeah. I agree.' He was tired. Just tired.

She noticed the physical distance between them. They didn't stand together like couples did. They were to be married and they trod in separate spheres. She wondered what it might be like to touch his hand. Would it be warm? She remembered heading home with one boy after a night out as a fresher, before she met Lewis. His hands were clammy. She recalled them rubbing up on her skin like cold oil, and how she squirmed beneath them, desperate to rinse her body of all traces of him. She hoped she wouldn't feel the same revulsion after her wedding night. Staring at Aryan, it was difficult to believe she would. She thought of the certainty of a wedding night. She almost keeled over there and then with the climbing anxiety.

'It's strange. We hardly know each other,' she whispered.

He nodded. 'If it helps, I'd never do what your ex did to you. I know that must have been hard.'

She looked into his eyes. She knew she didn't know him; however, something told her she could trust him. She had to go with that instinct. She couldn't remain where she was. She couldn't remain trapped. He held out his hand for her to shake. It was both a strange and completely natural thing to do. A deal had been struck, after all. But when Maansi thought of engaged couples, she imagined two people fawning over each other with hungry lips, disengaged from reality, their vision gliding through a film of diaphanous rose-gold. She shook his hand. It was warm. Not in the slightest bit clammy.

Within the next two months, arrangements were made. The Alekars wanted the wedding to be done in a hurry and her family, not quite believing their luck, agreed. Her gentle father enjoyed the news in quiet solitude, while her mother ranked up the phone bill, boasting to every relative and friend in the address book. Her daughter was going to marry the handsome Alekar boy!

'You see, Maansi. Everything is working out for you. This so-called depression or anxiety thing of yours will go away,' her mother said, stroking Maansi's hair as she deleted rejection emails from her inbox. Although she knew her mother's comment was coming from a place of ignorance, she hoped she was right.

She hardly saw or spoke to Aryan as the preparations were made. Her parents relayed the message that he was occupied with work. They felt the need to remind her how lucky she was, having a hard-working husband-to-be with a fat pay packet. She should be grateful, her mother told her.

Aryan and she managed to trade a few words here and there, over the phone or over Skype. He was too busy to offer more of himself. She didn't mind. She'd be living with him soon enough. How much more of him could she want? Besides, there was no going back.

Before she knew it, her female cousins were decorating her hands with *mehndi* and probing her for answers regarding the man she was about to marry. What did he do? What was his star sign? These questions accosted her from every angle. Aryan's relatives hounded her from every corner, eager to introduce themselves and ask more questions she hadn't answers to. Her own auntie proudly confirmed his sign as Scorpio. Yet, what that meant or whether astrology provided any real insight to his character, Maansi was unsure.

'Oh, you're a Pisces. You're both water signs. Very auspicious,' said the superstitious auntie. When it came to love and compatibility, she believed the stars could be gentle guides or the highest of authorities. 'Scorpios can be jealous and be possessive. Be warned.'

'Does that sound like him, Maansi?' one of her younger cousins asked, as she massaged turmeric paste on to her forearms. Maansi gulped. She honestly couldn't say.

Before she had a moment to catch herself and process what was happening, the wedding arrived. Fresh garlands were exchanged to connect the two families. With a hundred pairs of eyes witnessing, Maansi and Aryan circled a spry fire, bound to each other with crimson fabric. As they circled, Maansi noticed the faces around her wilted into one form, dark and motionless against the swells of the lapping fire. Everything around her was surreal. She felt woozy as her heart raced. After the seventh circle, their vows to each other were complete. They were married. They were showered with blessings and proclaimed husband and wife.

The reception took place the same evening. Although they had little time to plan, the Alekars' wealth ensured there was a certain degree of opulence, letting the Cavale family know their pockets were seamed with gold. On her wedding throne, beside him, Maansi looked out at the number of people flocking to the dancefloor, watching how his and her family blurred together. She found Sejal and Rakhee at a table, huddled together and exchanging whispers. Her stomach fell like a stone into a well as she realised how terribly she had treated them. In the past couple of months, she had only texted her friends, never bothering with more than a line or two. She longed to abandon her position to apologise but she couldn't abandon her new husband. She looked at Aryan and he looked back at her. He seemed as overcome and lost as she did. Recognising their own feelings in each other, they both released a weak laugh. A small laugh that captured their mixed feelings of amusement, fear, uncertainty and the nervous anticipation building for later.

CHAPTER 7

It was the first time she had entered his flat. It was minimalist, exhibiting mostly neutral shades of greys, whites and browns. She thought she'd enter and immediately discover him pasted across the interiors. She expected to see posters of his favourite bands, or takeout boxes from his favourite restaurants strewn across tables. She supposed, him being in his early twenties, he'd be living like a student. Instead, she was faced with an almost clinical environment. The facets of his life and personality were hidden from sight, leaving her face to face with a kind of showroom – plain but attractive, like a fresh sheet of paper in a new notebook. He walked through the living room and opened the door to his bedroom. Their bedroom, she reminded herself. She followed him in, holding her breath.

There wasn't much to see. The walls were painted a cool grey and the bed was laid with a deep-plum spread. The walls were naked. The curtains bland. The en-suite bathroom revealed a little more, although nothing more exciting than Lynx deodorant bottles, a toothbrush with flayed bristles and a few other toiletries.

'This place is really clean,' she said, self-consciously perching on the end of the bed. She noticed the mattress was firm. He nodded and mentioned something about a cleaner coming in every week. Maansi was still clad in her scarlet lehenga. She wanted to get out of it. She peered into the bathroom.

'If you want to change, I can leave?' he said, picking up on her hesitancy.

'No, it's fine. I'll just change in the bathroom.'

Maansi walked into the bathroom clutching a silk, drawstring bag with her wedding lingerie in it. At the time of buying it, it seemed like a good idea, but now she felt ridiculous putting on the sheer, lilac dress with its matching French knickers. She cringed at her appearance in the wide, light-studded mirror. She couldn't walk out like that, but nor did she want to step back out in her heavy lehenga. She opened the door slightly and peeked through the gap. He wasn't in the bedroom. She ran and fetched her dressing gown from her suitcase, thankful she packed it.

In the safety of her Hello Kitty gown, she left the bathroom and climbed into the stranger's bed. The firm mattress was unwilling to accommodate her, already teasing an ache along her spine. Her heart capered in her chest. They were going to sleep together. She waited for him to return, wondering if it would be weird to ask to sleep on the sofa. Still, another part of her wanted to become acquainted with his touch. Was it delicate? Rough? She ached for a glass of wine, hoping the rubicund grape would douse her worries. She thought about asking for a glass, but worried he'd find such a request suggestive.

As he entered the room, she surrendered to cowardice and feigned sleep. She could feel him standing over her for a moment, trying to work out if she had indeed dropped off. Moments later, she could hear clothes as they landed on the floor. She half-opened her eyes to peep and caught sight of his bare back. His golden-beige skin looked smooth and inviting to touch. He faced the standing mirror, and she could see a defined six-pack reflecting back at her. Excitement returned to compete with nervousness in the pit of her stomach. The bedstead cut off his lower body, leaving her blind to it.

After brushing his teeth, he slipped into bed and turned off the lamp. He lay on the edge of his side of the bed, facing away from her, the way she chose to face away from him. She could feel miles of distance laid between them and wondered how to cross over to him, or whether she should make the journey at all. She decided she'd wait for him. But he did not turn, or make a sound, and she grew terrified. The fear gradually unshelled itself, like a chick hatching from its egg. She was frightened about having made a mistake. She had married a stranger and this – this unromantic, nerve-racking disaster – was her wedding night. Her, on the other side of the world from him, alone. Her heart hammered against her chest and the old panic monster began to creep out of its habitat, step by step. She jumped out of bed and dashed into the bathroom. She slammed the door shut and turned on the taps so the water whooshed out like miniature waterfalls. She focused on her breathing and counted backwards and forwards until she felt calmer. She looked at herself in the mirror.

'You can do this. You can do this! This was definitely a good idea,' she attempted to persuade herself. The woman in her reflection was not buying it. 'I have exceptional communication skills, I am positive, confident...' she imagined telling the hard-faced interviewer. She remembered she didn't have it in her to sell herself any more. She couldn't do it. Down came the stamp with the fat red letters. Still, she fought through and cleared a passage for her breathing. It took ten whole minutes for her body to find equanimity again and for her chest to feel lighter and free of burden. She walked back into the room, nursing her heart in her mouth.

'Are you all right?' Aryan asked from beneath the sheets, still facing away from her.

'I'm fine. Are you?' she whispered.

'Fine.'

As she climbed back into bed, he turned on the lamp and

flipped round to face her. She was struck by his glassy eyes, as if it were the first time she was seeing them. They travelled through her, then down her body. She covered herself with the duvet.

'Are you sleeping with that thing on?' he asked. Maansi stuttered, failing to provide an answer. She held the duvet against her with her chin and, with difficulty, removed the dressing gown.

'I can look away, if you want. But if you didn't want me to see you in that, you could have worn something else.'

'Well, I thought things might go differently.'

'How do you want things to go?' he asked. Her eyes fell towards his lips and she felt a strong hunger surge through her body. She quickly looked away. Her cheeks warmed and prickled as her mind dared to collate what she had envisaged for her wedding night. She hoped he couldn't see the trailer streaming across her forehead. The same images must have surfaced in the forefront of his mind, as he tentatively placed his hand around her waist, surprising her and leaving her feverish with fear and anticipation. He moved in and pressed his lips against her slender neck. She let it happen, frozen like a woman preserved in paints. He tugged at the lilac bows and gently glided over her breasts with his fingertips. She now stirred and tingled. Soon, his hands were travelling up her thighs while his mouth became familiar with the curves of her body. As he undid the lace garments, she inhaled sharply and pulled the duvet over her. He stopped.

'Are you OK?'

'I'm sorry,' she mumbled. 'It just feels a bit strange.'

'That's OK. We don't have to. I thought you...'

'I'm sorry,' she said again. He shook his head and told her not to give it a second thought. There was no natural progression to this moment, and they both knew it. She didn't even know if he found her attractive. It bothered her. 'I don't even know what you think of me...' she trailed off.

'I think you're beautiful. I should have said so earlier. You really are.' As he spoke, his eyes softened.

She fiddled with the ring around her finger, not yet used to its weight. She wasn't sure she could believe him. 'Maybe, we don't have to go all the way. I know it's the wedding night but maybe remove the pressure?'

'If that's what you want.'

'Yeah. I think that would be better.' She slipped back towards him. He read her yearning and moved forward to meet her lips in their first kiss. At first, she gave his tender mouth little response, but she soon softened and succumbed, pressing her lips softly against his, before he led her into a sequence of passionate, careless kisses with his mouth teasing hers open, leaving a gap for the inclusion of wet, reaching tongues. She moaned and melted, her hands wrapping around his neck, her nails biting into his skin. He placed his hand on her neck and she felt she could burst. Yet, as he unburdened her shoulder from the lace strap of her garment, she moved off again.

'I can reduce the light.' She nodded and he dimmed the lamp. She worried about her body and how it looked... different. The darkness of it, the lack of 'pink' bits. Even with the low lighting, she thought he would move away, but he seemed magnetised to her, lapping her up as if she was something precious not to be wasted. And she burst with a thousand colours beneath the work of his skilled hands.

When they had punctuated the ends of their explorations of each other's body with quiet quivers, they did not hold each other. To hold each other would mean to breach the place of intimacy that did not yet welcome them. To hold each other would mean to love. Yet, love was a tiny foetus in the womb of time, soon to grow. Soon to gash the air with its shrill cry of arrival. Soon.

Aryan and Maansi Alekar retreated to their sides of the bed and slept for the first time as husband and wife.

CHAPTER 8

They decided against a honeymoon. At least, for the time being. Aryan's spotless flat already gave off the feeling of somewhere foreign and new. The moving men brought up her boxes from the van and left them in the middle of the living room. This was her home now. When her eyes fluttered open that morning, she'd forgotten where she was. She somehow came to believe she was back in student accommodation, waiting for her alarm to rouse her for an afternoon lecture. When she felt her back protest the firm mattress with a brusque spasm, the memory hit her around the head. She was too afraid to roll to look at the man next to her: her husband, she reminded herself, though thinking of herself with a husband seemed ludicrous. How could she be a wife? She still loved to watch cartoons and still struggled to fry an egg without breaking the yolk. But now she was someone's wife. She chewed on the word. It had a bitter aftertaste.

From the light coughing and clanking sounds flowing from the kitchen, she realised Aryan was already up. She washed up and fixed her hair. She gently dabbed a bit of foundation on her face, unprepared to be completely au naturel in front of the man she barely knew. She recalled the activities of last night and felt an army of butterflies take off in her stomach. Their wings beat faster at the thought of seeing him again. She tiptoed out of the room. She found him standing in the kitchen, sipping freshly brewed coffee.

'Morning,' he said, the smallest of smiles resting on his lips.

'Good morning,' she replied, wishing she had prepared more words. They sat down at the dining table to eat their slices of toast with jam. Their conversation was stilted and dealt with painfully stretching comments, such as 'this jam is really tasty' from her, and 'it's organic' from him. She took in the spaciousness of the spick and span flat, good enough to become the set of a Flash commercial, and tried to keep from smiling. Who could ask for a better home? Wasn't this piece of luxury telling her that her life would transform? That the deep blues and blacks surrounding her would transmute into lighter shades of gold and yellow? She clung to that hope.

Aryan agreed to help her unpack. He unpacked his half of the boxes with an unmatchable speed and was done in under half an hour. Maansi took her time with each item she fished out and accompanied the tiresome task with music from the charts. She felt him watching her as she added splashes of colour to his minimalist flat with sundry ornaments and decorations. She hummed along to Bruno Mars while placing figurines on the bare mantelpiece. His face soured as he gazed at the row of pensive fairies. When she asked if he minded them, he shook his head.

'This is your flat too. You can add what you like.' He bit down on his index finger before pulling out a copy of the *Economist* from a magazine rack. She searched the archives of her brain for a good conversation starter, but he left the room before she could arrive at one. He emerged a short while later, dressed in a suit and tie. 'Listen, I need to get to work,' he said.

'Wait. Why? Your dad can't give you time off? We just got married.'

'It's pretty urgent. Look, make yourself at home and I'll be back soon. I've left a key for you by the fruit bowl.'

He was out of the door before she could even say bye.

Maansi admired the living room, noting how her colourful ornaments had torn apart its once choking austerity. If only he was there to see the finished result. She felt irritated with Aryan's departure. She wanted to use the day to unpeel him, to deshell him and place his secrets on plates for her eyes to feed off. Who was this man? Well, if he couldn't be there, she would seek him out herself.

She made for the bedroom and began opening drawers that were not designated for her use. She jumped as she opened his bedside drawer, but what appeared to be a gun was nothing more than a novelty cigarette lighter. She found a casino membership card, designer watches, a copy of *A Game of Thrones* and a thirty-six pack of condoms with thirty condoms still encased in plastic. She winced. The absence of the six would torment her for days. She threw the items back in the drawer and continued her search elsewhere. Opening his wardrobe, she discovered his clothes leaned towards one side of the colour spectrum, showcasing blacks, greys and dark blues. Aside from quality garments, there was nothing more.

She didn't understand. She'd brought DVDs with her, her favourite books, treasured keepsakes and posters. It was easy to learn who she was from her things. Aside from the few items in his drawer, there was nothing she could use to uncover him. She searched beneath the bed and yet, not even a dust bunny was removed from hiding. Was he boring? Were his things at his parents? Maybe he just moved here and his things had yet to follow. She needed to know. She couldn't remain married to a stranger. It was reasonable to want to know her husband. She surrendered herself to the plush, leather sofa in the living room. If she wanted him to share himself with her, she would need to gain his trust and create the beginnings of a bond.

She knew what to do. She would cook for him. People always said the way to a man's heart is through his stomach. She switched on her laptop and pored through her bookmarks, searching for winning recipes she might have saved when she once wished to impress Lewis. She came across a chickpea, coconut and spinach curry. She remembered cooking it once. Her mother had expressed her approval by only offering one mild criticism, rather than seven drawn-out lectures about everything she had failed to do.

'Why did you not add jeera? Do you know the difference jeera can make? No, I know you haven't put it in. I know,' her mother's strong Indian accent raged through her ears. 'And why do you always put in too much chilli powder? Do you want to put your father in hospital?'

She'd make the curry for Aryan. Finding his kitchen sparsely stocked, she grabbed her new key and took off to buy the ingredients. She hoped she'd get it right. She wanted more than anything to impress him – to make their marriage work. She heard his words again: 'I think you're beautiful. I should have said so earlier. You really are.' Those words made her an air balloon among clouds. She played the words again, until they wore thin and crumpled in her hands like sweet wrappers.

She felt exhilarated, if a bit antsy, walking around Canary Wharf. She enjoyed the natural beauty of river frontages and green parks, balancing alongside the arrays of shops lining the streets. The place was abuzz with life and movement. The tall buildings brushed against the skies and preached to those peering up at them of unlimited possibility. There were all kinds of people walking the streets, brandishing their cameras and pointing in opposing directions. She saw businessmen and businesswomen with their briefcases, their phones attached to their ears. The wind danced with English, French and

Mandarin words, mixing them together until they became one cacophonous but strangely sufferable sound. The world was faster in London. She picked up her pace to match.

When she finished familiarising herself with the area, she popped into Waitrose and bought her ingredients. Just the other day, she was mired in self-pity in her mess of a life. Now she lived in Canary Wharf in a luxury apartment with an attractive, wealthy husband. The world already seemed to glow brighter, like freshly set morning dew in the younger days of March. There was life and vigour in the centre of London and her feet caught it in every step.

When she returned, the flat was eerily silent. She checked the time. It was only ten past two. He hadn't told her when he'd return. She grabbed her phone and lay next to the electric fireplace, opening unread messages of congratulations from friends and relatives and looking at the wedding photos she was tagged in. Sejal left a kind comment beneath a flattering photo of her, twirling under a spray of magnolia petals. She remembered how much she wanted to apologise. She wrote her a message. 'Hey Sejal. Thanks for coming to the wedding. I am sorry for the way I've behaved towards you. I didn't mean anything I said. You know I love you.'

She spent the next couple of hours completing personality quizzes and enjoying viral videos of kittens at play. When it struck four, she rose to cook. She was sure he'd be back around five, and then they could enjoy a lovely meal together as newlyweds. He'd see. She could make a damn good wife.

The fragrant scent of coconut and jasmine rice meandered through the flat in dizzy waves, setting her stomach churning with hunger. She waited patiently, drumming her fingers against the dining table. As she waited, thoughts rose like bubbles to the main platform of her mind. A good wife? Don't be ridiculous. You failed at your only relationship, remember? You weren't good enough. What makes you think you'll ever be... She heard the key turn in the door.

'Aryan,' she harped, running towards the door to greet him. She saw his face twist in confusion, almost as if he'd forgotten she'd be there. He stepped in, a carrier bag hanging off his arm with the words 'Mr Chippy' printed on the front.

'Hey,' he said. 'What's that smell? Did you make something?' Aryan asked, detecting the fusion of jasmine and coconut swimming in the air.

'A coconut chickpea curry,' she said in a high la-di-da voice so unlike her own. She coughed and lowered the register. 'I see you've already brought something.'

'Uh. Yeah,' he said, lowering the bag on to the coffee table. 'Sorry. I didn't know. Guess we could have both.'

'I guess that's fine. Should we eat?'

She led him into the kitchen and began plating the coconut curry.

'You didn't have to do this, you know,' he said.

'But what else was I supposed to do today?' She didn't mean for the comment to sound scornful. He shifted uncomfortably in his seat, no doubt thinking her petty. She dropped her spoon and hastily changed the conversation. 'I got to explore the area today. It's so beautiful. So many banks. I'm glad you don't live with your parents.' She remembered visiting their house to discuss wedding plans. She was reduced to shock by the immense size and sumptuousness of their home. The marble floors, the chandelier with a thousand eyes, the oriental rugs with golden trimmings... they mesmerised her. 'Even if it is in Knightsbridge.'

'Me too. At least we get some privacy,' he smirked. He tried a spoonful of the curry and murmured his approval. 'This is really good.'

She was pleased he liked it. As she watched him, she noticed he hadn't buttoned his shirt to the top, leaving a liberal area of his chest exposed. She wished she could reach out and stroke the region with her fingers, but she wouldn't dare do such a thing. They had yet to merge into each other's comfort zones. She wondered when the imperceptible barrier between them could bear penetration until breakage.

After finishing his meal, Aryan collected his and Maansi's plates and washed them. He scrutinised the kitchen and frowned at the mess she created. Grains of rice were scattered across the floor, the kitchen counter bore food remnants and open packets of food and there was the oil spillage by the stove. He looked uncomfortable and she noticed.

'Since you've cooked, I'll clean up,' he said.

'No, you don't have to. I made the mess.'

'It's fine. Seriously.'

'Well, I'll help then.'

She soon regretted her offer. He dictated where things should go, becoming agitated when she tried to adjust or ignore his system. Of course, the onions don't go there. No, it wouldn't be simpler to move those there. That's not how you tackle an oil spillage. By the end of the cleaning session, Maansi was exhausted.

'Well, if you cleaned up while you cooked…'

'I didn't have to cook for you,' she pointed out, doing her best to refrain from barking at him.

He froze. 'You're right. Sorry. This whole living with someone thing is, well, an adjustment. Excuse me.' He opened a drawer and pulled out a packet of Marlboros and a lighter. He headed for the balcony.

After some time spent shuffling her feet and scanning the flat some more, she joined him on the balcony. She approached him with caution, afraid she was trespassing on his territory and risking prosecution. He said nothing as she stood by him. Maansi leaned over the balcony. Below them, she could see a couple holding hands and kissing. The woman stood on the points of her feet like a ballerina to reach her lover's lips. The man held her to him, his hand lost in the loose waves of her chestnut hair. Aryan watched them too, with an intensity that would surely unsettle the couple and shatter their romantic trance. Twists of smoke reeled out of his mouth like Egyptian belly dancers, masking Maansi's view of the scene.

'You ever thought about quitting?' she asked. He nodded, taking another drag from his cigarette.

'I stopped for a while. But I guess we all need a vice.'

The grey clouds above groaned as they broke, releasing a slow, rhythmic patter of rain to the earth. Despite the growing cold, Aryan showed no intention of retreating indoors.

'I'm sorry about going into work today. I've taken time off now,' he said. 'What would you like to do tomorrow?'

At this news, a bit of warmth rekindled in her and she peered up at the sky with gratitude. 'Anything. I really want to get on to the London Eye,' she said. 'Oh, and maybe we can go to the London Dungeon.' She had, after all, never been to London before. 'Or, alternatively, somewhere we can just talk. A bar maybe?'

'All right, if that's what you really want.'

That night, they didn't talk much. Even though Aryan said he wouldn't be heading to work, he sat at his laptop for most of the night working. She sat next to him, leaving a gap between them of a few respectable centimetres, and watched *Pretty Little Liars*. He shook his head at her programme choice and dished out insults during his small breaks. After four episodes of unrealistic plot twists and constant key-tapping, they headed to bed.

With her pulse racing, she agreed to let him go further this time. They were married. It was ridiculous to hold off, she thought. Besides, her latest daydreams were dedicated to the temple of his body. It began soft and slow. His skin cared for hers and sought the grooves and turns to conjure the kaleidoscopic world pulsating beneath her, working it towards eruption. She soaked in his kisses and responded with her hands, moving them across his entire body. He entered her with care and was mindful of this being a first. When she dared to look into the smouldering sunsets of his eyes, he changed, as if her look threw him off. He decided to change the tune, moving faster and with more passion, yielding to more carnal desires. She blindly felt her way along the line towards a complete pleasure as he worked until their bodies were moist with sweat. After he finished, he turned to his side to sleep, leaving her libido in a pendulous state, several stops away from her desired destination.

'Night,' he yawned, switching off the light.

'Goodnight.' She listened to his breathing deepen as he slipped into sleep. She clutched herself in the dark and attempted to silence the voice in her head that tried to tell her she made a huge mistake.

In the night, she noticed, with horror, that even though she was in a different place, thrown into a different life, a seedling of pain remained, and it was growing. Like weeds snatched from the ground, it was making a return, emerging through the cracks. She was still a failure. She was still a bad person. She was still not good enough. And that depression was alive and breathing. But she couldn't cry into her pillow any more. There was somebody beside her now. She swallowed down the stubborn feeling that strove to erupt from her. It'll be gone soon, she told herself. It can't stay.

CHAPTER 9

'Come on,' Aryan said as the carriage doors opened, stepping towards them so quickly she was unable to reach for his arm. Everyone shuffled on to the carriage, packing themselves in like sardines, bound together through the stench of body odour and synthetic perfumes. She held on to a sticky handrail, her body pressed into Aryan's while the breath of another passenger ran moist across her neck.

'The tube is horrible. It's so warm,' she said. 'How do people do this day in and day out?'

'You get used to it. We could've gone to a bar nearby. This was your idea...'

At the next stop, the people beside her shuffled out of the carriage and were replaced by a mother and a child. Leaning over her mother's shoulder and looking straight at Maansi were the bright eyes of a baby.

As they jerked forward, the baby shrieked and began howling, as if its lungs were filling with battery acid. Maansi was overcome with sudden nausea. The carriage transformed into a tighter, more suffocating space. There was no room to breathe. The baby's face was inches away from her, reddening as it screamed at her.

'I want to get off,' she said impulsively, rotating towards Aryan. He screwed up his face. As the baby screamed louder, she reasserted herself. 'I want to get off now!'

'We can't just get off. We'll be there soon. Are you claustrophobic?'

As space opened up and the baby drifted away from her, she still couldn't handle herself. Aryan frowned. She could see the question dangling from his lips. He didn't ask it.

Her chest moved up and down rapidly and she folded her arms across her stomach. The baby's cries ascended an octave and there was no escape. As she watched its face twist in agony, she was stolen back to the cold clinic.

'What's wrong?'

'I'm fine,' she said, gaining composure and trying her best to ignore the child. The dark thoughts tiptoed in and knocked against her brain, letting her know they'd returned. On cue, she recited the familiar narrative, telling herself she was an awful person. A selfish and stupid girl.

Once they were at the stop, she was the first one out of the carriage. She left with an artificial strut, paying strict attention to how the left leg would follow the right and vice versa. Before she could get too far, Aryan pulled her back by her shoulder.

She rewrote the expression on her face, forcing on a passable smile.

'Sorry. I don't know what came over me,' she said. 'It's just suffocating in there.'

He seemed taken aback and she noticed her eyes smarted with tears. She bit her lip, hoping he wouldn't prod her further. He gradually nodded and led the way towards a bar.

The bar basted in pink light and the soft, temperate sounds of acoustic music. Young, trendy people entered to fill their hankerings for fancy cocktails with wacky, pun-driven names. Maansi and Aryan ordered their drinks and sat at the bar. Aryan pulled out an electronic cigarette from his pocket and began nursing off it. His face took on that same contemplative look of a philosopher. She didn't want to suffer any more silences. She'd force his thoughts out of his head and into the open. This time, she was prepared.

'So, I found this website that tells you how to fast-track a bond with someone. All we have to do is ask each other thirty-six questions and then look into each other's eyes for four minutes.' As she made the proposal, she realised how strange the activity sounded. The idea of forcing a bond seemed a bit creepy. He was unimpressed. Her shoulders drooped. Great, silence it is, she thought.

'You can ask three questions.'

'I can?' She perked up. She reached for her phone and scanned the list of questions, searching for the right one. 'OK, great. Here's one. For what in your life do you feel most grateful?'

'Money,' he said, without hesitation.

'Seriously?'

'Yes. Next.'

'You're not even going to elaborate?' He said nothing. 'OK… If you could change anything about the way you were raised, what would it be?'

He carefully meditated upon the question, little bursts of vapour pouring from his lips. 'Less pressure.'

'What do you mean?'

'Just some freedom to make more of my own choices. Less pressure when it came to exams. That kind of thing.'

Maansi knew Asian children generally had to deal with pressure growing up. A yearning for financial and academic success was rooted in Indian culture. When it came to education, she herself received little pressure from her family. As long as she went to university and got herself a degree, they let her get on with her life. She tried to imagine what kind of pressure

79

Aryan fell under. Since he wasn't in the most loquacious of moods – though being a non-communicator could be core to his personality (how would she know?) – she decided not to ask. She found just the question to coax him out.

'If you were to die this evening with no opportunity to communicate with anyone, what would you most regret not having told someone? Why haven't you told them?' That was a good question. One that would go a little deeper and nudge free those parts of him he kept hidden.

'Pass.'

'Pass?' she repeated.

'Pass.'

She shoved her phone back into her bag. That was it. She had enough. She was about to fire a series of challenges at him but stopped at the trigger. His eyes became crystal balls full of storms.

'I need to use the bathroom,' he said. With that, he got up and left her at the bar. She slapped her forehead with her palm. He was too difficult to handle. She ordered another drink and sluiced its courage-forming qualities down her, crinkling her nose as the spraying bubbles of the blended coke tickled her. She mulled over her next move.

'Hey, gorgeous. What's your name?' A man with a raspy voice slid next to her. She turned to face him. This man wasn't the bar's desired punter. He wasn't upscale or trendy. His nose was crooked, his hair was a peroxide blonde and he reeked of tobacco and body odour – both serving as middle and top notes on a base of something harsh and tangy. With her instincts driving her, she quickly deserted her seat and hurried to the back of the bar. The seats at the rear end were empty and there wasn't anyone around. Before she realised it wasn't the best idea to move off somewhere isolated, he was behind her, seizing her arm with his sweaty hand.

'Don't be rude. I was only giving you a compliment,' he said, revealing a set of yellowing incisors. 'You waiting for someone? Where's your boyfriend?' His free hand travelled towards the curve of her backside.

'Get lost,' Maansi hissed. She gripped her bag. Her heart awoke in her chest and started rampaging. She prepared herself to run past him, though at the same time told herself to keep cool. He couldn't do anything in public anyway, right?

'I don't think I like your attitude,' he said, tightening the grip around her arm until she cried out in pain. 'You should be more appreciative. Guys don't normally look at girls like you.'

'What do you think you're doing?' Aryan emerged from the men's toilets behind them. The blonde man faced him. Maansi saw the stranger's nostrils flare and his eyes blaze with an unquenchable lust for trouble. He squared up to Aryan and tried for a response with a swift thump to his chest.

'What you gonna do about it then?'

Aryan thumped him back. The man foamed at the mouth with dirty expletives. He prepared his punch, but before he could make contact, Aryan caught his arm, twisted it behind the man's back and flung him to the floor. Maansi heard a thud as the man thwacked his head against a table. He wailed.

'Ah. My head. My fucking head.' Hearing his pained howls, people began gravitating towards the back of the bar, their heads craning as they susurrated among themselves.

'What's going on back there?' shouted the barman from behind his station. Aryan took Maansi by the arm and led her out of the pink-washed bar. She inhaled the fresh air like a drug as they slid out of the doors.

'You all right?' he asked her.

She was shaking. She could handle her feelings if that encounter was the only bad thing to happen. But the ride on the tube was too much. She saw Aryan before her. She saw his strong arms and remembered the warmth of his skin. She allowed herself to fall into his arms. He made an 'uhrm' sound and awkwardly patted her with one hand.

'Just please try,' she pleaded, burying her face into his shirt. 'All I want is for you to try.' After a long pause, he wrapped his arms around her.

'Sorry,' he said.

'How did you stop that guy like that?' Maansi asked as she hung up her coat. They arrived back at the flat. It was a more welcoming flat with a loud, extraverted personality, thanks to her additions. Aryan had yet to say anything about the improvements.

'I'm into MMA.'

'Oh. Learning something new about you every day, Aryan.'

He smirked at her. She tingled at the new piece of information. There was something especially attractive about a man that could protect her. She shuddered as she reflected on the day. A part of her wanted to slip beneath the covers and allow herself to crumble, but more than anything she wanted to distract herself from those menacing feelings. An idea popped into her head.

'Teach me something then,' she said, backing into the wide space between the living room and the bedroom. She formed her hands into tight little fists and prodded him. He grinned, his eyebrows arching. She awaited the spate of mocking remarks, but he agreed.

'All right, fine. I'll teach you how to jab.'

He taught her how to stand in the orthodox stance, with her left leg in front of her and knees slightly bent. He positioned her arms up in front of her face. 'This is your guard,' he told her. She let him move her as he pleased, trying not to recoil from his assessing eyes as they checked her body from head to toe, making sure she was in the correct fighting position.

He demonstrated how she should step forward on to the left foot, twist her ankle and hips and generate power to throw a punch. She copied him, and he laughed at her feeble attempts. She drove forward to thwack his chest, but he grabbed her arm and, very gently, pushed her back. She pouted.

'Do it again,' he said, unassuaged by her inflated lip. She repeated the movement. 'No. Look. You're not moving your hips correctly.' He placed his hands on her hips and held her back against his own body. She could feel his warm breath brush against her ear lobe. His hands crept up to her waist. Like ice caressed by midsummer heat, she began to melt. She pushed off from him and threatened him with her stance.

'Come on then. Try it,' he dared. She was too afraid to hurt him, so lightly punched his chest. He mocked her, so she went again, but harder. He blocked it with ease.

'Let me get you,' she giggled. He caught her fist, grabbed her by the waist and tossed her on to the sofa. 'Oi!'

He leaned over her and she was certain he was going to dive in and kiss her. She puckered her lips, preparing for an act of concentrated passion. Instead, he backed off. 'What's wrong?' she asked.

'I should be asking you.' She knew what he was going to say. 'What happened, on the tube today?'

She suspected her behaviour wouldn't escape his mind. On their first date, she told him with confidence that panicking was not a regular thing – that her mental health was sound. Then they signed the marriage contract. She didn't want him to know. Lewis left her, in part, because he couldn't handle her depression. What if no man could? Her mother had countless stories of men leaving women because of their 'damaged heads'.

It wasn't uncommon for secret depression, schizophrenia or bipolar disorders to surface once an arranged marriage was made. They never worked out. Partners felt betrayed and preyed upon. Without love as a foundation, the baggage was too much to carry. Maansi wanted this marriage to work. Besides, she could deal with her problems herself.

'I'm sorry. I was just reminded of something that happened in the past.' She hoped that would be enough to satisfy his curiosity, but his face beckoned for more information. She sighed. 'I'd rather not talk about it.'

'We're married now. Whatever it is, just tell me.'

She hesitated. 'I can't.'

He crossed his arms. 'Then that's what you want? For us to have secrets?'

He was one to talk. She hadn't learned a single intimate detail about him. Maybe if she opened up, he'd learn to too... 'I had an abortion while at university. I didn't want an abortion. But I had no choice.' Her throat tightened. She said 'abortion' twice. She never dared to use the word, even in the privacy of her mind. When she booked her appointment, she said she needed a termination. Since she didn't hear the word used as often, it carried less power.

She searched Aryan's face. He seemed only mildly stunned at her disclosure. 'So, getting the abortion still affects you now. Like this?'

'Yes. Not all the time. I mean... just a little,' she forced herself up from her prostrate position. 'My mum used to tell me that everyone has a soul and when people abort, you mess up someone's cycle of birth. It screws with my head.'

All of a sudden, the demon living in her body leapt into action. It moved through her, willing her to collapse into a foetal position so it could break her down to a state of numbness. She struggled to resist it.

'That's ridiculous.'

'Excuse me?'

'Look, I don't believe in God. But even if I did, I don't think you'd have the power to mess up someone's cycle of birth, if such a thing even existed.'

'There is such a thing, and just because you don't believe...' She crossed her arms over her chest, digesting his words. 'You don't believe in God? So you're not even a little bit Hindu?'

'Atheist.'

'Great. How can an atheist and theist be together?'

'They can!'

She flinched. His voice was swathed in red-hot, metal gauze. He withdrew to a corner for a moment to breathe and cool down. What was that about? 'So, you didn't want to have an abortion?' he continued.

'I couldn't think about what I wanted. It was abortion or risk being disowned by my family and, well, the community. You know how it is.' She felt ashamed of what she had done. Mostly because she wasn't sure she would've opted for an abortion if things had been different. Indian girls couldn't get pregnant before marriage. Those that did were shamed. Those that did were 'coconuts' – brown on the outside and white on the inside. They usually belonged to a tree of coconuts. People without culture, as they saw it.

Aryan's setting silence ignited those familiar feelings of shame. She brought her knees to her chest, wanting to fold herself away into a box. Could she explain it to him? Would he understand? She wasn't sure she could understand it herself. As she tried to cement her frenetic thoughts together into a clear picture, he put his arm around her and drew her in. He held her to his chest, close enough so she could hear his heart drumming away.

'Sorry you went through that,' he said. 'I understand.'

Those words were magic to her. She let go of her breath and the tension barred in her muscles vanished. Her burden dispelled into their dusty boxes. It amazed her, just how safe she felt in his arms.

To her own surprise, she fixed her lips in the dip between his neck and collarbone and kissed him. She kissed hard, and seconds later her hand slipped beneath his T-shirt and travelled the wide planes of his chest. His breathy exhale told her he welcomed the trespassing. She wanted him. She wanted him badly. He kissed her on the lips with a butterfly-light touch, before stepping away from her.

'It's frustrating,' he said. 'Why should anyone have to hide or make a choice they wouldn't otherwise make, just because people will speak? Your parents should've let you make your decision, instead of making threats.'

She winced. 'They didn't know. There were no threats. Nobody knew.'

'Oh.' He rubbed his neck. 'I see.'

'You must think I'm pathetic.'

He sighed. 'No. I don't. I just wish we'd all stop caring. Do you know, when I was younger, my dad would spend all his time reading around philosophy and literature. He'd spend time reading Sufi poetry and Shakespeare – not because he enjoyed them. He didn't. He just wanted people to believe he was intellectual. Being a successful businessman wasn't enough. He needed to be impressive. All people seem to care about is what others will say about them, not about what they want.'

'That's sad,' she said. Her father-in-law already woke to torrents of respect. 'But Aryan, if I hadn't done what I did, I wouldn't have been Maansi any more. I'd be the girl that had a baby outside of marriage. And those who weren't spouting crap about me would just be silent. Who can deal with that? I'm not so brave.'

She sunk into the sofa, lolling her head over the top and closing her eyes. Speaking about something she'd shrouded in silence was tough. She shuddered, as it hooked its thorny feet into her reality, pressing in to form a fresher pain.

'Brave?' he said.

'Hey. Maybe I would be if you taught me more fighting moves.' She pushed herself back up, determined to change the subject. 'So, when did you first learn to fight? At school?'

He didn't respond. He stared into outer space, his fingers fiddling with his wedding ring.

'Aryan?'

'Yeah, around then. But I wasn't so good at fighting.' He glanced at his watch. 'We haven't eaten yet. I'm thinking some cheese toasties. Sound good?'

She grabbed Aryan's hand before he walked off. 'Thanks for understanding. And I know I seem like a bit of a mess, but I swear I'm fine.'

He blinked at her. 'It's OK.'

CHAPTER 10

As the week went by, they visited a few notable sites across the city. They spoke, but of nothing with much substance. The barricade tape ran between them, cutting short any conversations that steered them towards deeper subject matter. Once the week ended, Aryan returned to work, leaving Maansi alone to handle her new life.

She realised her and Aryan's bank accounts had joined into one and she expected a scintilla of excitement to spark within her. After all, not long ago, the mention of money would have her stomach turning like buckets on a waterwheel. She didn't have to worry about making money. But with all the money and all the time she could wish for, she didn't know what to do. This was her fresh start. She wondered how she'd colour herself into the pages.

Guilt crawled into her belly. Who was she to be so free? Who was she to be spending his money? The questions haunted her. She obsessively cleaned to maintain the pristine condition of the flat. She did the laundry, bought groceries and made sure food was laid on the table for the two of them every evening. She was contributing in a significant way, she told herself. Sometimes, her mind would arrest itself of any thought at all and a faint flutter would lift off in her chest as she realised how lucky she was. At other times, she could only feel the gratitude as a touch of sunlight on her skin and not as the internal flame that comes from drinking whisky, as if it were slowly extinguishing.

Aryan often worked late and, when he got back, required space to 'recharge', leaving her to loiter outside a closed bedroom door or potter near the balcony that kept him. She continued to tell herself everything was great. Everything was better than it was.

She tried to invite Sejal to London, thinking if she just had a friend alongside her she could go after the joys of London.

'Sorry, Maansi. I've started that new PR job. It's so stressful. It even keeps me busy on the weekends,' she told her over the phone.

'Don't worry, lovely,' she said. 'And wow, PR sounds great. Not sure I could do what you do. Anyway, I've got to go. I've got so much to do.' She hung up the phone and turned back to her new life.

She realised it a month after her marriage. The joy-suckling monster was as powerful as ever. As she aimlessly shifted from place to place in the daytime, becoming nothing more than a stultified zombie, she felt it stir. It only chose to show its full repugnant face when she met the red-haired beauty that lived next door. Lana Priestley stepped out one morning, dressed in a pencil skirt, a fitted blazer and a pair of stilettos. Maansi was at her flat door with the groceries, a baggy hoodie on and her wind-beaten hair straggling about her face. Although her full name was hung in gold letters on her flat door, she introduced herself to her.

'Hello. I'm Lana.'

Maansi heard her airy voice as it sprawled itself on a low vocal register and evoked thoughts of chocolate treacle and rich velvet. Lana's hair was thick and wavy – the kind that would billow in the frolicsome hands of the wind. Her lips were brick red. 'You must be Aryan's wife.'

'Oh, yes I am,' Maansi replied, her voice squeaky and fuelled with uncertainty. She coughed. 'My name's Maansi. You know Aryan?'

'Yes. We spent quite a bit of time together when he first moved in.' Maansi remembered the thirty-six pack of condoms. 'I haven't seen him for a while though. We've both been very busy with work.'

'What do you do?'

'I'm a solicitor,' she said. 'What do you do?'

'Um. Nothing at the moment. I'm still settling.'

'Oh, don't worry, you'll find something. These things take time,' Lana simpered. 'Anyway, I must be going. Lovely to meet you. Tell Aryan I said hello.' Maansi could have sworn her bottle-green eyes glinted as she spoke his name. She watched as Lana strutted down the corridor, her heels commanding attention as they clacked against the marble floor.

Once in the flat, Maansi dropped on to the sofa. Lana Priestley seemed to be the ghost of who she could have been. Who she had been. A put-together woman with ambition. But her depression had obliterated her ambitions into a million, unfixable pieces. Into paper confetti, with nothing to do except sweep them into a dustpan. Since the abortion and the break-up, she stopped caring. She lost her hunger for a first-class degree. She didn't want to fundraise or fulfil committee roles on student societies any more. She didn't want to work towards the university employability award, or take advanced French while studying for her international relations degree. Her five-year plan fell apart. The five-year plan that involved getting on to the Civil Service Graduate Scheme, doing a master's and obtaining her first position with the United Nations, preferably in Geneva. Once upon a time, Maansi Cavale was going to make a difference. But things were different now.

She reminded herself she was married to the future CEO of Alekar Co. He was wealthy and handsome. And he provided for her so she didn't have to join the rat race. While making herself breakfast in the mornings with fresh, organic ingredients, she'd tell herself out loud: 'No pressure, no desperation for money, no restrictions. Life can't get much better than this, Maansi.'

But she couldn't help but feel less than the Lana Priestleys of the world. She tried to convince herself, yet again, that she was contributing. She'd just bought groceries, hadn't she? Still, her mind spurted words like 'useless' and 'bad' at her. Still, the demon tapped and tapped on the inside, reminding her she was undeserving of joy. Still, she wondered if she could've been someone in a world without the pain.

When a few more days of endless persuasion proved ineffective, she made an appointment with the doctor. For the first time ever, she decided to see a professional.

'Fluoxetine,' the doctor said in monotone. 'One a day.' She ushered her out of her room, failing to deliver a reassuring smile. Maybe the damn doctor needed the fluoxetine, she thought.

Maansi tucked the pills into her underwear drawer, uncertain about taking them. But as days slipped by, she wasn't sure she could silence her cloaked tormentor without them. She retrieved the packet and popped a capsule on to her palm. She wouldn't tell Aryan about it.

It was the visit from her mother-in-law that changed her mind about her position in life. She made her first visit around noon. Maansi wasn't expecting her and wished she'd had the courtesy to call beforehand. She opened the door to Damini, still in her bunny-themed pyjamas with her hair uncombed and face unwashed, tiny bits of crust still tacked to the corners of her eyes.

'Hello,' Maansi said, wishing she had brushed her teeth.

'Hello, *Ma*,' Damini corrected her. She scraped past her and settled in the living room.

Growing up, Maansi had been subjected to her mother's Indian serials, which often sewed strenuous relationships between mother-in-laws and daughter-in-laws into the plot's fabric. The portrayal of daughter-in-laws and mother-in-laws as foes was standard practice. Even her own mother tried to inspire fear in her, forever remarking, 'What will your future *saas* think?' whenever she baulked at domestic chores.

Maansi dashed into the kitchen to make a cup of tea. As she poured boiling water over some PG Tips, she wondered if it'd be better to make chai. She threw open the cupboard doors in a frenzy, trying to track down the correct ingredients. No cardamom. No cloves. Nothing. She'd serve her regular English tea instead. That was OK, right? 'Chill out, Maansi,' she whispered to herself.

Unlike the mother-in-laws on television, Damini Alekar wasn't someone to fear. She was a meek woman with a small voice. When you could hear her, you could pick up a faint Indian accent diluted by the years spent in England. To Maansi's relief, she sipped the tea without complaint.

'How is everything?' Damini asked, her mouth falling into a thin, straight line.

'Yeah. Everything is going well,' Maansi said. 'How are you?'

'You're both getting along? Well?'

'Yes, of course.'

'And how has he been... behaving?' The rim of the cup compressed Damini's bottom lip. She waited for an answer, unable to sip until it came.

'Uhrm. Aryan is great. A really nice guy.' She wasn't sure how to answer the bizarre question. Damini's face remained hard and unflinching. She didn't seem to believe her. Feeling like a schoolteacher delivering a behavioural report, she reassured her mother-in-law that Aryan was good to her. They were doing well.

'And he isn't coming home too late?'

'No, no. Right on time,' she lied. Maybe her mother-in-law thought she was falling into boredom, since she didn't do anything all day. 'Anyway, it's fine. I'm going to start looking for jobs,' she continued. She didn't want her thinking she was leeching off her son and squandering his hard-earned cash.

'Oh, there's no need to do that.' Damini set her cup down on to the coffee table with care. 'It's no good, if you both come home late. Who will cook dinner and work at home? The marriage will not prosper.'

Maansi failed to respond. She did not, for a second, expect a woman of such social standing to think of working women as a bad thing. She considered her mother-in-law. Perhaps she had never worked a day in her life. Maybe she was wholly dependent on her husband. Was she looking at her own future? Did she want to comply to this woman's view of marriage? The tired feminist under the depression shook her head.

'Good values,' Damini said, peering at the statue of Lord Ganesh on the mantelpiece. 'Maybe Aryan can learn from you. Oh, I have this.' Damini withdrew a paper bag from her handbag and passed it over to Maansi. 'A gift for you.'

Maansi opened the bag. Inside were assortments of lipsticks, blushers and eyeshadows from MAC and Bobbi Brown. She examined the items, trying to contain a squeal. All of her favourite things in a bag! She was about to thank her and tell her how much she adored those brands, when she felt something else arrive on her lap. It was a battered, spiral notebook with a drooping daffodil pictured across the front.

'I have written my recipes in here. Let me show you.' Damini leaned in and showed her all the recipes she had jotted down over the years. As she turned the pages, she highlighted Aryan's favourite meals and went into elaborate detail on the preparation processes behind them. Maansi frowned. This notebook made one thing clear. Damini saw Maansi as her son's keeper. Her purpose was to keep him happy. And the make-up? Was she supposed to beautify her face for herself, or for him? Her ambitions rose from their graves and shook themselves off. Just like that, something else became clear. She wasn't meant for this. She knew she would have to get a job.

Once Damini left, Maansi switched on her laptop. She was not her mother-in-law's puppet. She'd find herself a job, then her mother-in-law would see her worth. Pages and pages of opportunities presented themselves, making her straighten up in her chair and crack her fingers, ready to apply. But as she read the requirements for each role, she sunk again. The daffodil looked at her menacingly with its kissing mouth – a new logo, advocating the lifestyle of a permanent housewife. She took the recipe book and stuffed it into a drawer.

When Aryan returned, she was in the middle of writing a cover letter – a terrible letter, drenched with clichés and trite phrases. She called herself a team player and said she maintained the ability to work independently. She claimed she had a 'can-do' attitude and a strong work ethic. She couldn't think of anything fresh and eye-catching to add. The letter made her completely forgettable. Aryan peeped at the screen.

'Don't start dear sir or madam, you want to find out the person's name,' he said. She glowered at him. 'Just trying to help.'

'When have you ever had to apply for a job then, mister my-dad-is-my-employer?'

'All right, fine. Don't listen to me,' he said, shrugging off his blazer.

She rolled her eyes. 'OK fine. Help me. I didn't do so great at university.'

'What do you mean? I thought you got a two-one?'

'Oh. I guess you could say I was affected by that circumstance. The one I told you about.' She hung her head as she showed him her CV. The first lie, exposed. She prayed he wouldn't despise her. He skimmed through it with an unreadable expression, while her heart raced, expecting him to sling contempt and scorn at her like an angry primate.

'Write your cover letter and then I'll send it over with your CV to someone in HR. Get them to fix it for you.'

'Can you do that?'

He nodded. 'What are you applying to?'

'To a publishing house. They're looking for a marketing intern,' she said. 'I could probably do that.'

'Probably. Anyway, I'm going to change and then I'm off for a run.' She figured as much. He always needed to be alone after work, whether this meant a solitary run or keeping his own company in a separate room. She tapped away on her laptop, trying to sell herself with stylish brevity. She was relieved Aryan didn't oppose her decision. It'd make her more interesting anyway. What did she ever have to say to him? She was so bored with her own company, it was astonishing anyone else could tolerate her.

Within an hour, she edited and polished her cover letter. She saved it, but instead of satisfaction from a job well done, she felt an unusual, stabbing pain in the left side of her stomach. She squirmed in her chair and her pores opened to release thin rivulets of sweat. Her throat began to relax and she felt her stomach leap.

She ran to the bathroom and dropped to her knees, her face hanging over the toilet bowl. She heaved for a good ten minutes. Her arms shook and her knees trembled as they balanced on the hard, unforgiving tiles. She heard Aryan re-enter the flat and tried her best to be quiet as her last meal slopped out. She was fine. He didn't have to know.

When she left the bathroom, she was pale and sweaty. Aryan was there in the bedroom, shedding his active wear. She drooped on to the bed, trying to look healthy and alive. He didn't seem to notice the state she was in. Without so much as a nod in her direction, he locked himself in the bathroom. She listened as the shower sprung to life from the nozzle, focusing on the rushing sound to soothe her.

Over the next few nights, she awoke with palpitations, covered head-to-toe in a film of her own sweat. She felt she'd been dragged through a horror film as the tortured protagonist. She clamped her hand over her mouth, gagging. She was terrified of the changes occurring in her body. Her doctor said the first two weeks would be a struggle, explaining the side effects would soon ebb away and leave her aglow with a positive feeling in the hollow pit of her body. She wasn't sure when or how that was going to happen. As she suffered through the nights, Aryan slept soundly by her side, none the wiser.

She reached for his hand beneath the covers and found his fingers wrapped around something rectangular and hard. He'd fallen asleep clutching his phone. She removed it from his grip and peered at the screen. Light erupted from the device and filled her head with a group of colourful stars. He was messaging someone called Omari. Aryan had texted him: 'Does he know?' To which this stranger named Omari replied: 'Of course he knows. I had to tell him. You know I did. When you free bruv?'

Unable to endure the harsh light, Maansi placed the phone on the bedside table and rested her head on his shoulder. He first flinched at the contact but dropped back into restful sleep.

She buried her head into his shoulder, wishing the plethora of side effects away. She felt sick to her stomach and worried Aryan would wake at the feel of her tears dribbling down his skin. She was unwilling to detach herself from him and he was too far gone into sleep to notice.

CHAPTER 11

'Here. They've pimped your cover letter.' Aryan motioned her over to him. She leaned over his shoulder and skimmed the document off his laptop screen.

'Whoa,' she said, in disbelief over how a simple turn of phrase could make her sound worlds above the person she really was. It was the art of deception at its finest. 'It's... perfect.'

She sent in her completed application to Hyland Publishers and almost instantly received an interview invitation. She gulped as she went over the details. 'It says there will be a panel of interviewers. Exactly how many interviewers make up a panel?' She felt a very real anxiety build a house over her drug-induced anxiety. 'I can't do it.'

'You'll be fine,' said Aryan. 'What is there to be nervous about?'

'Don't you ever get nervous?'

He took a second to deliberate. 'Not really.'

'You're not human.'

He winked at her.

On the day of the interview, she was shaking like an autumn leaf preparing to part from the bough. She sat in a waiting area within the publishing house, dressed in a two-piece suit and a pinstripe blouse. Her thick hair had been forcibly tamed into a ponytail and held down by rows of hairpins. She was queasy and afraid. At home, Aryan had tried to squeeze out every irrational thought and nervous bulb from her body through his lengthy and, at times, condescending pep talk. From what she understood, his position at work put him in control of staff and he had become impervious towards the nerves of common people. It meant, however, she could practise answering interview questions in front of a harsh judge.

'Always shake their hands,' Aryan had told her. She walked into an air-conditioned room where the smell of marker pens and the upholstery of office chairs spun through the air. There were four people on the panel. Two women and two men. One of the men, with tufts of grey hair on his egg-shaped head and his hands shuffling through some files, seemed to be the main man. Maansi shook everyone's hand and flashed her best, Colgate ad-worthy smile. She sat down into her designated chair, pressing her knees tightly together. The voice in her head attempted to break through and remind her of that red marker pen, of the fact she was a fraud. She waved it off. She tried to think of Lana Priestley. Perhaps, she could emulate her – pretend she wasn't Maansi Cavale or Maansi Alekar for a short minute. After a bit of small talk – asking if she was all right and if she'd found the place easily enough – they got right to it.

'So, what made you apply for this position?' said the main man. He leaned forward. Aryan had asked her the same thing.

'What made you apply for this position?' Aryan had said, his eyes narrowing and his lip stiff, notepad and pen at the ready. He was trying to intimidate her. It took her twenty goes to give a satisfactory answer. She delivered the same one seamlessly to the main man. It was difficult answering the following questions and she stumbled several times or tripped over words and had to divert left, right and back left to finally arrive at an adequate answer. Then, the dreaded question arrived.

'Your A levels and GCSE scores are exceptional. However, we cannot help but notice your degree classification is lower than what we would expect. Can you talk to us about it?'

She froze. She didn't know what to tell them. She had asked Aryan if it was all right to be honest and admit to her struggles during university. He shook his head and told her it would make her look weak. He told her one of the employees at his workplace was unreliable and always used his mental health as an excuse. He said he couldn't understand why people didn't just suck it up and get on with it.

'That's the most inconsiderate thing I've ever heard,' she told him. He merely responded with a 'maybe'. She didn't argue with him or show him the error of his thinking, in case she exposed herself. She knew she'd been right to keep her problem a secret.

'I suffered with depression in my final year and this had an impact on my final grade, but I completed my first two years with an upper second class honours,' she replied. 'And I am fine now and eager to work. As you can see from the experience I gained in my first two years, I am a dedicated, hard-working person.'

They nodded. She wasn't sure she'd done the right thing by telling the truth. Or if she had done the right thing by following that truth with a lie. The interview wrapped up and she gave herself permission to breathe again.

'Thank you, Mrs Alekar. We will be in touch.'

She rose, doubtful she'd impressed them. She glanced at them to assess her chances. Their faces were glacial.

As she left the building, she kept her eyes pasted to the ground and fast-walked, desperate to leave the vicinity. As she turned a corner, she bumped straight into a passing man, knocking a cup of coffee out of his hand. The liquid fled from its Starbucks cup and spreadeagled across the pavement, filling the cracks.

'Hey!' he yelled.

'Oh, my God. I am so sorry.' She held her breath and awaited the barrage of critical words. None came.

'Don't worry about it. It's only coffee,' he said. She faced him and was momentarily paralysed by the blue of his eyes. They had a soft sheen to them like polished sea glass. His hair was lightly tousled and indecisive about shade, settling somewhere between golden and light brown and his cheeks were lightly flecked with beauty spots. She couldn't help but notice he was a good-looking man.

'I'll buy you another one,' she suggested, guilt possessing her as he stood dabbing at the coffee stains across his sleeve.

'Oh, don't worry. It's no problem.'

'No please, I insist. I'd feel terrible otherwise.'

'Uhm. All right. If it'll make you feel better,' he said. 'I've got to head back in soon, though.' He gestured towards the Hyland building. They dipped into a Costa next door and she ordered him a coffee to-go.

'Thank you...' He paused for her name.

'Maansi.'

'Thank you, Maansi,' he said. 'Got to have caffeine pumping through my veins at all times.' He flashed a scintillating smile, the signs of playfulness tugging at the edges of his lips. Sometimes, it was easy to spot good humour in strangers.

'What do you do?' she asked him, as they sauntered outdoors again.

'Graphic designer. I design book covers.'

'With Hyland Publishers?'

'Yep.'

'I just had an interview there for an internship. I'm not sure it went well,' she said, following this statement with a profounder sigh than she'd intended.

'For what position?'

'Marketing assistant.'

'Was a guy called George interviewing you? Grey hair, funny shaped head?'

'Yes! He didn't even smile once,' she repined, kicking at an abandoned paper cup.

'He's a nice guy really. I'm sure you did better than you think.'

She very much doubted that. 'I really badly need a job.' She stopped at the entrance of the Hyland building.

She must have looked wretched as he reached out to pat her shoulder. 'Don't give up just yet. You never know what's around the corner,' he said. 'Anyway, I better go. Thanks again! Hope you get what you want.'

He disappeared behind the revolving doors and out of her life. To appease her mood, she dipped back into a café and bought herself a mocha layered with a generous lump of cream before heading back home.

Unlocking the door to the flat, she remembered she needed to fix dinner for her and Aryan. She held her queasy stomach. Thinking about food was the last thing she wanted to do. The fluoxetine had impaired her appetite. She glanced at the clock. Aryan wasn't due back for a while. She'd get away with a nap.

She woke up an hour later, to a smattering of kisses along her neck. Aryan was on top of her, his hands releasing her blouse buttons from their captors. Her nausea immediately amplified.

'Aryan,' she said, pushing him off. 'Aryan, don't.'

'What's wrong? Come on, I'm really in the mood,' he said, his teeth snatching at the skin of her neck.

'No!'

'OK, OK,' he sighed, clambering off. 'Fine.'

'We can just cuddle or something instead?' she asked, but he'd already left the room. She lifted herself from her bed and staggered after him.

'No food today? Or did you actually put things away?' he said, taking in the untouched kitchen. His tone was sour and sharp-edged.

'No. I didn't prepare anything. I fell asleep. Sorry.' There was no way she could cook. Her motivation had hung itself up at the door like a weather-beaten hat.

'Fine. I'll get something from outside.'

'Aryan, wait,' she said. He paused and she placed her arms around his neck and kissed him. His lips were rigid at first, but they eventually gave in and kissed her back. 'Aren't you going to ask how my interview went?'

'Oh, sorry. I completely forgot.'

She shrunk. How could he forget? 'It doesn't matter. I don't want to talk about it anyway.'

Once he'd left to fetch their dinner, she crawled back into bed. She was looming on the edge of slumber when her phone rang. She answered with a croak.

'Maansi? This is George Ibbotson from Hyland Publishers. I'm just calling to let you know we have decided to offer you the marketing assistant position.'

She froze.

'Hello?'

'Oh yes, I'm here. That's... that's amazing!' she exclaimed.

'Brilliant. I'll pop you an email with all the details and HR should contact you tomorrow to talk you through the offer, the pay and start date.'

'Great. Thank you very much.'

'It was lovely to meet you. Have a good day.'

When she put the phone down, she leapt back on to the

bed and hugged her pillow, squealing into it with delight. Doubts would taunt her, and she'd worry about whether she could fulfil the role, but at that moment, she was glad. She was now a wealthy, married woman with a job – well, paid internship – but she'd take it. Her life was unwrapping in front of her, revealing a gift at a time and the promise of a happier development in her tale. This reassured her, but she was still drained to the bone and sleep came to her easily.

CHAPTER 12

'Thank you for giving me this opportunity,' she said, following George as he gave her a tour of the building. He led her into the main open-plan office where she'd be spending all her time. It wasn't a plain or bland office by any means. One of the larger walls had a built-in bookshelf stacked with paperbacks, and the others were mounted with abstract art which, to her, seemed less like art and more like sploshes of paint hurled on to canvas by a group of overexcited children. Nevertheless, it was a pleasant and bright room with smiling, straight-backed workers.

'No problem. I liked your dedication, experience and your honesty. Logan put in a good word for you too. I didn't know you knew him,' George told her. She hadn't the faintest idea who he was talking about, until she saw the young man with the tousled, dark blonde hair sitting across the office. With earphones in, he drummed his pencil against the table, spellbound with his own thoughts. Maansi couldn't believe it. He had no reason for helping her. She spilt coffee on him, for goodness' sake! He owed her nothing. 'Sally will get you started. She'll be over in a minute. If you have any questions, don't hesitate to ask.'

'All right. Thank you very much.'

She continued watching the kind stranger from her safe distance as he wiggled and hummed in his seat. She thought Logan was a lovely name. His co-worker whinged at him and clouted him into silence. He held up his hands in apology, but once his co-worker busied her hands again, he snatched her notebook from beneath her.

'Logan, it's not ready. Give it back,' Maansi could hear her say, as he held her off with his arm, passing his eyes over her work and spawning jokes that made her flush and thrash about like a hen woken from sleep.

The woman called Sally came over and set Maansi to work, seating her with the marketing and communications team at the other end of the office. On her first day, she was to assist with the promotion of crime novels. Sally told Maansi there would be a meeting in a few hours and she should attend and even contribute some of her own ideas. Maansi stared at her to-do list and deflated. The antidepressants had yet to elevate her out of the pit. She was anchored to the ground, unable to kick off into her work, as if there was a titanium gate between her and her computer screen preventing her from rushing in and revelling in it. She was both there and not there. The impending meeting lurked over her and made the hairs on her neck stand up.

As she expected, the meeting was disastrous. She didn't contribute a single idea. Though deep down she knew it was her first day as an intern and ought to cut herself some slack, the voice in her head raged at her for being incompetent and inferior to everybody there. Instead of returning to her desk after the meeting, she made a beeline for the ladies' toilets, suspecting she'd talk herself into tears. As she tried to suppress the soaring panic in her body, she thought of Aryan and how unsympathetic he could be towards the people he managed. He attributed the display of emotions in the workplace to weakness. Was that really what she was? Weak? Her brain responded with a confident 'yes'. It was a while before she could step back out into the office again.

'Hey, Maansi.' Logan was standing outside the toilets, pouring himself a cup of water from the water cooler. 'How's it going?'

'Hi. Hey!' she said, trying to come across as though she was totally fine. 'Logan, right? I didn't get your name the last time.'

'Yeah. Logan Reeves. That's me! How's your first day?'

'Fine. George said you said nice things about me. I don't know why you did, but that might have helped me get this job. Thank you. Honestly.'

'Ah, no worries. I mean, my word doesn't mean much anyway, but you looked like you needed a break.'

'Thanks.' She brushed her hair away from her face. 'It's pretty intense here. I went blank in that meeting.'

He leaned back against the wall. He appeared calm and cool, like the snow-layered streets of winter mornings – soft and untouched. 'Don't worry about it. It's your first day. It's OK to be a little lost.' He leaned towards her and she could smell something akin to lime rising from his skin.

'My first day here I broke the printer and pissed everyone off. It's fine. Honestly. Don't be afraid of being human.' He winked at her. His cool demeanour was contagious. She felt calmer already. She wished she wasn't on the other side of the office from him. She wanted to shrink him down and put him in her pocket, ready to take out for a bit of perspective. More than that, she wanted to get to know him. She could use a friend.

'Oh, you're married?' Logan asked, signalling towards her ring.

'Oh. Yeah. I only just married, actually.' She felt a strong need to disclose she hadn't been married long.

'Wow. Congrats. What does your guy do?'

'He works for Alekar Co. It's a property development company. Have you heard of it? He'll be taking over as CEO in the future, fingers crossed.'

He nodded, suddenly silent and peering away from her. When he glanced back, she saw the warmth had been stolen from his eyes.

'Awesome,' he finally said, his hands fiddling with the water cooler tap. 'Anyway, I have to get back to work.'

She wondered what she said.

The day at work flew by and she walked home devoid of energy. As she approached the flat, she could hear Aryan's voice tangoing with another. She found him standing in the corridor with Lana Priestley. They were close together, their eyes fastened to each other. She was flirting with him, resting her hand on his shoulder, pushing her hair to one side to expose her smooth marzipan neck. Aryan, without moving an inch, devoured upon it.

'Aryan!' Maansi shouted, as she strode down the corridor towards them. She threw her arms around him and shot Lana a look. One, she hoped, confirmed her territory and told her to back off. Maansi had never been that jealous, but something about that woman troubled her. Lana delivered a brief hello before leaving for the lasagne she claimed to be baking. She gave Aryan a drawn-out goodbye, her cherry lips parting to show off her polished pearls. Did she want him? Maansi took her husband by the arm and dragged him into the flat.

'Can't wait to get your hands on me, is that it?' he said,

letting her lure him into their den. She let go of his arm. He tried to coax her towards the sofa – no doubt to prompt a session of passion, but his efforts weren't fruitful. Maansi whacked him away as if he were a persistent fly given to circling her at every opportunity. Alone on the sofa, he huffed, his right leg bouncing up and down: inconsolable. She feared rejecting him would tempt him towards their red-headed neighbour, but making love wasn't an option. She couldn't even feel anything any more. She tried stirring herself, the day before, to see if anything still worked but the sensations had been cruelly numbed by her medication. She told herself she'd continue being intimate with Aryan to keep him happy and to trap his focus on to her – an anti-feminist move again, she was sure. But in that moment, she couldn't yield. She was tired after having a normal, adult day with a condition that made her feel lesser than an adult and lesser than normal.

Only a few minutes after Maansi had changed and sat down to relax, Aryan was chastising someone down the phone again. His words cut like blades. The power behind them could leave you trembling in your sleep. It wasn't hard to figure out his work personality. Aryan was a corporate man. A man born to lead, to generate profit and care little for the people beneath him. He was usually composed, she evaluated, but quick to anger at incompetence and at people with thoughts and ideas subversive to his own. She heard him shout: 'Well, it isn't the right way. You'd have to be foolish to believe that'd work.' He retreated into the bedroom, shutting the door and locking it behind him as he continued ridiculing whoever had the misfortune of answering his call.

After a while, he returned to the room. 'How was your day?' he asked her. But before she could fumble with an answer, his phone rang again.

'Great,' she muttered.

'Hello,' he began. 'What's wrong? Are you OK? Why are you crying?'

She noticed his tone had killed its fire.

'Is everything OK?' she asked him. He whipped away from her, keeping her in the dark.

'What? No, you're not useless. Don't listen to him. He didn't hurt you did he? I don't care if it's been a year. If he's touched you again, I'll call the police this time,' he continued over the phone. 'It's not crazy, Mum. Staying with him is crazy. Can you please just listen to me?'

After a few more moments of pleading with her and getting nowhere, Aryan ended the conversation.

Maansi was speechless. From what she'd heard, it was easy to guess the topic of conversation. She sat there as the hushed secret of domestic abuse unravelled itself before her, lengthening its foetid form across the room. She was an outsider looking in. She'd seen Dhruv. He was terrifying. He had dead eyes, a tall body and hair slicked back like some kind of mafia caricature.

'What happened? Is your mum OK?'

'I don't know.'

'Does your dad... hurt her?'

'Sometimes. But she defends him. He never means to, apparently.'

'Couldn't she report him? Why does she stay with him?'

He shrugged his shoulders. 'She's too scared to be without him. She married young and he told her she didn't need to work and he hired domestic workers. She's never had to be independent. And she worries what her family will think of her if she left him. Obviously.'

'Are you OK?'

'I'm fine.'

'Do you want to talk about it?'

'No. I'm fine.'

Later in bed, Maansi thanked herself for forging through her pain and working outside. She'd had a bad day, but if she didn't even try, she might've surrendered all her personal power and become like Damini.

As she lay there, a clump of questions budded. She wanted to ask Aryan if he had similar experiences with his father growing up. Whether he too had faced abuse. She guessed not, since he was privileged enough to be sent to a posh boarding school. She looked over at the lumpy shape beneath the duvet. After the trying day she had, she didn't want hostility. She reached out to caress his shoulder, regretting it almost instantly, as he misread her gesture and turned to trace her body with his hands.

'I really don't think now is a good time,' she said. He let go of her.

'Fine.' Fine. The word fine, again – blunt and flippant. He used it so often she thought he might squeeze it from a tube of concentrated 'fine' and brush his teeth with it every morning. He turned back around and left her behind to travel the realm of sleep.

CHAPTER 13

Although still in battle with the demon inhabiting her body and mind, Maansi's time at work became less taxing over the next month. She'd been asked to complete numerous tasks, such as running social media accounts and writing blog entries for new and upcoming books. Thankfully, her negative self-talk had been quelled. It was as if the *vroom* of a car engine had dissolved into an almost inaudible purr of a house-cat. She could just about focus.

She recently had a performance review and was relieved to hear positive feedback from George. In fact, George branded a recent piece of work 'exceptional'. He told her to try to be more vocal and outspoken in meetings – to have confidence in her ideas. With the positive comments adrift in her mind, she left work feeling good about herself. She was still cautious, for she was walking a path she hadn't mapped out for herself in a five-year plan. She trod on a rougher course, barefooted and wincing at the feel of jagged stones. A career in publishing, while unexpected, didn't seem like a terrible idea. She couldn't lie to herself and say she felt comfortable. The marketing and communications team were planning a book launch and she was assisting. The stress from being involved strengthened her demon with nourishment, but the pleasure from her performance review meant it wasn't gorging itself. A kind of satisfactory balance had been struck!

She promised herself she'd be more vocal. She was putting in so much effort to produce work and take care of herself at the same time, she found it difficult to manage friendships at the workplace. She liked to speak to cat-loving Amy who sat next to her in Aztec patterned clothes and tortoiseshell glasses. She also had conversations with Rani – an Asian girl who worked in the editorial team. It seemed natural for the only two Asian girls to band together. That shared experience alone made the other feel familiar and warm.

Aside from succeeding with Amy and Rani, Maansi wasn't trying with the others. She hadn't seen much of Logan either. She noticed he hopped between groups and slid into circles with enviable ease. He waved at her from time to time; other times, he'd walk by her as if she were invisible, and the smile meant for him would expire on her lips. Amy said Logan was a daydreamer and lived in his own world, oblivious to his surroundings at times, so Maansi put his behaviour down to that.

To celebrate her performance review, she persuaded Aryan to take her shopping on the weekend. He wasn't pleased about the idea.

'Why are you torturing me with a shopping trip? Can't we just go for a drink instead?'

'Aryan, I've got good news and want to celebrate. Can you not be supportive?'

'I just, don't see... All right. Fine.'

He patted her shoulder with his palm, unbending and outstretched, as if striking an ambulant insect, speaking the words 'well done'. He didn't think of her news as a big deal. She did. He put on some clothes, stuffed his wallet into his jeans and off they went.

They shopped at Oxford Street. He followed her into the clothing stores, grunting when she asked his opinion on the floral blouses or jersey skirts. She wanted to stock up on clothes that made her feel her best. She read somewhere that if a woman looked good, she'd feel good. She'd do anything to keep herself out of that pit. Anything. After a good couple of hours browsing shop shelves and clothing racks, trying on shoes and purchasing jewellery, she finally agreed to a break. She suggested they get some food. According to Aryan, there was one place for it: Borough Market.

The market was crowded with people yearning for street food. The area was smothered with the smell of steaming, juicy burgers on grills; simmering exotic curries and fried dessert snacks. Aryan paid for hotdogs and they devoured them like famished wolves. She had hers with onions and he had his without.

'No onions? Not sure I want to be married to you now,' Maansi joked, hoping he'd lighten up. Behind him, she caught sight of a man in a graphic T-shirt with a guitar case strapped to his body. She nudged Aryan, almost knocking his hotdog to the ground.

'That guy over there is from work. Let's go say hi,' she said. She dragged Aryan through the throngs of people hovering around the market stalls. Logan was by the vegan stall taking a generous bite into his meat-free burger. Ketchup spurted from the bottom of the bun and rambled down his arm. He put his arm up to his mouth and started to lick it off like a schoolboy, unconcerned about manners and too lazy to hunt for tissue.

'Hiya!' said Maansi. He peered up at her, his arm still in his mouth. He quickly released it.

'Oh hi,' he said. 'How are you?' The volume of his voice plummeted towards the end of his sentence. She followed his line of vision to Aryan.

'Oh! This is my husband, Aryan,' she said. She still had to say husband slowly, stretching it out in her mouth like gum. Aryan didn't bother plastering on a smile.

'Hi,' said Logan.

Aryan nodded at him and then glanced around himself, as if he had somewhere more important to be.

'So, are you here alone?' Maansi asked.

'Yep. I am.'

'Well, you could come around with us, if you'd like.'

He looked back again at Aryan, then at the ground. 'That's kind of you. But I think I may have a migraine coming on. I was just going to finish this and head home. I'll see you at work, all right?' he winked at her and smiled.

'Oh. OK, look after yourself,' she said. Maansi watched him disappear behind a gaggling group of teenage girls. She couldn't blame him for rejecting her offer. Aryan was an inimical king upon a throne of ice. His lordship couldn't be bothered offering anyone the time of day, let alone the two measly syllables in 'hello'.

'If he wasn't telling the truth about the migraine, you'd be the reason he lied. Why can't you be nice to people?' she said. He didn't answer. 'Whatever. Shall we get some fries as well then?'

'I'm not hungry. You go.' He turned heel and marched off into the crowd behind her.

'Where are you going?' she shouted after him. 'Aryan!'

Selfish idiot, she thought. Instead of following him, she firmly planted her feet in line for fries. This time, she wasn't going to cave into his will. She thought about men like Logan. Nice men. Then again, Lewis Bingley had come across as a nice man. Those layers of cotton-candied wool were hiding the real him. She was at least thankful that Aryan didn't care for pretences, even if his capricious moods made her sour. She finally felt settled but still felt something was amiss between her and Aryan. Their relationship needed work. She wouldn't give up on it so easily.

When she returned home, he wasn't there. She hung around the living area, waiting for him to walk through the door. She waited three hours, before beginning dinner without him. She placed lentils in a pressure cooker along with onions, garlic and a range of spices and left it to simmer. While she waited for the daal to cook, she decided to capitalise on her positive mood and look at other things to do outside of work. Before the depression took her, she wanted to learn to paint and planned to take lessons. Aryan disappeared twice a week to attend his MMA club, so she thought it was high time she did something too. Now that she could see improvements, maybe she could look forward to something. She laid the plates of finished daal on the table. He still hadn't arrived. If he thought she was going to wait for him, he had another thing coming. Besides, he was lucky she cooked for him at all.

As she scooped the last spoonful of yellow lentils into her mouth, the front door creaked open.

'Not daal,' Aryan muttered, as he entered the flat and parked himself at the table. A word of thank you didn't drip from his lips. His eyes didn't meet with hers. Instead of eating the dinner, he slid his spoon under the lentils and fiddled with the bed of rice, eventually ploughing mounds of it on top of the soupy curry before lowering to taste it.

'Where have you been?' she asked him, laying her spoon down. He didn't answer.

When he finished, he swept up their plates and dropped them into the sink at such an alarming height, she was shocked they hadn't smashed into shards.

'Do all men wink at you like that?' he asked. His shoulders were high, his eyes narrow slits and his knuckles were turning white as he clenched his fists.

'Excuse me?'

'I saw the way you looked at him. Stay away from him.'

She hoped he was going to thaw into laughter, jeering at her for her gullibility. But he didn't laugh. He washed the dishes and dried them, his hands infused with a trembling aggression.

'Oh, my God. Don't tell me you're the jealous possessive type. He's just someone from work,' she began. 'What's the big deal?'

'He was flirting. Just stay away from him,' he snarled. 'Why is it that you need to work anyway? We have enough money.'

She couldn't believe he was being serious. She rewound her time with him, searching for clues, anything indicative of the unreasonable man in front of her. She wasn't stupid. She knew entering an arranged marriage with someone you barely knew was like holding a dozen scratch cards. But they were shiny and promising. She never imagined the words beneath the layer of UV ink could be anything close to 'jealous prick'. 'First of all, I have a life. I'm not some submissive woman waiting for you at home. I want to work. And what about you? With that Lana girl? You don't flirt with her?'

'That's different.'

'Oh, really? How is it different? Honestly, it looks as if you two have had something going on,' she challenged back, her cheeks burning. She dared herself to ask it. 'Have you slept with her?'

There was a suspicious delay before he spoke. 'I'm not going to dignify that with an answer.'

'That's what people say when the answer is yes!' she shrieked, tears gathering in her eyes. Oh my God, she thought. Was she getting upset? Why was she crying? He threw the teatowel on to the counter and strode towards the front door. 'Where the hell are you going?'

The thud of the door slamming ricocheted in her head and afflicted her with a sudden headache. She knew it. The six missing condoms had been expended on the Priestley woman. She only ever spent words on Logan, yet he vilified her. Don't see him? Because he dared to smile at her? Her entire picture of Aryan distorted and became disordered like Cubist art. Lana and Aryan must have been laughing at her with their faces shielded by their hands. Hands that wandered across each other's bodies. Her mind tortured her with questions of whether he brought a roughness to Lana's bed, or worshipped her with gentle, skilled devotion. She could hear the chocolate-syrup moans escaping from Lana's pretty throat. She pulled at her hair. They would have to move. She couldn't live between the pages of his history. The walls were closing in on her... 'Get a grip, Maansi.'

That night, they occupied their different sides of the bed again. She listened to his breathing. It was shallow and he sporadically sighed into the darkness. She knew he was awake. She heard him open and close his bedside drawer. A light bounced into the dark as his touch activated his phone screen. Was he texting? Playing a game? Browsing his gallery? Googling how to apologise to your wife? She couldn't take the mystery any more.

'Aryan, what are you doing?' she asked, turning her body towards him. He dropped his phone.

'Nothing. Sorry. Go back to sleep,' he said. His voice was laxer and woolly. She guessed he wasn't in the same vindictive mood. She edged closer to him. Her eyelids were drooping but she couldn't close them until she had at least a scrap of peace.

'I'm cold,' she tried. He took the hint and put his arm around her. She nuzzled her face into his chest and he stroked her hair. 'Do you love me?'

'I love you,' he spoke, never having once said so before.

'I love you too,' she said, not knowing if she truly did. It didn't matter. He was her husband. This marriage was her decision. Love was still growing, its stumps becoming arms and legs that would eventually stretch themselves out and shake off the aches of hibernation. She knew deep inside she couldn't hate him for his past. It would be unfair. She couldn't hate him for his jealousy either. After all, she had been jealous of Lana.

She shelved the day's incident in the back of her mind, where she hoped it would choke behind layers of dust and cobwebs.

CHAPTER 14

The following weekend arrived. She hadn't seen much of Aryan, both of them having been caught up with overtime at work. The air between them remained frigid and dense. She wanted to inject their weekend with peace – to lay under the covers with him and speak of sweet nothings, forgetting all that had happened. They'd never spent a morning that way. When she imagined getting married, she pictured cuddles beneath the covers, unable to feel the elapsing of time as they talked and laughed. Somehow, she wasn't sure Aryan would ever blend into the dreams she had of them.

She traipsed to the kitchen, her Hello Kitty dressing gown hugging her body and her hair a frowsy mess. Aryan was in the kitchen, mixing himself a smoothie. He drank the same one most mornings – a banana blended with peanut butter, oats and almond milk, a pinch of cinnamon on top. He'd knock it back, wait half an hour, attack a coffee and begin his pre-planned day. She preferred the idea of drawn-out mornings and big breakfasts – lounging about on the sofa and deciding to go somewhere on a whim – no plans in place.

'Morning,' he greeted her.

'Morning, Aryan,' she said, perching at the mini breakfast bar. His face stuck to its usual stolid appearance. 'Can we talk?'

'Well, you're already talking…'

She still had questions about Lana – things she was aching to know. Were they ever romantically involved? How often did he see her? Did he, at one time, see a future with her? But she knew better than to ask. 'I was wrong to accuse you of having slept with Lana. And anyway, even if you had, I can't get upset over who you've been with before we got married. That would be stupid.'

'OK.' He hit the button on the blender. The sudden noise ripped through her eardrums. He let the blades spin longer than necessary, until the quiet scent of burning folded through the kitchen.

'That's it? Don't you have anything to say to me?'

'About what?'

'You got mad at me for having a male friend. Don't you think you were kind of out of line? And then you told me I didn't need to work. I mean, hello? What year is this?'

He poured her a glass of the smoothie and placed it before her to try. 'All right, all right. I take it all back.'

'Were you jealous? Why did you get like that?'

'We're still trying to get to know each other. It's weird to me you'd be getting to know some other guy.'

She raised her eyebrows. So, he felt insecure?

She reached for his hand. 'Look, I know it's not easy for us to bond, but we're getting there, aren't we?' A brilliant idea thumped her on the head. 'You know what... let's go on a honeymoon, Aryan. Let's go to Paris. We'll have nothing but time then. What do you think?'

'Urm. I don't know. I have a lot of work,' he said.

'Aryan!'

'OK. OK, we'll go to Paris.'

She felt a warmth trickle through her chest. This is just what she and Aryan needed. A weekend in Paris to enjoy each other. He was always at work and scarcely had time to indulge in the decadent pleasures of romance. Paris could transform their relationship. She could imagine them, holding hands and strolling along cobblestoned paths, losing themselves in the shimmering lights of the Eiffel Tower while sharing a selection of macarons. The faint notes of 'La Vie en Rose' would amble on the wind and frolic through her hair. They could stay at the Renaissance Arc de Triomphe and drink expensive champagne, getting drunker (she hoped) with love as the clock ticked on. She linked her arms around his neck and hugged him.

She began to assail him with kisses. 'Going to try to defend yourself now?' she said, her hands grabbing at his collar.

'Sorry, Maansi.' He pulled her off. 'I'm not in the mood.'

'Oh.' She let her arms fall limp at her sides. She rummaged for something to say to him. 'Oh. Your mum texted me last night. She wondered if we wanted to go over this weekend.'

'I don't think so.'

'Are you sure? Aryan, we hardly ever go!' She wasn't desperate to see her in-laws. Her mother-in-law was sexist and her father-in-law scared her, but they'd have to go eventually and she wanted to hurry up and get the first visit out of the way.

'I see my dad at work every day. There's no need. We'll just go another time.'

'What about your mum? Don't you want to see her?'

'I'll call her later.'

Maansi didn't understand. She suggested visiting her parents once and he told her he was happy to tag along. When it came to his own parents, he turned glum and would lend no explanation for his behaviour. He saw his father during the work week and frequently called his mother. Yet, he grew uncomfortable with the idea of visiting his parents' house. Something about being there, sitting with the two of them in a more personal and intimate setting unnerved him. If she brought it up, he'd shut down and retreat into his own space, or he'd tell her he lived there throughout university and was sick to death of the place. She didn't believe that for a second. She bet she could get to the bottom of it in Paris.

'So, what are your plans today?' she asked him. 'Do you want to take me out somewhere?'

'Actually, I was going to go see an old friend.'

'Oh, you have friends?' she joked. Although, a part of her did wonder. They'd been together a while and she hadn't got to know Aryan's friends. 'I'd like to meet one of your friends.'

'Not this one,' he said. 'He's from school.'

'So, one of your oldest friends, right? Go on. Are you worried he'll have embarrassing stories to tell?'

He hesitated. 'OK. I'll tell him to pop over for a few minutes. Just introductions. OK?'

She agreed. It was better than nothing.

While they waited for Aryan's friend, they idled around on the sofa, engrossed in a new Netflix series. At least, she was. Aryan's foot tapped impatiently against the floor. His eyes kept roaming towards the door. As soon as the knock came, he bounded for the door like a hunted hare. Maansi scrambled to get a look at the stranger. In the doorway stood a tall man dressed in a gaberdine trench coat. His skin was dark and his eyes were big shiny conkers. He had a sophisticated demeanour, which lasted a few seconds before crumbling at the sight of Aryan.

'Mate, it's been months. Way too long!' he said, as he and Aryan shook hands and pulled each other in for a hearty hug. Aryan backed off and scrutinised his friend.

'What the hell are you wearing now?' he derided him.

'Shut up. I take care of myself.' The man became aware of Maansi's presence in the background. Aryan glimpsed at her, his Adam's apple moving up and down as he gulped a few times. Why was he nervous?

He waved the man in and stood him before her. 'This is my old friend, Omari,' he said. 'And Omari, this is my... This is Maansi.'

Omari stared at Maansi, as if she were part of an unknown species that ignited both fear and admiration. An alien of some kind.

'Hi,' she said, tugging at her sleeves. Something about Omari made her feel naked beneath a bright spotlight.

'Hi,' he said. He stuck out his hand and she took it. They shook hands, slowly, as his eyes adjusted to her and captured her face, inch by inch, for his memory. 'So, Maansi, how are you settling in?'

'Great, thanks,' she said. She noticed she nodded too much as she spoke. 'Come in and sit down.'

'No, better not. I've been stuck in lectures all day today.'

'What are you studying?' she asked.

'Medicine.'

'Really? Oh wow.'

'What do you do?'

'I work in publishing. Marketing.'

'How about that,' said Omari, beaming at her. She thought there was something off about him. His smile might have been wide but the skin around his eyes didn't crinkle – a sure sign of insincerity.

'Anyway, we need to go,' Aryan broke in. Omari delivered a curt nod and they both departed, arms hanging around each other, like the best of friends reunited. She could hear them as they travelled down the corridor, laughing and naming their favourite bars.

Omari. She recognised his name. She found it on Aryan's

phone that night. He had asked Omari if 'he knows'. She contemplated who 'he' might be and what it is 'he' knows. She logged the memory in her mental notebook, captioned: 'bring up in Paris'.

She lay in bed, preparing to read a book she'd soon have to promote. It was a novel about a woman in love with her best friend's husband. She'd already consumed a few chapters, finding the plot tedious and the writing lacklustre. Somehow, she'd have to write effective copy to promote the boring drivel. As she opened the bedside drawer to retrieve her copy, she saw that box of condoms and felt a pang of anger. He no longer needed that box from the past. She was on the pill and they were rarely intimate anyway.

Irrespective of her efforts, she couldn't desist her mind from travelling there. The image flooded forward and almost immobilised her. She imagined her husband and Lana, the bed creaking, the smacking sound of sweaty skins as Lana moved up and down, up and down. She slammed the drawer shut. What if he still liked Lana? He'd never cheat on her... would he? And what about her? She committed to a man she doesn't know – committed to being with him and only him. She was working on growing love between them, but she wondered what would happen if it developed with someone else, naturally and without effort.

When Aryan returned he reeked of liquor and cigarettes. He planted a kiss on her forehead.

'Did you have fun with Omari?' she asked.

'Yeah,' he sighed, stroking her back. 'Yeah, I did. It's been a long time since I've seen him.'

'What did you guys talk about?'

'Just our school days. Old memories.' He removed his hands from her and stripped off his jacket.

'What old memories? Anything you want to share? Or would I rather not know?'

He flopped on to the bed and closed his eyes. 'There's too much to tell. A whole chunk of my life was spent at that school. Maybe some other time.'

CHAPTER 15

At work, Maansi was compiling two lists. One for the best pick-up lines in literature, and the other for the top romantic heroes – all in preparation for Valentine's Day. She worked at a languorous pace, knowing once she finished she'd have to check all was ready for the upcoming book launch. Dealing with the launch made her shoulders curl. She much preferred the trivial task at hand.

She released herself from her chair, her body aching from being still too long. She wandered over to the water cooler, stopping for a moment at Logan's abandoned workstation, where she passed her eyes over the work trailed across his table. She leaned in and examined his creations. In front of her was an elegant design printed on a page of sharp white. On the cover was a silhouette of a man looking out to sea. He appeared to be holding a briefcase. Logan had intermixed cyan, shades of white and black to create a book cover that spoke of self-discovery – of a middle-aged man done with the verisimilitudes of life – of a being burdened with the staleness of his soul.

'Busted!' Logan's voice came from behind her.

She jumped. 'Oh, I was just...'

'It's all right.' He laughed. 'Still a work in progress.'

'I really like it.'

'Thank you.' He hopped back into his chair and swivelled it round to face her. 'How's it going?'

'Great. Sort of. Getting a bit stressed about the book launch.'

'Everyone always gets worked up about launches. You read the book?'

'No.'

'Me neither. Don't read much, to tell you the truth.'

'But you work at a publishing company,' she giggled. He had on a pair of jeans, a graphic T-shirt and a khaki utility jacket. He got away with casual wear. George would fire disapproving looks at him, but in reality didn't mind. He put it down to Logan being an eccentric creative.

'I was thinking of heading out for lunch. Want to come?' she asked, sweeping her hair to one side. She felt bold asking. Of course, she questioned why he'd want to spend time with her anyway, but she made it her mission to subdue those pesky thoughts. Have some confidence, she told herself.

'Uh,' he paused. 'You know what? Sure. I'll buy.'

They made their way to a retro, American-style diner nearby. The floors were tiled, the booths and the walls were a destabilising combination of red and pink; a wide, single wall stood deluged with old adverts for Coca-Cola and motorcycles. People tapped their feet beneath their tables as bubble-gum pop surfed from a neon-lit jukebox. You half expected to witness a girl in a polka-dot dress, leaning into her date, a tall glass of strawberry milkshake between them with two straws for sharing – just like in the old American movies. Logan and Maansi seated themselves at a table. She ordered a hamburger and he got the vegan burger with fries.

'When did you decide to go vegan?' she asked as she brought her burger to her lips. Its juice glistened beneath the hard lights, intensifying her hunger. How anyone could give meat up was beyond her, though she'd been taught that was the way to be a 'good' Hindu.

'Trying to go vegan, actually. I always give into cheese. I've been vegetarian since I was about six though.'

'How come?'

'Animals are people too,' he said, as if the answer was so blindingly obvious. 'Honestly, nothing disgusts me more than when I see people gnawing on the flesh of defenceless, innocent animals.' Maansi dropped the burger on to her tray and stuttered. He exploded into laughter. 'I'm kidding. Eat up.'

'That isn't funny!' She admired how his eyes twinkled like the surface of Christmas baubles when he was amused. She brushed his leg beneath the table with her foot. 'Oh. Sorry!' she said. She pushed her chair back a few inches, butterflies taking off in her stomach. Get a hold of yourself, you're married, she thought. 'So, are you coming to the book launch?'

'No. I'm not,' he said. 'Actually, after this week I'm not returning at all.'

'Why?'

'I've been offered a new job.'

'Oh.' She didn't know why her heart plunged into the depths of her stomach. It wasn't as if she and Logan spoke often. Still, she knew she'd miss glancing at him during her mini breaks from the computer. She'd never admit it to anyone, but he was a handsome man and his presence made for a pleasant view from her office chair. 'Congratulations,' she said. Before she could ask him questions about his new job, he changed the subject.

'Can I ask you something? Though, I hope you won't get offended.' She urged him to go on. 'Have you had an arranged marriage?'

She hesitated. 'Yes. Although not a lot of Indians do any more, I swear. Even in India, more and more young people are finding their own partners. I just chose to.'

'Right. Is it weird? I mean, didn't you want to meet someone on your own? Fall in love?' His gaze speared through her as he spoke. In that moment, she was thankful for her dark skin.

Without a doubt, her cheeks would have transformed into two Rome apples.

'It's complicated. But Aryan and I get along. We're fine.' There was that word again: 'fine'. He nodded, then resumed his attention to his burger. From the way his face warped as he chewed, she guessed the burger wasn't particularly flavoursome.

They finished up and returned to the office, exchanging only a few words as they walked back. He told her he was tired, so she put his sudden quietness down to that. When she returned to her desk, Amy nudged her in the ribs. 'So, Logan Reeves, eh?' she said.

'I'm married, Amy!'

'I keep forgetting! You're so young yet,' she said. 'Anyway, good. It means I can have him then.' Maansi laughed and resumed typing. Her fingers slackened at the keys, as the thought of Amy and Logan crept into her mind, maddening her. She swatted it from her mind. She was married and had no reason to be jealous. After all, Aryan was attractive, even if he wasn't the most affable of people. A shy smile stretched along her face. She couldn't wait to be alone with him. Her Valentine-themed lists had her dreaming about Paris.

Even during the season of love, the sepals of her romantic vision were watered down by the bludgeoning of regrets. They always found a way to rise. It would all expand from a drop of rain into a pool of unhelpful memories and thoughts, preparing to drown her. The abortion, the break-up, her inability to cope and her successive failures. How she let go of each important aspect of her life, one by one. She took a necessary breath. She was getting on well now. That's what she needed to remember.

After she double-checked catering was in place for the book launch and contacted authors for a separate speaking event, Sally arrived at her desk and asked to speak to her. Maansi followed her into her office, her arms studded with goosebumps.

The spacious office was filled with the cloying scent of lavender, making Maansi's head whirl. She lowered herself on to a chair, waiting as Sally gathered her paperwork. She admired Sally. She was an accomplished middle-aged woman with a direct, no-nonsense approach. Everybody respected her and noticed her when she stepped into a room. Sally could always be found in a colourful shift dress with a bold, matte pink swiped across her lips. She completed her job with both competence and style.

'So, you had your performance review with George and that went really well,' Sally said. 'I know you still have a couple of months of your internship to go, but seeing as you've been progressing well with us and have a good work-ethic, we would like to offer you a permanent job with us.'

Maansi's mouth fell open. 'What? Really?' she said, fighting the urge to turn around to see if Sally was indeed addressing her and not someone standing behind her.

'Of course, you! You don't have to accept now. But I wanted to let you know. We're impressed with your work. I can send you the salary details and another copy of the job description. Then you can let me know by Monday?'

'Thank you,' said Maansi, not quite believing her luck. She'd done it. She beat the voice, worked hard and achieved something. 'Thank you very much.'

She left work with a skip in her step. She felt like Mary Poppins and was as dangerously close to breaking into song as she tracked back to Canary Wharf. She flung open the door of the flat and sashayed through. Aryan's shoes were on the shoe rack. He was home early for once! She pranced to the bedroom, where she found him perched at the foot of their bed.

'Aryan, guess what! They offered me a permanent job at work today. Can you believe it?' she yelped in a frisson of excitement and leapt towards him.

'Congratulations,' he said. His voice was monotone. He was frowning. Just like that, the air balloon of her happiness descended back down to earth.

'What the hell? Is this what you call supportive?' she asked.

She saw he was holding something silver in his hand. A blister pack rustled between his fingers.

'I thought you said you didn't have any problems?' he asked. He held up the pack so she could see the yellow and blue capsules nestled in their plastic moulds. 'You said you were in perfect health. Physically and mentally, before we got married. I thought you said your problems were all in the past.'

'They are all in the past,' she whispered. 'Aryan, forget about that. Did you hear what I just said?'

'I know how it goes. That's what people do. They lie about their mental health before an arranged marriage to trap people. Like my auntie agreed to an arranged marriage with my uncle and found out later he had schizophrenia. No wonder he went down the arranged route.'

'That's hardly the same thing.'

'No? Clinical depression isn't serious? That isn't something someone should know about their partner before getting married? Are you telling me you didn't lie to my face?' He threw the pack on to the floor and rose to his feet, his hardened face demanding an answer. A reason. Maansi didn't know what to tell him. She could feel the honey gold of happiness slip between her fingers. She wanted to trap it. To always have it.

'I'm getting better anyway,' she asserted. 'I've controlled it around you. Aryan, right now, I'm happy. I wasn't trying to deceive you.' She held her arms out and stepped towards him. He backed away.

'I wondered why you didn't want to be touched,' he said. 'This is why, right?'

'Excuse me?' Is that what he was boiling it down to? Sex? 'I've done my best to keep it under wraps. To be normal.'

'I don't know you. You're a fucking stranger.' He was inches away from her face now. His lip curled and there was a sharp, menacing glint in his eye. 'What is it that depresses you, then? The abortion? Get over it.'

He was trying to impale her with his venom-drizzled words. She knew it. And it was working. 'Aryan, it was a small lie. It hasn't affected you. Why are you being like this?'

'I don't want the complication. I never wanted…' he took a deep breath. 'You lied.' It was a final statement. He stormed out of the room. Just as she prophesised in that moment, the slam of the front door followed. Weakened by the shift from glee to anxiety, her body surrendered to the bed.

Why couldn't Aryan be understanding? Why couldn't he see that she had never once asked him to support her in the battle against it? She had done her best to function, while the depression festered within her core. Suppressing it was no easy task. She drew her knees up to her chest and let the hot tears tumble down her face.

CHAPTER 16

He sank into a corner of the pub, where he could observe the bubbles rising in his citrine-coloured drink in peace. He was fuming. She had lied to him about her mental health. As if he needed something like that to deal with. Life made sure he already had his fill of drama. The pub was teeming with people with laughter-filled bellies and foghorn mouths. They packed together in the centre of the rustic-style room, covering every slab of hardwood floor. Aryan was the only one alone and unhappy. His ill-lit corner made him invisible in his black shirt.

He saw a crowd of young people chatting to each other, wearing similar jackets with their university logos printed on the back. He envied them. They were still stuck in their dream bubbles, protected from reality by NUS cards and brittle schedules. They didn't have wives. They didn't have responsibility. They were winged creatures. He was a worm squirming in mud. Sure, he was being a little dramatic. He knew his reaction was a tad on the extreme side, but he was always going to explode at any small issue. He never wanted to marry. He took a sip of his drink, hoping to forget what it meant to be young and happy, but then his childhood charged at him and almost knocked him out of his seat. He was there.

A part of Aryan knew he'd be there. Since seeing him at the markets he did what he hadn't in years and checked out his social media, learning this was his favourite place. He was with four others. Two men and two women. He was doing most of the talking, his hands flailing in the air as he narrated a story, his eyes wide and shiny like an anime character's. They all clung to his every word and burst into laughter as he reached the punchline of his story. Aryan saw he still wore a beanie hat and covered his arms in countless wristbands. He even caught the gleam of the same old chain and pendant around his neck. The beanie-hat-wearing man smacked his forehead as he continued speaking. He was probably telling another self-deprecating tale. He always did that. Found his failings and shortfalls funny and would share them openly with the world.

After approximately fifteen minutes, Aryan watched him hug his friends goodbye. They asked him if he really had to go, a girl tugging at his shirtsleeve. He apologised and, seconds later, headed out the door. Aryan's heart skipped a beat. It was now or never. There may never be another chance. He swung back a large mouthful of his drink and dashed through the pub doors.

As he stepped out into the drizzly night, his eyes hopped left to right, trying to find him. The wind howled, flapping at his jacket as it hung off his broad shoulders, taunting him and pushing him back with its uncanny strength, announcing its pitiless intention to slow him down. The lamps along the street burned like tired candlewicks. Still, his vision didn't fail him. He saw him by the kerb, hailing a taxi. Aryan fast-walked towards him, hoping he wouldn't get away. He sprinted as the man reached for the door handle of a black cab. He was there in an instant. Aryan grabbed his shoulder and he spun around, panic plain in his face. He skimmed Aryan's face and sighed, though with anything but relief. They stared at each other and time seemed to stop its endless marathon to respire. Aryan's breath was shallow. His tongue tied. The wind menacingly thrashed about his ears, screaming at him to do something.

'You,' the man spoke. 'What do you want?'

She believed a decent man would have reacted with sympathy. Aryan hadn't, so he wasn't a decent man. Yes, she lied to him and felt terrible for it. But a person could get depression at any time. If it had come about after marriage, how would he have responded then? Would he still cast her aside like gone-off milk?

She was fixing dinner for herself, not caring about placing items in the wrong cupboards, in 'illogical' orders or in 'impractical' places. Once she ate, she swore she'd leave the dishes in the sink. Nobody decreed they needed to be washed straight away anyway. He couldn't demand it from her. She cut into the carrot, finding a satisfaction in dividing its tubular body into coin-sized pieces. She considered Logan and his attitude towards vulnerability – his reassurance that it's perfectly OK to be human. Aryan didn't think so. Where Logan was a placid lake, Aryan was a fire that could glow, or burn, or explode across the room like fireworks, blinding you and forcing you to jump for cover. He careered between two poles like the pirate ship ride at the fair. Hot and cold, left then right. She was on board now and unable to get off.

While her dinner simmered on the stove, she poured herself a glass of fruit-infused wine and gave herself permission to check out Logan's online profile. She was bored with kidding herself. She was infatuated with him, or at least the idea of him. On his page, she found videos of him busking in the different boroughs of London, a group of appreciative people circling him. The comments and likes beneath the videos were plentiful. She listened to his playful, stripped-down renditions of pop songs. He had a captivating, soft voice that left her legs weak and her cursor wandering by the replay button. In his photo albums, there were pictures of him among different sets of people. He was the popular sort and had a way of befriending anyone and everyone at the office. Cruising through his profile, she found he unapologetically filled his profile with pictures of his family. The captions pointed out his father, his cousins, his grandparents and his sister. She too had golden-brown hair and deep-sea eyes. She thought of Aryan's glassy, nut-brown eyes and the false warmth captured within them.

Maansi skimmed through the albums, eager to forget her husband for a moment. Then, she saw it there, tucked away at the bottom – an album titled: 'Boarding School'. She hadn't realised Logan was another rich kid. She opened the album. The first image she landed on almost made her spit out her wine. She had to look it over twice, to make sure her eyes hadn't tricked her. There was an image of Logan and Aryan. Both of them, together, in powder blue shirts, black blazers and three-toned ties. They were flanked by two boys and a couple of girls, their arms around each other, as if they were good friends. She rubbed her eyes. She couldn't believe what she was seeing. She looked closer to make sure she wasn't mistaken. They were entrenched in the later teenage years, perhaps sixteen or seventeen, all of them flashing sunny smiles.

She didn't understand. If Logan and Aryan knew each other, why did neither say anything? She remembered Aryan's coldness towards him; his inexplicable aggression towards her as he commanded her to stay away from him. They must have been friends in the past. Something must have happened. Something big to make Aryan behave that way towards him. She couldn't tear her eyes away from the picture of the two boys, happy in their youth.

CHAPTER 17

The two boys slipped the rodent through the open window of their English classroom.

'That'll teach Miss Miller for being a tight arse,' spoke the boy with lighter hair.

'We do our homework for once and she gives us detention? What kind of system are they running?' complained the other.

'I know! She never said we couldn't use Wikipedia,' by which, of course, the fairer-haired boy meant plagiarise.

The tawny mouse scampered into the classroom, its nose up in the air, sniffing out its new environment. It stood on its hind legs and eerily transfixed its eyes on the *Of Mice and Men* poster tacked behind the teacher's desk. The boys watched it with their heads tilted, unsure of whether their plan would work out.

'Oi! What are you two boys doing?' boomed a voice from behind them. The headmaster was speed-walking towards them. 'Who goes there?'

'It's Mr Lane.'

'Leg it!'

They both darted through the entrance of the Humanities block and ran down the corridors, not stopping until they reached the safety of the boys' toilets and were locked in separate cubicles. They listened through the doors for the sound of an angry, paunchy man with a receding hairline. He bounded through the door, huffing and puffing like a man unacclimated to daily exercise.

'Mr Reeves and Mr Alekar, I know you're in here.' They didn't panic. They knew he couldn't force the doors open, or they'd just point the finger and call him a 'perv'. Aryan, at that point, decided to relieve his bladder and Logan made convincing evacuation sounds in the other cubicle. Hearing the offensive noises, Mr Lane doubted himself. He peered under the doors to find single pairs of feet in their expected positions for usual bathroom activity.

'Who is in this cubicle?' he asked, knocking on one door.

'David Wallace, who is asking?' said Logan, shedding his distinguishable Northern accent for Received Pronunciation. Aryan smothered his laugh behind his hand.

'Oh righty-ho,' said Mr Lane, embarrassed and unwilling to try the other door. He bumbled out of the toilets to look for the two year seven boys he was after. They both snuck out of the cubicles, self-satisfied grins smacked on to their faces.

'You know he'll just pull us out of next period,' Aryan said.

'I'm counting on it. I've got a speaking test.'

'Do you think we should rehearse?' Aryan said, swinging his stodgy backpack over his shoulder as they trundled out of the Humanities block, safely off Mr Lane's radar.

'OK. What you on about, Sir? I left my pencil case in there and was trying to grab it from the window. I knew you'd think the worst of me,' rehearsed Logan. 'Hang on. What mouse?'

'That's not what I meant,' Aryan sniggered. He hoped Miss Miller was standing on her table, shrieking as if the mouse circling her was a hungry shark circling a dinghy.

'Oh right. French. Can't be bothered. *Je suis fatigué.* Did I say that right?'

'Your accent's way off, mate.'

As they walked, they discussed their hopes and excitement for the rest of the year. It was the start of spring term. April showers were few and the sun had grown curious, peeping its blazing head out from behind the clouds, letting its rays filter through classroom blinds and on to the heads of pupils. Teachers were not yet bilious (except Miss Miller) and the students were brimming with a considerable amount of motivation – at least, enough to pay attention for half of each class. This wouldn't last long, of course. Attention waned faster in the spring term as students thirsted for the sunny fields, their daydreams sewn with daisy chains and football games on the dry field.

Aryan felt better this term. Finally, he was getting on at Brookside Boarding School. When he arrived in September, he wanted nothing more than to leave. He'd sulk in his room while the other boys were socialising, his father's words flipping about in his head: 'You have to go. It is best for you.' He told him it was so he'd get the 'best education', but Aryan was certain he just wanted to get rid of him. In the first term, he squeezed his pillow and wished himself out of boarding school. But when the first annual break arrived and he was allowed to swap his tiny room for his Knightsbridge home, he was introduced to a good reason to stop pining for it.

'What happened to your arm?' Logan asked. Aryan rubbed the plum and lilac splodge on his forearm, as if the simple action would make it fade quicker. 'Nothing. I fell over during PE.' He pushed his arm into his trouser pocket, out of sight. His dad said it was out of love, to help him be better after he left the oven on, but he knew better. Being at Brookside meant no more of those. That was something.

With five minutes to spare until the next class, Aryan took Logan by the arm. 'Listen, maybe we should cool it this time. Miss Miller deserved that, but Mr Lane will flip if we do anything else. My dad said if my behaviour reports didn't improve, he'd send me to a boarding school in India, or kill me. Whichever I think is worse.'

'It's fine,' Logan patted his shoulder. 'Mr Lane's soft anyway. But if you want, we'll get serious. Start thinking about our education and careers or whatever. Imagine working for MI5.'

'I think I'd like to be a lawyer someday,' Aryan mused out loud. Maybe the television shows he watched glamorised law and were full of inaccuracies, but he didn't care. Something about that future appealed to him. There was something about law he felt he could step into.

'Really? All right then. We'll study this time. Watch. Your dad will be proud.'

They tried to study throughout the remainder of year seven. But they quickly concluded year seven was only year seven after all. Everyone knew if you were going to mess around and have fun, you do it in year seven when nothing truly mattered. They spent their free time together playing football, plotting pranks and sometimes, if the mood struck them, devoting a smidgen of time to their work. Joining forces with their respective roommates: Omari Akintola and Christopher Harris, they adopted dangerous habits, like sneaking into each other's rooms at night, when the night warden's ears were apt to prick at the sound of footprints in the corridors. They huddled together and watched horror films past curfew, and whoever fell asleep first (usually Omari) fell victim to the attack of marker pens. Omari would wake to a face covered in cartoon genitals. The artistry always proved difficult to rub off without the assistance of industrial-strength soaps and it became common for Omari to be dismissed by teachers and told not to return until the marker was off.

'I will kill you guys. I will kill you in your sleep,' Omari forever fumed. It always had them in stitches.

Soon, Aryan forgot about home and how it provided a sickly-sweet mix of comfort and misery. Brookside became his new home.

'You know what?' Aryan said to Logan one night, as they stayed up watching *Saw* on low volume with the lights switched off. It was just the two of them. 'I'd hate boarding school if you weren't here.'

Logan swung his arm around him and brought him into a headlock, the smell of buttered popcorn coming off his clothes. 'Me too. You're probably my best friend.'

'Probably?'

'Most likely,' he grinned. 'And you will be for a long time.'

They stuck together throughout their time at school, never stepping away from one another, until college hurtled towards them and forced them into thinking about their futures.

The moment they became adults, life grew complicated.

CHAPTER 18

Aryan and Logan tucked into their cheese and cucumber sandwiches, neither talking for a while as their thoughts jumped around like a flea circus, trying to determine what life would bring for them once this chapter had ended. It was their final year at Brookside Boarding School. The concrete walls that contained them for years seemed to melt away, uncovering sections of the new world they were promised to. All the exams and lectures they endured were going to finally bear fruit. And now, more than just Brookside hung around the bend.

'So, let me guess. You're going to take to the streets to sell your art and sing to passers-by outside Primark?' Aryan said.

Logan grinned at him. 'I mean, I was looking forward to university, but your idea sounds better. You finished your application?'

Aryan shook his head. 'I don't know. I can't figure it out. I don't think I've ever been in this position before. You know what you're doing. Omari knows what he's doing.' Aryan gestured towards their shared friend who was standing several feet away, his questions about human biology keeping a teacher from her lunch. He was desperate to get as much advice as possible before making his application to medicine and would speak of nothing else. Aryan looked towards his roommate, Chris, who loitered near the tennis courts without a single slice of ambition in his hands. They were all about to embark on different journeys. Aryan would walk the ones marked for him, while his friends skipped between them, driven by an untrammelled and childlike curiosity, their passion-swathed university applications in hand.

'Why are you even going to university if all you're going to do is work for your dad? You could do that right away.'

'Nah, he wants me to get a business degree.'

Logan snorted at him. 'Mate, there's the issue. *He* wants you to get a business degree. Do what you want to do. I saw those books under your bed.'

Aryan scowled at him. 'What drove you to look under my bed?'

'Don't know. But you've been banging on about studying law since we were eleven. Forget your dad.' He stuffed more bread in his mouth than it could hold and mumbled, 'Follow your passion. Like I do.'

Aryan tutted at him. 'You're going to die poor. You know that?'

'Yeah, yeah. And you'll die miserable. What a life.' For a moment, Logan's eyes wandered towards the tennis courts, where a tall shaggy-haired boy that Aryan knew as Brad had arrived. 'What if I don't get my grades?' Logan sighed. For as long as they studied there, Logan couldn't keep his grades up without Aryan's help. No matter the subject, he could never focus.

'You will. I'll help you study.'

'You're a terrible tutor. The minute I get something wrong, you're out the door. Anyway, I've found someone to help me.' He gestured towards Brad.

'Him? Seriously?'

'Yes. In fact, I'm going to go ask him a study question right now.' He picked up his skateboard beneath the bench and rode towards Brad.

Aryan scratched his head. Brad wasn't exactly academic, he thought. Brad belonged in secret parties and student drug circles. He lurked in corners and knew everything about the town, as if he were more than a caged hen cooped up in a boarding school. Then, he remembered. When he was up all night studying for his exams, worried about failing, Brad offered him some 'study aids'. Was that the kind of help Logan was after? He observed as Logan spoke to Brad. His hands were thrust deep into his pockets. His eyes shifted side to side. He gripped his skateboard tight, as if ready to leap on and ride to his escape. Aryan wondered if Brad had given him something to conceal in his pockets. Why wouldn't he just tell him? He knew he was a little scatterbrained, but unprescribed amphetamines weren't the answer. Idiot, he thought.

'Got something you want to tell me?' Aryan asked him the moment he returned.

'Maybe later,' he said with a half-laugh. 'Let's grab Omari and Chris and get this over with.'

They scoffed the remainder of their sandwiches and made their way to the nearby computer labs. Aryan made a mental note to confront Logan later, though how he'd remember with university dominating every corner of his mind, he didn't know.

Every computer screen in the lab had UCAS open. Aryan had already filled out most of the sections. His A levels were business studies, further maths and economics, followed by sports science – a soft subject to satisfy his own interest. He'd been predicted As and A stars. He was in a fortunate position. But when the moment came for him to begin his personal statement, his fingers froze at the keyboard. Why did he want to study for a BA in Business and Economics? The question almost winded him. For the first time, he was stuck. He rubbed his forehead. When it came to schoolwork, he could write an essay the night before a deadline and still achieve a high grade. He never once needed a first draft, despite the advice teachers gave. Words just flowed from his brain. Yet, when it came to answering this question, his expansive rivers of words were too dry to draw from.

'Great,' he grumbled. He looked over at Omari, who was agonising over every detail of his completed statement. Chris was on his left. He bet he hadn't got much down, but then again, he was considering skipping university altogether.

'Where are you with your statement?' he asked him.

'Last paragraph,' Chris shrugged, as if finishing his statement was like finishing a Netflix show. He took long swings of his energy drink, humming to himself as he continued.

'Do you need help?' Omari asked, furiously typing away, committing his eyes to the screen. He didn't even hear Aryan's emphatic, 'Yes.'

'Logan. A little help,' Aryan groaned.

'Whoa. You're asking for my help?' Logan leaned back in his chair, fiddling with the cross he always wore around his neck. Whenever he plunged into deep thought, his fingers would rub at the bit of sterling silver. 'Wheel over. Read mine.'

Aryan read it twice. Logan made a very convincing argument about why he should be admitted to the study of graphic design. The entire letter was daubed with thick, clotted passion for the subject. Aryan wasn't sure he could mimic Logan's style. It was too much for him. He didn't feel that way about business. He could write about his grades, his achievements and all he had done, but the pressing question of 'why' remained.

'Guys, you're not supposed to be helping each other, remember?' Omari warned, gesturing towards the teacher hovering nearby. Aryan wheeled himself back before the bespectacled woman in drab clothes noticed. Logan wanted to work in graphic or web design. Omari wanted to be a doctor. He, Aryan Alekar, was going to be… an Alekar. What was so exciting about that? He began constructing sentences about his life-long, burning ambition of running a successful business and how it's what he always wanted to do. The paragraph he was left with was barren of honesty and stood propped up on the backs of clichés.

'I'll catch you guys later. It's not working for me today.' He swung his backpack around his shoulder and headed back towards his accommodation, feeling something he rarely felt – a sense of failure.

He entered his room. It was clean with two desks on either side of the room and a bunk bed in the middle. The walls were a calming duck-egg blue. He reached beneath his bed and pulled out the dense textbooks on law, one being *A Guide to Studying Law at University*. But his dad wanted him to learn about business, so that he could work for him. It was, his dad once said to him, his greatest wish for him. He wondered why he was following that path. Why did he care about what his dad wanted? What made him agree? Just at that moment, his phone vibrated. He let the phone ring three times before answering.

'Hello Dad... Yes, I'm good... I have been working hard... No, I'm studying now, I swear... Of course... Hi Mum... I'm eating fine... I promise... Yes, I'll come home next weekend... OK... That's fine... They are fine... Great... Bye... *Jai Shree Krishna*.' He threw himself on to his bed and closed his eyes. He wouldn't be going home next weekend. Since the beginning of term, he'd gone home for a few weekends and important holidays, like Christmas and Diwali. He missed his mother. Sometimes, he missed his father and they'd embrace awkwardly when he stepped through the door.

Home could be heaven. Whenever he returned, his mother would prepare his favourite curries – in other words, any dish featuring paneer. She'd make him hot aloo parathas when he woke in the morning and would boil chai on the kitchen stove, swaying like wind-stroked wheat fields as she hummed along to the songs of Mohammed Rafi, a sweet reflective smile on her face. The concoctive scent of cardamom, cloves and fennel seeds was consoling and rich with her love.

In the afternoons, she'd succeed at coercing him to attend *mandir* with her. Despite his commitment to atheism, he'd go with her to make her happy. He'd never classify himself as selfless but when it came to his mum, he didn't mind making little sacrifices. She'd beam at him, appreciating the time he gave up for her and there'd be harmony in the household. Then the evenings would arrive. His father would settle at home and her colourful, vivacious personality would dampen. She'd become embittered by his father's tendency to spray speared criticisms from the comfort of his chair. Sometimes, on the odd occasion, he'd hear her sob with her full body behind her bedroom door.

'The reason Indians are so successful is because of discipline and hard work,' his father would tell him. The way his father spoke made Aryan believe it was a common thing in Asian households – as if hitting and yelling was just a part of their culture – that this was surely the discipline he spoke of. Only, it wasn't culture at all. It was just him.

Whenever Aryan would leave for school, he'd leave angry with his parents. Angry at their failure to love each other. Angry that they lived in a smog of tension. When he was sent to boarding school, he was incensed with their decision to get rid of him. But he soon learned that boarding school was a blessing. He could think with clarity, away from the soporific air of a home mired in hostility. Among others, they were thought to be a fortunate family, with shiny cars, a majestic home and respect from the community. Aryan knew different. He knew that the flashes and flickers coming off their wealth distracted from the poverty they were in. They lived off paltry bits of happiness. Not enough to fill the hungry belly.

After twenty minutes of lying there thinking about his home and his personal statement, he could hear Omari's earth-moving voice pouring through the corridor. They were on their way back. Laying there, listening to his friends, the truth dawned on Aryan. Boarding school was coming to an end. The plain walls that encapsulated him in a separate world would fall away and expose freshly laid paths and walkways. What was he going to do?

'Hey! Write a personal statement for law,' Logan said as he entered, hurling a notebook at Aryan's chest.

'What?'

'I've written a template for you to use,' Omari chimed in. 'I've emailed it to you.'

Aryan blinked. 'What are you guys talking about?'

'Just try writing an application for law and see if it's easier for you,' Logan said.

'It's a waste of time.'

Logan and Omari looked thoughtfully at each other, then

picked up all his law textbooks and walked out the door with them.

'Hey. What are you doing?'

'You don't need these! These are for law students.'

He sighed. He already felt his brain sizzling from excessive thought, but as he considered writing a personal statement to study law, the ideas rose and spilt over in his mind like an opened cola bottle after a good shaking. After all, a career in law was generally considered a great career. Lawyers were respected. It wasn't as though he was asking to go to drama school. His dad dreamed they'd work together someday. But he had his own dreams. Maybe it was time he began to make his own choices.

A Chloe Orchards was tagged in the picture. She had wavy blonde hair and big hazel eyes. Aryan's hand rested on the small of her back, just inches from her backside. There were signs of intimacy there, whether real or desired, it was impossible to tell. Maansi sipped her wine, wondering why she had never asked about his previous relationships. He must have had girlfriends. She always presumed anyone who'd agree to an arranged marriage struggled to find a partner, but Aryan was a high-ranking male in the looks department. Of course, there was also Lana.

She asked herself why he agreed to her in the end. She remembered him explaining it to her in the café. 'It's hard to find girls ready to commit,' he said. She grimaced. From Aryan's love for solitude, it was difficult to ascribe a need for commitment to him. She remembered him telling her girls 'play games'. He and his mother had a lot of nonsense opinions on girls. Maybe a girl had played with his heart and left it crushed on the floor. Maybe a girl damaged him and he gave up. Maybe that girl was this Chloe Orchards. Maansi visited her public profile.

Chloe Orchards graduated from Oxford University with a Master's in Physics. Maansi found a post in which she expressed her happiness at getting a place on the NHS Scientist Training Programme. With her master's under her belt, she'd be heading into medical physics. Clever girl, Maansi thought. She slowly invented a story in her head. Maybe this Chloe Orchards could no longer handle Aryan's moods. Maybe he flipped out one day because she dared to be human. Or maybe she just looked in the general direction of another male and he became possessive and jealous, telling her she couldn't speak to another guy. She, being Oxford material, would have been far too intelligent to submit to him and moved on, leaving his ego broken on the ground. Maybe that's when he started MMA, needing an outlet for his anger. Maybe he then gave the responsibility of finding him a girl to his parents. She smiled at her story, thinking it was rather good. Plausible, even.

She picked up her blister pack of antidepressants and held it to her chest. She wasn't ashamed. She was angry. How could he treat her that way? She picked up her phone, her finger hovering over the call button beneath his name. She put it back down. She'd give him the opportunity to cool off. He managed to calm down after the Logan incident. She'd give him a chance. Somehow, she could endure the pain he inflicted on her.

She had Logan's number saved on her phone. If it came to it, she could ask him all her questions.

CHAPTER 19

Omari expressed zero interest in going with them to eat peri-peri chicken. Scratch that. He had zero interest in anything other than achieving his grades and getting into university. That was paramount. He wouldn't even loosen his revision schedule to make room for a bit of television. Shocked at that kind of determination, Chris, Logan and Aryan went ahead with a group of others to their favourite restaurant, leaving Omari behind. Aryan couldn't figure out which was sadder: that Omari wasn't going to Nando's or that Logan was but wasn't planning on eating any chicken. He and Chris always tried to tempt him with a leg heavily marinated in peri-peri sauce. The answer was always no.

'Why?' one of the girls of the group asked.

'Because chickens are people too, apparently,' said Chris. Logan nodded. She didn't understand.

'I fully believe that when we die we come back to Earth as whatever animal we've eaten. So, you know, chickens.'

'Really?'

'No!'

There were four girls and six boys. Chris dragged Logan and Aryan along. He was invited by two of the boys, who were invited by one of the girls, who was asked by the other girls. They were all chained together through vague connections but felt tightly knit together in the larger world outside their protective educational dome. Aryan sat next to Chloe. She was voluptuous and had blonde, wavy hair, scrunched with bubblegum scented gel.

'Guys, curfew isn't for a while. My cousin lives nearby. We could all go there for a booze-up afterwards. What do you say?' she asked. As students on the cusp of adulthood and ready for daring experiences, they weren't going to object. They quickly gobbled up their meals for the promise of alcohol.

They wound up in a flat crowded with furniture and inundated with the smell of cannabis. Chloe's cousin was indifferent about their ages and supplied the alcohol. Raucous music boomed from the sound system and multicoloured fairy lights were switched on. As they tippled, they spread out across the flat. Chris landed on the settee, trying out celebrity impressions with two of the guys. Aryan and Logan were with Chloe and her petite and pretty friend Nora. They stood in a corner, drinking cheap beer from cans. As Aryan spoke to Chloe, he felt an inexplicable pull towards her. Through her flirting, he knew she felt it too. She leaned into him.

'Let's get them together,' she whispered. 'My cousin has popped out and her flatmate isn't here. There are at least two spare rooms…' Aryan smirked at her suggestion. He peeped at Logan and Nora. She was resting her hand on Logan's arm. She edged closer to him every second but he seemed oblivious, yammering on about his Extended Qualification Project. He was terrible at interpreting the signs. Aryan excused himself from Chloe and pulled Logan to one side.

'What?' he asked.

'I'm going to get with Chloe.'

'OK. You need a wingman?'

'No. I think it's in the bag. Nora is trying to make a move on you, man. Read the signs!'

Logan blinked rapidly. He was clueless. 'Oh… so I should kiss her?'

'Well yeah. If she's up for it, do more than that,' he said, pointing towards one of the rooms.

He looked uncertain. 'But I don't have any...' Aryan had a couple of what Logan needed in his wallet. He slipped one into his pocket.

'You're welcome.'

As Aryan returned to Chloe, from the corner of his eye he saw Logan dive in and kiss Nora. Chloe mimed applauding. 'Now we can leave them to it,' she said, biting her lip. She took Aryan's hand and led him into one of the rooms. They locked themselves in and didn't come out for a good, long while.

When they finally emerged, the others had already gone. With hair dishevelled and clothes creased, they escaped the flat, realising they were in danger of missing curfew. Aryan forgot about Logan and failed to check whether he'd left. His head was still woozy from alcohol and the rush of hormones.

Once they hit the cool air of the outside, Chloe levelled with him.

'This means nothing, OK? I don't have time for boys.' She patted his face. 'This was just for fun.'

'Sure,' he replied, raising his eyes up to the sky to express his disbelief. She giggled.

'What's the plan then, Aryan?' she said, facing him as she trekked backwards on the wide, empty roads shimmering wet with rain. Her hair wafted in the wind. Though a little intoxicated, she still emanated a degree of elegance.

'Business and economics,' he answered.

'How dreadfully boring,' she said, shaking her head. He didn't bother disagreeing.

'What is your plan then?'

'I want to study physics, to unlock the mysteries of the

world,' she said, twirling and waving her hands in the air, reaching for the gold dust cascading from the streetlamps. She laughed, enthused by the cool and gusty wind.

'I would never have guessed.'

'Oh? Why is that? Because I'm a girl? Well, I'll be studying in Oxford, if all goes my way.'

'You'll make a sexy physicist.'

'I'll make a damn good one,' she corrected him. She tripped and almost fell. Aryan caught her by the wrist and drew her towards him. She looked directly at him and briefly lost herself. 'Oh, I'm sorry. God, you are a looker, aren't you? No girlfriend?'

'No.'

'I must say, you've a bit of a reputation,' she said, raising her eyebrows with knowing. 'I don't blame you. Too young to settle. You're a little bit wild. I like that.'

He wasn't sure he'd consider himself wild. He was, after all, trying to walk with anchors hanging off his ankles. 'Is that why you don't have a boyfriend?'

'I don't want a boyfriend. But if I did, you'd have to work for it.' Her hazel eyes were lined with kohl, giving her the look of a feline. He was magnetised by her. She stowed high doses of confidence in the curves of her body. She was wearing a basic striped T-shirt, jeans and suede boots. Yet, she moved as if she wore a tight, sleek dress and a pair of stilettos. It was then he knew he wanted her. He could see she knew the effect she was having. She played him like an instrument with her feminine wiles and her complete lack of need for him. The other girls had just been girls, bound to their stubborn immaturity and eager to belong to someone. This girl, in front of him, was more. He finally felt more than a weak mixture of apathy and arousal.

He dipped into a dream-like state for a long moment,

pinning snapshots of her to walls. When he jumped back to reality, she was a small figure in the distance. She turned.

'Aren't you coming?' she called. He smiled to himself and picked up the pace, a fox on her tail.

His housemaster pointed to his watch and shot him a look when he re-entered Rushton House. He failed to get indoors before the rain sprung from the skies. He was drenched.

Omari and Chris were in his room, practising their French with each other in exaggerated accents. They raised their eyebrows as they noticed the imprints of lipstick on Aryan's skin. The rain hadn't watered the cerise away.

'Wondered where you got to,' grinned Chris. Omari shook his head, feigning disappointment. He pointed to the lined paper on Aryan's desk.

'Lay off the girls and make some progress.'

The page was covered in scribbles and crossed-out sentences. He still couldn't write a decent personal statement. He had never felt so incompetent. He scrunched up the paper and tossed it into the waste bin. He'd better write something decent soon.

'Or maybe, you won't have to, if you want to take that gap year in Thailand,' Chris pointed out.

'You're going?' Aryan asked.

'My parents said OK. Logan's dad said fine, if he funds it himself with a part-time job. Just got to decide first. Yes? Or no?'

Aryan shrugged. 'Where is Logan?'

'Thought he was with you?' said Omari. 'He wasn't in our room when I checked.'

Aryan didn't tell Omari and Chris about Logan and Nora. He locked himself in the bathroom, removed the wet clothes clinging to his skin and purged himself of the day beneath the comfort of a hot shower.

CHAPTER 20

Aryan grabbed a lunch to-go and went to find Logan. He hadn't seen him since Saturday night. He wasn't in the common room, or his own room and he didn't have any classes scheduled. That left two places: the art studio or the music rooms. His gut told him the art studio and he was right. He found him there, on the floor with his sketchbook open but his attention captured by the black and white pages of a popular manga. Logan scanned the pages, bobbing his head to the music streaming through his headphones. Aryan yanked them out of his ears.

'Hey!' Logan said.

'I thought you came here to work. How is reading *Death Note* work?'

'On a break.' He twitched beneath Aryan's gaze. Usually, he'd speak more than three words. In fact, he'd speak too much, and with his new manga in his hands ready to review, he should've been talking Aryan's ear off. Something was wrong.

'Everything OK?'

Logan didn't answer. Aryan snatched the manga from him and tossed it aside. 'What is your problem?' Logan groaned.

'Did something happen? Haven't seen you since Saturday night.'

'No, it's fine.' He didn't elaborate. He picked up his sketchbook and flicked through the pages.

'Well, how did it go?' Aryan nudged him in the ribs. 'You still a virgin then?'

'Leave off.'

'Why? Something happened. You're being weird.' He settled next to him and started unwrapping his lunch. 'Could you not get it up?'

Logan furrowed his brow. His pencil vehemently scratched against paper, weakening it until the nib caught itself in the resulting hole. 'I didn't do anything with Nora. I made an excuse and I left.'

'Oh. Why? Didn't you like her?' Aryan asked. After all, Logan had agreed, on more than one occasion, that Nora was a solid nine out of ten. Logan looked at him, his eyes shot with apprehension.

'I need to tell you something,' he said. 'But I'm scared about what you'll think of me when I do.' He looked around the studio to make sure they were alone. He leaned in, opened his mouth, but instead of speaking, he sighed and hid his face in his hands.

'What?' Aryan pushed. 'Just fucking say it.'

Logan drew in a few deep breaths and said: 'I don't like girls.'

'I know she's a bit immature mate, but—'

'At all,' Logan said. 'I don't like girls at all. I'm... gay.' His voice was barely audible and crackled as he handed over the last word. It was there now, in front of them, unmissable like a sex-fused billboard on a motorway. Aryan frowned.

'Yes, very funny, Logan. What's the real reason?'

'No. I'm gay,' he said, with more assertion this time. Aryan assessed his face. Logan was terrible at keeping a straight face when he joked. But his cheeks didn't spasm, the skin around his eyes didn't crease and his lips were stiff like a mannequin's.

Aryan pushed his lunch to one side. For the second time that year, he couldn't find the words. He could see Logan's eyes were imploring him for some sort of reply, but he couldn't physically speak. It was as if his vocal cords had been sealed off with heavy duty tape.

The door creaked open and their heads whipped round like cats caught on the kitchen counter. Omari and Chris strolled in.

'There you guys are. Want to go watch the auditions for the school musical? It'll be a laugh,' said Chris. He sensed the unease in the air and fell quiet. 'What's wrong?'

'I'm gay,' said Logan. His body was a paradox; his chest was puffed out but his eyes cowered as he confessed. The small splashes of shame were concentrated and etched in his faintly speckled face. The room fell silent as Omari and Chris processed the information.

'Well, I didn't see that one coming,' said Chris. 'Are you sure?'

Logan gave a feeble nod.

'Oh. Well, thanks for telling us.'

'You're... not weirded out?' asked Logan.

'Nah,' said Chris. 'Why would we be?'

Omari took out a Snickers bar from his pocket and unwrapped it, unfazed.

'I kind of feel sorry for you,' said Omari. 'Having to look at this every day and knowing I'm straight.' Logan rolled his eyes, the muscles in his face loosening.

'So, have you... you know. Been with a guy then?' asked Chris. Omari made a high-pitched 'ooo' sound and they sat themselves down to listen, like children promised a scary story regarding the empty house over the hill. They didn't want to know, but they couldn't accept not knowing.

'Maybe,' was all Logan said. 'But I guess I shouldn't say with who.'

'At this school?' said Chris.

'I know who it is. Crap. It's so obvious now!' said Omari. Aryan could almost see Omari's brain rewinding through, picking out past moments with tongs, observing them and the way they didn't make sense. 'Brad! He ain't smart enough to be a tutor.'

Aryan winced. Brad hadn't been supplying him drugs then.

'Whoa. I did hear he was gay. Is he your boyfriend?'

'No, no,' Logan jumped in, waving his hands in the air. 'It was more of a... um... physical thing.'

They all winced. 'Gross, man. Not because you're gay, but because I share a bloody room with you,' said Omari. Logan had to reassure him nothing happened on or near his bed at least three times before they could move on.

Aryan wasn't listening to their drivel. He only noted Logan wasn't a virgin either. What else didn't he know about his so-called friend?

'Does your dad know? What did he say?'

'How can you be Christian and gay?'

'Who, in your gay opinion, is sexier? Me or Chris? No, don't answer,' Omari held his hands out as if halting applause. 'I know it's me.'

They both bombarded Logan with dozens of questions. He outright refused to answer some of them, forcing Omari and Chris to criticise him, since, as Logan's friends and boarding school family, they believed they had a right to know everything. They were packed with myths and facts about gay men, with an inability to distinguish between them. Logan tried to rewire their thinking over a few minutes, eventually deciding it wasn't something that could be achieved in a few minutes.

'I'm just glad you're OK with it,' Logan said. 'Want to watch those auditions then?'

Omari jokingly suggested Logan audition for the musical, since being gay 'obviously' meant he harnessed a secret love for them. Chris and Omari walked out together, speculating out loud what would happen if they were to tell their families they were gay. There was no drama or shock towards the revelation. No disgust or criticisms. They were normal. The dynamic between Aryan's friends remained intact.

Logan and Aryan were alone together. Logan was waiting for him. Aryan had always been proud of his poker face.

'How long have you known?' he asked him.

'Since year eleven.'

Aryan struggled to look Logan in the eyes. He kept his mouth shut for almost two years. Two years! He had Logan down as an open book. He was supposed to be somebody he knew inside-out. His best friend. 'Why did you never say anything?'

Logan shuffled his feet and fiddled with his tie. 'I was going to tell you, in year eleven. I don't know why I didn't. I was worried I'd lose friends, or that one of you would think I was into you or something.'

'And you're not?'

'Of course not!' Logan couldn't help but grin. Aryan grinned too, though he wanted to be mad. He wanted to tear out the pages from Logan's sketchbook and stuff them into his friend's mouth. He wanted to tell him to stop talking!

'Listen. You guys are the first people I've told at school, aside from Brad. Being a gay guy at a boarding school, where I'm living with guys, well… it's better kept quiet. I'm not ready. But it's no big deal, right?'

'Yes.'

A part of Aryan wanted to reassure him that if anybody found out and said anything, he'd be there. Instead, he kept quiet. He was still trying to digest the information. He glanced at Logan, already perceiving him in a different, unnatural light. Like the sketches in Logan's book or the pages of the manga, a play with shading was occurring before his eyes. He wasn't sure how he felt about the transformation of what was once a familiar and valued piece.

'To the auditions then?' piped Aryan, desperate to toss the situation out of the window. Once they'd walk out of the studio, he'd pretend nothing happened.

'Sure. I think Chris secretly wants to audition. He's actually a pretty good singer. We should stop telling him he's terrible.'

They left the studio. Aryan's breath felt stuck somewhere, as if he exhaled only a fraction of what he inhaled. He felt unsettled. In some sense, betrayed. But everything around him continued as normal.

CHAPTER 21

With some free time flowing and a bountiful supply of money in their accounts, the only logical thing to do was to throw a party. The weeks had been wearisome and everyone's thinking caps turned defective. Aryan felt brain-dead. He finally wrote up a personal statement with ten different tabs open on his laptop, each leading to exemplar personal statements, and an old thesaurus to prevent him overusing the word 'passionate' – a word that held no meaning any more. Its symbol of a red, fiery rose withered to dried plant remains in Aryan's hands. He rendered it meaningless with his claimed passion for something he hadn't once cared about. Hadn't once dreamed about. He wondered if he was naïve for thinking dreams mattered. Life wasn't a Disney film, after all.

Aryan helped organise the party. He and a few boys from his dormitory had gone on a weekend to book a hall from an unsuspecting elderly lady.

'No, madam, of course there won't be alcohol at this party,' they reassured her. 'We only drink squash.'

Aryan turned eighteen earlier than the others and was responsible for supplying the alcohol they had sworn off in front of the old woman. Of course, the party couldn't break curfew, so it was going to be an unorthodox party, starting in the early evening and finishing around eight.

Aryan was in the mood to get drunk. He'd finished his personal statement and his coursework had come back marked with glittering As and A stars. He stepped into the hall. The atmosphere was threadbare, carrying a few lights and a table of flat coke. Chris helped him carry in the vodka and beers. Under Aryan's insistence, their DJ (a self-proclaimed musical genius from economics) turned up the volume of the music. Soon enough, students were either dancing or pouring generous servings of booze into paper cups. He saw her on the dancefloor, her hair a wild mess and her eyes smoky.

'She's so fit,' Chris said.

'Indeed, she is,' Aryan replied. He downed his drink and moved towards her.

'Aryan,' she said his name softly as he approached. 'Can't keep away? Dance with me.'

They danced close up against each other. He could feel the heat of her body. The lush scent of flowers radiated from the base of her neck and possessed him. She twirled and giggled, and then danced in that uncontained way as people do when nobody is watching. She was so comfortable in her skin and it made her that much more attractive. He wanted to get closer to her. When the music came to a halt, she led him away by the hand to talk.

'Aryan, listen, it's important to me that I put my ambitions first. My studies are my absolute priority...' she began. He'd find out later that if he continued listening, he'd have heard her say, 'but I do quite like you, and I suppose it wouldn't be the worst thing if we saw each other. If you'd like?' But his attention had been nabbed by the unfamiliar figure entering the hall. Aryan squinted and recognised the stranger as Brad. He looked different, with his face bare and unobstructed by curtains of coal-black hair. Instead, he sported a simple crew-cut. It suited him. He watched as Brad roved through the room to Logan and swung an arm around him in a semi-hug. He whispered something in his ear, drawing an unfamiliar grin from Logan's lips. Their eyes skipped across each other's bodies. They looked as if they hungered for each other. Aryan took another swig of his drink.

'Aryan? Are you listening?'

'Yeah. Yeah, I am.'

He liked Chloe, though the more she spoke about her future ambitions, the more he realised pursuing a relationship of any kind with her would be futile. She was astute, beautiful and everything he wanted in a woman. But she was firm in not wanting a boyfriend. If she did turn around and tell him she wanted to be with him, she'd lose her appeal for retracting her statement. Yes, that was how he felt. He was sure.

He clenched his jaw as he watched Logan having a good time. People flocked to him. He was funny, sociable and somehow, despite the years spent in boarding school, still in possession of a regional accent that made him all the more approachable. It must have been because he spoke to his family on the phone every night and visited most weekends, keeping one foot decisively rooted in Yorkshire. He reminded Aryan of a Labrador puppy with his high energy levels and desire to connect with people. Sometimes, he found it irritating. At other times, he didn't, and he supposed he'd say he found it endearing, although 'endearing' wasn't quite the word to describe your best mate. A more appropriate word evaded him.

'Chloe, I wanted to tell you I like you, a lot, but I know...' She had walked off. What did he expect? He hadn't listened. He sighed as he stood alone. She was the kind of girl that wouldn't pander to him. He kicked a paper cup rolling towards him along the floor. Why did he sabotage himself? Was pursuing her really that futile? He didn't know what to do and his party mood started to wane, leaving him desperate for a night in with the television. He could hear Logan's voice drift across the room like dense miasmas of smoke. When he saw Logan alone with Brad once more, he weaved through the crowds to reach them.

'Hey. Everything OK?' asked Logan. Brad nodded at Aryan. He didn't nod back.

'No, actually. I'm not feeling this party.'

'Really? I thought you were up for it?'

'No. Let's go.'

Brad pulled a face and Logan grimaced. Logan wasn't required to leave with him, but Aryan was feeling selfish and didn't care. For whatever reason, he had to separate Logan and Brad. He knew Logan would return with him if that's what he wanted. Besides, he'd been drinking. If he pretended he had a fair few, Logan would never let him leave alone. 'Um. OK. Yeah. See you, Brad,' Logan said. Aryan saw Brad's face drop and felt oddly sated by his disappointment.

He and Logan strolled towards the bus stop. The frosty air nipped at their ear lobes and noses, reddening them to a shade of deep cherry. Aryan rubbed his hands together, his teeth chattering. If only he'd taken a last generous dose of booze, then maybe the wintry cold would feel like fronds of a gentle feather instead of a mass of iced needle-points. Logan leered at him, reminding him, as he often did, that Northerners never get cold.

'Want to wear my jacket? I don't need it,' he offered.

'Save it for your boyfriend, mate.'

'Again, he's not my boyfriend,' he reminded him. 'Anyway, I thought tonight was the night you were gonna win over Chloe? Don't tell me you bombed.'

Aryan didn't bother launching into an explanation. Logan took off his gloves and handed them to him. Although he couldn't place why, Aryan hated the gesture. He took them, smacked Logan round the head with them, then threw them into a nearby bush.

167

'Hey! What the hell is wrong with you?'

As Logan knelt to fetch his gloves from the prickly foliage, Aryan caught sight of their bus bobbing down the road. The bus stop wasn't far off. If they ran for it, he was convinced they could make it.

'Come on! Bus!' Aryan hollered, racing towards the stop with Logan still digging around for his gloves.

'Oh for the love of...' Logan ran after him. Reaching the bus stop, they stuck out their arms like aeroplane wings.

'Got your gloves?' Aryan panted. They clung on to the rails in a near-empty bus, trying to catch their breath. Logan nodded, his face blotched a docile pink. 'OK good. Give them here, my hands are cold.'

He clouted Aryan with his sullied gloves.

'Why did you want to leave? I've never known you to leave a party early?' Logan asked as they entered Rushton House.

'No reason. Tired. I'm going to nap.'

'You serious? I've left this party for you. Let's have a quiet drink at least. Omari's gone home for the weekend. You owe me the company.'

Aryan hesitated, but remembering he wasn't the sort of person to pass up on a drink nor the sort of person that napped on a Saturday night, he agreed and followed him into his room. The schism in the room was still evident. Omari's desk was clean and neatly kept, while Logan's furniture pieces were covered in socks, T-shirts and sweet wrappers. Nothing had changed.

'We can still have fun here,' Logan said as he took off his jacket and abandoned it on the floor. Out of habit, Aryan picked it up for him and hung it on the back of the door. He waited as Logan rummaged for bottles of warm beer in his wardrobe. They settled on to the floor, dragging out Omari's secret stash of sweets and chocolates from beneath the bottom bunk. They'd been borrowing from his box of treats for years without his knowledge. Logan logged into Spotify.

'Do you remember this?' he asked Aryan as they listened to the introduction of a soft acoustic guitar. It was 'Sleeping with the Light On' by Busted. Aryan grinned the moment he recognised it. When they started school in year seven, they both loved Busted. Logan had been more open about his love for the band than he had. Aryan thought it was social suicide to like them unless you were a girl, so he denounced Busted in front of others. He only listened to them with Logan when they were alone, each taking an earpiece of Logan's headphones as they plugged into an old mp3 player, its LCD display failing to capture the song titles. They used to know all the lyrics to their songs. Logan bet they still did.

'I feel her slipping through my fingers, now she's gone. I'm sleeping with the light on...' they sang, their brains already addled by excess alcohol. Aryan stopped his singing. The last time he and Logan had listened to the song, they were thirteen and Logan was crying into his pillow. Their teenage years began with the loss of Logan's mother to lymphoma. Aryan recalled how Logan couldn't come to terms with it. He tried to pray. He tried to get angry. He tried to call a helpline. In the end, all he could do was play that song and the tears finally streamed down his face, as the truth sunk in and welded itself into his body. Aryan lay with him all night, and they listened to that song on repeat, until Logan fell asleep, coincidentally, with the light on.

Relaxing on the floor, now at eighteen years old, they were going from 'Sleeping with the Light On' to 'What I Go to School for' to their old favourite: 'You Said No'. They always sang that one with passion, making sure to shout the words, though not too loud, or the warden would castigate them for the fiftieth time that year.

'Can you believe how much time has passed? Our last year here. Then a whole new adventure,' Logan said, slurring his words slightly.

'You been thinking about deferring for a gap year?'

'Mm. My dad's given me the thumbs up. I haven't thought much about the money, though. I'll get around it somehow. Wish I had as much money as you guys. Hate being one of the poorer students at this school.'

'Why do you care? You should be proud. You got here through a scholarship. You're here because you're good.'

'Whatever, man.'

'What? Your art and designs and whatever are amazing.'

Aryan noticed a pile of art on the bedside table. He retrieved them to make a point. He found himself gazing at intricate drawings, fabricated with symbols, animals and helical scripts.

'Like whatever these are. Wait. What are these?'

'Brad wanted a tattoo done, asked me to design a few for him. Then his friends asked me to do the same. Thought I'd have a go.'

'These are pretty good,' Aryan said. Brad's irritating and pockmarked face flashed into his mind. 'Design me one.'

'What would you want?' asked Logan, before imbibing the remainder of Corona in his bottle.

'I don't know. A cobra would be pretty cool. On my arm.'

'Give me your arm.'

'Are you even sober enough to draw now?'

'No,' said Logan, sticking his hand beneath the lower bunk for a stray pen. He scooted next to Aryan, rolled up his sleeve and started drawing a cobra on his forearm with a pen that leaked watery ink from its nib in runnels. The moment Logan touched Aryan's arm, the black ink swam into the minuscule lines of his skin, illuminating them and their likeness to branches. 'Logan, this isn't going to work. Change the pen.'

He scrutinised the rubble on his desk and shrugged. 'Never going to find one.' He continued, unable to control the movement of the image, or Aryan, who struggled to stay still. The fine-tip tickled him as it travelled in long, S-shaped curves. The finished image wasn't too bad, for the work of a drunk artist with the wrong tool and a slippery canvas. A dark, shadowy aura hung over the indistinct snake. It compounded the sense of villainy created by its gaping, fanged mouth. It could have been labelled abstract. Maybe.

'Done,' Logan said, throwing the pen down in victory. He flipped back a strand of hair from his forehead.

Aryan admired the ireful cobra, wishing it'd take up permanent residence on his arm. He was about to tell Logan to draw it for him on paper, once he sobered up. Instead, he said: 'You have ink on your face.'

'What? Where?' Logan vigorously rubbed where Aryan pointed, spreading the ink across his cheek. He looked like he'd fallen face first into dirt.

'It's all over your hand, you idiot.'

Aryan used his thumb to scrub away the dark smudges from Logan's face, softly laughing at him.

'Ow! You don't have to rub so hard.'

He stopped and assessed Logan's face for any remaining ink. All of a sudden, his hand glided towards Logan's dark-blonde hair and – without thought – his lips propelled forwards and joined with his. For a moment, there was stillness in the soft seal of their lips.

Logan pushed him off and stared at Aryan like a startled fawn. Aryan opened his mouth to speak, but the words perished in his mouth and he stared, dumbfounded.

'Uhrm…' Logan began.

'I…' Aryan's words were caught in a web. What had he just done? He spurted a thread of incoherent sentences and half-words, before angrily thumping Logan's chest. He stormed out of the room, taking from his stock of curse-words to carry him out. After slamming the door shut, he heard Logan shout after him.

'You drunk… idiot!'

'Fuck. Fuck. Fuck!' he said to himself. How much had he had to drink? He hoped Logan was drunk enough. Maybe the devious workings of booze would tamper with Logan's memory and he'd wake up in the morning having forgotten the whole thing, he told himself. Aryan paced backwards and forwards outside the room, agitated and tending to a new-born animosity towards his closest friend.

In the shower the next morning, he scrubbed aggressively at the cobra with soap, until the inked lines broke into curls and fell away. He swirled the murky puddle on his arm with his index finger, then watched it run off on to the ceramic floor beneath the downpour of water. He had woken up to an uncomfortable cocktail of nausea and irritation. As he lathered shampoo into his hair, he thought back to the moment he leaned in and kissed Logan. This exacerbated his condition to the point he was sure he'd capsize and throw up. What an idiot, he thought. Whether he meant himself or Logan, he didn't know. He watched the foamy shampoo edge towards the drain and felt determined to toss the memory of last night down with it. Even the best bits. Busted were childish anyway. And he wouldn't ever tattoo a cobra on his body.

CHAPTER 22

Every Thursday, since the beginning of the year, Logan and Aryan played a friendly game of football with other year thirteen boys. After his study sessions in the library, Aryan would usually drop by the music rooms to wait for Logan so they could head towards the field together. This time, he headed straight there without him.

He stripped off his clothes at the rear end of the changing room, hoping Logan wouldn't find him. But despite the enormous amounts of money pumped into the school, the changing rooms were small and he found him the second he stepped in.

'All right?' Logan asked, in that Northern way that sounded more like 'Oreyt.' He studied Aryan with his head tilted, sensing there was something amiss – like a dog, Aryan thought. He turned from him, unable to bear the shine of his tinsel-fringed eyes. 'I saw you heading here from the windows in the practice room. You OK?'

'Yeah,' Aryan responded, rushing to pull on his gym clothes.

'All right then.' Logan started unbuttoning his shirt. 'By the way, I'm going to catch the train home tomorrow night.'

'Yeah, you always go home on alternate weekends. Isn't exactly news.'

'I was just saying. I didn't think you kept track of my schedule.'

'Whatever. You have a freakish, unhealthy dependence on your family. Got it.'

Logan slipped off his shirt to uncover warm, ivory skin and a defined set of abs. He let his shirt crumple over Aryan's folded clothes on the bench. Aryan couldn't get a handle on his growing agitation.

'What is wrong with you?' Logan asked him.

'Nothing,' he replied. 'I'm going to wait outside.'

He marched out of the changing rooms and waited on the fields, bringing his attention to the way the wind bristled the stretching fingers of coarse grass. He needed to blow off some steam with a game of football. He had struggled all afternoon with a series of maths problems. Normally, he worked well with numbers and sometimes – though he'd never tell a soul – found a thrill in solving mathematical problems. But lately he couldn't pay attention and his mind became languid. It rambled on like an elderly, drunken man burdened with fatigue. He hoped a game of football would mend it and return it to full functionality.

They were split into red and blue teams. Aryan wound up on the red team and took the leadership role. For as long as he could remember, he'd always been competitive. He always demanded a win, whether the game was 'friendly' or not. It was this 'type A' personality that drove him forward through life. However, this time, he was content with just playing.

As he rushed across the field, the cool air decimated his stress and packed him with a new lease of life. Somewhere between cheering for his team when they scored and swearing when the other team did, he stopped caring about his problems. Aryan travelled up the field with the ball at his feet, sweat emerging from his forehead and his heart leaping like a river dancer. He was moments away, biting his lip, preparing to strike for another goal, when something hard knocked into his body and sent him crashing to the ground. He squirmed on the grass, his back burning.

Slowly, he hoisted himself up into a sitting position and brushed off the clumps of mud clinging to his shorts. Blood trickled thinly down the top of his left shin. His skin had been torn by the studs of football boots. He peered up to find Logan standing over him, flicking mud off the front of his T-shirt, guilt slapped across his face.

'Shit. You OK?' he said, proffering his hand. Aryan smacked it away.

'Don't touch me,' he spat as he climbed to his feet.

'Sorry. Let me help.'

'You can help by watching where you're going,' Aryan growled, shunting him. Logan tried to come forward to apologise once more, but he shoved him again.

'Don't push me!' Logan shoved him back.

'Come on then, let's start. You fucking fag.'

Logan froze. His eyes widened. Before anyone could stop him, he charged forward and tackled Aryan to the ground. With fists flailing and their legs kicking, they rolled around on the damp ground. The others crowded around them, some gasping, some cheering and only one yelling at them to stop. They both struck each other in the face, trying to make impact with their elbows and knees.

'FIGHT!' screamed a couple of the boys with all the foolish excitement of primary school children. Fully fledged fights rarely ever happened at Brookside. This was a rare spectacle. Logan straddled Aryan and was about to serve a punch but lost the chance as Aryan headbutted him in the stomach and winded him. Aryan rolled him over, ready to deliver a blow to his face, when the arresting voice of the PE teacher cut through the chants and severed his chance of victory.

'Stop right now! That's enough!' The stocky teacher, Mr Langford, forced the two of them apart and dragged them to their feet. They tried to slip past the barriers of his arms to get to each other. They failed and only made Langford angrier. They were in deep trouble. The teacher escorted them off the pitch to the medical room, where they were plastered up and sent straight to the headmaster's office.

Déjà vu rang its bell through the room as they sat on the other side of Mr Lane's desk. Mr Lane listened to the account of events from the PE teacher while Logan and Aryan sat in silence, making sideways glances at each other to figure out how much damage they had inflicted on the other. They had succeeded in blackening each other's eyes and drawing balls of blood from their lips. Aryan pronounced himself the winner. With his body sore and tender, he couldn't sit still in his seat.

'I am appalled! Absolutely appalled. Look at the state of you two!' shouted Mr Lane. His pudgy face was inflamed with scarlet and spit flew from the corner of his mouth like sparks from a lighter. Aryan had never seen him so angry. 'This kind of senseless violence will not be tolerated! Do you hear me? Do you?' He closed his eyes and waited for the panting to subside. 'Now, tell me, in your own words, what happened. And why. Why you thought it was OK to behave in such a disgusting, barbaric manner.'

'He shoved me to the ground. He started the whole thing,' said Aryan, crossing his arms as he slumped in his chair. He knew he was acting like a child. He didn't give a toss.

'What? You *are* kidding? You know that was an accident.' Logan rolled his eyes. 'Sir, I accidentally bashed into him during the game. He got pissed off, called me a fag and tackled me to the ground.'

'Bullshit, you tackled me!'

'Language!' warned Mr Lane.

'Because of what you said,' said Logan.

'Let me understand this. He called you a name and you thought it was acceptable to incite violence?' said Mr Lane, sighing deeply as he leaned back into his armchair. He shook his head in disappointment and massaged his temples. 'I have been through this with you both once before.'

'Well, it hurt,' snapped Logan. As he said it, Aryan knew he wasn't talking about the punches. His ears burned. They didn't confess their feelings. Not even to each other. Aryan turned to face him. Logan's eyes were swimming with tears. 'I thought I could trust you. Not to say anything, for one, and to just be cool.'

'Well, why did you have to say anything in the first place? You made things weird the other night.'

'The other…? You kissed me! I did fuck all.'

'Language!' shouted Mr Lane, rising to his feet and propelling himself forward, his hands splayed on the desk. He bit down on his bottom lip as he processed the other bit of information. 'I beg your pardon?'

'I'm gay. He kissed me. And, apparently, that's my fault. What the actual fuck?'

Mr Lane stammered, unsure of what to say. His teacher training hadn't prepared him for this, Aryan thought.

'I was drunk,' Aryan hissed.

'I beg your pardon! Drunk? You were drunk?' Mr Lane was overwhelmed with information at this point. He lowered himself back into his chair – a man delivered news he couldn't endure.

'Exactly, I didn't make you do a damn thing. All of a sudden, you're calling me a faggot, just because I knocked into you. Grow up!'

'You've ruined things. You're different. It's like I don't even know you any more. You've been hiding this for two years. And you know what? No, I don't want a gay best mate. Thanks.'

Aryan could see that stung him. He watched Logan shrink

into his seat. 'Fine. You go ahead and hate me then.'

Aryan cringed. He didn't hate him. He wanted to punch him in the face and swear at him some more, but he didn't hate him. Even so, he wasn't going to correct him. Before Mr Lane could begin his lecture and assign their punishments, Logan stood up and left the office.

'Mr Reeves. Get back here!' the headmaster called after him. Logan didn't turn back. Mr Lane grunted and took a sip of his coffee from a tawdry mug that stated 'I'm a head teacher. What's your superpower?'

He slipped on his reading glasses and flipped through a contact book. He only addressed Aryan now. 'You're both banned from football. I'll have to gate you and I'm going to have to call your parents,' he said. He paused and lowered his glasses to the end of his nose, so he could centre Aryan in his gaze. 'Logan's father asked me to keep an eye out for homophobic bullying. He was worried people might find out about his, shall we say... affliction. I'm sure he'll be surprised it's come from you, Mr Alekar.'

'Whatever,' he said. He heard the word affliction. At least Mr Lane understood it for what it was.

Maansi picked up her phone, rolling the device from back to front in her hand, before surrendering and dialling for Sejal. She needed to tell someone. Her secrets balanced on the backs of each other like a house of cards and were ready to tumble.

'Sejal,' she began, once she answered. 'I've been so stupid.'

'Maansi? What's wrong?' The sound of wind and cars driving in the background raged through the phone. 'I'm just walking back from work. Are you OK?'

Maansi took another sip of her drink, the wine lapping against the sides of her glass as she thumped it back down on to the table. 'It's Aryan. He yelled and stormed out of the house. He's really mad. I'm not sure I can fix this.'

'Why? What happened?'

Here we go, she told herself. She took a deep breath. 'Well, he told me he wanted a specific kind of girl. Someone fun and outgoing. I mean, I used to be that way, but I pretended I still was. And he found my antidepressants. All he kept saying was that I'm a liar. We married on a lie. Like it's some huge deal!' she said, fighting to keep her tears at bay.

Sejal didn't reply straight away. 'You're dealing with depression? Since when?'

'Um. Since last year of university.'

'What? Why didn't you tell me?'

She scored little 'x's along the surface of the table in front of her with her long nails – kept so not because of a preference, but because grooming took a back seat when in battle with depression. 'I don't know. I didn't want to drag you down. You're so extraverted and fun and I didn't think you'd want to...'

'Oh my God. Are you crazy? Of course I'd want to see you. Look. I went through it too for a while. Literally, I used to just stay in bed and watch puppies and Lilly Singh videos. That's all I could do. I get it.'

Maansi's heart was in her throat. Sejal had been through it too?

'Do you know what caused it? Or did it just happen for you?'

'It happened after... I had an abortion.'

Maansi fought to keep her composure as she endured another episode of silence. 'I'm sorry... What?'

'The only person that knows is Aryan. I never told anyone.'

179

'Maansi! You mean you've been dealing with that all alone? What the actual hell? Girl, you should've spoken up. I would've come with you. You didn't need to do that by yourself.'

She couldn't cage her emotions any more. Maansi allowed her tears to flood forward and all over her face. 'Really?'

'Of course! Hon, why are you crying?'

'Oh, God, I don't know. I love you so much!'

'I love you too. Stop. You'll make me cry! Now, what are we going to do about your dickhead of a husband?'

Maansi generously topped up her glass with more wine. 'You don't even know the half of it. He's so secretive. I think I'm going to have to play detective.' If she'd found out Aryan knew Logan through the internet, perhaps there were other parcels of information stored as clickable data, ready to impart just a little more knowledge – even just a single drop more would help. All of a sudden, a message popped up on her screen. 'I'll call you back, Sejal.'

With Imran Khan playing at low volume in the background, Aryan flicked through his textbooks. He could hardly focus. Why did Logan have to spoil everything? He thought of all the time he played wingman to Logan, trying to set him up with girls. Logan never said a word. He went along with it – kept quiet. Aryan's face burned. Logan probably thought he liked him now, thanks to that stupid drunken kiss. He had to be cruel with him on the field. He had to be clear that wasn't the case.

He didn't understand how men could enjoy being physical with each other. He didn't even understand what it was they did between the sheets. He tapped his fingers against his desk. He supposed there'd be no harm in finding out. He accessed a proxy server, as students habitually did at boarding school, to conceal their searches and pass through search barriers imposed on them by an establishment with no regard for 'teenage needs'. He hesitated at the keyboard, looking over his shoulder and hoping Chris wouldn't burst through the door. He wouldn't be able to explain it to him. After a spell of indecision, he searched. Returned to him were approximately two million videos. He mindlessly clicked on the first and observed as two men appeared on his screen. Their tongues battled together and their hands slipped down each other's toned, sweat-brushed bodies. Their breaths escaped in flurries and one man let go of an elongated moan. Aryan clicked out of the window, his stomach lurching and his cheeks hot. He took a sip of water. He didn't know how others could accept it. He never thought he had an issue with gay men. He had never targeted a gay man or expressed any disapproval. He had never cared. In fact, he thought he supported it. Yet, there he was, struggling with the notion.

He thought about Logan's teary face. Logan was never angry, choosing to live some kind of 'hakuna matata' lifestyle, as Omari had once called it. He pictured Logan's warm, ivory skin, pressed up against the whiter skin of Brad's. He pictured Brad biting into his neck, allowing his hands to move freely across the rest of him. Aryan hurled his pen down on to the desk. It sickened him. He withdrew a pack of cigarettes from his drawer and proceeded to the window to stick his head out and smoke. What he saw through the window vexed him even more. Just what he needed, he thought. Chris and Chloe were outside, their hands joining together.

He watched as the beautiful Chloe adjusted his friend's collar and cuffed him as he made some kind of joke. He watched as Chris went to kiss her cheek, missing his destination as she pulled him in for a passionate, open-mouthed kiss. It was no short event. When they paused to breathe, Chris peered over his shoulder. The guilt was plain on his face. The fool didn't even realise he was standing right outside their bedroom window. Aryan poked his head out.

'So, I see you've downgraded. Thought you were the on and up kind of girl,' he called. Chloe turned and blushed at the sight of him. Chris gulped and took several steps back, freeing his neck from his tie as if it were a tightening noose.

'I told you I'm not looking for anything,' she called back, her hand positioned on her hip.

'I know. But something is better than nothing, right?' he winked. Chris grew frantic. He hastened his goodbye to Chloe and ran into Rushton House. The door handle turned minutes later.

'Aryan, I know you're mad. But you have to realise... Shit. What happened to your face?' Chris said.

'Nothing. And I don't care what you do with her,' Aryan said, resettling himself at his desk. He didn't mean what he was saying but the anger was driving him towards it. 'You know she's been around.'

'And so have you!' challenged Chris. 'In fact, that's the reason I thought it was OK to go for her. You go through girls like a pack of tissues. I actually like her.'

'I like her too,' said Aryan. 'A lot. I told you.'

'She said you ignored her at the party. You didn't want anything to do with her.'

Aryan's phone rang. He peered at the screen. It was his father. He palmed his head and groaned. Exactly what he needed.

'Aryan?'

'Just shut up for a second.' He answered the phone. 'Dad...

182

I know… We just got into a scrap… It's nothing… I wouldn't have been expelled over that… I don't need to quit football, they've banned me from playing… No, I've just submitted my application, I won't hear until March… I am!' He angrily hung up. His phone started buzzing again. He hurled it across the room, where it rebounded off a wall and popped its battery out, cutting off the ringtone. He reopened his textbook and came face to face, yet again, with that insoluble equation. His chest rose and fell rapidly. Everything was getting on top of him.

'Aryan?'

'Leave me alone.'

'Aryan, wait,' called Chris. Aryan stormed out of the room and slammed the door behind him. Once he was out, he picked up the pace of his walk and broke into a jog. When he was ready, he sprinted. Something in his body told him he could outrun the problems. Maybe he could sprint fast enough to leave them suspended in the past, as he pressed on into a new and simpler present. He saw an upcoming tree and charged towards it, his palms stuck out before him. As they met the bark, he hauled his body over his arms, flipping himself over and landing on his feet. The landing was imperfect. He walked backwards to an acceptable distance from the tree and tried again. The school once had a parkour workshop. He'd been obsessed ever since. It was unsafe to practise alone, outside of a safe practice environment, but he never cared. He tried again. And again. Until his landing was perfect. When he'd done it, he felt better. Lighter. Unchained in some way. He sprinted off in another direction.

By the time he finished running, the sky was a royal blue plunging into the black of night. He stood outside his door, listening to Chris's movements inside. He didn't want to see him. He headed towards Omari's room and let himself in.

'I'm revising, man. You want to stay here you better work,' Omari said, as Aryan sat at the available desk. 'Is everything OK?'

'Chris wants to be with Chloe. Looks like she wants the same.'

Omari closed his book – something he never did unless absolutely necessary. He wheeled his desk chair round to face Aryan. 'Why would Chris do that to you?'

'I don't know.'

'You really liked her?'

'I don't know,' he said. On the desk before him, he saw a sheet of paper scattered with drawings of cobras. They were impressive – a few psychedelic and pieced together with clever, fractal patterns – a combination of spirals and arrowheads. He studied them closely, his fingers tracing each image.

'Those are pretty cool,' said Omari. 'I'd get Logan to do me a tattoo design, if I didn't think tattoos were stupid.'

'Whatever. Since Logan's gone for the weekend, can I sleep here?'

'In Logan's bed? After your fight? You sure he'll be OK with that?' Omari returned to highlighting passages in his textbook. 'I wouldn't. I don't know when that boy last changed his sheets.'

He thought about Logan and Brad mingling beneath those sheets. 'I'll bring my own. I just don't want to deal with Chris today. I'll shower and come back.'

When Aryan returned, Omari wasn't there. He texted him to say he'd gone to revise with a group of boys from biology. Aryan stripped the top bunk of its sheets and replaced them with his. Exhausted, he slipped in and shut his eyes. As sleep took hold of him, images of the two men from the video unfurled like moonflowers in the night. He was watching them again, although this time there wasn't an 'x' button to make it stop. There was a stirring near his groin and an inviting warmth spread across the southern region of his body. His eyes shot open. The bulge in his underwear called for his attention. He thought he was losing his mind and scolded himself, burying his face into the pillow. For the next hour, no matter how he tried, he couldn't expunge the images from his head, nor the incessant throbbing from his body. He picked up his phone to see if Logan had messaged him. He hadn't. He didn't expect him to. Even so, he kept his phone next to his head for the remainder of the night.

CHAPTER 23

'Hey. I heard you got married. I just wanted to say congrats. That's great news. And I wanted to say sorry, if I ever upset you. Good luck!'

She blinked twice. Had he really just messaged her that? After all the time that had passed? 'Sorry if I ever upset you.' It was just like Lewis to deliver the world's worst apology. Of course, he upset her and he knew it! She thought about all the pain she went through because of him. He wasn't even worth it! And now there was Aryan. Would she have to suffer at his hands too? No way. They'd talk it out and she'd let him know he couldn't mess her around or judge her for what she went through.

Seeing Lewis's pathetic apology made her realise he was probably never the one for her anyway. He left her and immediately went off with another woman, before she could even get over her abortion. He was scum – even if he never knew she was pregnant. He was still scum! She wondered if she and Aryan would have babies. They'd never discussed it prior to marriage. Yes, she knew it was stupid to leave the subject out, but they hardly knew each other! It would have been awkward and strange to bring up babies. What if he didn't want kids? What if he hated children? She couldn't imagine him being a warm, paternal figure. Oh, God. She needed to speak to him desperately. She needed to know if he wanted children!

She wasn't about to get ahead of herself. She didn't plan on having children until much later. She was excited about her career, about becoming a fully-functioning member of society. She wondered what Aryan would have become if his father wasn't a wealthy businessman. Who was he without those things? It didn't seem to matter how much time she spent with him, she could never find him. Instead of him in front of her, plain and raw, he was packaged with layers of cling film. You could see him, but the same way you couldn't bite into cling-filmed foods was the same way she couldn't experience Aryan.

Maybe an arranged marriage wasn't the best idea. Maybe she should've waited for love. But what if love was always going to be imperfect and difficult? What if this was all it could ever be? When she was younger, love looked like princes and princesses, exercising their melodic voices on white, noble steeds. Maybe love didn't look much different to her and Aryan's situation, and maybe nobody admitted it. The world's best kept secret.

Aryan liked Sophie because she was intelligent and governed debate club. She wasn't Chloe and he didn't like her the same way, but she captured him anyway. He liked that she could form scorching arguments to shoot at her opponents like a skilled archer with a taste for sadism. They usually left with emotional, second-degree burns. Mostly, he liked her because she was beautiful and had lips slicked over with a peach-coral gloss. He liked kissing her behind B block before class. She'd enter her classes with the gloopy gloss caught in her cupid's bow, a strand of hair out of place from where his hand had pushed it aside. It made him feel powerful, in some sense.

He held Sophie's hand as they walked down the corridor.

He wasn't much of a hand holder, but she insisted on it because 'that's what boyfriends and girlfriends do'. He didn't recall making her his girlfriend but didn't challenge her. Suddenly, William stepped out in front of them and stretched out his arms, obstructing his way.

'Move,' Aryan growled.

William ignored him. 'Hello, sweetheart.' He looked Sophie up and down. He was her ex-boyfriend and he looked pretty pissed off. 'What are you doing with this sand monkey?'

Aryan felt her hand slide out of his. Sand monkey? He hadn't heard that one in a while.

'Say that again, prick,' Aryan said, shoving William. Before William could push him back, someone grabbed the hem of Aryan's T-shirt and pulled him back.

'Whoa,' said Logan. 'We don't want any trouble.'

'What are you doing here?' Aryan said.

'Walking back from lunch. Is that a crime?'

'Oh, you are kidding me? What's with your accent? Sounds like you should be wearing a flat cap and be on your way back to the factory workers you call family.' His friends hooted and cheered him on, though William's insults were never very good. 'Well, the school does need to let a small percentage of disadvantaged people in, I suppose.'

'Disadvantaged? My dad's a university professor and I'm here on an arts scholarship. Being a posh toff doesn't make you better than me.'

'Oh, congratulations. Well done,' William replied in a slow and patronising tone, his hands clapping together in the imitation of a toddler. 'Now. Why don't you and your Paki friend—'

In a flash, William was on the floor, squealing as blood spewed from his nose and poured down his sky-blue, Ralph Lauren polo. William's friend tried to punch Logan back, but Aryan knocked him to the ground with almost comical ease.

'Dicks!' cried William. 'Fuck off to wherever you came from,' he said, pointing his finger at Aryan.

'Oh, fuck off!' Sophie screamed at him, throwing in a quick kick of her own.

William and his unhurt friend shored up the supine loser, groaning and snivelling on the floor. They staggered off in the direction of the medical room. Logan nursed his knuckles with the moisture of his mouth.

'What the hell did you do that for?' Aryan said.

'I don't know. Should have let them have you,' Logan said.

'Wait here, Soph,' Aryan said to Sophie. He followed Logan as he walked back to Rushton House. 'For me? You realise I devote a lot of my damn time to learning how to fight. I don't need any help from you.'

'Yeah. That's why I got a few punches in the last time.'

Anger brewed insidiously beneath the surface. The words 'sand monkey' and 'Paki' played in his mind like a set of perfectly matched chords. It wasn't the first time he'd heard them. He'd got worse through the years at school. 'Curry muncher' was the most deplorable. The international students from India got it all the time. But he wasn't different in the same way. At least, he didn't think so.

Logan let himself into his room and collapsed on his bed. His knuckles were a pronounced pink – a beautiful, sore testament to having punched the pompous 'toff' in his privileged, alabaster face.

'What the hell happened to you being a pacifist?'

'He made fun of Northerners.'

'That's not why you punched him.'

'Whatever. What he said was bang out of order. You're not even from Pakistan. Not that Pakistani people should deal with that. No one should,' he said. He yawned and nestled into a cocoon he created with his duvet. As William's bloodied face popped into Aryan's head, he couldn't help but feel an injustice had occurred.

'Why did you interfere? It isn't like we're speaking.'

Logan groaned. 'So stop speaking and leave me alone. I just want to nap. I'm getting a migraine. You know they get really bad.'

Aryan wasn't cruel enough to fight him during one of his migraines. They were punishment enough. 'Fine. But I don't need you fighting my battles next time, all right?' He wanted to have done it. It should have been him. He'd got his friend, sure, but the satisfaction of impacting William's nose with his own fist would have been unsurpassable. It would have been delicious.

'All right.'

There was a knock at the door.

'Logan Reeves, if you're in, open this door please,' came a booming voice.

'Shit! Don't open the door,' said Logan, recognising the voice of the housemaster.

'I can hear you. Mr Alekar, I can hear you too. Open up or I'll let myself in.'

'We're doomed,' Aryan smiled at Logan. He didn't smile back at him.

Aryan's own knuckles were sore that day. After hearing what the headmaster had to say, he struck the wall.

'You will be gated for the next month. Outdoor privileges are now abolished and you will complete homework in the housemaster's office,' he'd said.

'Are you being serious? And what about Gillingham?' Aryan asked.

Mr Lane couldn't respond.

'Unpunished,' Aryan stated for him, disgusted with the so-called man in charge. 'Because his dad's a massive—'

'Aryan!'

'Donor.'

Everyone at the school recognised the name Gillingham. William Gillingham's father was always praised for his large contributions. They went on and on about his generosity at every event or ceremony funded by his obese wallet. His son was to go unpunished and Aryan and Logan were to be severely punished to placate him. Mr Gillingham called the shots.

On top of detentions, he and Logan were expected to clean the corridors and kitchenettes before bed. Since Logan had a migraine, they began the following night. While Logan polished the countertops, he mopped the floor. Neither said anything for a long while. The silence was too much for Aryan to handle.

'I'm sorry for before. For what I said.' The words loosened themselves and flew forward without Aryan's permission. Part of him demanded to know what he was saying sorry for. What happened to being totally justified?

'For calling me a faggot, you mean?' Logan snorted. 'Since when do you apologise?'

'Come on, Reeves.'

'OK. Whatever.'

'I was just angry. I've been on edge. I didn't mean any of it. I'm really sorry, all right?'

Logan heaved a sigh. It was a weary sigh. One of exhaustion and defeat, rather than a willingness to forgive. But Logan forgave. He could be relied on to forgive. He believed, unequivocally and without doubt, that if a person should ask for forgiveness, you should forgive. Aryan once called him naïve, sentimental, an idealist… but he was glad in that moment that Logan didn't hold on to every bit of anger, like a miser held on to every gleaming or dulled coin in a pouch clutched to his chest. Logan strove to keep peace there instead. 'Fine. I guess we can forget what's happened then.'

Aryan paused, put down the mop and leaned against the wall, trying to regroup the thoughts derailing in his head. A realisation took the shape of a sizeable skeleton key and it began trying the doors he was too afraid to open. The ones he longed to keep closed.

Logan stepped out to take the bin outside and Aryan followed him. As soon as they were out in the cold, he began. 'Look, when I kissed you…' he trailed off.

'I know, I know. You were drunk, it's forgotten,' said Logan. He tied up the bag and hauled it into the larger bin. 'Just forget about it.'

'I think I meant it.' The words came out in a strangled whisper. As they escaped, he hoped the wind would immediately kill them.

Logan's eyes flickered towards him. They could see each other's eyes beneath the deep blue wrap of a fledgling night. Aryan waited as Logan checked him for the signs of a poor joke.

'What?' Logan said. Aryan could feel the warden watching them from a window. 'What do you mean?'

'I don't know. I kissed you. I wanted to. It didn't feel wrong,' Aryan said while staring at the ground, surprised by what he was saying. His voice seemed to be cruising through without concern for consequence. 'But I'm not gay like you. I like girls. A lot.'

'OK.'

'OK,' confirmed Aryan. He turned away, heat washing over his face. Logan had always been the kind of person who knew what to say. He forever butted himself into a group of new people and tore down the walls of unfamiliarity and discomfort. But Aryan had rendered him awkward and speechless.

'I'm going round the corner for a smoke,' Aryan said.

'I'll come with you.'

They walked around the corner and stood at the mouth of an open field. Their breath shed their screens of invisibility and streamed through the cold air in white wisps. Their eyes lingered towards the sky, where the stars were quashed by groups of ravenous clouds. They were conscious of each other's movements; of the way their chests rose and brought the cool air into their lungs.

'Listen, it was literally just a kiss. There's no need to be weird. You were drunk,' Logan told him. Aryan withdrew his pack of cigarettes and offered one to Logan, which was a strange thing to do. He knew Logan didn't smoke. 'But what did you mean by it didn't feel wrong?' Logan asked, rubbing the back of his neck.

'I don't know.'

'Do you ever think that way, about guys?'

Aryan slipped him his answer through his silence.

'So, you gave me a hard time for liking guys. Why? Because you're questioning your own sexuality?'

Aryan felt sick. 'I like girls. If I had to choose, it'd be a girl. I just... wavered.' Yes, that seemed like the right word. He was woozy and directed by alcohol, if not outright pushed. He was like a puppet beneath a puppet-master, meaning to move his left arm, but finding his right flapping. He wavered. He could feel Logan's eyes assessing him, peeling away the layers – trying to work him out.

193

'Maybe you're bi. Or just curious,' Logan said. 'Maybe you thought, hey, I want to try some of that.' He ran his hand through his hair and winked, simpering and trying to crumple the mood like old newspaper, because at the end of the day, Logan was made to tear down the walls of discomfort and unfamiliarity.

'Piss off,' Aryan said, rolling his eyes and submitting to a frail laugh. 'I don't know.'

Logan looked directly at him. 'It's OK, you know, to like guys too, whether less or more than girls. And it's OK for me to like them.'

Aryan agreed with him.

'So... Sophie, huh?' Logan nudged him in the ribs. 'When did that become a thing?'

Aryan smiled at him. 'It isn't really a thing. I don't know what it is.' She wasn't Chloe.

'All right. Well, shall we get back to cleaning?'

'Sure.'

Aryan walked a little behind Logan. He dropped a message to Sophie and hoped she'd be up.

Aryan's page provided no answers. Maansi's curiosity piqued and would not be conciliated until she had an answer. She chewed her fingernails as she waded through Logan's information. She came across pictures of him in a rainbow-coloured T-shirt, with shades on and a couple of men hanging off his neck. He stuck his tongue out, his face splattered with powdered colour and paints. The other men playfully puckered their lips and waved flags of hashtags and bold statements.

His T-shirt read 'love is love', with Mars and Venus symbols interlinked in varying combinations. A small laugh escaped her. Was this man who she had secretly been infatuated with gay? She was slightly disappointed. He'd never find her attractive! Yet, maybe this oversight of hers provided an answer. Aryan was intolerant of mental health conditions. Perhaps, he was intolerant of homosexuals too. Wouldn't that make sense? Could that be why a friendship between them extinguished? Maybe they weren't ever friends and their picture together did nothing but trick her into believing they were. Perhaps, they were people who connected in a fragment of time, to be forgotten the following day and never recalled upon. That could be a possibility. She'd never know unless she spoke to him.

The vacant holes puncturing Aryan's completed picture – a man she thought she was beginning to understand – grated her and forced her to pace the flat. He'd left her in a state of anger and now she couldn't shake the feeling that there were buried secrets beneath her feet that couldn't be unearthed. If he couldn't be open about his past friendships, what could he be open about? Where had he slunk off to? She'd had enough of the mystery. She picked up the phone and dialled.

'The person you are calling is currently not available. Please try again later,' came that infuriating, robotic voice. How angry was he? Was he ignoring her? Would this escalate into the destruction of their marriage? She dialled again, hitting the keys with so much force her fingertips whitened against the screen. 'The person you are calling is currently not available. Please try again later.'

'Urgh!'

She bet he'd switched his phone off, just so she couldn't reach him. She was fed up. Looking back over the weeks, he had proved himself to be possessive, secretive and a complete insensate. Slowly, he was revealing himself to her and she was terrified about what else he was hiding. She could only guess what she'd find when she pared his outer edges. What was he at his very centre?

CHAPTER 24

When Aryan came out of the shower in the changing rooms, he found Logan freshly washed and waiting for Omari on a bench. Everyone else had showered after the cross-country run – another one of Mr Lane's great ideas to reduce stress (and increase misery) during the exam period.

'Aryan,' Logan began, as Aryan finished dressing. 'Have you thought much more about a gap year?'

'Sorry, I'm not going.'

'Is it because you're pissed off with Chris? I heard about Chloe.'

Aryan shook his head. It had nothing to do with that. He just couldn't persuade his dad to open his wallet for full moon parties and life-changing adventures when there was an education to pay for.

'Is that it then? Once we finish here, we won't really see each other.'

Aryan didn't like the sound of that. 'You know I want to go. Maybe when you're both back—'

Logan gently hushed him. He raised his eyebrows and pointed to the occupied shower cubicle on their left. They could hear Omari singing a beyond unacceptable song from his shower cubicle.

'Bieber Fever,' Aryan diagnosed.

'Better cool him off. Grab that bucket,' Logan said, pointing behind Aryan.

As Logan stole Omari's clothes from the shower rail, Aryan

grabbed the grimy bucket and filled it to the brim with ice-cold water. As if by the intervention of fate, Omari turned the shower off the minute they were positioned and ready. Logan drew the curtain open and Aryan chucked the arctic water at him.

'Motherfu—' Omari shook like a fish out of water, squealing as the cold coursed to the centre of his bones. Logan and Aryan darted out of the changing rooms with Omari's clothes and room keys. They could hear him cursing after them as they sprinted off.

They ran straight into Rushton House, into Logan's room and locked it, half panting and half laughing until Logan was plagued with a torrent of hiccoughs.

'Oh cr-' he hiccoughed, '-ap.'

Aryan fetched a bottle of water from his drawstring bag and handed it to him.

Logan knocked it back, choked and spilt the rest of it down his shirt. 'Well done, Logan,' he scolded himself, coughing.

Aryan laughed. All of a sudden, an uncomfortable sadness burgeoned in the pit of his stomach. 'I'll miss this.'

'What, me?' grinned Logan. His smile faded, as he recalled the bad news of the afternoon. No gap year together. The missing would happen sooner than they thought. 'I'll miss you too.' Aryan was struck by the soft and sincere tone with which he spoke, as if the words were cut from fragile glass.

'We'll visit,' Aryan reassured.

'You've hardly spoken to me, mate,' Logan said. Aryan felt guilt creeping up on him. It was true. He hadn't been speaking to him much since that night on the field.

'It's my fault. I let my feelings get in the way,' said Aryan, finding it difficult to wrap his tongue around the word 'feelings', seeing as he never discussed them and associated 'feelings' with the weak.

'Is this about me being…?' began Logan.

'No, it's about me probably being bisexual, or maybe not, I don't know,' he said. Logan's blue eyes arrested him. They were effulgent balls of cobalt blue that sparkled with kindness whenever Logan laughed, smiled or sympathised. But they pierced like a pack of blades when he was serious. Aryan struggled to get the words out. 'I don't want to say anything that might jeopardise our friendship.'

'Our friendship is already in jeopardy,' said Logan. 'Just say it, candidly. You secretly like me. Or, I don't know, maybe I've got that wrong, but I don't think I have.' He paused, before saying, 'I like you too.'

Aryan's ears burned at this disclosure, collecting crimson in the flaps as he doubted what he'd just heard. 'What are you talking about? Since when?'

'Since recently. I don't know. You're my best friend so we already have that. And you're, you know, attractive.' He laughed nervously and shook his head, his cheeks flushing. 'I was going to like you at least a little, but what was there to do about it?'

'Oh,' said Aryan.

'Yeah.'

They both looked around the room, one stroking his neck, the other twiddling with his shoelaces.

'Now what?' asked Aryan. Logan shrugged. Aryan was going to suggest they check on Omari, when he noticed Logan's eyes wander towards his mouth. His blue eyes snapped back up, but the moment was caught in the net, thrashing and wrenching – demanding his attention. Aryan leaned in and planted his lips on Logan's. They kissed, slowly at first, and with uncertainty, as if trying a foreign delicacy for the first time.

Kissing a boy didn't feel too different from kissing a girl. This time, instead of being accosted with a heady floral scent, Aryan could smell sandalwood and citrus rising from Logan's skin, and it made him kiss harder. He carefully placed his hand below Logan's neck, where his fingers travelled along his collarbone. He could feel their friendship move into a whole new game. But he continued kissing him, boldly moved through the dangerous minefield, while a desperate Omari banged at the door.

'Guys! Let me in. I don't know whose towel I've got wrapped around my crotch. This ain't a good feeling,' came Omari's voice. He banged again. 'Guys!'

Logan and Aryan ignored him, too busy running their hands across each other's chests, tugging with frustration at their T-shirts. They breathed heavily. Aryan's skin smarted from the uncontainable desire rising within him.

'Come on, I'm cold!' pleaded Omari. 'These year sevens are laughing at me, man. Piss off, you little twats!'

Logan pulled away. He glanced at the door and opened his mouth, probably to suggest they put Omari out of his misery, but Aryan drew him back towards him again before he could utter a word.

'Logan! What would Jesus do? What would Jesus do?'

They tore away to laugh.

'Maybe we should let him in,' Logan said.

'Maybe.'

Neither got up. Aryan gave in again to the natural urge that mangled his thoughts to rest on the one thing that mattered: the boy in front of him. He kept his focus on Logan's lips and not the stirring of electric pulses in the lower depths of his body. He couldn't begin to think what would follow the kiss. He knew, as he met the mouth of fresh boyishness that he was moving towards a form of hell. But he hoped that, if he was going to burn or wind up in a world of trouble, Logan would be there. As he had been, from the first day they met.

CHAPTER 25

They took the scene and froze it in time. The opportunity for development was halted; a bookmark jammed at the cliffhanger. They would return to it later, thumb through the preceding pages and acknowledge, wholly and completely, what had followed. In the meantime, May's final exams summoned for their undivided attention.

Regardless of their decision to temporarily forget the lust-stippled snogging session, things weren't normal. The change was nuanced and subtle, like a gradual shift from burgundy to maroon. When they revised with Omari and Chris (who Aryan had finally forgiven), they stole glances at each other. When they sat together for lunch, they'd let their knees graze against each other's. There was something chemical occurring that couldn't be controlled. It was strange. Uncomfortable, at times. It challenged the sturdy foundations of a friendship, built on brick by brick. Yet, the rocking of the structure wasn't as frightening as it was thrilling.

Though it was his idea to avoid discussing the aftermath of the kissing, Aryan found it difficult to forget it. It needed to dance on the front stage of his head. It wanted to perform itself repeatedly, like a ballerina twirling as she ascended from a child's music box to the ongoing tune of 'Für Elise'. It was responding to his muted calls for an encore. He'd view it again, when he found Logan in the corridors, engaged in conversation with a boy he hadn't met, or when he caught him in an impromptu game of one-on-one basketball with a boy he knew of, but was unaware of any connection between them. Although Logan stopped seeing Brad, Aryan bore the influx of 'what ifs' as they tunnelled through his brain like assiduous moles. What if there was something more in the words Logan gave the boys he spoke to? What if the flash of white teeth meant more than just an expression of amusement or friendliness?

Aryan came out of the exam hall, following a gruelling two hours of maths. He drowned out the chatter of students discussing answers with his headphones. He took a glimpse into the future. This time next year, he could be at the London School of Economics, completing his first year of a business management degree. Logan had cancelled his UCAS application, set on applying the following year at the London School of Arts, or Edinburgh.

'Why Edinburgh?' Aryan asked, as they sat in the outdoor eating area, enjoying the rarity of sunshine. It was unfair, the way the sun chose to come out of hiding when students were suffocating in exam halls and stuffy libraries.

'Why not Edinburgh?' Logan replied.

'With that logic, then why not Timbuktu?'

'Because Timbuktu is a desert town with most of its residents living in poverty,' Omari cut in, lowering his lunch tray as he seated himself. Logan nodded, pretending he knew all about it. 'Meaning, my friend, there is no university. Although, there did once exist the university of Timbuktu, which was an association of mosques in the twelfth century that offered Islamic-centred learning. Something tells me they wouldn't have studied graphic design.'

'I was just trying to make a point,' Aryan said. His friends could be impossible.

'I know what you're really saying,' said Logan. 'You'd miss me.'

Aryan scowled and tossed an empty juice box at his head. 'Not bloody likely.'

Aryan and Logan traipsed to the nearby shops, in hunt of snacks to get them through their final revision sessions. Aryan bought cereal bars, dried fruits and almonds. Logan bought party-sized packets of Jaffa Cakes, Oreos, Haribo and a few tubes of Pringles. Aryan warned him he'd be getting diabetes if he continued that way. At the till, Logan turned to him, his expression serious. Aryan thought he was going to bring up the subject they were avoiding. He waited for the 'So, what does this make us?' talk with a tight jaw.

'Listen, I was thinking, do you want to come over this summer?' Logan said.

'To York?'

'Yeah. We haven't visited each other these past few summers. We could go camping.'

'Uhm. I don't know,' Aryan said. 'I mean, we haven't even spoken about, you know.'

'Come on. There are no expectations. We'll just hang out as we always do. You'll be off to uni. May not see you for a while.'

Aryan was affected by that possibility. If they were splitting off in separate directions, what would they need to talk about anyway? This newly discovered attraction towards each other was pointless. There would be no opportunity to mould something out of the lump of clay. 'I'll think about it,' he said.

As they sauntered back to Rushton House with their snacks, they witnessed a glossy black Lexus manoeuvre into a parking space allocated for guests. Aryan instantly recognised it. 'Shit.'

'Shit,' Logan concurred.

They scrambled up the stairs to Aryan's room. Since the final exams had started, Aryan's cleaning habits had slackened. He gathered the KFC bags by his bed and added them to the congestion building in Chris's bin. Logan, as trained over the years, withdrew small statues of Hindu Gods from Aryan's cupboard and placed them meticulously on his desk and windowsill. Aryan made his bed and Logan moved cigarettes, packets of weed and other taboo items from Aryan's drawers to Chris's. They left notebooks and textbooks open on Aryan's desk and untacked posters of bikini-clad women and Lamborghinis. It was as if Ofsted had arrived.

'You still have this?' Logan asked, finding a thin, introductory book on law jutting out from beneath Aryan's bed. He flipped through the pages. 'You've highlighted it.' Aryan had spent a good couple of hours reading it. The book crammed a surfeit of information in its pages, using the tiniest possible font and forgoing illustrations to fit it all in. It hadn't put him off. He devoured the information.

'It's nothing.' He took hold of the book and slipped it deeper under the bed.

'Aryan, just tell him.'

'I will.'

'You've been saying that for ages. Don't be a coward.'

'I'm not!'

There was a knock on the door. Aryan sprayed some cologne on him, hoping it'd mask the faint smell of smoke clinging to his clothes. He had reduced the number of cigarettes he smoked by an impressive amount, though since he'd had an exam, he allowed himself the one that day. He smoothed his clothes and hair down and opened the door.

'Dad. What are you doing here?' he said, feigning surprise. Dhruv Alekar stepped through the room, his nose elevated and his eyes crossed, like an inspector or detective with a hunch.

'I was driving through. Thought I would come check up on you. See how my son is doing.' He noticed Logan standing by the desk. 'Hello, Logan.'

'Mr Alekar. Good to see you.'

Dhruv nodded, as if in agreement that it was, naturally, good for anyone to see him. 'How are you? Your studies going well?'

'Yeah. Good. Last couple of exams left.'

'Good. What are you going to do afterwards?'

'Graphic design. Although, I might just take a gap year first.'

Dhruv delivered a curt nod. Aryan watched Logan shrink. Dhruv was skilled at provoking fear and shame. Logan excused himself. He told Aryan he'd see him later and wished Dhruv the best, avowing once more that it was *really*, very good to see him again. He scuttled away, leaving Aryan to deal with his father alone.

'Imagine spending all this money for your son to work in design. How is the other friend of yours? The bright one?'

'Omari. He's fine. Studying.'

'As I hope you are,' he said. He picked up Aryan's books and nodded in satisfaction at the proof of highlighter blotting the kaolinite-coated pages. 'I'm pleased to hear your exams have been going well.'

'Yeah. Dad, listen. I've been thinking about studying something other than management.'

His dad faced him. His eyes were fashioned from the crystalline glass of winter ponds. His facial muscles were twitching. 'What do you mean?'

'Well, law might be a good option for me.'

Dhruv heaved a sigh. 'Might be? There is no room for might.'

'All right then, it will be good for me.'

'I understand the attraction to law. But I know you'll love working with me better. People are mistaken. Lawyers slave away and still don't make nearly enough. At least in comparison to how much you'd make with me. And you might not even be any good.'

Aryan winced. Of course, he'd be good. Even if he didn't take to it at first. Even if he needed to study harder than everyone else. He had his doubts, but he had a strong drive and a mind that absorbed information like an unused dish sponge freshly birthed from its packet. He'd be good.

'Well, I think you're wrong. I don't want to work for you, or take over from you. I just don't want that.'

'Excuse me?' he advanced towards Aryan, his face hard and, despite his golden colouring, empty of warmth. 'Why would you say this now? We've been talking about this for years. I built this company for you.'

Aryan's feet were stapled to the ground. He looked his father in the eyes. 'I am not doing it. I want to choose my own course.'

'Aryan.'

'I'll take out a loan and live at home. I'll even study locally. I won't ask for anything.'

Dhruv sneered. 'Stop this. Why can't you see that becoming a lawyer is a good option for others, but not you? You'll be sacrificing a certain lifestyle. You won't be able to send your sons to boarding schools.'

'Do you ever hear yourself? You're so damn selfish,' Aryan snapped. He should have predicted what was going to happen. Dhruv struck him before he even registered the slipping off of the favourite sapphire ring. The one with the chequerboard cut. He felt the impact of his dad's sharp backhand upon his left cheek. With his skin stinging, he clenched his fist and convened a large sum of strength to stop himself from hitting back. He breathed and told himself to take it out on a punchbag later. His father slipped the ring back on to his middle finger.

'That is not how we raised you to speak. How can you be so disrespectful?' he said in his resonant voice. 'You'll receive no allowance for a while, until you learn some manners.'

'I don't care.'

'Aryan. Stop getting upset. Pull yourself together. I've big plans for you.'

Dhruv's phone rang from his shirt pocket. He answered. 'Hello... Yes, everything is in hand... Of course... I will have someone see to the matter immediately... Yes... All right... Bye.' As he hung up, he turned to Aryan.

'I know, you have to go. Bye,' Aryan said.

'Study well and everything will be fine,' he said, stroking Aryan's hair. 'I shall see you at home in a couple of weeks. *Jai Shree Krishna.*'

'*Jai Shree Krishna,*' Aryan whispered back.

Once his father had gone, Aryan grabbed the notebooks from his desk and flung them across the room. He kicked his desk chair over and panted. His body shook with irrepressible fury. He needed to go somewhere. Anywhere. He stormed out of his room and straight into Logan's.

'Ever heard of knocking?' Logan said, buttoning his blue, checked shirt. 'What's up?'

Aryan snatched Logan's hands away from his shirt and kissed him. He removed his lips and told a bewildered Logan: 'I'll come to York. If that's still OK.'

'Really? Good, I'm glad,' Logan said, his eyes glinting in soft, halcyon delight. He slipped a jacket on. 'Look. I'll see you later. I'm going to pop into town for a bit.' He squeezed Aryan's shoulder. 'Hope everything went all right with your dad.'

He left Aryan in his conflicted state. His fists were clenched but his head was light and higher than a kite.

CHAPTER 26

'Aryan, good to see you again,' said Logan's father. Andrew Reeves patted him on the back and took his luggage from him. He had the same blue eyes as Logan, though his hair was a rich, coffee brown. He wore a tweed jacket with elbow patches, over a quiet lilac shirt and beige chinos. He certainly looked the part of the sagacious professor. 'Bet you're glad this is all over now?'

'Yeah. Definitely,' Aryan lied. In truth, there was a hole in his emotion-bucket. He couldn't feel anything and submitted to numbness.

'Louisa, you remember Aryan.' Logan approached Aryan with his seven-year-old sister attached to his back, her arms swinging around his neck. Her blonde hair cascaded down Logan's shoulders in waves, hosting purple and turquoise butterfly pins with glittered wings and a detachable pink braid.

'Hi Aaron,' she piped.

'For the last time, it's Aryan,' Aryan told her.

She stuck out her strawberry-pink tongue in response. 'Are you coming to stay with us?'

'I am.' She struggled off her brother's back. 'We just bought a new trampoline. It's so much fun! Promise you'll jump on it with me!'

'Sure.' He turned to Logan. 'Have you said goodbye to everyone?'

'Yup. We should go say goodbye to Chris and Omari once more, before they leave.'

Chris, Omari, Logan and Aryan came into a group hug and said their goodbyes a final time before separating from each other, gradually, like petals from a fading flower. Brookside had been home for an ample chunk of their childhoods. It was painful to say goodbye to each other and Rushton House, though easy enough to the school itself.

Aryan and Logan jumped into the blue Honda Civic – the humble car against the lines of BMWs and Mercedes. Louisa claimed the front seat, leaving them to squeeze into the back. Aryan's bags took up most of the left side, forcing him and Logan to push up against each other. Half an hour in, after some chatter and music, Logan and Louisa drifted off into sleep. Logan's head gently lolled on to Aryan's shoulder. Aryan pressed his cheek into his hair, feeling a tenderness towards him and relishing the whiff of peppermint swaying off his freshly shampooed hair. His head sprung back up as Andrew peeked into the rearview mirror, almost catching the tame affection.

After a few hours in the car, they arrived at a quaint, semi-detached house. Stretching his body out of the car, Aryan refamiliarised himself with the Reeves's house. The front garden was outfitted with assemblages of perennials and annuals. Terracotta pots flanked the front step, boasting an array of vibrant flowers. Attached to the front door was a rustic, wooden sign with the word 'welcome' painted across it in white. As they entered the house, Aryan caught the alluring scent of cinnamon and baked goods. The house bathed in it and brought back memories of his previous visits. He popped his head into the living room and saw the old, cosy fireplace and the buttercream walls. Corny proverbs were marked on wooden signs and hung up, like the classic: 'the home is where the heart is', which hung proudly above the cedar dining table. The living area was messy, with settees supporting teddy bears, colouring books and their sleeping Golden Retriever – Cheddar. Most surfaces were stacked with endless rows of academic papers and history books. Even with the mess and the cheesy quotes, there was no denying the Reeves's household felt like a home.

Logan led Aryan up to his room. The Reeves family had a small, three-bedroom house. Whenever he visited in the past, he and Logan shared a room, and often the bed. Whenever Logan visited Aryan, it was a different story. They couldn't stay up and talk or play video games, not even on mute in darkness, since his dad would point out Logan would sleep better in a room to himself and he'd be ushered out before they had the chance. Aryan would be restless all night, waiting for the morning to resume the fun.

Logan's room was colourful. Both artsy canvases and music posters were stuck to the parrot green and bright blue walls, along with a basketball net, which hovered directly above a laundry basket. There wasn't much to see, since Logan's stuff was still in his bags. The room begged to be filled.

'I'll stick your stuff here,' Logan said. Aryan nodded, without registering where Logan meant. He couldn't remove his focus from the bed. Sharing a bed with Logan made his palms moisten and his head flood with questions. Images of him entangling himself with his friend, his best friend, beneath the sheets were a little scary. What exactly would Logan be expecting?

'You have a sleeping bag, right?' Aryan asked.

'Yeah. I told you I'd lend you one for camping.'

'No, I mean for tonight.'

'Oh.' Logan scratched the back of his neck. 'I guess, I'll look for it before we sleep. What do you want to do right now?' What did he mean by that? Aryan thought of the things they could do together and felt his temperature rising.

'Maybe we could... play Fifa?' he finally suggested. That's what they'd normally do. Logan agreed and unpacked his

PlayStation to connect to the television. He handed Aryan a controller and they began playing. As they settled on the edge of the bed, Aryan was aware of Logan's knee slightly pressing against his. 'All right, Alekar. Winner picks the movie we watch later. Let's go.'

'Don't think I'll go easy on you.'

'Wouldn't dream of it.'

As soon as they began playing the game, Aryan started to forget his anxieties about the night. Within a few minutes, he drew the ball away from Logan and straight into the goal. 'Too bad, Reeves! I forget how bad you are at this.'

'I got it. I got it.'

Aryan watched Logan bashing the buttons in a random order and tutted. 'Mate, you've got to develop some kind of strategy. This is why you keep losing.' Aryan scored another goal.

'Oi! Ease up.'

As his confusion grew again in his mind, Aryan dropped his focus and let Logan take the lead.

'So… question. The rest of your family are Christians. Are they all right, you know, with the whole gay thing?' Aryan wondered why he was asking. By talking about the 'gay thing', he was removing the normalcy from their friendship again and bringing to light those same bed-related questions.

'Oh. Yeah. They're fine with it.'

'How did you tell them?'

'I didn't exactly. My grandad found out first. He caught me kissing one of the regulars out back. Pretty embarrassing. Oh… man! I could've scored that.'

'Oh.' Aryan never knew there were other boys. He thought there was only Brad. He wondered what other information Logan had withheld. What lay behind the tight flaps and coverings? 'What did they say?'

'They were surprised. And I thought they'd say it was

wrong. But then they said if something is done out of love and isn't harming anyone, it can't be wrong. What is it that Hinduism says? I wondered.'

Aryan shrugged. 'I don't know. Culture and religion are so tangled, it gets kind of confusing. Culturally, I know it's unacceptable, but I'm not sure what Hinduism itself says. It's like sex within Indian culture is a taboo subject, right? But within religion it's a pure and sacred thing. It's weird.'

'Sounds it. You can't even talk about it at home, can you?'

Aryan snorted. 'My mum thinks *EastEnders* is too raunchy. What do you think?'

Aryan scored another goal and Logan threw down his controller. 'OK. Break.' He spread himself across the bed like a starfish.

'So, did you tell your dad about studying law?'

'I tried,' Aryan said.

'And? How did he react? What did he say?'

'Nothing. Leave it alone.'

'Why? Go on. Tell me.'

'No.'

Logan propped himself up. 'Aryan. Come on.'

'He said no and whacked me across the face.'

'Oh.'

Logan grabbed Aryan's hand and squeezed. Aryan snatched his hand away and looked towards the door. Even though there was nobody there, nobody to play witness or taunt him, it was too much in that moment.

'What's wrong?'

'Just don't. OK?' He was conscious of how his palm retained the heat of Logan's hand. He never understood handholding, but he'd be lying if he said the experience of holding Logan's was unpleasant. 'Let's just continue playing. I'll go easy on you.'

When they finished their game, Andrew was in the middle of marking dissertations. He handed Logan a wad of cash for food. They ordered two large margarita pizzas and potato wedges and settled in Logan's room to watch *The Lord of the Rings*. They watched it so many times over the years, they could speak along with the characters. When they were younger, they'd re-enact their favourite scenes. It was the height of amusement, taking hold of the mop in the Rushton House kitchenette, transforming it into a staff and screaming 'You shall not pass!' like the old wizard they venerated.

Louisa snuck in halfway through the viewing, insisting she was, no matter what 'Daddy' said, old enough to watch it. Logan told her she wasn't, so she stamped her foot and widened her eyes, her lip sticking out and quivering.

'Just let her. It's only *Lord of the Rings*,' Aryan said. She wedged herself between Logan and Aryan. Her mouth hung open for the remainder of the film. She hid her face into Aryan's arm when the orcs appeared, shuddering with a mixture of fear and bliss.

'They're so ugly,' she cried in horror.

'That one looks a bit like you,' Aryan pointed to the bulky, leading orc with a fanged mouth and bluish veins ascending his face.

'Logan!' she shrieked. 'Tell him!'

'He's right. God, Lou. You should have auditioned for the film, maybe then we'd have more money.'

She left the room to tell her dad they were being cruel to her, returning once she realised she couldn't possibly admit to watching the film without his permission.

Once the film finished, Logan and Aryan were both exhausted, having spent their energy on last-minute packing and travelling. Aryan slid into the sleeping bag that they managed to bring down from the top of Logan's wardrobe. In the dark, he listened to the rise and fall of Logan's breath. As the minutes passed, the tempo of his breathing slackened and he was sure he was asleep. He glanced over and thought he was being ridiculous, sleeping on the floor. They shared a bed hundreds of times in the past. Just as he thought of abandoning the bag and creeping into the bed, the bedroom door opened and a small outline of a figure stepped in.

'Logan,' Louisa whispered. Logan stirred in his bed, grumbling, but did not wake. 'Logan.'

'What's wrong?' Aryan asked her, propping himself up on his elbows.

'I can't sleep. I can't stop thinking of the orcs and Daddy's not in his room yet. Can I sleep here?'

'I don't think he'd say no,' he said. 'Just get in.'

She tiptoed across the room and slithered beneath the duvet. She curled up by her brother and rested her head on his outstretched arm. Aryan missed his opportunity. 'Didn't they scare you?' she asked Aryan, wriggling round to face him.

'No, of course not.'

'Do you ever get scared? Of anything?'

'No.'

'Not even of the dark? Or spiders? Or ghosts?'

'No.'

'But Logan says everyone gets scared sometimes.'

'Did he?'

'Yeah. He says his biggest fear is losing people, like me, or Daddy. He said losing Mummy was the scariest thing in the world. But he says it's silly to worry about things like that.'

'He's right. That's why I don't bother with fear. Now go to sleep, OK?'

'OK. Goodnight,' she said in a sleepy voice.

That night he dreamed Logan was no longer a part of his life. The loss of him was terrifying.

CHAPTER 27

They arrived at the Dales the next morning. The weather was kind, teetering between clement and cool. The dazzling sun lay recumbent across the clear sky and decanted sheens of light to the earth. The wind whined, straddled by a hostile cold. The grass of the camping park was fine-tipped and bright and the birds tweeted summer songs as the caravans hummed in the background. Logan sat on the grassy bank, watching the battle between Aryan and a two-man tent.

'I'm telling you, you're not doing it right,' Logan said, for the third time.

'I know what I'm doing,' Aryan said. It was a lie. He hadn't the foggiest idea about how to pitch tents. Suffering with the condition of hunger, he did not have the patience to have someone teach him. How hard could it be, anyway? Common sense was all you needed, he declared. Logan told him he was being ridiculous and should swallow his pride and listen, but soon decided to give into Aryan's will. Now he sat there, laughing at Aryan's struggles and adding to his irritation.

'It's defective,' Aryan announced, unable to make the tent rise.

'You've not done too bad. You've got to thread the poles through the clips in the corners now.'

'I know that!' he growled. He hadn't seen the clips. When Aryan had enough and commenced kicking the tent, Logan jumped to his feet and rushed towards the tent to take over. Aryan fell to the earth, reaching into the cooler bag by him for a can of beer. Logan erected the tent before he'd taken a third sip. Smug-faced, Logan explained to him, step-by-step, the correct process of pitching a tent.

'Oh, piss off!' Aryan replied.

They trailed over to a place called The Knight's Table to mollify their grumbling stomachs with generous portions of pizza, chips and (for Aryan) a grilled chicken breast. After Aryan ate, his mood thawed, transforming him from stony cold to tepid. He was ready for adventure. As soon as they paid the bill, they embarked on a journey across the grassy landscapes of the Yorkshire Dales, in awe of their surroundings and energised by the volatile gales fronting them.

'If we were younger, we'd probably pretend we were on a journey to Mordor. Just leaving the Shires,' Logan said, skimming the hills ahead.

'Probably. I'd be Samwise. You'd be Frodo.'

'Dream on. You'd be Frodo.'

'You can be an elf. They can't grow proper facial hair either.'

'Hilarious.'

They found themselves on a bridge, watching the River Ribble tumbling into a series of mini waterfalls ahead. Aryan leaned over the stony bridge wall and focused on the frolicking water. Their silence wasn't awkward. It was serene. Being out in nature, away from exam halls and classrooms, made him feel free. There was something about being on a bridge, gazing at a river that made you think with clarity, as if a misty haze had dislodged itself from behind your eyes. Logan pointed out a few birds to Aryan. He explained how he and his dad used to birdwatch when he was younger, and how he was never patient enough to look for birds but found pleasure in identifying them when they flew into sight. He told Aryan he liked the tree pipits best. He liked calling them tree pipits. They both started repeating the word 'pipit', childishly finding too much humour in the word. Aryan uncrossed his arms and allowed them to dangle. His hand brushed against Logan's hand. Impulsively, he took it.

'So, what happens now?' Aryan asked.

'I don't know. We just be as we've always been. Throw in a few benefits.'

This only raised a hundred more questions. 'Like what? What exactly is it that you…?' Aryan hoped Logan mistook the pinkening of his cheeks as a reaction to the cold. He hated being out of his depth. He knew what to do and how to do it (and excel in doing it, he'd argue) with a female, but he wasn't sure what to do with a male. Wasn't it the same sort of thing? He did what he imagined most people did when considering the nature of gay sex: he jumped to penetration, picturing one man on his fours and the other behind. For him, it was an image of nightmares, depending on which role he'd have to take. If he could keep his usual role, he supposed it was all right. Still masculine – or was it wrong to think that way? What if being with a guy was nowhere near as good as being with a girl? His mind was ready to fulminate.

'Hey. Nothing you're uncomfortable with has to happen. You know some gay dudes never do it the way you're thinking. It's all down to preference. No rules.'

'So, if not that, then just everything else?' Surely, not as good as being with a girl then.

'I guess. Like I said, no rules,' Logan replied, punching his arm. 'Relax, will you? You think too much. Come on.'

They hired a pair of bikes and continued their journey across the Dales. They discovered waterfalls leaping over rocks and sheep grazing in fields. There was such an abundance of fresh air, the crispness of it was overwhelming. They zigzagged through groups of trees and raced down steep, tortuous paths.

Aryan gave him a head start and still won the race, though Logan refused to count it because, he claimed, a bug flew into his eye. After they had taken in as much greenery as they could, they wheeled their bikes back to the campsite, where they drank hot chocolate from Styrofoam cups, topped with globs of clotted cream and marshmallows. As they relaxed, Logan strummed a few tunes on his guitar. He tried to show Aryan how to play a couple of chords. Unable to get a clear sound out of an F chord, Aryan decried the guitar a useless instrument. Logan laughed and Aryan was thankful he chose to follow him to York.

In the tent that night, it was cold. Aryan shivered, much to Logan's amusement. It seemed Northerners really didn't get cold.

'Here. Unzip your sleeping bag,' Logan said, undoing his. He took the ends of their bags and zipped them together to form one, enormous bag. He scooted closer and Aryan's heart thumped aggressively. 'I'll keep you warm.'

Logan's arm rested on Aryan's chest. They were facing each other. A torch shone from a netted pouch, illuminating the tent. Aryan was captivated by Logan's irises. They were electric blue flames. Like gas-fire erupting from the stove. He reached out and stroked his face with the back of his hand. Then, without hesitation, soared forward and kissed him. Aryan felt Logan's hand climb up his skin beneath the layers of clothing. Logan gently nibbled on his neck. His mouth was warm. He sat up and removed clothing from the top half of his body, baring his smooth and toned body. He began tugging at Aryan's clothes.

'It's freezing,' Aryan protested, though the sight of Logan's half-naked body made him feel a little hot.

'I promise, I'll keep you warm,' he whispered, unzipping Aryan's jacket. Aryan stripped his layers off. His hands eagerly ran across Logan's chest. Their breathing quickened, as they absorbed each other's body heat, closing any gaps between them. Logan bestowed kisses on Aryan's body, moving south and pressing harder with each one. Eventually, Aryan's remaining garments were below his knees. Logan stayed at his middle, performing for his pleasure. At first, Aryan's reaction was to panic, to push him off and curse him. He thought he'd detonate with anger. But he felt a rush of pleasure that his body couldn't contend with. He ran his fingers through Logan's hair and, to his surprise, told him not to stop. When he passed the final goal, Logan rose to lie by him again. 'OK?'

'More than OK.' Aryan kissed Logan. He was about to reciprocate, preparing to move down Logan's body, but he was stopped.

'You don't have to. If you don't want to,' he said, stroking Aryan's neck. Aryan grabbed his arm and pinned it above his head.

'I want to,' he said. He lunged for his neck. Logan gasped at the sudden movement. Aryan journeyed across his body, arriving at the place that wrested quiet moans from his lover's mouth. He dug his fingertips into Logan's back, feeling his gentle convulsions and endeavouring to produce more. He never once cared for another person's pleasure before.

After their amorous exercise was over, they put their clothes back on. Logan fell asleep first. Aryan gazed at him beneath the glow of the torch. His hand couldn't be deterred from reaching for his sleeping partner's face. They had always been comfortable with each other, but now, when he touched his skin, there was a difference – an electrifying effect whirling at his fingertips and seeping to the base. He remembered when he was gifted an expensive watch. He kept tracing the face of it with his finger, ogling at the value of it – examining every precious detail. He was doing the same now. Yet, some part of him somewhere still wanted to deface him with marker pens; or play the clownish prank of placing whipped cream in his hand, before tickling the edge of his nose with a feather; or take embarrassing pictures to blackmail him with. But then he wanted to protect him and play with his hair, while he dozed in his vulnerability.

Logan felt like home and a hotel in a foreign country. He was a brand-new adventure and a familiar promenade through the neighbourhood. He was the Yorkshire Dales. Laying there with him in a wind-battered tent as the rain pelted outside, Aryan knew he wouldn't have liked camping, if he didn't equate it with everything that was essentially Logan.

CHAPTER 28

'Hey again,' Maansi spoke to Sejal over the phone. Maansi's eyes were fastened to the clock. It was getting late and her husband still hadn't returned home. 'Maybe I was right in the first place. Maybe arranged marriages are a terrible idea.' She suddenly felt overcome with emotion. She dabbed at the corners of her eyes. Alcohol had a way of drawing out the rest of her emotions from their locked cells.

'Yeah. I'm sorry I told you it could be destiny,' Sejal said. 'I was distracted by his stupid good Avan Jogia looks. We're smart. Why do we do dumb things?'

'I know! This is so ridiculous. I know nothing about him. He could be a drug dealer. I mean, he smokes. How much of a jump is it from cigarettes to drugs? I mean, really?' She waited for Sejal's playful castigations. Of course, she didn't believe that for a second. 'Hello? Sejal?'

'I'm here. Listen, Maansi, maybe he is like that. I mean, I heard rumours but I never thought much of them.'

Maansi remembered Sejal tried to tell her about the rumours circling Aryan, but she had silenced her, too proud and too desperate for change to listen.

'Tell me,' she asked, on the edge of the chair now. 'Go on.'

Sejal hesitated. 'Well, I know one of his cousins. I just mentioned Aryan when I saw they were mutual friends online. He said ages ago Aryan was sent to India, to curb his addiction.'

'Addiction? What addiction? Oh God, I was joking about the drugs...'

221

'Sex addiction.'

Maansi froze. There was a bubble rising in her chest. She didn't know whether it was to be a laugh or an incredulous gasp. 'Excuse me? Sex addiction? What sex addiction?' She punched each syllable forward, demanding to be answered.

'That's what I've heard. His parents found out he couldn't keep it in his pants and they sent him to India, to find God and be healed or whatever. I know it sounds ridiculous, but do you think it's true? Maybe he's relapsed and he goes to sleep with other women. Isn't that what an addict would do? I don't know. I didn't even know it was a thing!'

'Oh, come on. That's crazy. We haven't even been sleeping together much. He isn't sex-crazed.' But what if he was? Maansi thought. What if his anger towards her depression was a deflection from the real problem? He announced he understood why she'd been rejecting him as he held the blister pack, focusing on the absence of intimacy as a symptom. It sounded perfectly logical. Or maybe the wine was clouding her mind. 'If you knew this, why didn't you tell me? You'd let me go off with a sex addict?'

'You didn't want to listen and it was only a rumour. The cousin mentioned drugs too! Who knows if it's true? Even if it was, his cousin said his parents sent him to India for a whole year for treatment. So, he must be all right now. Right?'

'I don't know what to believe,' she said. 'I need to go and call my husband, find out where the hell he is, find out about his previous relationships and find out the truth about this so-called addiction he has. Sorry *might* have. Then, I need to ask him what his problem is with my co-worker. Well, ex-co-worker. God!'

'Yikes.'

'Honestly, I wish I hadn't married him. Nothing is ever easy.'

'You can always dump his arse. Let people talk.'

'I know. I'll ring you back.'

She hung up the phone and dialled Aryan's number once more. She remembered, again, her struggle to understand his reason for marrying young. The puzzle of his parents' insistence. The confusion of how his hot head could even allow him to cede his freedom.

'The person you are calling is currently unavailable. Please try again later.'

CHAPTER 29

'You sure you still want me to come with you?' Logan asked.

'Of course.'

Logan helped haul Aryan's bags and suitcase downstairs. The driver took the bags and loaded them into the car. Aryan reminded Logan this was his family's servant, or as he was supposed to be called in Britain, their 'domestic worker'. His name was Minal. Minal had golden skin and deep-set dimples in his rounded cheeks.

During the car journey, Minal and Aryan held brief conversations in Hindi. Logan was always impressed by the way Aryan could easily switch between languages without thinking. Without a pinch of effort, he could transition between English, Hindi and Punjabi. He remembered how angry Aryan got when he once referred to Hindi as 'Hindu'.

'Hinduism is a religion. Hindi is the national language of India, Logan, it's not fucking hard!'

Logan liked the way Hindi sounded. The words seemed to flow into one another. He remembered staying with Aryan a couple of summers back. Aryan was ill one night and retired to bed early. He wasn't up for sleeping, so he sat with Aryan's mother and watched a Bollywood film. He didn't remember the name of it – not that he'd be able to pronounce it anyway. He couldn't always keep up with the subtitles and found the sound effects jarring and much of the storyline unrealistic, if not senseless. Yet, he enjoyed it. The dance numbers and the poetic language they used in songs. The rich and ornate clothes. The intense action scenes. The profound declarations of love. He savoured the whole thing, which was an achievement, considering the length of it. Aryan's mother was pleased he loved the film. She told him she didn't understand why more people didn't take an interest in their culture. Even Aryan lacked an appreciation for it at times.

The journey to Knightsbridge took four hours. By the time they were out of the car, Logan's face turned pale green. 'I'm fine,' he said, trying not to hurl up his innards all over the pavement. As he entered Aryan's home, he was instantly distracted from the griping churns of his stomach. No matter how many times he visited, he was always astounded by the sumptuous elegance of the Alekar home. The floors were marble and there was a spiralling staircase. Hung upon walls were family photos encased in golden, leaf-patterned frames. Amber light glimmered from the crystal pear drops of the grandiose chandelier. As they stepped in further, the paintings of Gods with sky-blue skin and meditative eyes appeared, one of whom held a flute to his lips, an awestruck doe strolling beside him. In the middle of the hall, pressed against the wall, was a bookshelf displaying books on Greek mythology, the philosophy of Stoicism and the full works of Shakespeare.

Aryan's mum appeared, wearing a designer fuchsia dress, with a string of pearls hanging from her neck. As she hugged them, Logan caught the delicate aroma of rose on her skin. 'Boys! You're finally here. Come, come have something small to eat before dinner.' She led them to the kitchen, where she had plated slices of fruit cake and laid out cups of spiced tea upon a table garbed in rich, brocade cloth.

'I'm telling you Mrs Alekar, every time I come here, I'm amazed by this house,' Logan said, enjoying the sweetness of the candied sultanas.

'Thank you, Logan,' she said. 'Have some more. Make sure you finish it. Here.' She gave them another three slices each. Aryan and Logan eyed each other. How they were going to get through the fruit cake was beyond them. But, of course, as always, Aryan's mother would push for them to take every crumb. She hummed to herself and watched Aryan, her face aglow.

'Are you OK, Mum?' Aryan asked her.

'Yes, sweetheart. So much happier now that you're home. I've missed you so much.' She stroked his hair and he rolled his eyes. Logan grinned at him as he shied away from her affection.

With fruit cake weighing them down, Logan followed Aryan upstairs. Inside Aryan's bedroom, the walls were a gleaming white, the floor a mid-tone grey and his bedding black. Save one canvas of a motorbike on the wall, there were no other embellishments. 'Your room is so boring,' he remarked, though every surface seemed to sparkle.

Aryan seized Logan's wrist and drew him towards him, sending his heart sprinting. He expected a passionate kiss to follow, but his hope crumbled as Aryan unbridled his greatest worry. 'My parents can't find out. OK?' he said. In the centre of his dilated eyes collected an almost tangible fear. 'If they do, everything will be over.'

'But—'

'No buts. Or ifs. Just no. All hell would break loose.'

Logan knew they had been glossing over the parent problem. It was why he knew he couldn't take their relationship seriously. This was probably a bit of fun for Aryan. A genuine relationship that transcended their friendship wouldn't work. He felt stupid for thinking otherwise. 'OK. I get it. No problem.'

Damini called for them and they made their way downstairs to the dining table. Aryan's father had arrived and had taken up his position at the head of the dining table. He saw Logan and Aryan and said, 'Hello.' Aryan and Logan murmured their hellos. Logan didn't know why Dhruv wasn't throwing his arms around Aryan, expressing his joy over his son being home and congratulating him on finishing school. Logan plopped down on a chair, his shoulders turning inwards as Dhruv passed his eyes over him, like a judge in a courtroom. Dhruv didn't exude the same easy affability that Aryan's mother coasted in. The plates were placed in front of them. Dinner was a potato and pea curry garnished with coriander and served with steaming, cumin-infused rice.

'Here, Logan, it might be too spicy for you,' Damini said, as she poured some yoghurt on his plate to cool his palate.

'Oh, don't worry about it, I'm all right with spice,' he reassured her. She bore into him with incredulity, then heaped more yoghurt on to his plate. Aryan snorted and Logan delivered a quick blow to his knee beneath the table. Everyone ate dinner in silence. It was an uncomfortable scene. He couldn't remember it being this bad before. Eventually, Dhruv struck up a conversation.

'So, you want a career in graphic design then, Logan?'

Logan jumped as Dhruv's voice drilled through the quiet. 'Oh, I don't know. I guess so. Or illustration or something.'

'You mean, a career in drawing pictures,' Dhruv said. 'Why is that? You've been schooled at a fine institution. Is there not something more lucrative to do?'

Aryan met his father with a glare. Damini cut in. 'He's following his passion, aren't you?' she offered with sympathy. 'If you're good at something, then why not?'

'Yeah. And you can make design lucrative. Maybe start your own design agency…' Aryan continued.

'That's your ambition?'

'N-no, I haven't really thought about it.'

'Well, planning is the first step to success. You must think of everything, from every angle, to achieve your goal,' Dhruv said. 'Create a timeline and write down practical things you'll do every day to get where you want to be. That's what I did. That's what I've taught Aryan.'

'Do we always have to talk on the same subject?' Aryan asked, an acrid quality surfacing in his tone and his foot tapping against the floor. Dhruv lowered his cutlery and stared at Aryan with an unreadable, yet chilling visage until the tapping stopped and Aryan refocused his attention on his food. Damini drained her glass of water.

'Any more yoghurt, Logan?' she asked.

'No, thank you.'

'More curry? Rice? Have some salad.'

'I'm great, thanks, Mrs Alekar.'

They ate in more uneasy silence, before Dhruv reignited the conversation with: 'So, boys. You've finished at Brookside. Do you think you'll get good results?'

'Well, Aryan helped me study a lot, so I bet I will,' Logan said.

'And Aryan?'

'You know I will,' he said.

'So, how is your family?' Damini asked Logan, veering them away from the same-old talks about education. 'How is your little sister?'

'She's doing well, thanks.'

'And will she be attending Brookside too?' Dhruv asked.

'Maybe when she's of secondary age. Though, it depends on whether she wants to,' Logan replied. 'I don't think she'd want to part from Cheddar, to be honest,' he laughed meekly.

'Excuse me?' Dhruv asked.

'Oh, sorry, our dog. His name is... Cheddar.'

'Cheddar is a type of cheese,' Dhruv stated, creases forming along his forehead.

'I know... it's just...' he let himself trail off. He feigned biting into something hot and swallowed a few spoons of yoghurt, as if it were medicinal syrup. He thought it'd be best if he kept his mouth shut.

After finishing their dinner, Logan and Aryan left the dining room and collapsed at the kitchen table, tired from the lashing tensions of dinner. As they consumed cups of coffee, Logan rubbed his stomach, regretting eating so much. Damini asked if his stomach was all right.

'Uhrm. Yes,' he answered. 'Does she think I can't handle a curry because I'm not Indian?' Logan whispered to Aryan as she fetched something from the cupboard. Aryan confirmed the theory. She returned and placed a jar on the table, covered in orange and yellow wrapping, the word 'Hajmola' bouncing across the front in supersized letters.

'What is that?' Logan asked Aryan.

'It's for digestion. I don't think you could handle it.'

'Why does your mum think... what do you mean handle it? I can handle it,' he said, sitting up in his chair. 'Why couldn't I handle it?'

'Because you're white,' Aryan teased. 'You can't handle it.'

'Oh, really?'

Aryan winked and pushed the jar towards him. Logan unscrewed the top and took a whiff. He burst into a fit of coughs. 'What is that smell?' he asked. 'Pepper?'

'It's Ayurvedic medicine. It's made up of a bunch of herbs. It's popular in India.'

Logan dropped one into his hand. It was an ash-brown,

round tablet, compact with herbs and spice. 'What will happen?'

'Nothing. You just suck on it and it helps your digestion. Used to eat them as a kid. Just for fun, really.'

Logan examined the tablet with suspicion. 'For the record, there is nothing wrong with my stomach,' he said, before launching the Hajmola into his mouth. He could handle it. He hated it when Aryan assumed otherwise. He sucked on it slowly, his lips pursing and his face contorting as the overwhelming, pungent taste took over. He jumped in his seat, his cheeks in spasms. He cupped his hand over his mouth.

'Told you, you can't handle it,' Aryan chuckled, amused by the display of Logan banging his fist on the table. 'Just spit it out.'

'Mmm… no… handling it…' he said. He made the intrepid decision to bite down on the tablet and chew. It was as if somebody decided to squeeze every available herb and spice in the world into one, single tablet. As he ground the last of it down and swallowed, he shuddered. He swept his tongue over his molars to get the last grains.

Aryan took a Hajmola himself and tossed it into his mouth. He chewed on it as if it were a soft mint – something considerably more palatable – without so much as wincing or moistening his tear ducts.

'Show off,' Logan muttered.

Sitting through dinner with the Alekars exhausted Logan and he longed for the safety of a soft bed. He expected to be offered a spare bedroom, following in the line of tradition, but Aryan invited him into his own. 'We aren't kids any more. They're not going to separate us to make sure we sleep.'

In bed, there was distance between him and Aryan. He didn't believe they were going to venture across each other as they did in the tent. He could tell Aryan had fallen asleep from the sound of his breathing, like a tide moving on and off sandy shores. He found it difficult to fall asleep next to him with hands twitching, aching to touch. He squeezed his pillow and after a period of tossing and turning, his attention was snatched by a low, wailing sound. At first, he thought it was a cat yowling outside. As it continued, he realised it held a more spectral quality and spilt like molasses through the house, in long, tired drawls. It continued for a while and came to bother him. He left the bed and tiptoed on to the landing, keen on locating the source of the sound. It led him to outside the master bedroom. The hiss of lacerating words came from inside and a deep, plaintive howl radiated through the wall.

He tiptoed towards the door to listen.

'He'll be going to university soon. He's already an adult. You sent him away from me for his childhood. From his own mother.'

'Because that's what is best for him. You're being selfish. If I could give him the best, why wouldn't I? We had nothing growing up. You know my father was ill. I had to give up my education. I'm giving him everything I wished for.'

The conversation then switched to Hindi, or Punjabi, he had no way of telling. All he knew was they were having an argument.

When he re-entered Aryan's room, the bedside lamp was switched on. Aryan was awake. He rolled towards him. 'Where have you been?'

'I heard noises. Your mum's crying. Really crying. Think your dad's arguing with her,' he whispered.

Aryan groaned. 'They'll never change.' He ran his hands through his hair and huffed.

'It's so strange. Your mum's warm when your dad's not around. Together, they freeze up the place,' Logan said, repositioning himself in bed. He twisted his body round to face Aryan. They were only a hand's width apart.

'They have a loveless marriage. They don't love each other and no one here knows how to love. Or how to even recognise it.'

'You think you can't love or recognise it?' Logan asked, struggling to picture a family barren of affection. He considered the Alekar family. Their tongues were tied like military knots and their eyes were eternally lowered, as if seeking discolouration on their already perfect floors. They argued. They did not speak. They barely touched.

'I thought that. Before.' Aryan's eyes locked on Logan, almost propelling him out of his skin. He didn't want Aryan, for a second, to think he was unwanted. The eggshells beneath his feet crunched and he no longer cared for the protection of his own feelings.

'I know it's soon. Well, it isn't, I've known you for bloody ages, really. But I want you to know, that I think I… I mean… I do. I do know that I…' he stammered.

'I love you too,' Aryan said. Logan was stunned into silence. Aryan's eyes were hard but sincere. He discharged those words like a cold fact, but it didn't diminish the meaning behind his words. It gave them bones.

'Good. I love you too… too,' he whispered back. He quietly rebuked himself. It was embarrassing, being reduced to a pack of nerves before his friend. Aryan smiled and scooted closer to him. His lips were so close to his. Then a worry came over Logan. 'Would a relationship between us ever go anywhere?'

'Mm. My parents probably wouldn't accept a blonde, Christian girl. Forget a guy,' Aryan said. 'It's always had to be a girl, preferably Hindu-Punjabi, or at least Hindu, from the same caste and from a respected family.'

'Then what's your plan? Never to tell them?'

'I don't know. I just know they've already made every decision for me. They can't make them all.'

A stretch of heat rose into his face. 'You know what? They shouldn't be making any. Like if you don't want to study management, don't! If they don't give you money, then go for a loan. Go for bog standard accommodation, get a part-time job. There could be scholarships and hardship funds. You might not be able to afford London, but wherever you go you'll be fine,' he spoke ardently.

'I haven't worked a day in my life.'

'So? You have to start somewhere. Why are you so desperate for your dad's approval?'

'I'm not!' Aryan snapped. He fell silent and began to ponder. 'Maybe you're right. But I can't reapply for the coming academic year. What do I do for the year?'

'Come stay with me,' Logan said. 'Get a job. Save the money. Take some of what I earn. I'm not desperate to go abroad.'

'I'll never take your money. Isn't it a bit too soon to live together?'

'Um. Hello. We lived together at Brookside,' Logan said. 'Look. If this doesn't work out, it won't get weird. We'll always be mates first. Agreed?'

Aryan smiled. 'Agreed.'

Wrapped up in the warmth of this certainty, their eyelids flickered shut and they fell asleep. When Logan woke a few hours later, he found he was comforted by the warmth of Aryan's skin upon his. Aryan's breath tickled the side of his face. It connected him to him. This wasn't the same as what he had with anyone else. With others, like Brad, everything was purely physical. Brad never had his heartstrings in the palm of his hand like Aryan did. He tugged at them like a child with a kite string: gently, but with enough power to stir him.

CHAPTER 30

Logan was mumbling in his sleep again. It woke Aryan up in the early hours of the day. His LED alarm clock flashed 8:00 at him in lurid red. He grabbed his laptop from the bedside table and climbed out of bed, trying to be as quiet as possible to avoid waking his slumbering friend. As he trod on to the landing, he could hear his parents shuffling about downstairs. His parents rose as early as the blackbirds and robins do for the dawn chorus. Even on weekends. He could hear Minal praying as he lit the *Agarbatti* in the prayer room and his mother speaking in rapid Punjabi down the phone. His brain automatically translated the words to English. 'Of course, everyone here is fine. Aryan will be going to university soon. As if I haven't suffered enough with him being away for boarding school.'

He stole away into a spare room to be alone. He had to do this now. He couldn't wait until results day. If he achieved his grades and got a congratulatory letter from the university, he knew he'd become an addlepated mess. He wouldn't toss aside the pleasure of success, even if the success was wrong for him. He needed to end it now. He allowed the cursor to hover over the withdraw button for a few moments. The questions began to sprout, one by one. Was this the right decision? Had he thought this through? They piled on top of each other, each pushier than the last. He forced himself to stop thinking. When the modicum of pure silence arrived, he clicked withdraw. He confirmed he was sure and his application to LSE – on which he laboured for days – vanished.

He climbed back into bed, his stomach in knots. He wanted to tell Logan what he'd done but he was still asleep. He stroked Logan's hair and listened with amusement to his asinine mumbles. He was a strange one. Aryan buried his face into the back of his neck, into the little, invisible blonde hairs that tickled his skin. What he had just done was unprecedented. Sure, he had used distance from his father to practise autonomy in boarding school, steering away from what he should have been doing. But this was new. This would be mutiny in his father's eyes. This was more than a little bit risky.

'I'm not afraid of him,' he remembered telling himself at twelve, noting the way his purple bruise faded into the same yellow of turmeric-stained nails. He wiped away his tears and said he'd never cry again. It was his tears that turned his skin mauve. It was his tears that disgusted Dhruv so much and drove his hand. So, he learned to use logic. But now, he needn't protest at all. He was a man. He should have the freedom of one. Though he was resolute in that, his heart beat to an unsteady rhythm. He sighed.

'Aryan,' Logan yawned and turned towards him. 'You awake?'

'No. I'm asleep.'

'You're so bloody pleasant in the mornings,' Logan tutted. Aryan sought Logan's hand beneath the sheets and stroked it. The tips of his fingers were tough and calloused from his habit of pressing guitar strings to a fret board, yet the caress had the same comfort of a soft throw. 'What's wrong?'

'I cancelled my application.'

'Fuck. You did? That's great!' He squeezed Aryan's arm. 'If you do find yourself needing to escape, I meant what I said. You can come stay with me.'

'Thanks, Logan. You're a good mate.'

Aryan slated his choice of words. He was calling him a

good mate, when only last night he told him he loved him. He replayed the reveal in his head. He said the words with conviction and he meant them, but he still felt weaker for having spoken them, as if he'd offered something vital to his own survival to Logan for safekeeping. He supposed they'd call it his heart.

'Do you want to rehearse?' Logan said.

'To get out of trouble or for the speaking test?' Aryan mumbled, wishing he was stuck with those choices again. Now was the time to deal with a more serious situation. 'Go back to sleep. I've got this.'

He paced the floor outside the living room, hoping for windstorms of courage to take hold of him. With a firm anticipation for war, he entered the living room. Dhruv sat on his plush, leather armchair, a newspaper in his hands, his spectacles concealing the steeliness of his eyes as they balanced on the end of his streamlined nose. Aryan stood before him and let the news peel from his lips like hot wax from skin. 'I've withdrawn from university. I won't be studying business management.'

Dhruv folded the newspaper and placed it on the coffee table. In his own time, he removed his reading spectacles and entrapped them in their case. He looked at Aryan – his face grave. 'Why have you done this?'

'Because it's what I want to do. You created your own life from scratch. You did what you wanted to do and nobody stopped you.' He spoke with an expanding chest and balled fists. His voice was coarse and steady. He waited for hellfire.

'Fine. It is done,' Dhruv said. 'I am disappointed because

I believe I know what is best for you. And I just want to give you everything you deserve. But if this is what you want, then fine. I will not stand in your way. Just don't come crying to me if you are wrong.'

Aryan's shoulders drooped. 'So, that's it?'

'Yes. But you can't idle around this year. You will still work for me. Who knows? You might like it, you've never given it a chance,' he said. 'Otherwise, find your own way. You are a man now.'

Aryan was speechless. He uttered what vaguely sounded like a thank you and left the room. His father had given him the reins to his own life. He was in charge. He was in the cockpit. It was all up to him! His chest inflated with pleasure. Though a part of him – the part that knew best – feared his dad would change his mind.

CHAPTER 31

'Come on, Damini. Let's go,' Dhruv said, already dressed and ready to leave. 'You know what will happen if we keep Renu waiting.'

'Yes, yes. I know what that woman is like,' Damini said, slipping her feet into a pair of high-heels.

Aryan and Logan were settled in the unlit living room, their eyes stuck to the television screen and their hands submerged in a tub of popcorn. 'Will you boys be all right?' Damini asked. They nodded. 'OK. See you later then, sweethearts.'

Moments later, came the definitive sound of the front door slamming shut.

'So now what?' Logan asked, setting the popcorn aside.

'Hmm?' The film hooked Aryan. He watched as Leonardo DiCaprio tried to piece together a complete picture in the dark depths of the patients' ward, his character's skin clammy with sweat and his hands unsteady. He watched fixedly, awaiting the next twist. The tension built as DiCaprio trod further along the narrow corridors, his footsteps echoing into the gaping maw of darkness. Before the scene could unfold itself, the television switched off. Aryan heard the thud of the remote as Logan dropped it on to the leather sofa.

'What is wrong with you? Put it back on!' He went to snatch the remote, but Logan got there first.

'Me? What is wrong with you? Your parents are gone, your servant dude is not here either...' He swung one leg over Aryan and stroked the nape of his neck.

'We can do this later. They'll be gone ages. Stick the film back on,' Aryan said, taking the remote off him and switching the television back on.

'Are you being serious?' Logan asked, slipping off his shirt. Aryan gazed at his bare skin, then back at the television. Then back at his bare skin. He couldn't stop his twitching fingers from coursing along their territory.

'Next time DiCaprio,' he said, resigning as he pulled his own top off. Logan leaned into him and began on his neck, while Aryan kissed his shoulders, occasionally peering behind them to check on story development. The television pitched musical suspense from the film across the living room. Doors slamming, keys unlocking. Thuds and echoes. He and Logan were writhing, stroking, gasping... but the largest gasp rose from their chests when light bled through the room, catching them in their passion. They froze beneath the eyes of Dhruv Alekar.

They clambered off each other and reached for their T-shirts.

'Dad,' Aryan began. No words followed. He could see the veins in his dad's face bulge as he gritted his teeth. Aryan's breath remained captivated behind his throat. Dhruv reached for a sequinned gift bag from behind the sofa and strode out of the room. Logan and Aryan both flinched at the sound of the front door slamming.

'Shit. Shit. Shit!' Aryan cried.

'What's going to happen?' Logan asked. He tried to reach for Aryan's arm to soothe him but Aryan thumped him across the chest.

'Don't. This is your fault!'

'Mine?'

'Yes. Could you not just keep your hands to yourself? We could've just been watching the film.'

Logan rubbed the pinkened skin of his chest. 'I'm sorry,' he said. 'I didn't think.'

'No, sorry. It's not your fault. I don't know.' Aryan paced up and down the room, his frenzied hands pulling at tufts of his black hair. 'You have to leave.'

'What? No. I'm not leaving. You can't just deal with this on your own.'

Aryan gripped Logan's shoulders. 'Listen. You have to. Things will get ugly.'

'Maybe it won't. If we just explain it.'

'I belong to a traditional Indian family. Believe me, this is not OK.'

'Maybe they'll understand.'

'No, Logan, they won't. This will bring them shame and that's all they will see. Please, go upstairs and pack your bag. I'll call a cab. I'll pay for your ticket. If there are no more trains, I'll pay for a hotel stay. Just go.'

'And what will happen to you? You think I never noticed the bruises growing up? Sports my arse. I'm staying.'

Aryan couldn't make him see sense. Why wasn't he listening? 'No. You can't. And I'm not a child any more.'

'Just come with me.'

'I can't. If you want to help me, you need to leave. He'll see you and will become angrier. He might even hurt you and if he does that, I'll hurt him and make it worse. Just, please, wait here. I'll grab your bag.'

Aryan raced upstairs. He cast Logan's straying items into his bag, zipped it up and slung it round his shoulder. He opened his drawers and withdrew a packet of notes from beneath a mountain of socks. Old Diwali money he hadn't spent. Logan waited for him at the foot of the stairs.

'I've called Omari. I'm going to stay with him,' he said.

'What? In Kent?'

'Yes. I'm not going up north. How will I get back to you if I need to?'

Aryan was about to argue but he knew Logan could be as stubborn as he was. 'OK. I'll come to you when this all blows over. Do you know where to go? How to use the tube?'

'No. But I'll figure it out.'

Aryan handed him the bag and money. He pulled him in for a quick embrace. 'Sorry, Logan.'

'Don't be. It'll be OK. Please ring me.'

'I will. Now go."

Aryan stood on the porch and watched Logan walk off until he became a miniature dot, no bigger than a full stop, in the punishing distance. He returned to the settee and tried to occupy his mind with the rest of Scorsese's film, but the psychological torment of the key character failed to quiet his own. He turned the television off and waited, soon dozing off and reliving the events in his dream.

A couple of hours later, he awoke to the slam of car doors. His mother sighed as she entered the house, kicking off her heels before launching into complaints about the quality of food she'd eaten. Both his parents passed by the living room and drifted towards the kitchen. Aryan could hear the tap running. Perhaps his dad was moistening his throat in preparation of the upcoming screaming match, or perhaps they were discussing his punishment beneath the babbles of gushing water. Eventually, his mother entered and sat next to Aryan on the sofa.

'Your father is in a bad mood,' she sighed. 'Nothing new, I suppose. One day he'll smile and won't ruin the evening.' She stroked his cheek and crooned, as she usually did when she detested Dhruv beyond measure. Aryan didn't relish being her only comfort. He should get her a dog. 'Where is Logan?'

'He had to go. Family emergency.'

'*Hai*? Is everything OK? What happened?'

'He couldn't say.'

'Well, I hope he'll be all right. He's such a lovely boy. I hope nothing's wrong with his dad. He doesn't even have a mother any more, *bechara*. A boy needs his family.'

Dhruv entered the room. He did not sit down. He stood over them – a God ready to pass judgement. Aryan gulped and averted his gaze. He couldn't predict the words that would come from his father. They had never spoken about relations. The word 'sex', as in most Asian households, had no place. When he was younger, he didn't know how to break through the online child locks at Brookside and so learning about sex and puberty was a trying task. He could never ask his father about the gooey product he was waking to in his underwear, so he sealed his mouth shut and unpicked answers from the low murmurs of night-time conversations across the boys' dorms. In his parents' eyes, even stolen kisses between young boys and girls stripped them of their innocence. It was all wrong. Unmentionable. He awaited his father to breach the barriers and open the subject.

'So, he has gone then?' he began. His mother concurred.

'Family emergency,' she said.

'Yes, not for his family. For ours. It's good he's gone. I have never been so angry in my life.'

'What are you talking about? Maybe we should talk in private,' Damini said, obviously fearing for her marriage. Aryan could see she thought this was about her. In all her years of marriage, the threat of divorce hovered over her, never landing. She was protected by her husband's shared fear of gossip, no matter how much she wailed into the night or how much he criticised her.

'Ask your son. Ask him what he was doing with his friend.' Damini glanced at Aryan. 'Go on. Ask him.'

'Aryan?'

'He was cavorting with him. Both of them, where you are sitting.'

'Cavorting? *Iska matlab kya hai?*' Damini asked, not understanding the word's informal usage. Her shoulders rose to her ears. Aryan knew she had an inkling of the meaning. She'd soon find her worst nightmare confirmed.

'They were kissing. Feeling each other. Their shirts removed. Here, in our house,' Dhruv said. Once she was sure she hadn't misheard or misunderstood, Damini clapped her hand over her mouth. Gradually, she stood up and stepped away from Aryan, shaking her head in disbelief. She took her position next to Dhruv. They both loomed over him as he slunk further into the sofa, hoping to fall into the cracks and never return.

'Why?' she asked. 'Aryan, you wouldn't do that, right *beta*?' Her eyes were already welling with tears. Her hands already trembling.

'Mum...'

'Shut up. Don't try to confuse her. What you were doing, it was wrong. Disgusting. Is this what you do? I let you choose your own path, and this is what you choose? *Sala Kutta*. I should kill you,' he growled. 'Get up!'

Aryan stood and his father advanced towards him. He stood, inches away from Aryan, his nostrils flaring. 'How long have you been doing these heinous acts for? Is this what you've been doing in boarding school? With how many boys?'

'Just one.'

Dhruv jeered at him. 'Do you hear him? Just one. Just one! Why? As part of some sick experimentation?'

'No.' Aryan dared himself to stare into his dad's mercury eyes. 'No. It isn't. I'm with Logan. I love—'

Dhruv smacked him across the face and then grabbed him by the collar. 'What were you going to say? You love him?'

Aryan fought the urge to strike back. He could hear his mother whimpering. He'd have to endure it. 'What do you do with him? Go on, tell me.'

'What do you want to hear, Dad?' Aryan said. 'If you're wondering if we've done more than kiss shirtless. Then yes, a hell of a lot more.'

Dhruv released him and gawped. He turned to Damini who was sobbing, Aryan knew, both out of disgust and pity for him as he dealt with his father's wrath. Dhruv told her to look at her son; to look at what she had created. He seemed amused. Calmer, for a moment. Then, he whipped back towards Aryan and struck him again, his ring cutting into his skin and drawing blood. Aryan collected the trickle of blood on to the back of his hand.

'I will beat it out of you, whatever poison is running through your system.' He raised his hand again, but this time, Aryan blocked the hit. He pushed his father out of his personal space.

'I'm sick of trying to respect you. You try to hit me, I'll hit you back.'

Dhruv's eyes widened. This was overstepping the line and Aryan knew it. 'Where is your bloody respect? It's this western culture. It's ruined you!' he shouted. 'And that boy. God knows what that boy has done. How he has influenced you.'

Aryan turned to his mum, who continued to shake. He pleaded with her. 'Mum, you know Logan. You know he's a good person. You say it all the time.' She clamped her hands over her ears, refusing to listen.

Dhruv paced up and down the living room, swearing in Hindi. 'We should have sent you to a boarding school in India, away from these *goray*. These English people have no shame. All the time, sex, drugs, nudity. Now you've lost your values,' Dhruv concluded, chewing on his reasoning, absorbing it into every bit of his flesh. It was Logan's fault. England's fault.

Damini took Aryan's hand and sat him down with her. Her tears poured freely, leaving shadowy streaks of kohl and mascara down her rouged cheeks. 'How can you be so stupid?' she asked. 'What do you want to do? Marry this boy? You cannot even have children. I don't know of a single Indian man like this. Do you know what people will say about you? About us? We are held in high respect in our community.'

'He's selfish. Bloody selfish,' Dhruv lashed out, stabbing his finger in the air.

'I don't care what people will think,' Aryan said. 'It's exhausting to live life for your satisfaction. I'm attracted to men and women and it just so happens the one I like now is a guy. You just have to deal with that.'

'If you like women, then be with a woman! Why are you bothering with him?' his dad argued. He flung his hands in the air like a conductor running on too much caffeine. 'Gay people don't have a choice. They have to be with men. Why would you intentionally ruin your life?'

He wouldn't have said gay men couldn't help it, if Aryan claimed to only like men. Aryan couldn't tolerate it any more. The more his dad spoke, the more he realised the hopelessness of the situation. He stood up to leave the room.

'You see that? Why aren't you saying something to him? Say something!' Dhruv said. He shoved Damini and she fell to the floor. Aryan ran to his mum's side.

'Are you OK?' he held out his hand, but she refused to take it.

Aryan grabbed his father by the collar, just as he had grabbed him moments ago. Dhruv started to laugh, sending tremors through Aryan's hands.

'Don't touch him,' Damini told Aryan. 'I won't forgive you if you do anything to your father.' He let him go. Even though he was capable of physically dominating his dad, he wasn't sure he could ever bring himself to do it. What lunatic could hit their parents? Aryan huffed and charged straight out of the room, trying to keep himself from crumbling into tears.

'Go! I can't look at your face any more. If you think you can leave this house or use your phone, you're wrong,' his dad called after him, as he trudged up the stairs.

Now, the second argument could begin. The one between his mother and father. He positioned himself at the top of the stairs, eyeing the front door. He could leave. He hadn't unpacked his bags yet. He could grab them and storm out of the door, meet Logan in Kent and head to York in the morning. Instead, he listened to his father shout at his mother, telling her it was her fault. She sobbed louder and asked God to forgive her for her son's sick mind.

'*Hai Bhagwan, hai Bhagwan,*' she cried. Oh God, oh God.

Soon, the shouting and high-pitched cries fell into low conversation. Aryan guessed this was the part where they'd discuss a strategy or a plan for punishment. They'd come up with something to ensure he wouldn't have those 'unwholesome' thoughts or urges again. His phone vibrated in his pocket. Logan had texted him.

'Are you OK? Ring me when you can. I'll keep my phone with me all night.'

He didn't bother responding. He picked himself up and resigned to his bedroom.

What only felt like moments later, his parents invited themselves into his room. It was time to talk. He stood to face them.

'Well? What do you want to do with me?' Aryan asked,

folding his arms. His father's fist was still clenched.

'We are all leaving for India soon for your cousin's wedding. We think it would be best if you stayed there, for a while,' Dhruv said.

'Why? What does a while mean?'

'You are confused by western ideas. Being in your home country will cleanse you.'

Aryan's mother took his hand in hers. She squeezed it. 'I want you to get better, *beta*.' She couldn't stop using terms of endearment. Her eyes were red and puffy from her tears.

'Better? Mum, I'm not sick.'

'Yes, you are,' Dhruv said. 'This is a mental illness. You'll go to India, see family, reacquaint yourself with God and go to healing centres.'

'Healing centres?'

He smiled, almost callously. 'You said yourself you wanted to travel. Take a gap year. When you are not in recovery, you can explore India. See what you want. You can even take a luxury trip to Goa. But you will go.'

'And if I don't?'

'If you don't go, I will not support you through university. Everything I have given you, you will lose. And why would you want to hurt your mother?'

'Really? As if I don't know what would actually hurt her,' Aryan spat. 'And if this healing doesn't work?'

'It will work,' Dhruv said. 'You will no longer like men. Even if you still do, you will at least realise none of this is worth it for some boy. You will consider your family. You will not do something so unnatural.'

Dhruv left the room, leaving Aryan alone with his mum. She slowly lowered herself on to the bed and kept her gaze fixed on the wall opposite her.

'I don't know what I did wrong. He worked to provide

for us and I stayed at home. The way you turn out is my responsibility. I don't know what I did to confuse you... I've never seen your father like this. It scares me.'

'Mum, you've done nothing wrong. The way he treats you is wrong. It's abuse. I swear, if he hurts you again...'

'It's you who is hurting me, Aryan. Not him. You're my only son and you're my pride. You can't do this.' With that, she rose to her feet and staggered towards the door like a drunkard, sniffling and fighting to keep her body from caving in.

'You know you can always leave him,' Aryan said to her.

She turned. 'And do what?' She looked through him, as though he'd made the stupidest suggestion in the world – as if life outside of a marriage was not a life at all. She was stuck in a cage of her own making, designed by her belief there was nothing for her to be aside from a wife and a mother.

Aryan's phone buzzed in his pocket. He withdrew it and rejected the incoming call, ignoring his trembling heart. He was going to India.

CHAPTER 32

The first doctor told Dhruv Alekar that homosexuality was not treatable. 'You see, it is not a disease. It is a normal variation of human sexuality,' the doctor said. He lowered his spectacles to the end of his hooked nose. 'And one that we must come to accept.'

Dhruv wasn't having it. 'How much? You are the best sexologist in Delhi, tell me how much.'

'Mr Alekar, please. I will not treat your son. He is not sick.'

Dhruv snarled in response and deserted the doctor's office, refusing to shake his hand before departing. Damini shuffled after him, concealing her face behind her dupatta.

'Thanks for your time,' Aryan muttered.

The doctor squeezed Aryan's shoulder. 'Good luck,' he sighed. He too saw Dhruv's resolve. It was as salient as red carpet unfurling across a white floor.

They crossed off the first doctor. In Delhi, there were others. There were plenty of doctors happy to provide cures and treatments to feed the bellies of their pockets with rupees. Alongside these scheming money-grabbers were doctors who believed in their treatments and thought, with sincerity, they were helping those with abnormal urges. Ungodly urges. Dhruv Alekar searched for a doctor far and wide.

'Yes, of course, Mr and Mrs Alekar, we can help your son,' Dr Gupta reassured Dhruv and Damini. They sat in his beige-toned office. Dr Gupta had a round and patchy face that reminded Aryan of broken pani puri, before it is stuffed with potatoes and chickpeas. The doctor's voice droned on. 'After treatment, he will get better. I guarantee he will stop liking men and start liking women.'

Aryan didn't even bother telling this doctor that he already liked women. The point was he still liked men and that needed to change.

'I treated a twenty-four-year-old man. His parents were worried because he was having relations with men. He is now married to a woman and has fathered a child.' He beamed, proud of this success story he surely delivered time and time again to distressed parents of homosexuals.

After more pointless chitter-chatter, the doctor asked Damini and Dhruv to stand outside, so he could examine Aryan. Once they left, his broad smile decayed and he asked Aryan, in a cool and clinical manner, to unzip his trousers.

Aryan hesitated. 'Why?'

'To medically examine you,' the doctor said with a waspish voice. Aryan unzipped his jeans. The doctor took a magnifying glass to his personal area. He stayed there a while, poking with gloved hands, forcing Aryan to wince and squirm. He resurfaced, wheezing as he steadied himself back into a chair too tiny to support his weight. He wrote some notes. Aryan strained his eyes, trying to make out what he was writing.

'So how many times do you have anal sex with men?' the doctor asked bluntly. Aryan frowned. He had never had anal sex, but, of course, this man wouldn't believe him.

'Nearly every day,' he lied. 'I just can't stop.'

The doctor nodded and continued to take notes as he fired more questions at him. Aryan told him what he wanted to hear, because if he didn't he'd be branded a liar and the doctor would inform his father about his unwillingness to comply. The doctor then asked him questions about his diet, how much he weighed and whether he took any medication, as if any of it mattered. Aryan counted the bleach-bathed tiles as Dr Gupta took detailed notes. Once the interrogation was over, his parents were invited back into the room to discuss the next steps.

'I think hormone therapy will be very useful for your son. In many cases, gay men do not have enough testosterone. What we will do is give him testosterone and that should lessen his desire for men.' To this 'simple' answer, he pinned a hefty price tag.

His dad adopted a cool stride and hummed with satisfaction as they left. Aryan knew his father. Dhruv wasn't going to take any chances. This wouldn't be the only therapy Aryan would undergo.

As they battled through India's infamous road rage, Aryan thought about the Yorkshire Dales, where it was quiet aside from the birds singing – where you could cycle across the grass-bordered paths and throw stones into still bodies of water. Where time seemed to stop. Now, he was in Delhi. The scooters growled and the horns of cars and yellow rickshaws blared. The Delhi heat beat down on him and suffused his cheeks with a reddish hue. Sweat keenly fled his pores and created a squelching seal between his back and the car seat. He opened the window. He wasn't getting enough air. Even with it down and with the car soon moving at considerable speed, he wasn't getting enough air.

A few days later, he was taken to a counsellor. The question hung from her painted lips the minute she knew she was dealing with a queer.

'Have you ever suffered child abuse?'

'No.' Aryan sighed, engulfed in fatigue. He sunk into the armchair as the musky scent of incense loomed over him. 'I've had a happy family life. Great, in fact.' Then, she questioned whether he considered his father weak. Because somehow, weak father figures removed barriers and made space for homosexuality.

Once they were done there, he was taken to a yoga centre. His mother told him that the influential Baba Ramdev believed homosexuality could be cured through yoga. According to Baba Ramdev, anything could be cured through yoga. Although Aryan didn't believe for a second yoga was a cure-all treatment, he did relish the sessions. They helped him clear his mind and find a moment's peace. Whenever he felt ready to explode, he lowered himself down on to a mat and controlled his breathing. It kept him sane.

It was his father's final idea that broke him. It was because of the last doctor, with the skeletal form and the grease-slicked hair, that the yoga mat could no longer comfort him. The one who looked away as Aryan's chest aggressively rose and fell. His shaking hands clung to the metal handles of a bucket. He clutched his stomach and swallowed, the corners of his eyes moist and his face pallid. Yet, the doctor would not look at him, nor the two men tangled together on screen, their moans long and their movements fast. If Aryan stopped watching, he knew. He knew and he barked for him to watch, or it wouldn't end. Aryan watched through the mist clinging to his vision, waiting for the end.

When it was all over, the doctor removed the equipment and nodded at Aryan, indicating the end of session. He didn't pat him on the back or ask if he was OK. He didn't even apologise or provide a single sliver of comfort. Aryan left the room, his legs quaking beneath him.

'How do you feel?' Dhruv asked, standing outside the

building with his driver. Aryan staggered past him and fell into the back seat of the driver's car. He wiped his damp forehead, then cursed and clobbered the pristine leather seats of the Mercedes. Once he used up the last few morsels of energy, he dropped his head to his knees and groaned, his throat sore and stinging, the smell of vomit caught on his clothes. In the passenger seat, Dhruv readjusted the rear-view mirror to observe his son in the reflection.

'Are you OK *beta*?' he asked. Aryan didn't answer. For a moment, he thought he might have seen tenderness in his father's eyes through the mirror, but before he could determine what it was, the driver repositioned it, leaving father and son blind to each other.

CHAPTER 33

After his treatments, Aryan was allowed a brief reprieve for relaxation, before Dhruv put forth his next command. Aryan was given strict instruction from his father to board a plane and head to a branch of his offices in Mumbai. He hung up the phone, packed his bag and said goodbye to his mother and auntie. He was glad to leave.

As he waited to board his flight, he scrolled through his messages. When his phone vibrated violently, begging for his attention, each vibration more urgent than the last, he hadn't even glanced at his phone. He hadn't spoken to Logan since that night. Now, when not a single message came through, he couldn't stop scanning its blank screen, willing it to buzz, to ring, to notify him that he was thinking of him. He opened his notes application, where he had painstakingly practised the termination. From 'I don't think this is going to work out. It isn't worth it for me any more. I'm sorry', to 'This won't work out. I'm ending it. I'm really sorry', to 'All this drama isn't worth it. We're better as friends. This isn't going to work out, I'm sorry'. In the end, all he could manage to send was 'I'm sorry.' Not a word more. He received no reply.

The plane journey lasted a couple of hours. He hopped off at Mumbai airport and was picked up by a man named Jignesh.

'Aryan, so good to see you. How was your flight?' Jignesh said in Hindi. He patted his back, but his enthusiasm was dulled by the seriousness of Aryan's expression. 'Your dad says you're thinking about entering the business and to show you the ropes while you're here. Then we can arrange for you to travel. Are you excited?'

'Yes.'

As they travelled to the Mumbai base, Jignesh kept talking, his words whirling into the next without pause for breath. The quivering heat panning Mumbai did nothing to quell the man's energy and Aryan tolerated him with difficulty. Eventually, they arrived at the central office. Jignesh invited Aryan into his personal office to discuss the tasks he would be undertaking.

'You'll gain experience in every facet. You'll begin with acquisitions, helping us find land to build upon, then you will help us design a project. We'll teach you about finance, how to get planning approvals and how to organise construction. Then, later on, we can look at marketing and how to sell or lease a space. By the time you leave here, you will have the skills to become a good property developer.' Jignesh wanted to make Aryan believe he was going to be an integral part of their workforce. His fiddling thumbs told Aryan he must have been nervous. The big boss's son has come to India, with a serious face and a voice that knew his father's ear.

Aryan's first task was to conduct research on land for sale. He was led to the open-plan office, which sported a deep blue and cream colour scheme, as it stood saturating in the stench of tangy sweat and an overpowering, synthetic air freshener posing as Madagascan vanilla. The air conditioner rumbled noisily beneath the patter of fingers on keyboards. As he settled at his desk and pulled up his internet browser, he realised everybody in the office was staring at him. One of them even stood up to get a look. Aryan sighed. It was going to be a long day. He put his head down and began his quest for sellable land. He didn't know anything about India or property development, but he knew how to get answers. He fetched his

Kindle from his bag and downloaded a few highly rated books on property development to skim through during his break.

'*Namaste*,' said a young woman in a damson blouse. He swivelled round in his chair.

'*Namaste*.'

'My name is Kajol. If you need any help, let me know,' she said. She was holding a porcelain mug filled to the brim with coffee. He thanked her and accepted it. Taking the hot liquid to his lips, he noticed the workers were smiling at him instead of just staring like mindless galagos. As Kajol walked off, the man at the computer next to him scowled at Aryan and muttered something under his breath. He had a youthful appearance, his thick beard doing little to negate it. Aryan guessed he was still in his mid-twenties.

'Did you say something?' Aryan asked.

'Nothing.' The man suddenly produced a smile. 'Welcome, my name is Chirag.'

'I'll remember that,' Aryan said, in a matter-of-fact manner. He smirked to himself as this statement trickled down Chirag's back and beleaguered him with shudders, the insinuation of Aryan's words taking hold like a viral infection. 'And I'll remember all the invaluable advice you give me while I work here. And, of course, how I'll be thanking you for it too.'

Chirag jolted in his seat. 'Of course! I've been working here a while. I can teach you as much as you need to know. However long it takes,' he reassured him with an unnatural, shrill laugh. 'We can start at lunch?'

'Perfect.'

The workdays were pleasant. He sailed through his workload and even found and secured an impressive bit of land for development, to the disappointment of other, more experienced employees. He left them reeling in black holes, questioning their own competence. In his spare time at work, he jotted down tips, tricks and innovative ideas regarding strategic development from books. It became a daily challenge – an addiction, to surpass his own expectations. Jignesh relayed Aryan's progress to his father and, months later, he posed the question.

'Do you want to work for me?' Dhruv asked, over the phone. Aryan thought back to the humiliation he endured, the cold doctors and the unsavoury treatments. Of course, the anger. He was still angry. He'd always be angry. Then he considered the money growing in his account, the successes he was experiencing and the pleasure of helping generate profit. Mostly, he thought about the flinching and the nervous smiles he inspired in the employees, being the son of the big boss. He'd forget he ever lost power.

'I'll let you know.'

He hung up the phone and glanced at Chirag. Sandwich crumbs flecked the bottom of his plump lip.

'What do you think Chirag? Do you think property development is for me?'

Chirag hastily swallowed the moist bread balling in his mouth. 'Well, yes. You'd be very good. Was there something else you wanted to do?'

Aryan considered the path he wanted to follow. His past desires, once bathed in a frothy glow, now lay flat as paper. But it didn't matter. He had just discovered a lust for money and business. He thought of how he'd been reduced to a puddle of loose water. How he'd been driven to weakness. In the position he was in, there was strength. He could earn money and respect. He could have permanent, solid constructions against his name.

'No, nothing else,' Aryan told Chirag. 'I want to move out, make a ton of cash and buy a sports car one day.' He stretched his arms over his head and yawned. It was a good dream. One he could invest the whole of himself in.

'And have a wife and kids?' Chirag asked, taking a larger bite of his bacon sandwich.

Aryan could almost hear his mother rejoice, as he said: 'Sure. One day.' As long as he didn't allow himself to drop head-first into an illogical, hopeless love again.

CHAPTER 34

When Aryan's mother began lining up girls for him to meet, he didn't fight her. A permanent exhaustion had set into his body following the fiasco. That's what he called it. His brain refused to churn out the name of 'the boy' or what had happened. Whenever the details tried to creep forward, he'd blur them out with fuzzy television static, the sound of fireworks would replace any memories of words spoken and he'd label the event 'the fiasco' and move on. But, in truth, he couldn't move on. His mother was picking the wrong kinds of girls – girls that fit her criteria for the perfect daughter-in-law.

When he met Rakhee at the wedding reception, he struggled to stay in conversation with her. She was too controlled, as if he'd have to dig for days and would still never get to the heart of her. If he was going to move on, he needed someone more exciting and real. After watching him with her, his mother suggested Maansi Cavale.

'Her? Why her?'

'Aryan, you've complained that every other girl we've chosen is too dull, too traditional, too this and that. We think Maansi might be a good match for you,' Damini Alekar began in her stern voice. 'Her mother says she is opinionated, like you. I could see she liked to dance and laugh. You said you need a bit of fun. A bit of *masti*. Maybe she's the one you'll say yes to. She isn't my choice but...'

He sighed emphatically. 'But her?'

'You don't find her pretty? I know she is a bit dark.'

'What? No. She looks fine.' Attractive even, he thought. He'd never understood the obsession with fairness. His mother used the Fair & Lovely soaps so often that she could wallpaper the house with all the empty packets she'd thrown away.

'Then?'

Aryan shrugged his shoulders. She was a nice enough girl. More suited to him than Rakhee, that was for sure. But, was she too much? She suffered a panic attack that night and had got a little too drunk... Well, that was realness, he supposed.

'Look, we spoke to her parents. She is also a Brahmin and she is educated. I would have preferred Rakhee, or the other six girls we found. But maybe we should try the opposite type to get you to agree.' Aryan could feel his mother's fury growing as he shrugged his shoulders again. He kept his eyes fixed on the blank television screen in front of him. Why was it so important to marry him off? Did they really think he'd run after the past? 'Well, speak to her. I expect you to at least try.'

With her final words flung at his feet, she strutted out of the room.

He dropped his face in his hands and took a deep breath. He knew his mother was no longer willing to play the game. They were caught in an ongoing battle of chess and she'd finally flipped the board, fed up with the stalemates. 'Fine,' he said to himself. He'd drop her a message. Although, why she'd want to marry at a young age was beyond him. What if she said yes for the money?

After his first date with Maansi, Aryan couldn't believe he told her he was fine with taking it further. But the truth was, he had no fight in him, and he did enjoy himself with her. He liked that she was funny and a little clumsy. She didn't care what others thought and the way her dimples set deep into her cheeks told him she might bring a bit of sunshine into his glum life. And she was honest. She told him right away about her unfaithful boyfriend. That's what he needed. Someone honest, cheery and uncomplicated. He wasn't any of those things, but the boy with the blotted-out face had had those qualities. He thought, just maybe, something could blossom between them.

After their first night together as a married couple, regret hit like a bus. As he listened to her breathing – shallow, the rhythm broken with sighs – he knew she was awake too and expecting more from him. But the idea of letting her into his space made him shudder. Sex was easy enough, but holding someone afterwards, being close enough to feel their breath on his skin... it was too much. He even went to work to escape her.

As time went on, he wanted to turn from the wall at night, swing his arm around her and bury his face into her neck, but still, he couldn't. When he told her he loved her, he wanted the words to ring true. He wanted to let her in. He wanted his shrunken heart to expand and flower. But it didn't. He thought he'd eventually fall in love with the girl, but she wasn't the 'sunshine' he presumed her to be. She'd look worn out and exhausted most days. She added to his exhaustion and they existed in a weird, heavy fog. Then, he discovered she wasn't honest. He found the antidepressants nestled in her underwear drawer, though she swore she was in perfect health. She broke his trust.

Maybe he was being unreasonable. Maybe the whole thing wouldn't have upset him, if he hadn't been there at the markets.

As the aggressive wind flooded towards him, he imagined it taking Maansi away. In the end, she wasn't the person she was replacing. She wasn't the boy he loved nor the man he wanted to love. No. He was there, in front of him. Both of them were standing there, facing each other after years apart. His body jolted to life.

'You,' Logan spoke. 'What do you want?'

Aryan struggled to find words. Any words. He'd once plugged in a memory drive at school, only to find his documents on the Second World War deleted. Every word, every page he had written, made him secure in the knowledge that he was well prepared for the presentation. In the end, the computer picked up nothing. Here, in this moment, his mind was like that blank screen. It didn't matter how many times he practised what he'd say when he met the man in front of him. His brain refused to acknowledge his years of cogitations and supposed scenarios as ever having existed.

'Can we... can we talk?' he finally managed. Logan shook his head and tried to get into the cab. Aryan took him by the arm and slammed the cab door shut. The cab driver beeped, the sharp screech carving into their eardrums. Aryan waved him off with a sweep of his hand.

'What the fuck!'

'Logan, please.' He halted. The ease with which his name rolled off his tongue surprised him. He wanted to speak it over and over again, to feel his mouth warming to the memory of it, like an adult re-experiencing the sweet confections of childhood. He missed saying it every day. He hated that it had remained just behind his teeth, just on the tip of his tongue – in the backdrop of every freshly finished thought, for all those years. 'Please.'

'I tried to talk to you for a long time,' Logan said. 'Said please and all. You didn't listen.'

'I know. I know.' Aryan fell silent. He didn't know what he could say to persuade him.

'I need to go. It's cold out.'

'I thought the cold didn't bother Northerners,' he said. He thought about how once upon a time that would have made Logan smile and puff out his chest with 'Northern pride', and how he would have jeered and jabbed at him.

'I need to,' Logan held his head. His face twitched. He looked as if he was in pain. 'I have aura, so just back off, all right?' Aryan realised Logan was holding on to the lamppost for balance. His face was paling.

Aryan remembered what aura was. He'd forgotten all about the sufferings of his old friend. The unbearable pain of a migraine. His body was preparing him with a warning.

'I needed that damn cab,' he growled.

'I'm sorry. Look, I'll get you another one.' He hailed down the next cab. He opened the door and helped Logan in, jumping in after him.

'What are you doing?'

'Where do you live?' Aryan asked.

Logan muttered his address to the cab driver. He laid back and tried to focus on his breathing. He removed his beanie hat and buried his face into it, attempting to block out the light of passing traffic. He groaned. Aryan didn't know whether to put his arm around him or whether to pat his back. Logan probably wouldn't welcome any contact.

The cab stopped outside a block of rundown flats. Aryan paid the driver and proffered his hand for Logan to take. Logan ignored him and got out of the cab himself, stumbling as he did.

'Go home, Aryan.'

'No.'

'Seriously, piss off.'

'Just let me stay with you until this passes,' he demanded. His arms were crossed. It was impossible to bat down his stubbornness, so Logan submitted. He entered a code at the rusted gate and trekked up some stairs with Aryan following, his head swaying and his hands waving off what Aryan imagined were stars and stripes pirouetting around him. He unlocked the flat and tottered in, feeling along the wall for a light. It flickered on and a shabby, cheerless flat filled their vision. The walls were old and dented, the white paint peeling off in flakes. The cream carpet, besieged with mud-brown stains, had a mild mildew smell coming off it.

'Couldn't afford much else at London prices,' Logan explained as Aryan scrunched up his face. 'Listen, if you're going to stay, get me a glass of water.' He lumbered off into one of the rooms.

'Yeah. Of course.'

Aryan navigated through the unknown territory of the kitchen, in search of a glass. He looked around. The kitchen was a tip, with used dishes invading every surface. There wasn't a clean glass in sight. He took one from the sink and washed it with a tattered sponge. It was clear Logan was living with someone else. There was a bin rotation stuck on the fridge and dried, fat drippings on a meat grill. Logan was a vegetarian. Unless he wasn't any more. How would he know?

He entered Logan's room and sat on the edge of the bed, passing Logan the glass of water. Logan gulped down the cool water as if he'd been roaming a Middle Eastern desert. He lay down again, mumbling something about spinning. As Aryan waited for him to find some stillness, he surveyed the room. Logan hadn't learned to tidy up after himself. The floor was swamped with unfinished drawings and packets of sweets. His old acoustic guitar was supported by a broken guitar stand and his laundry basket was empty. His dirty clothes dangled off the sides of it and lay crumpled in piles along the floor. There were PS4 games and DVDs piled up by his bed. A skateboard balanced on his wardrobe door. Aryan smiled at detonation that occurred there. It reminded him of old times.

'What are you doing here, Aryan?' he croaked. 'You need to go.'

'Won't you be having a migraine attack soon?' he asked.

'I'm fine. Go home to your wife.' The words snapped like an elastic band.

'I don't want to,' he said. 'It was never even my choice to marry her. I had to, after what happened.'

'What did happen?' said Logan. 'Because I have no clue.' Aryan assessed his face. It hadn't changed much. His face looked slightly older and more chiselled. Other than that, it was a familiar face. A face that raised the same feelings as settling by a blazing hearth after a commute in the rain. He was so adamant in erasing Logan from his life when he returned from India. He blocked him online and deleted pictures on his phone. He did everything he could to shut him out, only getting a glimpse into his life through Omari or Chris, who let Logan slip from their mouths and faked their apologies.

'I didn't want to leave you,' Aryan began. 'But my dad would have turned on my mum. You know what he's like. Leaving was the worst mistake of my life. There hasn't been...' he trailed off. What was the point? He'd never believe him.

'You could've told me,' he said. His blue eyes were burdened with an aching that tore Aryan to shreds. 'I waited for you. Every day you were away, until I realised you didn't respect me enough to say anything. You didn't care.'

He could have told him, but he hadn't. The pain of saying goodbye stopped him. He'd been a coward.

'I'm sorry,' he said. He decided he wouldn't leave anything unsaid. 'You're the first person I ever loved, and I wish I could go back. Go back to Brookside.'

Logan blinked at him. 'I thought the goal was to get out of Brookside?' Aryan laughed a little at that. They used to call Brookside prison. He later realised he was freer there than anywhere else.

'I'm still in love with you,' Aryan whispered. There ensued a period of overdrawn silence.

'Aryan.'

'I know,' he cut him off. 'I just wanted you to know.' He dropped down next to him, laying close enough to feel the warmth from his body. Logan's skin still emanated a citrusy woody scent.

'Can't things work between you and Maansi?'

'No. No. I have to leave her. I can't do it to myself, or to her any more. It won't work.'

'If you think it's the right thing to do,' said Logan. 'But you'd be doing that, even if you didn't feel anything for me?'

Aryan reassured him he would. He liked Maansi. He did. He just didn't want to be shackled to her in marriage. While he cared for her, he possessed no love for her. He'd been waiting for it to grow. Waiting and waiting...

'How is your head?' he asked Logan.

Logan rubbed the side of it. 'I'll be keeling over in pain soon enough.'

'Can I stay?'

Logan hesitated. 'I suppose.'

Soon, Logan's migraine struck and Aryan was switching off the bedroom light for the kinder feel of darkness. Logan whined and twisted in pain beneath the covers. Aryan lay next to him on top of the duvet, waiting for him to drift off into sleep. Sleep was the only thing that brought him solace. His breathing soon deepened and his belly visibly rose. He murmured as he slept, saying something about 'Cheddar' – whether he was thinking of his dog or the popular variety of cheese, Aryan couldn't be sure.

He stared up at the ceiling, wondering how he was going to break it to Maansi. He didn't want to hurt her, and he really did think it could have worked, once upon a time. Maybe if he'd met her himself under normal circumstances, in a world where Logan didn't exist.

He traced Logan's face in the dark. Unable to resist the temptation, he reached out and touched his hair. It was matted with hair gel. Aryan remembered how Logan would run a dollop of VO5 gel through his hair before heading out the door. His hair always had to look like a 'styled mess'.

A few hours later, Logan opened his eyes. He announced his waking with a loud yawn and a stretch, rousing Aryan from his own shallow slumber. Logan switched the bedside light on.

'You're still here,' he said. Aryan frowned. He guessed he'd have to leave. 'I was dreaming about the Dales. Remember when I took you up there?' Logan continued. Aryan remembered it well. The memory was cosy and melted like butter. If he closed his eyes he could still recall the smell of greenery, the feel of a lungful of breath gifted by trees and, even more so, the feel of Logan's body as it shared its heat with him in the tight enclosure of their tent.

'How is your head now?' said Aryan. Logan told him he felt better, albeit a little groggy. Aryan waited to be told to get out, but the command didn't arrive. 'I've missed you,' he dared himself to say. Logan bore into him with his beautiful, just-woken eyes. They softened.

'I've missed you too,' he sighed. He seemed disappointed with himself for saying so.

'Do you think things could ever be the way they were?'

'Maybe,' said Logan, without hope. But to Aryan a maybe was still a shiny possibility, a silver coin in a mound of dirt, still retrievable.

Aryan leaned in to kiss him. Their lips brushed together, before Logan pushed him back.

'You're married,' he said.

'I thought you said nothing could be wrong if it was out of love,' Aryan said, his hand sliding along Logan's neck. He would still try. He revisited the mini birthmarks there with his fingertips. They were tiny prints of memories, reactivating with his touch. Logan shook him off. They lay there, on their backs, the edges of their hands touching beneath the duvet. The contact of their skin produced a ticklish warmth. Neither wanted to move their hand. They didn't want to be, in any sense, separate.

'Can you forgive me?' said Aryan.

'I don't know,' said Logan. He closed his eyes. Aryan moved his face closer to Logan's. He could feel his mojito-redolent breath cruise over his face, cooling his heated skin with mint leaves and lime.

'What would Jesus do, Logan?'

'Shut up,' he said. He opened his eyes and gazed straight into Aryan's. 'I still... you know. Love you too. I must be stupid.'

Aryan felt as if someone had released their hands from his throat, after years of difficult breathing. He reached for Logan's hands, interlocking his fingers with his. Although he knew Logan's shields were up and positioned against him, he didn't let go. They remained, joined in this way, until both floated into the arms of sleep. Aryan's ears reassigned the footsteps of Logan's flatmate to the inept warden, roaming the corridors at night to make sure the boys were asleep and undisturbed.

CHAPTER 35

The golden light of a late-winter sun gushed through the blinds and alighted on the faces of the two men, still caught in the apparels of slumber. It was the smell of buttered toast and bacon sizzling on the frying pan that woke Aryan, and his stomach shortly after. It grumbled as his mouth salivated. He soon noticed his fingers were resting on Logan's curled hand. The afternoon rays illuminated him, spinning his hair into a richer gold, revealing every mark on his skin, every hair comprising his dark brow. Aryan felt dazed. The previous evening was like a television show from the 1990s. The picture was fuzzy, affected by alcohol and the fatigue that accompanied the night. Now, Logan was in front of him, clear and unmistakable.

Aryan reached for the phone in his pocket. It was dead. Sitting up, he scanned the room and spotted a charger on the other side. He snuck out from beneath the duvet. As he knelt on the floor to charge his phone, he found a waste bin on his left, bloated with torn and scrunched up papers. He picked out a few from the top layer and flattened them out on the carpet. The creased sheets were granted life with a sequence of imperfect but charming drawings. He smiled as he remembered the drawings Logan used to show him. These drawings didn't belong in the bin.

From the corner of his eye, he spotted a scarlet card in the bin among the whites, calling for him to take it. He fetched it. On the cover of the card were two cartoon bears in an embrace, captivated beneath an arch of hearts, as polished and shiny as apples. The card read: 'For You This Valentine's

Day.' Aryan opened the card. Inside, written in blue fading ink, were the words: 'To Logan, I'm always thinking about you. Love, Charlie.' Attached to the blank side of the card were photo booth-style images of Logan and a boy with curly, russet hair and shamrock eyes. They moulded their faces into comical positions in all but the last. The last captured a private moment between them. Aryan dropped the card back into the bin, where he believed it belonged. As he stood, he saw dozens of photos pinned to a cork wall installation. He noticed Omari and Chris in a few, as well as Logan's family members, but mostly they were of Logan with people he didn't know, didn't recognise. He wasn't in any of these pictures.

There was a knock at the door. 'Logan, wake up! I'm going to Asda soon. Text me if you want anything,' came a husky voice. Aryan didn't even know who Logan was living with.

'Aryan?' Logan yawned from his bed. 'You're up.'

'Who are all these people?' he asked.

'Friends from university. From work.'

Aryan found the boy with the russet curls in one of the group photos. His grin was wide and self-satisfied. 'And who's this?' he asked, pointing to the boy.

Logan paused before answering. 'That's Charlie. My ex.'

'Why ex? When did you split up? How long were you together?' There were more questions furiously bubbling within him.

'Hm. Nothing like a morning interrogation,' he joked. 'I met him during second year at university. He was chair of an Amnesty society that I joined. We were together for two years. After he finished, he went abroad to teach. While he was out there, he cheated on me. So, I left him.'

'Was there anybody else?'

Logan shook his head. 'No, no more boyfriends, as such. Just short flings. A little dating here and there.'

'Right,' Aryan replied, uneasy at the thought of Logan meeting other men, for the purposes of pleasure or otherwise. He joined him, perching on the edge of the bed. 'So, this Charlie guy. Did you love him?'

'I did,' he said in a muffled whisper. Aryan followed the lines of light leaking in, watching it separate into bouncing, yellow discs across the sheets. He didn't really want to hear this. 'He was sorry. Really sorry. But I don't know. I couldn't take him back.'

'Right. So now you're working at a publishing company? There's so much I don't know. You're almost a stranger.'

'Well, I've left now. I've got something more flexible with better pay. It's you who surprises me. You aren't a lawyer.'

'No. I wound up doing property development anyway. I actually like my work. I'm good at it.'

Logan picked at the hangnails on his fingers, his smile sour like oranges grown without summer's hand to sweeten them. 'So, you finally got your dad's approval then?'

'What?'

'Come on, Aryan. You were happy to trade me for your dad. That's what really happened, right?'

'That's not true. I told you things would've got worse at home.'

Logan nodded. 'And Maansi?'

'It's over.'

'Aryan, I haven't even said we should do this.'

'It's still over.'

He said goodbye to Logan, promising he'd be back. Logan gave a shrug, suggesting indifference, but Aryan refused to believe that's how he felt. He was guarded and it was Aryan's fault. He'd fix it.

He stood outside his flat, clutching his keys tight, the metal scolding an outline into his skin as he tried to get his thoughts together. He unlocked the door and stepped into a room that accommodated the musty smell of old saree silk and jasmine. He knew that smell. It belonged to his mother on the days she visited *mandir*. She was sitting in the living room alongside Maansi whose face was dappled with the dew of tears. Dhruv took the one-seater sofa to himself, both his arms upon the armrests. His eyes were black clouds flecked with a silver glow. Throughout his life, Aryan had always taken the phrase 'every cloud has a silver lining' to be negative – a sure sign his father was enraged by a poor choice he'd made.

CHAPTER 36

Aryan hadn't returned that night. She waited in bed, all night, for the sound of keys turning in the lock. It never came. Clueless about what to do, she picked up the phone in the morning and rang his parents' house. His father answered. As his baritone voice came through, she remembered how Aryan loathed to spend time with him. Could it be because he was forced to go to India after all? For a supposed sex addiction? She'd had enough of the mystery. She told his family Aryan hadn't returned home and asked where they thought he might be. Instead of discussing possibilities with her on the phone, her father-in-law told her they were on their way, hanging up before she could protest.

They arrived within the hour. She opened the door with tears rolling down her face. She felt fragile, aches and pains leaping from limb to joint. They had only just started talking when they heard the rattle of keys. Aryan unlocked the door and stepped in. His hair was unkempt and he was wearing the same clothes as the day before. She could only imagine where he'd been.

'What's going on?' he asked, his expression blank. Maansi's muscles contracted. She struggled to even look at him without wanting to explode.

'We're comforting your wife,' her father-in-law spoke. 'She doesn't deserve this behaviour from you.'

'What are you talking about? Is this because of last night? I stayed with a friend from university. I meant to message.'

'But you didn't. Where were you?' Maansi asked. Her heart walloped and warred against the confinements of her body.

'Yes, where?' his mother joined in.

He scowled, twirling his keys around his index finger. 'Look. We've had our first argument and if you don't mind, I'd like to sort it out with my wife alone,' he said. 'I don't understand why you're here.'

'Maansi was worried, so we came to offer support,' Dhruv said.

'Well, there is no need to worry,' he said. His tone was spiked with a subtle poison. 'You can go now.'

Dhruv nodded at Damini and they rose from their seats. Maansi wouldn't leave it there. There were too many cogs and gears rotating in her head as all the questions came up at once. There were too many answers missing. She began with the very first. 'Who's Logan? To you?'

Dhruv and Damini stiffened, becoming immovable sculptures. From his reaction, she knew she hit a nerve. 'To me?' he asked. 'He's your colleague. What would he be to me?'

'Colleague?' Damini asked. 'You work with him?'

'And how do you know him?' Maansi asked Damini. 'Who is he?'

'No one!' Dhruv roared. 'Absolutely no one, am I not right, Aryan?'

Aryan gulped. He was about to say something, but she could see he was uncertain, vacillating as a boat upon waves. Second-guessing himself.

'Aryan!' Dhruv bellowed, demanding an answer and end to the setting silence.

'You're not right,' he said. He took a step towards her, his head lowered as he prepared his confession. She'd been waiting for this. 'Logan was my best friend at school.'

'Yes, they are old friends, that's all,' Damini interjected.

'Then why were you cold towards him?' Maansi asked. 'And why are you and your parents so shocked at my question?'

'Because our friendship turned into a relationship,' he said. 'A physical and romantic relationship.'

'What?' Her mouth dried. She suddenly felt parched. She needed a second to make sure she heard him correctly. 'What?'

'What do you think you're doing?' Dhruv said. 'You're single-handedly ruining your marriage.'

'It was a relationship that ended,' Damini said, her vocal cords tremulous. 'That's why they don't talk, but he isn't gay. He likes women, tell her Aryan! Tell her.'

'I'm bisexual. I like women too. I like you,' he said to her. He stepped closer to her now and took her hands in his. 'But I love Logan. I'm so sorry.'

'Why are you telling me this?' she asked, snatching her hands away. 'We're married. Why would you say you love him? Aryan, you can't be with him!'

'I was with him last night.'

It was all coming back to her now. The pain Lewis instilled in her. The glued pieces of her heart started to break loose again, bits hanging off and trembling, fighting against the force of gravity. By lying about something that happened to her, had she called it into reality? 'You cheated on me?'

'No. No. I didn't.'

'ENOUGH!' Dhruv's voice boomed across the flat as if projected through a tannoy. He strode towards Aryan with a quivering hand. Maansi recalled the secret of violence. It seemed Dhruv was struggling to hold his hand in place, his base instinct to strike his son hard to contain. She wasn't sure she'd care if he hit Aryan. The ensuing pain couldn't match the pain she felt from his confession. Everything made sense. All the loose ends were tying themselves up.

'I trusted you to make the right choices and to stop being selfish. But no, you have this mission to hurt your family, to hurt your mother,' Dhruv said.

275

Aryan's expression was vacuous. 'I think you should go,' he told his father. 'I need to handle my personal affairs. This is, after all, my marriage.'

'We are not going anywhere.'

'I'm not a child!'

'You have never been anything more than a child!' Dhruv's voice dropped to a hiss as he said the following words. 'You are a big disappointment to me. *Bhagwan* knows I am ashamed of you.' He signalled for Damini to start leaving. She stood, still shaking. The fabric of her saree tumbling off her shoulder bore wet patches of tears, pushing the purple shading towards a docile black. Before following her out, Dhruv held a finger up to Aryan and said: 'I will deal with you later. And if you dare end this marriage, we can't work together any more. You can't come home.'

As the door slammed, Aryan shifted to face her. She didn't want to hear anything he had to say. She scarpered into the bedroom and shut the door, locking it behind her and sliding down against it, knifed by the truth. He knocked.

'Maansi,' he said. His voice was smooth as balm. 'Maansi, I'm sorry. Open the door.'

She thought she wouldn't. She thought she'd remain shut in, but in a trice, she swung the door open. Strands of her black hair clung to her face, using her tumbling tears as their makeshift glue.

'So you want to leave me then?' she shouted. 'Just like that? I've done nothing wrong!'

'Maansi, I'm sorry.'

'No!' she said, pointing her finger at him. 'Don't. You say you love Logan, well then, from what I gather, you loved him before you married me. So why the hell did you marry me? Because he wasn't available then? Why would he be yours now? Explain it to me.'

'Even if he wasn't available, Maansi, I just can't be with you. I didn't come to you freely. I came to you because I had to. I had no choice.'

She pulled at her hair. 'And what about your sex addiction?'

His confusion zapped the rumour to smoke. 'My what? What are you talking about?'

She knew Sejal had been wrong. If she thought about it, she could predict why he might've been sent to India, but her head was clouded. The information she had was too much to handle.

'You'll ruin my life,' she sobbed. She held herself and collapsed against the wall. 'I'm too young to be divorced, forget bloody married. I'll have to leave here and go home. I'll have to leave the job that I'm starting to love. You'll put me back in the hole.'

'You can still live in London in shared accommodation. Your salary will cover it.'

'But I don't know anyone,' she sobbed louder. 'I'm alone in a big city. I'm depressed, whether you care for it or not. I won't survive.'

'Then go home,' he said. 'Get a new job! You'll be fine, all right?'

'No,' she said, standing upright. She stuck her nose in the air and smiled like a china doll from a toyshop of horrors. 'Besides, you can't legally divorce me because we haven't been married for at least a year. And even if we had, I wouldn't sign a thing. Not a damn thing.'

'We can separate,' he urged. 'Please try to understand.'

'No!' she screamed. 'You married me. I uprooted my life and followed you here. I'm not going anywhere. If you want to parade around with your boyfriend, then fine by me.' She fled into the room again and shut him out.

CHAPTER 37

Logan buzzed him in. He'd just come out of the shower, drops of water still trickling down his exposed skin, with nothing but a blue towel concealing his modesty. His body was doused with the fresh scent of limes.

'Where's your flatmate?' Aryan asked, unable to tear his eyes from him.

'He's visiting his girlfriend. He'll be back later.' Logan cast his eyes downwards and nestled on to the sofa, patting the space next to him so Aryan would join. 'Listen, Aryan. I don't think us being together is a good idea. We've moved on. It'll never feel the same.'

Aryan hushed him. He couldn't have him wandering down that path, away from him again. 'It can. We can leave off exactly where we were. Isn't it worth a try? Think about it.'

Logan dithered. He had to say yes. After the dramatic explosion Aryan set off at home, he had to. 'I don't know. I guess I need convincing.'

'All right.' Aryan grasped his hand and led him into the bedroom.

'What are you doing?'

'Convincing you.'

Once in, Aryan removed his jacket and let it drop to the floor. He unbuttoned his shirt at a leisurely pace, drinking in Logan's gaze through every inch of revealed skin.

'Come on, man,' Logan said. 'You're still married.'

'Legally, yes.' Aryan slid the shirt off his arms. 'But otherwise it's over.'

He advanced on Logan and freed him from the burden of his towel. Logan shook his head, smirking at him. 'Are you even sure you can handle this?'

Logan's hands voyaged across Aryan's chest, down his abs, lightly like the transfer of watercolour on to canvas. Their mouths met and they moved, still caught, towards the bed. There, they became reacquainted once more with each other's bodies. They had both changed. They had become broader and formed slabs of muscle where they previously hadn't any. To them both, it was all as familiar as embarking upon old stomping grounds. They kissed with passion and fire. They moaned and clung on to each other as if their lives were hanging in the balance. Yet, when the moment came to venture further, past where they'd ever been together, Aryan faltered.

'What's wrong?' asked Logan.

It was the painful memory that stopped him. It flashed before him like lightning: the image of the skinny man with his oil-slathered hair. The feel of metal as it shifted from cool to warm in his sticky hands. These images woke from their hibernation. His throat constricted as his stomach squirmed in remembrance. He backed off and grappled for air. 'Sorry,' he said.

'It's fine. It happens.'

'No, nothing like that,' he tried to explain. 'I just remembered something awful.'

'What do you mean?' Logan asked, scratching his head. He seemed offended. Of course, Aryan didn't mean his body was a reminder of something awful. He flopped down on to the pillow, holding himself.

'Just a therapy my dad paid for in India. I'm not even sure it was legal. It didn't work. It's just the memory of it...'

'What therapy? What do you mean? Like a conversion therapy?'

'I don't want to talk about it. Just give me a moment.'

Aryan tried to erase the experience from his mind. It was unbearably warm in Logan's room. If he closed his eyes, he could mistake the radiator's exertion for Indian heat. It made the memory more vivid.

'There's no rush,' Logan said, rubbing his shoulders. 'Here, let's put some music on. Get your mind off it. Tell me if you know this one.'

Aryan heard the introduction of an acoustic guitar. The voice came from the speakers: 'Along she came, with a picture, put it in a frame…'

'Sleeping with the light on,' he grinned. 'I haven't heard this song in years.' He toyed with the cross around Logan's neck. Its edges were chipped and a bronze tint started to encroach on the silver. 'You haven't changed.'

Logan scowled. 'I have. If you're expecting the same person from school, you'll be disappointed. I've had experiences, I've changed.'

'I know. Relax. I'm not expecting things to be easy. But you're worth the struggle.'

'Were you always this cheesy?'

'Shut up! I'm pouring out my heart here.'

'"My heart". Do you hear yourself?' Logan burst out laughing. Aryan brought him into a headlock and rearranged his hair. 'Get off!'

They stopped playing as Aryan's phone droned on the bedside table. Logan reached for it. Dhruv was calling. They both looked at each other, the vibrations impaling the light mood and dissolving their laughter behind strait-laced frowns. He handed it over. 'Are you going to answer it?'

'Nope,' Aryan said, hitting the reject button.

They pulled the duvet over them and lost themselves in the havens of their bodies, leaving no place undiscovered or stone unturned. The phone continued to buzz, but having thrown themselves into a world where only they existed and mattered, they could no longer hear it.

CHAPTER 38

Visions of Parisian cafés, of enjoying dainty macarons and champagne while cruising along the River Seine, of her hand in his, they all shattered into a million pieces. As her heart drained of affection, she tore the tickets into fragments, throwing them in the air so they fell like wedding confetti. She held herself as she sat on the floor, too disgusted to be on the bed. Their bed. Or his bed, now that he undeclared her as his. She hated herself then. How could she be so stupid? Love would grow? Yeah, right. It took off in her eventually, but for him the seed never germinated. He held no love for her.

She slid the ring off her finger, observing it. She concluded it to be a meaningless object. It offered nothing but unfulfillable promises. She then recalled Lewis and his promises. All the falsities. He too left her and got busy with a blonde in bed. She flung the ring, hearing a satisfying clang as it hit something and vanished from sight. She was in Canary Wharf, in one of the busiest and most impressive cities in the world, though she may as well have been on the floor of her student accommodation, cursing Lewis, crying as the fear of community drove her to commit something wrong for her. She dug her fingernails into her arms, leaving crescent moons on her dark skin. She could feel herself slipping back to where she used to be, as if the last few months hadn't happened.

Her depression took the opportunity to mount her and strengthen its hold. She instinctively scratched herself, wanting to rip off the skin and see blood. She didn't want to feel the weight of her situation. Oh, they must have laughed at her. Him and that man. She remembered Rakhee. It was almost her. How Sejal and her would have laughed when they discovered she married a man in love with a man, never seeing the pain of the situation, only the comedy at the surface. They would have patted themselves on their backs for being too liberal, too shrewd for arranged marriages, clinking their glasses of cosmopolitans together as Rakhee rolled her eyes at their transgressions.

She lay prone on the floor, focusing her attention on the ceiling, finding every mark and every blotch. As smooth as it appeared, there were marks. There was a roughness to everything. What was her next move? She couldn't remain in his room for ever. She saw the parcel of books given to her from work, balancing on the edge of her dressing table. She wasn't ready to leave work. She'd finally found something she could do. She'd have to stay in London. But where? In shared accommodation? With people she didn't know, having to pay rent in the most expensive city in the UK. She'd have to say goodbye to the luxury flat that was peppered with herself through careful redesign and sprucing up.

Perhaps, he'd let her stay. His dad's threat was empty. A father wouldn't fire his son. She'd demand to stay. He could leave and live with that man. She still couldn't picture them together. They weren't alike. Like the resulting sound of two incompatible keys pushed on a piano, the image of them together was discordant. You couldn't blend fire and water, without one dousing the other out, or one boiling the other until gradual evaporation.

She must have lain on the hard floor for an hour. Her back ached and a thin layer of dust coated her and made the exposed areas of skin itch. Damini rang her. She answered with a croaky, 'Hello.'

Her mother-in-law reassured her Dhruv was going to fix it. This was simply a phase. It went away before, it'd go away again. There was absolutely no way they'd allow Aryan to be with a man. The more she spoke, the further her voice trekked up its register, as if she were being pumped with a glut of helium. Maansi hung up. They were worried about their reputation. Their honour. He was concerned for his freedom. Only she worried for herself.

She rose from the floor and staggered to the dressing table, her legs barely able to carry her. She examined her reflection in the mirror. She pulled a cleansing wipe from its packet and swabbed away the clumps of wet mascara and streaky foundation. She tucked her hair behind her ears and saw her clean, bare face, swollen and pink from crying. She pressed her hand to the cool pane of reflective glass. Aryan wasn't in it. Neither were their families. It was just her. In the moment, in her own company, she saw she needn't let others affect her. She didn't want her pain to be in the hands of others any more. She was done with being helpless.

CHAPTER 39

'So, when do you start this new job?' Aryan asked. Logan poured some oil into a pan, stared at it in wonderment, before pouring in a tad more. After their lovemaking, their stomachs rumbled and they bickered over who was a better chef. Aryan bet Logan couldn't cook something remotely complex. So, he claimed with pride that he knew how to cook a Thai curry. In truth, he made it once with the assistance of a friend and a detailed recipe book, a good three years ago. He assessed his spice rack. What was it he used before?

'I start in a few weeks,' he replied, as he drained the tofu. 'But forget that. What about your job? Would your dad really fire you?'

'You know he would,' Aryan sighed. 'I'm going to start looking for another. I've got enough money to live off, and since you're not starting yet, I was thinking...' He didn't complete the sentence. Logan left the pan to cook the onions and joined Aryan at the kitchen table.

'You were thinking...'

'We could get out of here. Go abroad for a couple of weeks. Whatever continent, I don't really care.' There was a cool steadiness in his features. 'What do you think?'

'Where would you want to go?'

'Wherever you want to go.'

Logan stretched his hands behind his head as he considered this. A smile extended across his face. 'Thailand. It'd cost a bit, but we were supposed to go together. But are you sure you want to run away right now?'

'Yep. Forget them. I just want to focus on us.'

'What about Maansi?'

'I told her it's over. Maybe me leaving will be good for her. Give her some time to organise herself.'

Logan wondered what she was doing. If she was coping. He felt responsible for her pain. She was a nice girl, undeserving of all of this. All she wanted to be was his friend and this is what he did in return. Aryan stood. 'I'm just going to use your bathroom. By the way, I think the onions are burning.'

He left as Logan rushed to tend to his singeing food. 'Shit!' he said, as the pan spat at him. His phone rang upon the counter. He reached for it, knocking over a pot of chilli powder. He cursed under his breath. He answered the phone, propping it up against his shoulder as he scoured the place for a dustpan and brush. 'Hello?' The hairs on the back of his neck stood up as he heard the sonorous voice of a man from his past. He immediately abandoned his search and seated himself at the table. He lowered his voice to a whisper, afraid Aryan would hear.

'How did you get my number?... Excuse me? No... I won't... Speak to him... I don't think... This isn't any of my business!' He listened as the man went on, unable to get a word in. Eventually, a pause arrived, and the man urged him for a response. Something told him he'd regret it later, but he gave in to the desperation coming through the receiver in plumes. If it was so important, he couldn't say no. 'All right. Fine. I will.' He hung up and slipped his phone in his pocket. He resumed his cooking just as Aryan returned. 'Aryan, your dad—'

'Is it OK if we don't speak about my dad right now?' He planted soft kisses along Logan's neck. 'I'm going to have a look at some tickets to Thailand.' He peered into the pan. 'Hopefully, actual Thai food will taste better than whatever it is you're failing to make.'

'Hey! It's supposed to look like this.'

'Is the floor supposed to look like that?' Aryan pointed to the layers of red powder trailing along the floor.

'Oh. I forgot about that.'

'Relax. I'll sort it.' Aryan found the dustpan and brush lodged behind the fridge. Without complaint, he got on his knees and started to sweep.

'Listen,' Logan began, keeping his attention on the pan as he stirred. 'I'm going to pop out after we eat, to pick up my medication.'

'I can get it. I have nothing else to do.'

'No, no. I can go. I won't be long. If you want, you can go pick up some of your stuff.'

Aryan stopped sweeping and stared at Logan. 'My stuff?'

'Did you not want to stay here a while? You know, until things blow over?'

'Really? Yeah. Sure! Sounds great. I mean, if that's what you want.'

He grinned. 'Yeah. Why not?'

The last time he was in Knightsbridge was the night he and Aryan were caught. He remembered dashing out into the night, trying to locate a tube station. He'd clambered into a carriage, disturbed by the sheer number of people crammed in – their faces blank and funereal. London once overwhelmed him. He never thought he'd one day morph into a Londoner. The way of Londoners seemed frictional against his own. Nobody smiled at each other when passing, or gave thanks where 'thanks' would be scattered about like seeds back home with a show of teeth to match. It was a new world to him.

Though he became accustomed to travelling up and down London, into the different boroughs, sometimes for the sake of exploration and sometimes for a purpose, he still didn't think he'd wind up in Knightsbridge again. He stood in front of the stately home of the Alekars. Something ached in him. After he'd left that night, he wanted nothing more than to return. He listened. The neighbourhood was eerily still. He was told to come this evening.

The door creaked open and he was beckoned inside by the shadowy figure of Dhruv Alekar. He was dressed in black trousers and a crisp white shirt, the top few buttons undone, uncovering straggly, grey hair coiling from his chest. 'Come.'

'I'm not following you until you tell me what you want.'

'I told you, if you care about Aryan, you'll hear me out.'

Logan followed him into the hallway and up the marble staircase, taking care to leave a span of distance between him and Dhruv. The old chandelier wasn't lit and he couldn't hear the sweet hums of Mrs Alekar. Dhruv led him into his bedroom – a room he'd never seen before. 'Sit down,' he ordered, gesturing towards a bed swathed in rose-gold damask. Logan recalled how Damini wailed that night. How many times had the sheets been stained with ceaseless tears?

'I won't sit. Just tell me what it is you want.'

He pulled out a chequebook from a drawer and waved it in front of Logan like a white flag. In the light, Logan saw how much Dhruv had aged. His skin was lined like tree bark and his beard streaked with white. 'How much?' Dhruv said.

'Excuse me?'

'How much do you want? Surely, there's an amount that will make you leave my son. You're a graphic designer. You can't live comfortably.'

Logan fought the urge to laugh. He'd never heard anything so ridiculous. 'You can't be serious?'

'How much?' Dhruv asked again, louder this time.

Logan raised his hands in the air and stepped towards Dhruv, as if the chequebook flapping in Dhruv's hands was a weapon. 'I don't want your money. So, if that's all, I'll be leaving.'

'You don't care about him,' Dhruv growled. 'Do you know what he would have to give up to be with you? All ties with this family. He will be an outcast from his community. He'll be the centre of vicious gossip. Our community is not so tolerant yet.'

'So what if people talk? And you don't have to cut him out.'

'Yes, I do. His behaviour isn't right. If I am seen to be accepting of this, there will be repercussions. He isn't gay like you. He has a choice. He can have children, a wife. He can have a normal life, but you... you stand in the way.' He approached Logan, his hands pressed together. 'Please, don't let him choose a struggle.'

The image of Dhruv Alekar begging was bizarre. Logan sunk on to the bed, his hands clutching at the sheets. He wasn't equipped for this. He expected threats and irrational anger. This, on the other hand, was unprecedented. This man, despite his towering height and strong body, started to appear as he was: just a man. Logan's set of certainties fractured as Dhruv's words infiltrated his mind. It didn't make sense for Aryan to leave behind everything for him. If he allowed him to go through with this, wouldn't that make him selfish? No. What they had was love. It couldn't be wrong.

'I'm sorry,' Logan said. 'I can't.' He stood up and moved towards him with eyes gentle and moistened with pity. 'I'm really sorry, Mr Alekar. I hope you can understand. I care about Aryan. Maybe one day you'll be OK with it. It doesn't have to be a problem.'

Dhruv jerked his head from side to side, as if there were an unbearable ringing in his ears. 'Why can't you understand? It's unnatural. It's disgusting. It's wrong.'

Logan wanted to launch into an explanation. He wanted to find the words to help Dhruv understand, but his head warned him of an oncoming unilateral pain, preparing to slice into him like pastry. His vision shifted from sharp acuity to a vague blur. He felt for the wafer-thin paper of his prescription in his pocket. It was late now. He'd have to pick up his medication tomorrow. 'I have to go. You've got to just try and understand.' As he reached the top of the stairs, he was snatched back by Dhruv's tight grip around his arm.

'Let go of me,' Logan said, trying to free his arm.

'I love my son. I won't let you spoil his life. He's never been the same since you.' He knocked Logan on to the floor. An intense pain climbed his spine and shot through his head. Dhruv wrapped one hand around Logan's throat, mottling his skin with berry pink beneath the press of his thumbs. Logan's head became sodden with a shawl of blurs and electrifying pain from hitting the ground. He tried to lift himself but couldn't. The room spun in imperfect circles. Dhruv pressed his knee on to Logan's leg to stop him kicking and after a few seconds, released him entirely. Logan gasped and spluttered on the floor. Dhruv kicked him in the stomach, bringing him to his front again and pressed his spinning head down.

Logan's arm, fuelled by panic, swung backwards, trying to force Dhruv off him. Dhruv caught it and pinned it down. With his head pounding from the fall, he fiercely held on to the scraps of consciousness left before an imminent blackout. Then, for a measly second, Dhruv loosened his grip. Why? A question of ethics? A sound from somewhere in the house? It didn't matter. Logan twisted his body round and elbowed him in the jaw.

'Bastard!' Dhruv cried as he fell on to his back. He pushed himself up, blood seeping from his nose. Logan struck him on the side of the head, then did it again. And again. He couldn't stop. His fists kept bashing into his skull, his nose, until finally his hand was smattered with blood and Dhruv lay next to him, a twisted pile on the floor. Logan collapsed, panting and sopping with sweat.

Out in the cold, he shed his armour and let the tears accumulate in the corners of his eyes. For the first time in years, he felt overwhelmed, more than he did when he first arrived in the city. He clutched himself and did what he could: walk. He would walk away. He would leave it all here. As he counted the steps to the tube station, he promised he'd never return to Knightsbridge again.

CHAPTER 40

He rang the bell again. Logan should've been back by now. The pharmacy was only ten minutes away and he himself had been out for a couple of hours. He glanced at his phone. Logan would have texted him if he was going to be late. Maybe his phone died. Aryan leaned against the gate, a stuffed duffel bag by his feet. Perhaps he was in the bathroom. It didn't matter. He didn't mind waiting. He felt strangely satisfied. He couldn't be happier spending time with Logan. Even his burnt Thai food went down a treat.

As he waited, he spotted a crowd gathered at the street's corner. They were huddled together, whispering among themselves and wearing solemn expressions. He wondered what drama had unfolded. He tried the bell again. When he got no response, he swung his bag over his shoulder and walked over to the crowd, bent on feeding his curiosity while he waited. The crowd started to disperse as he arrived.

'What happened?' he asked an elderly woman with a trolley bag.

'A young man had a seizure. He was in quite a state. The ambulance has taken him, poor thing.'

'A young man?'

'Oh yes. Probably no older than you, love.'

He stopped listening, his attention taken by the flimsy bit of paper poking out from beneath his shoe. He bent over and picked it up. It was a prescription for Naramig, the name Logan Elias Reeves printed at the top. 'Oh no.' Dread rolled through him and liquefied his legs. 'Excuse me. Where is the nearest emergency room?'

The old lady shrugged. 'I don't know, dear, I'm only visiting. I'm from Nottingham.'

Once he got the answer from his phone, he wasted no time. He leapt into a cab and made it to the nearest hospital in under fifteen minutes. He raced to the reception desk, skidding across the floor and setting off a few grumbles from the nurses. 'I'm looking for a Logan Reeves. Is he here?'

The receptionist asked him to 'hold a moment,' as she checked the system. He drummed his fingers against the desk, biting down on his lip so hard he could almost taste blood.

'Well?'

'No. No one here with the name Reeves.'

'He was just brought in by the ambulance. He had a seizure.'

'One moment.' She rose from her seat and waved a nurse over to the desk. They spoke in hushed tones. She returned to Aryan. 'Someone will be with you in a moment. Just take a seat.'

He sat on a rickety chair, sandwiched between a man with a chesty cough and an elderly woman with sallow skin. Waiting was torture. This must have been because of his migraines. He must have fallen and hit his head, setting off a seizure. Aryan had never hated himself more. If only he'd gone to get the medication for him. He should have insisted. He should have known. His mind conjured up the worst scenarios.

He pictured a white-tiled room, reeking of sanitiser and cleaning detergents, as if they were trying to remove the smell of incipient death. He imagined pulling the wayfaring strand of amber-blonde hair from Logan's forehead, letting his fingers slide down his face, his neck... until he found the silver cross. He imagined shaking his head and trying his best to refrain

himself from cursing the God that was supposed to save him.
His hands would be cold. These were morbid thoughts. They
were thoughts he shouldn't have been having. Besides, people
don't usually die from seizures. But if his thoughts were ever to
translate into reality, he couldn't bear it. A nurse walked over
to him.

'There isn't a Logan Reeves in this hospital. The young
man that just came in with a seizure has a different name.'

'Are you sure?'

'I'm sure.'

With his arms limp and heavy at his sides, he traipsed back
to Logan's flat, criticising himself for jumping to conclusions.
At least Logan was safe. He pressed the bell at the gate and a
gravelly voice sprung from the intercom. It was his flatmate.

'Hello?'

'Hey. Is Logan in? Can't reach him on his phone.'

'No. He isn't.'

'Well, I'm a friend. Can I wait inside for him?'

There was a pause.

'You Aryan?'

'Yes.'

'You better come in.'

He was let in by a man decked out in peace tattoos with
frizzy, shoulder-length hair. He gestured for Aryan to take a
seat, but he refused.

'He's gone,' the man said.

'Gone? Gone where?'

'He didn't say. Only, he'd be back in a couple of weeks for
his stuff.'

Aryan kneaded his forehead. 'What do you mean? I don't understand. Back for his stuff? He's starting a job in a few weeks. Where would he go?'

'His job isn't in London, mate. Didn't he tell you? Sheffield, I think he said. He was going to leave in a few weeks anyway, but for some reason decided to go now. It was kind of sudden, but you know him, he's a bit impulsive. I just don't question it any more.'

'Sheffield? He never said.'

'He told me, if you came calling, to say you didn't convince him. Whatever that means.'

Aryan was unsteady on his feet. 'Oh. OK. I guess I'll be going then. Thanks.'

He slogged down the steps and out of the gate, his grip on the straps of his duffel bag loose. He didn't understand. He thought Logan was all right with him. He thought back to dinner. Logan was quieter than usual. He wasn't wholly there with him. Was it because he didn't want to be? But he invited him to stay with him. It was his idea. Unless it was a ploy to get him to leave for his bags. And why didn't he tell him about Sheffield? Nothing made sense. Nothing at all. No matter how many times Aryan dialled his number, Logan wouldn't pick up. He was in the dark, unable to contact him. Was this revenge?

CHAPTER 41

Maansi filed her nails, letting the resulting dust fall along his side of the bed. Her nails were even but she continued to grind them down. It gave her something to do while he roamed about the flat. He came back the day before, to pack a few things and move them to his lover's place. Then he returned after a few hours, the glee in his eyes vanquished and his things still in hand. They didn't speak much. When he came back, she spared two words and he gave back three.

'What happened?'

'He wasn't there.'

She didn't ask for more details. To tell the truth, she was amused. He got there, all ready with his bags, full of excitement and hope, no doubt, and Logan wasn't there. When she'd walk past him as he lay sprawled on the sofa, she'd see the phone glued to his ear. No one was answering his calls. Logan deserted Aryan. In that, she found some justice.

Days passed on and, like a ghost, he hung around the living room. She didn't care. She'd return from work and find him prone on the sofa, surrounded by empty bottles of beer and greasy chip papers. His expression was always vacant. She'd slam the door shut with force to see him flinch, but he wouldn't even do that much.

'Aryan!' she said. 'Aryan, you're not working and you do nothing all day. How are we going to continue living here?'

He groaned, covering his eyes with the back of his arm. 'What do you want from me?'

'Whether you like it or not, you married me. You have a responsibility to me.'

'I can't do anything. Not now. I'm not feeling great.'

'Neither was I. And what sympathy did you give me?' Her words skated on the back of frost. How dare he accuse her of weakness and berate her for depression, when he was succumbing to it too? She was happy to let him fester like an open sore. As much as she wanted to burst into angry flames and pour herself out in front of him, she chose cold hostility, refusing to spend even an ounce of energy on him.

After telling him up to twenty times, Aryan finally climbed the stepladder to unscrew the dead lightbulb. Maansi returned to her reading. She was absorbed in the book, finding an escape into another world comforting, but was taken away from the heroine's story by the sound of glass smashing. She jerked in her seat and observed Aryan storming out and into the bedroom. The remnants of glass were strewn across the floor. By the wall, with which the lightbulb collided, was a diffident grey mark – identical to the one she left when she once hurled a book, stung with too much pain to bear. She wouldn't sympathise with him. He deserved it. She remembered his promise to be faithful. It was as if life was playing a joke on her, wadding its belly with laughter as it flung bullets out into the world with its eyes closed.

As the night brewed on, Aryan didn't leave the bedroom. She couldn't sleep with him. She'd have to kick him out. She opened the door and peeked in. She could just about make out a clumpy figure beneath the duvet. She switched on the light and saw he had pulled the duvet right over him, so only the sward of his ebony hair showed. 'Aryan. Wake up.' He didn't stir. 'Aryan!'

When he rose into a sitting position, she saw his bloodshot eyes and the puffiness beneath them. He must have mopped up his face, but his collarbone remained wet from the spill of tears. 'Sorry. I'll sleep in the living room.'

As he stepped out of the bedroom, she swivelled round and sniped at him with his own weaponry. 'Get over it!' He froze, his back towards her. She waited for him to turn on her. She knew his temper now and she was ready for it, her arms folded, forming a shield across her heart. Instead, he walked away, shutting the door gently behind him. Tears trickled down her cheeks. She was angry at him for shedding tears for another and angry at herself for trying to bruise him with his methods. In the safety of the bed, she screamed into her pillow and sobbed until sleep and all its mercy took her away.

CHAPTER 42

She was cross-legged on the bedroom floor, flipping through her wedding album and recapping her first night with Aryan. Time had scarcely passed and their marriage was already over. They couldn't continue living together, remaining separate, as they were.

Another week had passed and he hadn't improved. Their supply of money to pay for the flat was dwindling. He was unconcerned and instead of working towards solving the problem, he spent his time barefoot on the balcony, relying on the succour from his cigarettes.

'Look. I'm sorry,' he said. She peered up from the album. He was standing in the doorway. 'I'm sorry for everything. You don't deserve any of this. I do know that. Please, forgive me?'

She was speechless. The arrogant, emotionless man that she met was now a depressed wreck, grovelling for her forgiveness. He was no longer the man she met, dapper in a navy suit with emotions contained in vacuum sealed bags.

'Aryan, before we got married, I was depressed. I still get depressed. I only married you to take me away from that. To try and start again.' She didn't want him to think he meant much to her. 'So I guess we've both wasted each other's time.'

He knelt beside her. 'I want you to know, I never meant to call you weak.'

'Good. Because you were wrong. I'm strong!' she said. 'So, if you want to hurt me, go ahead.'

He took her hand in his. His often hard coppery eyes

softened into buttery caramel. 'I never wanted to hurt you. I didn't get back with him to hurt you. I swear.'

Give me a break, she thought. 'But you have. You married me. Now you've gone off with someone else – a man for God's sake. What am I supposed to think, Aryan? An old friend? An old fuck buddy?'

'It wasn't like that. Look. Let me tell you the whole story. What happened between Logan and me. Why I married you. Why I've done what I've done. All of it.'

She rose to her feet. Had he lost his mind? 'I don't want to hear it.'

He stood and took hold of her hand once more. 'Come on, Maansi. Just hear me out.'

For a long time, she wanted to strip away the layer of mystery that wove itself around him. It was all she wanted. How could she say no when he was so willing, at last, to drop the cape and let her finally see him? 'Urgh. Fine. Tell me.'

It was hard to hear. The stories of the physical abuse he faced as a child and how he was afraid for his mother if he didn't comply with his father's wishes. How she dealt with criticisms and would weep the nights away. He spoke of his dad's attachment to making Aryan successful like him, since he grew up without a penny with a sick father who could do nothing for him. When he spoke of his and Logan's friendship, he could hardly hold himself together. She watched as the once cold, calculating Aryan she couldn't pry open came apart, bit by bit. Her heart didn't just hurt for her, but for him. 'God, I'm so fucking weak.'

'No,' she said. 'You're not weak.' She couldn't believe how much she despised him, and yet, how much she wanted to console him. She collected his tears on her thumb, clearing them away, before clearing her own. He had become a version of her former self. She could see it was effort enough for him to exist, to not escape into that state of somnambulism that netted him.

'Well, it's done. I have no family, no job, no Logan. Believe me, Maansi. It's probably best you leave me. I don't know how to support you. I can't take care of you.'

She hushed him. She wouldn't hear it. What was she going to do now?

'Wait here,' she sighed. She staggered to her feet and disappeared out of the room. She returned to him moments later, with his shoes and coat. She positioned them in front of him. 'Get them on. You can't give up now. You're going to York. He might have gone home.'

'York? Wait. What? What about... us?'

She fought the impulse to break into tears. She kept her composure, feeling as if she were walking on stilts. She was close to falling. 'There never was an us, Aryan,' she spat.

They were two people brought together because they couldn't handle their pasts. They made painful decisions and were hurt by those around them. They used each other to silence the past that wished to claw itself out. They were there because of '*log kya kahenge*'. That's all. She could see that now. 'Look. Whatever. I'll be all right. I'll survive, won't I? But I don't know if you can without him.'

She knew Aryan had a car, but had never once sat inside the sleek, silver body of the BMW. Cars never seemed to move on the congested roads of London. They were better off whipping out their oyster cards. They both shuffled by the car, unsure of what to say to each other. Her body sucked in all the anger, the pain, the pity. She'd process those emotions later, undoubtedly with the help of a gallon of ice cream. She told him good luck, but something niggling in her mind told her not to stop there. There was more she needed to tell him. If she didn't tell him then…

'Aryan,' she began.

'Aryan!' came a desperate voice, cutting Maansi short. A woman appeared before them, swamped in scarves and a large, quilted jacket. It was her mother-in-law. 'Aryan. Aryan, *beta*, I had to come see you,' Damini said.

'Mum, what are you doing here? Thought you weren't supposed to see me? Remember that?'

'Forget what your father says. How can I not? You're my baby,' she cupped her son's face, assuming that perfected look of a wide-eyed doe. 'Please, ask your father for forgiveness. Then he'll accept you again. He'll give you back your job. Everything will be OK.'

Aryan shrugged her off. 'Mum, please! He should ask for mine. Just go.'

'You want to give up everything for that boy? Do you know what he did to your father? He beat him. He broke his nose! He did that to your own father. *Kuch toh sharam karo.*' 'Have some shame,' Maansi translated with her restricted knowledge of Hindi. In her desperation to get her son back, she must've been spinning lies. As if Logan could hurt anyone.

Aryan stared through his mother, as if she were nothing more than a phantom he could slip his hand through. 'Goodbye, Mum.'

'No. Stop it. I won't agree to giving up my son. You and Maansi are here, together now. Stop this Logan business.'

'I've tried, Mum. I tried for you.'

'He'll hold this over me for ever, Aryan,' she beseeched him, grasping fistfuls of his shirt.

'Then leave him!' he snapped, wresting himself free of her.

'Being a wife or a mother isn't all you've got to be. Be brave, Mum.'

'Wait! Aryan, wait. You know I didn't do this because I hate Logan. Logan was a good boy, a sweet boy. We were just trying to protect you. You have to understand. But if you really do love him... Maybe somehow I can learn to...'

He punched the hood of his car, making Maansi gasp and draw back. 'It's too late for that. Don't tell me now you can accept it, because it's too fucking late for that.' He flung the car door open. Before getting in, he aggressively embraced Maansi, clutching her to him as if they'd never see each other again. She absorbed the warmth of his body. There was comfort in his arms and she didn't want him to let go. He delivered a single, tender kiss to her forehead before breaking away. He climbed into the front seat of his car and shut the door, without so much as glancing in the direction of his mother.

The car reversed out of the bay and swerved round, the tyres screeching against the tarmac. He shot out of the parking area and on to the road, the navigation system preparing a route to York.

CHAPTER 43

Aryan parked the car across from the quaint little house. The rustic welcome sign still hung on the door, worn and battered by the caprices of weather and the slow but sure plodding of time. He wondered if the house still basted in the sweet, luxurious scent of cinnamon and baked goods, as it did the last time he visited. He had never known if Andrew baked, or if the scent had lifted off from the melting wax of a Yankee Candle. He yearned to enter. It'd be like stepping back in time, to when nothing bad had happened and he and Logan were still drifting through the days, indolent and happy as two lotus-eaters.

He gripped the steering wheel, his stomach performing summersaults. He hadn't considered what he'd say to Logan. What if coming up to York was a mistake? What if it made him look desperate? He ejected the seat belt. Well, he was desperate. Please be here, he thought. If he wasn't there, he'd never find him. Logan had cut off every available line of contact Aryan had to him, the same way he had on his return from the motherland.

He rang the doorbell. The bark of a dog bounded through the house, followed by the weary calls of a man instructing the animal to quiet down. There was a brief shuffle and fiddle with the door latch. A young girl, around the age of twelve, opened the door and stood before him. She had long, wavy blonde hair and eyes the blue of topaz. 'Yeah?' she asked, zipping up her pink hoodie as the cool gales crossed over the threshold.

'Louisa? It's Aryan.'

She straightened up as she recognised him. 'Oh. I remember. What are you doing here?'

'Is Logan here?'

'No. Why? Why are you here?' He found her bitterness cutting. She once adored him.

'Louisa, who is it?' came a voice behind her. She stepped out of the way for Andrew. He had dark pillows of fat beneath his eyes and his hair was untidy. Aryan guessed he was up the whole night marking essays or researching. He had forgotten to ask Logan if his father still worked at the university. Andrew's eyebrows wedged together as he recognised the man in front of him. 'Aryan! What are you doing here?'

'Hey, Andrew. I'm looking for Logan. But Louisa said he isn't here. So, I guess I'll be going.'

'No. He isn't here,' he yawned. 'I'm sorry.'

'Do you know where he might be?'

'Lou, give us a moment,' Andrew said. She stomped her feet in protest but a stern look from her father forced her to slink away into the living room. 'Aryan, I don't know what's happened between you two. One minute he's telling me you're back in his life, then the next minute he isn't speaking to you. I don't think he's ever been this shut off. I don't know what's going on, but it needs to stop.'

'I understand. I do. I'm trying to fix it now.'

Andrew heaved a sigh. 'Aryan, he's demanding some space. He's in, but he asked me to deny you entry. Can I give him a message? Maybe he'll meet you himself.'

Aryan raked his restless hand through his hair, finding a jittering desperation powering through his feet, willing him to push past Andrew and run up the stairs. 'Can you tell him I'll be at the bridge within the Dales. Tomorrow at noon. If he sees me this one time, I'll never bother him again. If that's what he wants.'

He agreed. Aryan left before Andrew could say another

word. There was a hotel nearby. He'd arranged to stay there and would head off for the Yorkshire Dales the next morning. He prayed – though a positive atheist – that Logan would meet him there.

CHAPTER 44

The Dales didn't glimmer as they did before. The weakening light broke through patches of grey clouds, too dull to reach the tips of rain-swept grass. The air was a bitter cold and made his skin tingle. He gazed at the river, his face and hands numb and turning puce. He had been waiting for an hour.

When he'd given to shuddering like the leaves of nearby trees, the footsteps he was anxious to hear came towards him. He saw him, his head just visible beneath his hood, his hands concealed in his pockets. With caution, Aryan approached him, as if the path towards him was paved with fractured glass. He halted a metre away from him. For a while, they did nothing but take each other in, like the excess air surrounding them.

'Why did you leave?' Aryan asked. 'You've got to tell me why.'

Logan turned his attention away towards the river, the warmth that usually encompassed him quenched. 'I don't know.'

Aryan dug his hand into his pocket and retrieved a packet of medication. He offered it to Logan. 'Your medication. I got it for you.' Logan stepped towards him and took it. His thumb brushed the text as he checked the name.

'Thank you,' he said.

'I'm owed an explanation. What happened?'

Logan sighed. He picked up a cluster of stones from the ground and tossed them, one by one, aiming for the spilling waterfalls of the Stainforth Force. Aryan edged closer to him, rubbing his hands together to protect them from the assaulting cold.

'You couldn't think of anywhere indoors to meet?' Logan said, as he assessed the bitten skin of Aryan's hands. He withdrew a pair of padded gloves from his pockets and handed them to Aryan. 'Here. I don't need them.'

'Thanks.'

Logan drew his hood down and let the wind scuffle with his hair. He closed his eyes and meditated for a minute. 'I freaked out. I ran away. I'm sorry.'

'But why? I thought we were OK. We were planning to go away. What happened?'

'Your dad.' He passed a stone from one hand to the other. 'He wanted me to see him, so I went. He offered me money to leave you. And when I wouldn't take it... he... he tried to strangle me.'

'What?'

'My neck was purple. I couldn't even speak.'

Aryan could feel the bile rising in his body. The information hit him like bricks. 'Oh God. That fucking bastard. Logan, I'm...' Aryan touched Logan's arm and watched him flinch. 'Sorry. You should have told me. I'll kill him. It's a good fucking thing he's done with me. I want nothing to do with him.'

He was furious. His body stiffened and his hands were eager to punch out at something. He tried to keep calm, for Logan's sake. He knew then, he didn't care if his dad dropped dead. He wouldn't mourn him. Not for a second.

'What do you mean? Did he cut ties with you?'

'Yeah. Because I chose you.'

Logan hurled another stone into the river with all his might, then turned to him, a teardrop roaming down his face. 'I worry I'll look at you and see your dad.'

Aryan couldn't cope with that. His dad had spent years

308

shredding him to pieces, slashing his dreams and bruising his skin, his body, his face. To be a picture of his dad made him want to peel the flesh off his bones. He simply couldn't cope with that. 'Look at me then. Find out.'

Logan looked at Aryan, his dispirited eyes shifting from side to side, soaking up every centimetre of Aryan's face. He raised his hand and travelled along his cheek with his fingertips. 'I can still see the bloody child in your face.' A laugh ruptured from his mouth. 'God, this is exhausting me. But I do... love you.' He surveyed the downcast skies above. The bellies of the clouds rumbled and tiny droplets of rain fell and splattered on their skin and the greenery around them. They sought each other's hands and interwove their fingers together.

'I love you too. And I'm exhausted too. But I don't mind. Even if there's a speck of me left, I want to do the right thing, and just focus all my attention on you. I really do and I'm so sorry.'

'Don't apologise. None of it matters any more. We're here now. Here's a good place.'

'I promise I'm not going anywhere.'

Logan kissed him. Their ice-glazed lips hurt as they came to touch, yet the gentle pain of it was sanctuary against the callous weather reeling around them. All the bitterness of the past began to disintegrate like snowflakes – their once complex structures worn away by the warmth of joined hands, until they became nothing more than droplets of water, trickling off with the rain.

CHAPTER 45

She dropped to the floor, her arms sore and her back contracting from the heavy lifting that came with packing a life, box by box. She was done with the place. She'd already rejected the job offer that morning, severing all ties with London. Although she started to love her work, it didn't make sense to stay. Besides, they'd write her a good reference, so she could pick up and start again, far away from the Alekar family.

Into a box she put her wedding album, the cover of which was a photo of her and Aryan, forced smiles upon their faces. He looked so handsome in his champagne-hued sherwani. She was proud for a minute, knowing he was temporarily hers. She sealed the box with long slabs of duct tape. She didn't know what she was going to do with that particular box. She could toss it away and erase her mind of him and the months they shared together. Though she knew the memories would return in violent torrents, the minute the divorce papers arrived. And then there was the other thing, reminding her with its presence on a daily basis.

She blew her nose into a tissue, her whole head congested after the blitzes of silly tears. She'd been foolish. She married Aryan Alekar and believed love would grow and bloom without any problems. It hadn't. But she had. She'd moved away, fought through her depression and started working. This box was a testament to her strength and the heartbreak she survived. She didn't feel the same depth of sadness and didn't unleash plaintive howls as she had when her first love walked out on her. This time, love walked out of the door and she let it – supported it, even. His heart belonged elsewhere. At the core of all his pain was the threat of community. She could understand it and, in time, maybe even forgive it. She wiped the newer tears from her salty face.

'Maansi?' The front door opened and a familiar face peeked through, her once electric blue streaks now shocking pink.

'Sejal! You're here.' Maansi ran towards her and wrapped her arms around her friend, trying to keep any extra tears at bay. 'Thank you for coming.'

'Of course, honey. How are you feeling?'

'I don't know. I can't process anything. Especially what I know now.'

Sejal nodded in a mechanical manner, then took Maansi by the hand and led her to the sofa. 'Let's just take a moment, all right? After what you've told me, I've been thinking... It's OK, you know, if you want to get rid of it. I'll come with you.'

Maansi shook her head. She wouldn't even consider that option. 'No. I know that decision is right for some women. But it isn't for me. Believe me. I don't want to make that mistake again.'

'All right. But be prepared. I need you to be strong.'

She knew gossip would come from her community and her relatives. But she wasn't going to put her reputation first. Not again. She saw first-hand what that could do. 'Let them talk. I'm tired of all the secrets we have to keep.'

Sejal pressed Maansi's shoulder. 'And Aryan? Are you going to tell him?'

'Later.' She patted her belly. 'I don't even know how this happened. Maybe my medication made the pill stop working. Or, I don't know, I was throwing up a lot, so I probably wasn't absorbing it.'

'I don't know. But you have me.'

'Thank you.' She reflected on her wedding day and how it came to be.

Sejal grinned. 'Speaking of gossip. You wouldn't believe what's happened to Rakhee. She's only gone and fallen for one of the optometrists at her workplace.'

'Really?'

'Yes! And she's never had a boyfriend before and has never gone behind her parents' back. She's a nervous wreck. He's white. Can you believe it? But just think, Maansi. If she'd married Aryan… '

'I'm happy for her.'

Sejal helped Maansi shift the rest of the boxes outside and into the hired van. Maansi scrutinised the flat. It was bare and minimalist, as it had been when she first entered it. Their stories and their characters could not be read on the clinical, white walls. There was no evidence of the failed marriage, the secrets and the sadness that trapped them both. She took a deep breath and clutched her chest. Her life was now the walls of the flat – blank and ready for the next chapter to be written across it. But first, she'd have to tell the story up to that point and brace herself for what was to come.

CHAPTER 46

Maansi's parents sat with their breaths caught, unable to exhale or utter a word. They were still, the low whirring of the washing machine in the kitchen thinning the weight of silence.

Her father rose to his feet with a calculated steadiness. With his jaw clenched, he pulled out his mobile phone and stepped out of the room. Maansi and her mother glanced at each other, neither knowing what to do or whether to interfere.

'What the hell am I hearing from my daughter?' they heard him say in his cottony voice. It was strange to hear her father say 'hell'. He never shouted or cursed, not even when she'd misbehaved as a child. He was the kind of person that strolled with hands clasped behind his back, his eyelids heavy and making half-moons out of his soft eyes. Yet, there he was, responding at the precipice of anger. 'This is disgraceful.'

Maansi expected her mother to be on her feet, her voice a speakerphone, dictating what should be said to the Alekar family, and eventually getting so fed up, she snatches the phone and tells them herself. Instead, she sat across from Maansi, her eyebrows pinned together. Her father's voice faded as he walked out into the back garden – she imagined, to protect them from witnessing his descent into his version of rage. She didn't care to listen. She didn't want to know what excuse Dhruv was giving. She could only dream of the lies he would tell to protect his reputation.

'What a selfish man,' her mother finally said. 'Who marries a woman if he knows he is gay? Who ruins a life like that?'

'Not gay. Bisexual,' Maansi found herself saying. She wasn't trying to defend the man, but she felt it was important to remind herself he liked women, that she was enough in the bedroom for a period of time. Or maybe she wasn't. Maybe those extra hunks of fat clinging to her made his mind wander back to his male ex-lover. If Logan was his 'true love' then why didn't he crumble sooner? Why didn't he dash back to him before marrying her? When he was alone, surely there was nothing to do but plug his head with thoughts of Logan.

'It doesn't matter. Whether his lover was a man or a woman, if he knew he'd go back, then he shouldn't have married you. I have no problem with him being gay.'

'Bisexual.'

'Yes, yes. I'm not intolerant. I've seen that film, *Ek Ladki Ko Dekha Toh Aisa Laga*. I have a problem with him making a mess of your life.'

Maansi chewed on her bottom lip. Was it a mess? She tried to step out and look at the picture of her life, but despite her efforts to focus in and perceive each hard edge and corner, everything was a blur. When she thought of Aryan, she pitied him. But when she remembered who she was and where she stood, she hated him. Whatever he was and whatever mess she was, it clumped together within her and was glowing with life.

'Maansi,' her mother began, staring at her copy of the Gita on the mantelpiece, raking through her hair with electric fingers. She shifted her gaze towards Maansi. 'You have to forget that man. You have to erase him from your life. Completely.'

Maansi noticed her mother's eyes had wandered downwards towards her stomach and the significance of the last word pressed into her.

'What do you mean?'

'You know what I mean.'

Her mother's words swivelled around her head like a

bee before landing. She couldn't believe it. While her mother always defended a woman's right to choose, abortion went against their core values. 'But it's wrong. Against *bhagwan*.'

'Maansi,' she leaned forward, her fingernails slicing into the flesh of the pecan-coloured sofa. 'It will ruin your life. Obviously, marrying again will be hard. You know how Asian families are about single mothers. And you don't even have a job now. You'll waste away. You'll never reach your full potential. You'll never reach your purpose.'

'For God's sake, Mum, don't even start with my potential. Your head is stuck in the self-help section.'

She sighed. 'Fine. I read too many self-help books and I watch too much Oprah. My life needs something. I wanted you to marry Aryan so you'd have the best lifestyle and money while you figured yourself out. Not to be a divorced woman burdened with a child. What will your life be?'

'It'd be—'

'I won't help you,' her mother cut in. 'I won't do it. I won't watch you spoil your life and I am not going back to being a childminder. I've done my time.'

The room fell silent once more. Maansi revisited the days after the first abortion. The guilt had buried itself into her stomach the way a rat would bury into a wall, and it stayed there to fester. For months the mordant smell wriggled out of her pores and circled her. 'God won't forgive me.'

I won't forgive me, she thought.

Her mother inhaled deeply and closed her eyes. 'Well, I am telling you to do it. I am not giving you an option. God can punish me. You are clean. OK? You are clean. How can you seek forgiveness for something you don't have the freedom to choose?'

Her mother didn't know the half of it. She looked at her and saw 'clean'. But, she supposed, if she was already dirty, redemption was not possible. Without the baby, she could focus on a career. Without the baby, she could look forward to getting remarried. She could forget Aryan for good.

Her mum stood and delivered the final word. 'If you have this child, it'll be a mistake. Women aren't just born to be mothers, Maansi. You'll want your freedom. I won't support you in this.'

Maansi wasn't sure if her mother was lying – saving her, by removing the burden of choice, or if she really meant what she said. Either way, what choice did she have? How could she do this alone?

CHAPTER 47

Maansi left Aryan a text.

Please call me. We need to talk.

The app displayed two cyan ticks, letting her know he'd seen the message. An hour had passed and he hadn't called or messaged her back. She understood he wasn't in love with her. She received that message loud and clear. But how could it be so easy for him to pluck her from his life? Like she were nothing but an unwanted hair – to be thrown away, without another thought or look.

She took a deep breath and pushed the clinic door. It resisted, and after forcing it again she noticed the word 'PULL', bold and in block capitals. Great. They made entering harder than it needed to be. That little bit of extra effort made it plain to her that she was going out of her way to do this. It wasn't a decision she could float towards and carry out unknowingly, like a sleepwalker trotting along a pre-programmed course. This required action, not passivity. As she stepped in, the scent of detergent and something that reminded her of berry-flavoured vitamins swamped the space around her.

After confirming herself as arrived, she settled on a tottering chair in the corner. On the table beside her were old women's magazines with scratched surfaces and folded edges. She picked one up and flipped through, landing on an interview with Cheryl Cole. She started reading the first line again, and again, conscious of her foot tapping against the floor. Cheryl

317

Cole was slim. Well, at least she wouldn't puff up into the size of a house, she figured. Wasn't that a positive? Was it right to even console herself with that thought? No, she concluded. It was a ridiculous, empty way to comfort herself.

She walked over to the water cooler, her legs like straw. She filled the plastic cup, poured the water down her throat and then crushed the cup between her hands and watched it fall into a pile of discarded cups. As she stared into the dark mouth of the bin, the nurse called her name.

'Maansi Al...car?' called the voice. Even with the incorrect pronunciation, the name slammed into her like a truck. It was that name: 'Alekar', that separated this time from the last.

She followed the nurse down the corridor and into the second room on the left. The moment she entered, the hairs on her arms lifted. The room was like a walk-in fridge. Folding her arms over her body, she set herself down on the assigned chair. The nurse supplied her with information about what to expect. She'd take the first pill now, the second pill later. She was questioned again about her decision, and whether anyone was picking her up. She couldn't help but wonder... if she'd told Aryan the truth, would he be pulling up now, trying to stop her? Or would he be sitting by her, holding her hand, telling her she was doing the right thing?

'Do you need more time to think?' the nurse asked, her voice like hot vinegar. 'Any more questions?'

As Maansi shook her head, the nurse placed the pill before her and discharged more meaningless words from her mouth. Maansi closed her eyes as she picked up the pill. The tap was dripping this time. The powder rubbed off on to her fingers like chalk. Acid climbed up her stomach and into her throat, and rose with more power the more she swallowed.

'When you're ready,' the nurse said.

She tried to imagine what life would be like the moment

it was all over. She'd write applications again and endure rejections. She'd fight off guilt and think about what could've been. She'd eat too much some days, nothing other days. And maybe she'd do it all in her pyjamas. Everything would return to how it was before she met Aryan. This pill would do more than just get rid of the child. It would send her back in time.

'Everyone goes through the cycle of birth, death and rebirth until they can meet with God again,' her mother's voice echoed in the chambers of her mind.

She placed the pill on her tongue. She'd return to square one. And then what? The pain of that first unwanted abortion stuck a thorn into her side, and she wanted it out. She removed the pill from her mouth and let it fall to the floor. 'No!'

Without acknowledging the nurse and her roll of questions, Maansi rushed out of the room and out of the clinic, the bitter taste of the pill still slipping into her taste buds.

She stepped outside into the cold. Rain fell slowly like autumnal leaves. Before she could process what she'd done, her phone rang. She imagined it was her mother, calling to ask if 'it' was done, unable to call 'it' by its proper name. She wanted to accompany Maansi, but Maansi knew her mother's guilt would've only fed her own. She looked at the screen and her chest tightened. It was Aryan.

'Act normal, Maansi. Act normal,' she whispered to herself.

'Maansi, hi. I got your message. Are you OK?'

Her heart dropped. His voice was soft cashmere on a winter's day. It was sorcery, the way he could still make her feel for him. She wanted to tell him how scared she was and how much she needed him. But she needed to be stronger than that.

'I'm OK. How are you?' She then asked what she really wanted to know. 'Are you happy?'

She pushed her feet into the concrete ground as she received his answer. She was sure her heart would collapse if she wasn't careful. 'Good. That's good.'

'What did you want to talk about?'

Her hand hovered over her abdomen, her mouth still soaked with the bitter taste of what she'd almost done. She could feel the nurse hovering at the reception area, waiting for her to turn back around.

With just two words, she would hurl a grenade into the centre of his world and blow it into smithereens. The fresh smile would drop from his face, and he and Logan would talk, maybe argue. Would he be angry? Would he want to be there? For the baby? For her? Would he beg her to get rid of it? There she'd be between them – a barrier, a force to be reckoned with. She'd complicate his life. But didn't he deserve to know?

'Maansi? What is it?'

'Listen, Aryan…'

She didn't look back towards the clinic. She'd made the wrong decision once and she paid for it for a long time. But it was fixed now, right? Wasn't this redemption? Something stirred in her belly in response. Not a child, but a monster. The same one that called her body host and was happy to share its home. She could still feel its presence. But next to it, something was growing – a love that she hoped would tunnel through the darkness. A love that she hoped would make all she'd been through worthwhile. This was her second chance. And after all she'd been through, she was ready to take it.

BOOK CLUB NOTES

1. Do you think Maansi should have told Lewis about her pregnancy? Why do you think she keeps it a secret? Was she wrong?
2. Do you think Maansi and Aryan ever develop feelings for each other?
3. Why do you think Aryan reacts in the way he does when he discovers what's in Maansi's drawers? Is his anger justified? What is he angry about?
4. Which character do you sympathise with the most? Do your sympathies change throughout the novel?
5. Based on his behaviours throughout the novel, could we conclude Aryan is selfish?
6. Maansi appreciated Logan's warmth and kindness. What is your perception of him? Is he the good guy throughout?
7. Why do you think the novel is called *All The Words Unspoken*?
8. A common question asked within Indian communities is *log kya kahenge* (what will people say)? How does this question drive the events in the novel?
9. Consider the ending. Do you think Maansi tells Aryan the truth? Do you think she should? How do you think he'd react?
10. Compare Maansi's and Aryan's parents. Which values do they share? Where do their perceptions differ?

ABOUT THE AUTHOR

Serena Kaur holds a first-class degree in English from Loughborough University. Straight after graduating, she made a firm decision to chase her dream of becoming an author. When she is not spinning her daydreams into stories, she teaches English as a second language. She lives in Leicester with her husband and is currently working on her second novel.

Find out more about RedDoor Press and sign up to our newsletter to hear about our **latest releases, author events,** exciting **competitions** and more at

reddoorpress.co.uk

YOU CAN ALSO FOLLOW US:

 @RedDoorBooks

 Facebook.com/RedDoorPress

 @RedDoorBooks